For my parents, my brothers and sisters, and my children, especially Hannah, whose patience helping me put this together was greatly needed and appreciated.

Rob Wheat's memory was as organized and violent as a South Korean student demonstration. But he couldn't safely remember anything. There were rules. He just didn't know them all.

The guillotine doors of the big dishwasher crashed down, steam eddying up from edges. Perspiration stung his eyes. He could feel Hilda shuffling behind him, and then heard the sucking sound as she drew air in through her toothless mouth. Stennis, the assistant manager, had predicted two hundred. But it didn't really matter. Dishes, silverware, and glasses would come, and he and Hilda would run them through until they stopped coming. Tablecloths and napkins would be stuffed in laundry baskets. All manner of garbage would be thrown, sloshed, poured in the heavy plastic cans to be taken to the dumpsters later.

He had first met Hilda thirty years earlier, when her job had been peeling shrimp in the kitchen of another restaurant. A lifetime ago. Her skin was cold coffee brown, with lighter areas, as if some of the cream had separated. Every age line in her seventy year-old face was vertical, which contrasted with the horizontal lines of her eyes and mouth, and gave her look a kind of cubist feel. That mouth, bereft of teeth, puckered and sagged like a bellows. She spoke in a cackling frenetic language all her own, knowing she was not being understood and not caring. She singularly inhabited her universe. But there was a glint in her eyes, mischievous, yearning, a reminder of who she had been. And it reminded Rob of something.

It was the twenty ninth of May. Before his stroke he could remember a fact about almost every date on the calendar. Whether it was a family member's birthday, or that of a famous person, or the date of a famous battle or treaty or assassination or natural disaster, the combination of the month and the number of the day would open up something for him. He awoke that morning knowing the twenty ninth of May meant something, something personal, to him. But he could not put his finger on it. He had finally walked to the library, found an empty computer cubicle, and entered the date. Many things came up. In 1588, the Spanish Armada left the port of Lisbon for their appointment in the English Channel. In 1765, Patrick Henry, raging against the Stamp Act, said, "if this be treason, make the most of it." In 1923, the Attorney General of the United States ruled that it

1

was legal for women to wear trousers in public. He had left the library amused, but dissatisfied.

Irina came back from the dining room, a tray half-full of dishes balanced on her shoulder. She was tall, statuesque, her legs long, her movements coltish. Her features were fair, although just beginning to tan in the early summer. She had a small straight nose under wide-spaced blue eyes, and her mouth was bowed and compact, drawn in as if in a permanent, sensual pout. With blond hair, thin and wind-blown even indoors, she looked like an artist's rendition of Slavic beauty. Rob watched her, using the overhead glass rack to shield his eyes. She glanced over toward the grill line as she walked toward him, checking to see if her next order was up. Turning sideways and bending at the knees, she laid the tray on the counter in front of him and began unloading the plates and glasses, tossing cutlery into the bus pan. A wisp of hair fell from behind her ear. She didn't look up at Rob. He noticed a rising blush on her cheeks, and as she walked away her cheeks did the jelly-dance of sadness, a sign of some disappointment, or sorrow, or worry.

He wanted to go out back before the rush came, and nodded to Hilda as he shuffled by her. His left leg dragged, although he fooled himself into thinking that it wasn't too noticeable. Out back on the small landing above the ramp, the sun was still angled high in the sky. The wind was steamy from the southwest. He leaned against the doorjamb. From the kitchen radio he heard the strains of a Beach Boys' song drifting out, and he remembered hearing it first over forty years earlier, although it had been released years before then. Back then, in his early teen years, many of Brian Wilson's songs had given him a hint of pre-nostalgia, as if they held the kernel, in their lazy sunny sadness, of a further sadness down the road. The first time he heard this particular song it etched a new emotion in him he knew he would feel again.

He caught sight of the yellow triangle of a wind surfer sliding and chattering across the shallow Albemarle Sound waters. Further out a kiteboarder swooped under his chute. On the other side of the Sound the town of Manteo brooded in the haze. To the south, returning charter boats with high superstructures ducked under the causeway bridge, slowing and turning into the channel that led to their berths in Pirate's Cove. Clouds hung low on the horizon, but he was unable to tell if they would threaten or not.

2

He turned his attention back to the east. The sky was coral on the horizon beyond the big oceanfront houses on the other side of the highway. Traffic threaded north and south, hissing and humming along the asphalt. Full summer was a few weeks away, coming with the solstice as it usually did.

Rob held the railing and drifted part-way down the ramp and then turned and came back up, his left leg stubbornly reticent. The screen door flew open in front of him. Irina came out, cigarette held in her trembling fingers. She didn't acknowledge Rob beyond a faint unconvincing smile as she let him pass. As he entered the interior darkness of the hallway leading to the kitchen he turned to watch her. She fumbled trying to light a match, which sputtered and then went out. She paused as if collecting herself before striking another. She was clearly agitated, and struggling to regain control. He watched her as predator would, looking for a weakness. Most often Irina was very sure of herself, dismissive of her other Eastern European brethren and their false fashions and uncomfortable and silly heelless shoes. Her attitude at work was that she didn't need to be there, and there was the chance that at any moment she might drop everything and walk out the door, never to return. She had been in America for a few years, and with its relentless optimistic salesmanship, it had sold her on itself. To complement her tattoos she hung with a fast, and to her mind, dangerous crowd. Rob didn't think she knew what danger was. He could tell her. He could tell her things about violence and risk, about split second decisions you could never take back. But it would be like recounting another life.

Spencer had let Rob stay at the restaurant house...for old times' sake. It was a four-bedroom beach box on pilings built in the eighties boom. Spencer had had it enclosed underneath and had put in three more bedrooms and a bathroom down there with plumbing that backed up on a regular basis. In season there were anywhere between ten and fifteen people living and crashing at the house. It was an interesting mix; college kids, two Mexican brothers who washed dishes at one of Spencer's other restaurants, a number of Russians, Serbs, Ukrainians and Poles, most of whom worked two jobs and came and went at all hours. Stennis, the forlorn assistant manager who was temporarily, he said, separated from his wife and three kids, was also staying there, and Rob. There was some kind of party every night after work. Rob was downstairs, which at first bothered him, but then he realized he never would have been able to sleep otherwise. Since his stroke it was hard to describe what stood for sleep, although most of it was spent in the shallow end of the pool and floating just below the surface. It turned out that Irina was in the room across from him. She had another Ukrainian friend who spent most of her time there. Their voices came to him at night in haughty, guttural whispers, laughs that rose at the end. Irina's cell phone rang at all hours. They often had male visitors, although this array of students, acquaintances and strays always seemed to leave disappointed. Rob kept his door cracked and from his position on the bed he watched their room, sometimes for hours. They were inconsistent about whether they left the door opened or closed, possibly because it was still and stultifying on the ground floor. There was a small table against their back wall where they sat for hours at night in the long deep shadows, talking and smoking. Rob watched them with a gleeful perverted patience. He watched their long crossed legs bare in the lamplight, watched the cigarettes trembling in their long fingers, saw the swirling air from the oscillating fan ruffle their hair and heckle the rising blue smoke.

Often he would drift in and out of consciousness, hear their voices and others in his sleep, dream them sitting there as they sat, dream-wishing for some carnal accompaniment. He would see the backs of darkened forms arrive at their door, blocking out the light, hovering above them at their table. The visitors' voices would become pleading and urgent. Their replies in husky whispers, although Rob couldn't hear the words, were dispassionate and unyielding. But then Rob would be fully awake and their door would be closed and the light gone out inside. He would lie there, perspiring, trying to remember what was dream, and what wasn't.

In an instant, he half-remembered one feverish night. It had been a few weeks before. The bass had only just stopped thumping through the floor from upstairs. It must have been after three. With the end of the music came the end to the sounds of footfalls above. He had heard Irina creep in from the outside and sidle down the hall while the music was still playing. Peering through the darkness, he thought he saw her unlock her door and enter her room. She didn't turn on the light, but Rob could hear her moving, and thought he heard the scraping open of a drawer. Then he felt her sitting at the table across from him. He strained with every effort of his eyesight to penetrate the gloom, but he could see nothing.

He was about to give up and allow himself to drift fitfully toward sleep when there was the simultaneous hissing, rasping sound of a lighting match, and a yellow explosion, circumscribed but bright, rushed across the space toward him. As it settled into flame he saw Irina's face in profile, the perfect skin, the perfect lines, especially as they drew his eyes to her long neck. She had on a short nightgown because even in early May it was warm and humid, and he only just saw the rise of her breasts as she held the match to her cigarette and then shook it out, the flame thrashing wildly to its death. Then all he could see was the faint disembodied red glow at the tip like a tiny devil dancing in the air.

Rob wanted to get up and go to her, but the person he imagined crossing the space and being welcomed by her was not the person he was. That person he remembered, or imagined he remembered, was gone, and there was no chance he was ever coming back. That realization was like a depth charge concussing inside of him.

So when the music stopped, he was lying there, dumfounded, bathed in perspiration, feeling an alternate throb and then dissipation between his legs, trying to connect his brain to it, and wryly thinking about the many times in the past when he had tried so frantically to disconnect it so he could last just a few moments longer. He felt secure in his darkness, safe to observe. And then he felt his will rising to take over and control the situation. It reached across the hall and demanded that there be light.

The click of the switch completing the circuit and the blaze flashing across the hallway were instantaneous. Rob saw Irina leaning across the table, her hands still fumbling under the lampshade. Her nightgown appeared to be made of smoke so little did it clothe her. Her image was shadows and curves, brightly lit contours and dark secret places. Rob was hard and straining against his shorts before he completed the image.

He was just on the verge of willing her to turn so that he could gather it all in from another angle when a broad silhouette filled the doorway, having come silently down the hall. The shadow enveloped Irina, the room, the light. Rob was just thinking he recognized the outline when the form stepped into the room, and with the back of its hand closed the door and sealed out all light except at the base. Rob saw moving feet there trying to speak to him in some code, but he couldn't understand it. Nor could he understand the words that came across the hallway like a rush of pebbles in the shore break. And his will was just that quickly broken.

The dining room was filling. There was a bustle in the kitchen as orders were turned in, appetizers and salads picked up and delivered. Waiters and waitresses in black and white darted back and forth. In the dish room Hilda sat on the edge of her stool looking at the counter where some dishes had begun to accumulate.

Rob came around and got into position to receive the deliveries from busboys and wait people. As he reached for the sprayer he immediately felt as if he were on the verge of remembering something else. There was a strand as delicate as a spider's web connecting him to it, and he tried to be still to let it come.

"Where are you from?" the guy in the VW bus asked him.

"The Outer Banks," Rob said, and got a blank look. "The coast of North Carolina, Cape Hatteras?"

"Oh, yeah. We're from Santa Cruz," the guy said. "We've been up in Nicaragua. It got weird. When we saw soldiers throwing bodies off the cliff we decided it was time to go. Can you score any weed around here?" First things first.

"Yeah. Some Panamanian, they say. Colombian. The locals don't care, but I'd still be cool about it. How did you pick this place?"

"We didn't pick anything, just headed south. Man, the hills. Fifty-eight horsepower in this thing means ten to fifteen miles an hour up-hill. We came out of Nicaragua, and found a little town called Tamarindo. Got waves there. Just headed south. Didn't look at a map. Didn't realize we were on a peninsula 'til we got down here. Crossing the rivers was hairy, but the locals helped. You're the first gringo we've seen since we left Tamarindo."

Rob shrugged. "It's kind of hard to get here. Just the drive you took from up north, which most people won't attempt, and then the pedestrian ferry that runs across the bay to Puntarenas. I've been here six months, and only seen a few Europeans, and a couple of Canadian hikers."

"Surf?"

6

"Mellow, mostly beach breaks. If it gets big enough you can start looking at the points. If it gets really big from the south you can try to find a ride around inside Cabo Blanco and check those points. There's always something."

"If you've been here for six months, how are you surviving?"

"I live like a king. Nothing costs anything. There's a fishing camp at the south end of town. Yellowfin tuna, cirro mackerel, grouper, you name it. There are guys who go off the reef for langusta. Two for a buck. Vegetables and fruit by the side of the road. Little sodas where you can get a Tico Tipico plate, local food, for $2."

A beat-up truck squeezed by on the narrow road, a dark face under a straw hat nodding as the crate rattled by, dust pluming behind it. The heat shimmered in the distance. The low frondy branches on the sides of the road were all coated with a patina of reddish dust. On the west side the ocean could be seen through the trees, blue-green, and white where the small surf broke toward the shore. Rob's usual reticence evaporated. He hadn't seen any gringos, or spoken English, in a while. His pidgin Spanish made it difficult to communicate with the locals, and there were days at a time when there was no one at all to speak to.

"I've been working for this Swiss woman. She bought most of the land on the east side of the road for the next three miles." He waved vaguely toward the steep hillsides. "She got with some surveyor and they broke it up into 10 hectare lots. My job is to follow the lines, clear them out a couple of feet on both sides and then plant a line of hibiscus to mark them. It's too dry to plant now, so I'm mainly just clearing lines."

"Hot work?"

"Well, yeah, but I usually just work early mornings…when there's no surf."

"Where are you staying?" the guy in the passenger seat asked. He had been quiet, leaning against his door, eyes lazy and red beneath his brows. The breeze suddenly swooped down from the hillside, blowing through the bus's open windows.

Rob remembered. The tall young busboy was standing in front of him, a glass held suspended. Had he said something out loud? He turned to shove a rack into the maw of the dish machine, and then went behind it to unload the racks that had come out. Hilda was gone… not far, he knew…drifting through the kitchen, looking for a smoke. He knew her circuit, first to Eusebio, the Honduran prep guy behind the line, then to the wait station. She didn't even have to ask anymore. Someone would see her wandering around and drop a cigarette in her hand. She would always return to the dish room with a few plates or an employee coffee cup, and drop them off before shuffling outside.

The pace began to accelerate. A steady stream of waiters, waitresses, and busboys dropped and emptied trayloads on the stainless steel counter. Glass racks were filling, and balled-up napkins and tablecloths began to fill the laundry basket. Hilda returned, shuffling, smiling, mumbling. She stopped opposite Rob, and shooed people away as they arrived with their trays. He knew what she was looking for. And then he saw it, five ounces of red wine in a bulbed glass. The staff had been warned to dump all alcohol that came back to the dish room, and they usually did. But if it was busy, or they were lazy, they would sometimes ignore the order.

Hilda's eyes took on a hooded, secretive look, something reptilian, as she turned toward the broader kitchen to see if anyone was watching. Deftly, as she emptied the tray with her left hand, she picked up the glass by the stem with her right and held it under the glass racks to Rob. He hesitated, looking at the mottled brown skin and her gnarled, ruined knuckles. But then he took it and walked the few steps to the back of the machine to the rows of clean, stacked dishes and set it behind a pile of plates. When Hilda had emptied the tray, she shuffled carefully back to her station.

The kitchen radio was now tuned to the eighties station and the song "Ninety Nine Luft Balloons" wafted above the clash and clang of pots and pans and the opening and closing of oven doors, and the cacophony of voices. Rob ran some cups up to the coffee maker near the dining room door. It opened and a wind of cool air followed Irina through. She no longer looked sad, only serious and involved. She didn't look at Rob. He was a cipher to her. She never saw him, even when she was looking right at him.

Rob stepped aside as she gathered cups and saucers. On her left upper arm, just below the white of her blouse was the black and blue of a new tattoo. The eastern Europeans had only been coming to work summers on the Outer Banks for the last four or five years, and just in the last year, it seemed, the girls especially had gone crazy for ink. But you would never know it when you saw them fully clothed. All their tattoos were hidden. Only when a blouse became untucked or a button loosened could the snaky end of a design be seen disappearing into a bra or a skirt or a pair of pants.

Everyone was moving now. The kitchen chugged along like a noisy steaming medieval engine. Food hissed on the grills and in sauté pans, was arranged on plates, and was carried to the waiting diners. Empty dirty plates, glasses and silverware were returned.

Rob had seen different kitchens working like this on and off for more than thirty years. The smells of wasted, clotted food, the noise, the bright lights, the teamwork, the music rising and falling, cool air escaping from the dining room, beads of perspiration on servers' foreheads. People drifted out the back door to smoke or whisper. There were always secrets in these kitchens, some harmless, some essential, and many dark and urgent, complicating lives, intertwining secrets that sometimes led to intertwining arms and legs. It wasn't as overt as it had been in the eighties when the desperate hedonism was fueled by cocaine and the edges were as serrated as a steak knife. Everyone was prowling then, for a line, or a gram, the hard press of lips together. None of the people in this kitchen remembered any of that. Now though there was oxycontin and heroin and ice…their own joyless poisons.

Hilda was getting tipsy behind him. She would drift off to run plates and wander, teetering, staying out of the traffic-ways, humming softly to herself. Her position wasn't one of charity because she was there six nights of every week. What she lacked in speed she made up for in steadiness. She had worked for Spencer, the owner, for almost thirty years. She was old even then. At some point she moved into the dish room. Then she had a partner, a round smiling middle-aged man named Lester, who worked with her, doted on her. They ran the dishroom, making up their own rules, harassing whoever might break them. But Lester had died long ago and left Hilda to shift for herself. Rob guessed she drank back then, but he couldn't remember.

Dustin, the chef, rounded the corner and tossed an armful of sauté pans clanging into the pot sink. His eyes fell on everything as he moved. It was his kitchen. He didn't like Rob. Dustin remembered him from the old days

9

when Rob had been a waiter, and he, Dustin, had been a busboy. Rob hadn't done anything overt, just ignored him. He hadn't recognized the drive. When Dustin left to go to culinary school, it had corresponded with Rob taking to the road, and they hadn't seen each other for more than twenty years until Rob came back, stroke-lowered, speech-impaired, limping, asking Spencer for work. Spencer sent him to the Sea Horse and Dustin, and the roles were reversed. Dustin made fun of his speech, called him "Wheaties." He'd throw various pots or pans in the sink, and then call out that he needed a specific one. Rob would search through the greasy, soapy water, wash the one he thought Dustin wanted, but Dustin would always send him back, claiming it was not the one he was looking for.

Dustin was married and had two small children. But in his kitchen at night, he dogged the women, making lewd comments to the Mexican prep girls, openly leering at the waitresses and hostesses. He was always asking to see the European girls' tattoos. There had been complaints, and he had been spoken to, but the harassment hadn't stopped. Rob thought there was something artificial and forced to it because he had seen him doting and protective of his family when they visited some afternoons before the restaurant opened. There was a truth in that affection. You could see it in his eyes. And the look in his eyes as he brazenly stared at the chest of the eighteen year old hostess spoke of a disconnect.

"Wheaties, we need ramekins," he called as he rounded the corner to return to the line.

When Rob had been outside he had noticed low brooding clouds to the south. He went out again, knowing it would be the last break he would get. The clouds had pressed forward and risen. He saw the dark gray curtain where rain had hidden the causeway bridge and was pressing on toward them. Lightning licked out across on Roanoke Island. There was still a band of awkward shimmering pink running along the base of the western horizon, but it was losing ground to the oncoming storm. The air picked up the scent of newly turned earth and sent it forward on the quickening breeze. Rob went back inside.

There was a logjam of plates and cutlery when he got back to the dish room. Hilda was working to keep up, but she only had one speed. This was to be the start of the hissing, steaming three-hour slog. He would have to concentrate to keep his feet planted on the greasy floor, which was more important now because of his gimpy, unresponsive leg. He would keep his head down because as he became busier his ability to communicate suffered. It was not a matter of not knowing what he wanted to say, or how he wanted to say it, but he had lost some ability to separate his points of concentration. He could not jump from physical manual exertion to the verbal exertion of crafting and forming words. It was as if he had to turn one light off before he could turn the other on. Something was truncated between the two lines. He knew more concentration wouldn't help. Calming himself wouldn't help. The doctor had told him that at some point the barrier might start coming down. He had meant the barrier between thoughts, and shaping those thoughts into words.

Through the perspiration dripping in his eyes, Rob watched for Irina. He saw her across the kitchen, picking up her food, and his eyes followed her as she disappeared into the dining room. He anticipated her return, longed for it with a foolishness he didn't feel was a part of himself. Her sensuality, the way he saw it, had opened doors in his mind that had been closed. Or cracked them anyway. "I Want Candy" was on the radio with its rolling, syncopated African drums, its young (was she Filipino?) singer, its Spanish-inspired guitar riff. The thunder from the south was rolling up on them. Rob could feel it vibrating through the rafters. Then with a crack and a zizzing sound, the electricity went out. The kitchen was plunged into total darkness. Rob grabbed the railing of the dish table for balance. He heard titillated, nervous laughter from the dining room. Then the emergency lights kicked in. Over at the line he could see smoke lowering into the kitchen above the grill where the exhaust fans had cut off. There was a lot of frantic activity to not much effect. Rob took a clean wine carafe and drifted over to the kitchen service bar. He filled it with white wine and returned. Hilda stood at her usual position in a kind of daze. He held the carafe up to her face as he went by. The liquid looked like amber with dancing flecks of gold in it. He poured them each a glass and stashed the remaining wine behind the dish machine. Hilda drained her glass in a moment and clawed at a couple of racks of coffee cups to run them back to the coffee maker. Rob held up his hand to stop her. Even with the emergency lighting it was dark in many areas and with all the staff running around he thought it was too dangerous for her. She turned her glassy eyes up to his and shrugged.

Rob wandered over to the dining room doors and stepped into the room, though it was forbidden for the kitchen staff to be out there. There was brash light in each of the room's corners from the emergency lamps, and single twinkling candles in the center of each table. Outside the picture windows the seated group watched occasional flicks of lightning from the almost-spent storm, but the strikes now came less regularly and less violently. Rob stood in a dark corner, drying his hands on his knee-length apron. For a second he could almost have felt sorry for himself. This weakness had only come since the stroke. He had never anticipated a lessening of his physical powers, and that the strength and obedience of half his body had been stolen away in a second was still a mystery to him. He rubbed his heavy left hand absently with his right. He tried to lift his left leg, and only succeeded in dragging it a few inches along the carpet.

Irina was hovering over a table near the picture windows, a family of four. She had her hand on the back of the man's chair. At first Rob thought they were just tourists, but then he recognized the man. It was Steven Hart. Rob remembered him from the old days. He was about ten years younger than Rob. Steven had been a young carpenter in those days, a framer, or, in the vernacular, a wood butcher. But he was focused and industrious. Over the years he had expanded into general contracting, and then into the buying and selling of the land itself. He was a big realtor now, founding co-owner of a company that built and sold vacation homes. He drove a bulging white SUV, wore a solid and expensive gold watch, had pressed clothes, and a handsome family. It was his second family.

Rob had known Steven's first wife, Paula, very well. They had had a comfortable sort of affair that had lasted for years, from before she had met Steven until some years after they had married. She and Rob were fuck-buddies before anyone had coined the term. It was just something strange and natural between the two of them. It wasn't a threat to anything. Rob knew that if he saw her now they would look at each other with nostalgic half-smiles and part without any acknowledgement. And then he remembered she was sick, very sick, with cancer.

Rob looked at Steven more closely. Steven was a dog, always had been. He looked at his pretty young wife, wondered what kind of allowances she had made to live the life she did. If he knew Steven, it was an equation, the

12

parameters of which he was continually working to expand outward. That was his personality in most things, one of the keys to his success.

The lights flickered and came back on. Rob backed into the kitchen. A thin pall of smoke clung to the ceiling above the grills, but with the exhaust fans and the back door open it began to swirl out. There was a back-log of loaded trays on the steel shelf in front of dish machine. Rob went back to his station and began to work to clear things away. It was a steady two hours of numbing work after that. Rob drank white wine that came back on the bus trays, and refilled the carafe he shared with Hilda. He convinced himself that he wasn't getting too buzzed, but he lost track of how many glasses he had. By the time the pot sink filled up after service he realized he was unsteady on his feet. He was worried as he made his way gingerly over to the pots. He had been warned. He kept his head down and scrubbed.

An hour later most of it was done. The chef's crew had finished hosing down the line. The wait-staff was well into their clean-up chores. Trays heavily laden with clean glasses and silverware were carried out to the dining room to set it for the next day's service. Stennis buzzed in and out, checking on the progress. Rob tried to stay out of his way until he realized he wasn't paying much attention to anything except getting to the bar for his after-work cocktail. That was clearly the motivation for most of the front-end staff. When Rob finished up the pots and came back around to the dish machine. Hilda was almost finished running the clean plates, silverware, coffee cups, and glass racks back to their respective stations. Her dark eyes were glazed and tinged with a jaundiced yellow. He wondered how she did it, night after night, year in year out.

Rob heard Spencer's booming voice as he was beginning to hose down the dishroom floor. Spencer owned three restaurants on the beach. He also owned and leased the biggest shopping center, had his hand in many of the housing developments in the area, including a couple of the most expensive ones on the northern beaches. Rob knew he owned twenty or thirty rental houses, including four oceanfront mansions. He also had vacation houses in Cabo San Lucas and Monserrat, and an apartment in New York City. There were rumors that he had other far-flung businesses. Some said he owned a block in downtown Vail, where his wife now lived, and others said that he had mining interests in Montana and Wyoming, and owned thousands of acres on the Kenai Peninsula in Alaska. He had worked hard for years, expanding and consolidating his holdings with a combination of acumen and good luck to a point now where he was now probably one of the richest men on the Banks, maybe one of the richest in the state. He was semi-retired. His control over all his holdings, including his restaurants, now consisted of dropping in unannounced to check on things. Most times his visits were unremarkable. He would make a suggestion or two, but he took pains not to undermine his every-day management teams. If he did find problems however he could be a bear. His temper was legendary. In the old days when the Seahorse was his first and only business, his tantrums could start from nothing and build to spitting, plate-throwing frenzies. He no longer terrorized his staffs, but that was really a nod to the politically-correct new realities than to anything else.

Rob grabbed the heavy garbage can and wheeled it to the back door. He usually needed a waiter's help to get it down the slippery ramp to the dumpsters, but in this case it was just more important to get himself out of Spencer's path. The sky had cleared after the earlier storm. There was a breeze, but it was still heavy and wet. The moisture seemed to wash the stars, dimming their outlines. The horns of the new moon pointed at the heavens.

At the top of the ramp Rob realized he was stuck. An honest appraisal of his strengths told him he would not be able to control the food and drink-slurried plastic can once it began rolling down the incline. The left side of his body had not the strength or the grip to guide it. Nor could he lift it once he got it down to the dumpster. He stood on the small landing, his good right hand on the plastic handle of the can. He heard footsteps approaching the back door and turned. The door opened and silhouetted in the kitchen light was Spencer's broad shadow.

"Rob," he said, coming out, "you need help with that?"

Rob nodded and lowered his head, turning away, wary of the alcohol on his breath. They were both embarrassed, each holding their separate memories of the past. With a hold on opposite handles, they fought to get the can down the ramp. It was all Spencer's strength that lifted it over the edge of the dumpster and let the full bag slosh down inside. Spencer slapped his hands together and looked around for something to wipe them with.

"Rob," he said. "I have to ask you to leave the house."

Rob didn't say anything.

14

"You know there have been complaints. And then after the other night…well, it's just too much. I've got these girls living there from the other side of Europe, for Christ's sake. I can't have it. We go way back, but I can't have it."

"But I…"

"Rob, you were half-naked in the hallway at three in the morning, drunk, crying about your daughter. Those girls don't understand any of that. It's not fair to them. They're so far from home, and it's my job to protect them. Now, I know you wouldn't do anything, but they don't know that."

Rob stood there, looking at the ground, shaking his head. He couldn't line up the words to say what he was thinking so he remained silent.

"I can front you a couple of hundred, if that'll help." Rob shook his head. "You need to do something to pull yourself together, Rob, really. Look at yourself. Have you and Hilda been drinking tonight?"

"Yes, but just enough to keep me on an even keel." There was no use denying it. "I understand your position, Spencer. Don't sweat it."

"What happened to us, Rob?"

"We're getting old, some of us more quickly than others," Rob said, slapping his leg.

"What's happening with that?"

"It's getting better," Rob lied.

Spencer looked hard at him, and then something in his expression collapsed. He didn't care. Before he was forced to acknowledge it, he turned and moved toward the ramp.

"Find somewhere else to stay tonight, and you can get your stuff tomorrow. Come by the main office and we'll stroke you a check to get by. I'm sorry, you know that."

That was three, or was it four days ago. Rob rushed down the steps from the bathhouse to the beach. He knew the woman had called security. She had caught him showering in his surf trunks at the community's private cabana, looked at him and his backpack, and then gone back toward the parking lot and her car to get her phone, he was sure. He didn't wait for her to come back. He rinsed the soap off quickly and grabbed his stuff. He was a hundred yards down the beach when he looked back and saw the security guy with his creased khaki shorts and logoed pink shirt up on the deck scanning the beach for him. But it was only a moment before Rob realized the guy wasn't going to follow him. The clouds above the ocean were pillowy and brilliant white on top with ash gray edges underneath. Although the breeze was blowing smartly enough that there were whitecaps driven north along the horizon, the clouds above seemed to float aimlessly. The heat from the sun was warm and penetrating.

Rob had awakened that morning on an oceanfront deck next to a pool, surrounded by floats and beach chairs and collapsed umbrellas. He knew there was going to be trouble because he felt no sign, other than the gray felt feeling on his tongue, of any sort of hangover. The red dawn sun had winked behind the clouds. He had no idea how he had gotten on that deck and could remember little of the night before. There had been some kind of party after work. He didn't know how or if he had been invited, or how he had gotten there. He had drunk beer out of a red plastic cup, and then rum, first with coke, and when that ran out he mixed it with anything close by. His memory was that he had held it together for longer than he should have been able to. But then there was something else. It was the feeling he sometimes got, and he didn't know where it came from, that he had done something horrible and wrong, but he couldn't remember what it was. But what clearly remained was guilt.

He kept walking south. His backpack was slung over his left shoulder and it dug in. Walking on the sand was a penance because he couldn't disguise his infirmity.

He kept his head down. He crossed to the Beach Road at the old Dolphin Motel. It wasn't there anymore. It had been torn down and replaced with three ten bedroom pastel beach palaces, all complete with twelve bathrooms, in-ground pools, hot tubs on each deck, professional kitchens with two of everything; stoves, oven, microwaves, dishwashers, refrigerators. There was a small, private walkway between two of them. Rob opened the high gate and walked toward the Beach Road, limping as if he were carrying a cross. No one saw him, or acknowledged him if they did, as he slipped across the two lanes.

Crossing the five lanes of the by-pass highway was more problematic. The early summer traffic hummed both ways. He couldn't run. He waited, perspiration clutching at his clothing. His head throbbed. He was at a place where he knew he couldn't remain still for long. He had to move forward, and keep moving forward, to try to keep the blackness of the hangover behind him. Finally he could cross, a gap opening seemingly from nowhere. As he shuffled across the hot asphalt he waited for a car to appear out of nowhere, crush his body, and drag it to the south. But then he was on the land side of the highway and safe. He slowly drifted up the restaurant driveway, climbed the ramp to the back door. Salsa music came from the prep room behind the line. Lupe, the Mexican pastry chef, was working on the desserts for the evening. Dustin was in the chef's office on the phone. Rob passed quietly. He went back to the laundry room and pulled clothes out of his backpack, covered them with a layer of napkins and soiled tablecloths, and spun the knobs to turn the machine on. He was determined to keep that part of himself together anyway. He went into the employee bathroom and looked at himself in the mirror. Not as good as he had hoped, although he thought he had lowered his expectations enough. His hair was matted and pressed flat on one side. The gray in it seemed to grow faster and left a bushy nest around his ears. But it was his eyes that were most problematic. His left eyelid showed a laziness that dropped to his cheek and then to his jowl. Again he realized his best bet was to keep his expression as neutral as possible. To test it he smiled into the glass. The left side of his face was heavy, flaccid, dough-like. The contrasting animation on the right side looked garish and held up by invisible strings. He splashed himself with water and dragged a comb through his hair.

He slunk out of the bathroom and pressed open the double doors to the dining room. The feeling came on him in an instant. It wasn't an anxiety attack. It was something more sinister, more hopeless. Between his ears a chaotic struggle was going on, having to do with what he could remember and what he couldn't, what was true and what was conjecture and those things that were false, or could have been. He again got the feeling that he was guilty of something, and it was something he would not get away with.

The two hours until he could punch in and begin work were a penance. He paced the empty dining room, went out the back door and paced the Soundside deck. He descended the outside stairs and trampled the spongy marsh grass as he made his way around the building to the kitchen door and did it all again.

The early crew of the waitstaff began drifting in at four. If Irina didn't show up for her shift it would be the third day she had missed.

17

II

"Do you remember Paula, Steven Hart's first wife?" Chick asked.

"Sure." He looked at Chick, knowing he knew about Paula and him.

"Oh, yeah… I forgot," he said, and tried to reconstruct those days. "You know she's really sick…cancer."

"I heard that," Rob said. "I was just thinking about her the other night. I saw Steven out to dinner. His new wife looks good, a couple of nice-looking kids."

It was almost seven in the evening, steamy on the porch, and the mosquitos were beginning to drift in, murmuring in their ears. Chick was smoking, flicking ashes over the deck railing. His girlfriend, Tanya, was inside cooking them dinner. Chick had rescued Rob a few days earlier. There was no other word for it. It had been a week since Spencer had asked Rob to leave the employee house. Rob had treated it as if it were something that hadn't required immediate attention. It was almost summer. He had crashed on the beach, in open oceanfront cabanas, and one night he had stretched out on a pool lounge chair beneath the decks of a massive occupied oceanfront home. He didn't look on it as homelessness, not in the mild pleasant weather.

The front screen door creaked open and Tanya stepped out. She was small and round. There was an openness in her expression, a readiness to smile, a curiosity about the things around her that somehow almost always leaned to the mysterious and the occult. She was half-mother to Chick, jealously and efficiently taking care of his physical needs, the cooking, the cleaning, the marketing, the laundry. At first Rob thought Chick was taking advantage of her. It was her house, after all, and when Rob first saw them together there, it was clear that Chick was in charge. He was firm as he told her what and how he wanted things done. For her part, Tanya acquiesced, but without the hint of subservience that had usually marked Chick's relationships with women. So when Chick snapped an order or made a demand, her open readiness softened him in turn.

"I heard you mention Paula," Tanya said. "She died last night, you know? Cammie called this afternoon. Those poor kids."

It didn't register with Rob, and then it did. He experienced a momentary chill in the oppressive humidity. Then he saw her, Paula, as clearly as if she had been with them on that porch. It was a night thirty years earlier. She was tall, her skin nut-brown, her hair cut short. He was looking at her, up and down, all of her, and she liked it. She knew about Jane, and he knew about her boyfriend then. This was years before she met Steven. Neither cared. She had pulled him outside of the churn of the summer party, an impish, inviting smile on her face. She gently dragged him into the dark and kissed him before he could speak. From that tipsy germ something had grown, never acknowledged or pursued, something based on accidental or propitious meetings and an inchoate magnetism. And now the positive pole of that magnetism was no more.

"Those poor kids," Tanya repeated.

Two crickets began a clicking conversation in the flowerbed beneath the deck's railing. The three of them stopped to listen, each hearing and feeling something different. Chick sighed and shifted position. Rob thought he'd changed a lot, with Tanya's help. Apparently the frantic need to be jobbing everyone around him was gone. He'd long since given up fishing and taken up trim carpentry. From all reports he had a real flair, not just with the intricacies, but creatively. His reputation got him steady, reliable work, work that he took seriously. Rob felt funny thinking it to himself, but Chick was organized and responsible. His truck downstairs was a testament to that organization, everything in its place.

A late bee thrummed along among the flowers, bouncing awkwardly from one to another, bending stems over as it landed.

"This summer hasn't even begun, and it is flying by," Chick mused.

"It sure is," Rob said. "Every third day I wake up is Monday."

They were quiet, and the evening was quiet. Far away they could hear the traffic on the bypass droning and hissing eerily. A dog barked down the street and was answered by another. Rob knew better than to try to concentrate. He was relaxed in a way he hadn't been in a while, safe and inwardly quiet, with people he knew. He thought that for only a moment, and then knew it wasn't true. He wouldn't be able to stay for long without disrupting the fragile chemistry between Chick and Tanya. Did Chick deserve the peace and quiet? No, probably not, but that was not Rob's call.

"I'll have something for you boys to eat in a while here," Tanya said. "It's heating up on the stove." She opened the door and disappeared inside.

Rob leaned forward in his chair. He had not had a drink in three days. This morning he had awakened in a sweat, tangled in the sheet that covered him. There was an internal pain in his lower back deep in his abdomen, a stabbing ache. He still could not eat. It seemed to him that he hadn't eaten in a long time, as if food wasn't necessary to him anymore. When he was drinking, most days he was too hung over to be able to get down more that a few bites of anything, and now that he stopped he found that he just had no hunger for it. He knew it couldn't last, that the biology of it wasn't sustainable, but he figured he would let it ride.

"What's happening with that Russian girl?" Chick asked.

"Ukrainian," Rob corrected. "She's Ukrainian. She hasn't been seen or heard from in a week. No one knows anything. The police don't seem concerned. They think she might have gone to DC or New York. They all end up going to New York, but usually they wait until the end of the summer. But who knows? She's not the same as most of them. She's been in the states for a couple of years. I don't think anyone's sure what connections she may have developed. I've heard rumors about her and different people, but I don't know."

"You seem awfully interested in her. What's that all about?" Chick leaned forward and turned to look into the darkened house to make sure Tanya wasn't in earshot. "I see them riding their bikes, and, I don't know, they just look different... fuckable, you know."

Rob didn't answer about his interest in Irina, and didn't offer his opinion as to their overall fuckability. He was confused because something in his memory was letting him down again. He had lost his bearings. He knew something was there, but he couldn't conjure it up. The throbbing started in his back again. What did that mean? It felt as if an organ, his spleen or pancreas or something, had hardened and was turning gray or black. He had arthritis in his wrists, fingers, most of his joints. Sleeping out of doors hadn't helped.

Chick rocked back and forth slowly. "I wonder what JP is doing."

"He's not doing anything, Chick, he's dead."

"But don't you wonder what they see, what they know? I always got the feeling that once they were separated from us by it, by death, that they could see and understand everything that had been hidden when they were alive. If that's not the way it is, what's the point of being dead?"

"The one thing about it is that there is no point."

"I just throw up my hands, like to Paula now, and say 'OK, here I am. I thought this, I did that, and I'm doing this right now.'"

"Maybe that's why we bury them," Rob said.

At the corner a police cruiser turned on to the street and came slowly up the block. Rob and Chick both experienced a 'flight or fight' moment. Each had things from the past that could still potentially bubble up, debts that might be called in. But neither moved from their seats.

The cruiser did stop in front of the house. A tall young patrolman got out, adjusted his patent leather belt, and put on his hat. From above him on the second floor deck, Rob could see that he was in his mid-twenties, fit, with an erect posture and a military haircut. Chick stood and went to the railing.

"Can I help you, officer?" he asked.

The patrolman was still adjusting his kit, tugging at the heavy belt with its big holster as he came forward.

"I'm looking for a Robert Wheat," he said, looking at the notebook in his hand.

Rob didn't move. The patrolman was still approaching and disappeared below the margin of the deck floor.

"Come on up," Chick said in an easy, open voice.

Rob was still in the chair. His deadened left side would not allow him to rise. The apprehension became hard and calcified. The patrolman got to the top of the stairs and stepped on the landing.

"God damn," Chick said. "Davy? Davy Todd, is that you? How's your mom?"

The cop clearly didn't recognize Chick, and threw him an embarrassed smile.

"It's Millie Todd's boy," Chick said to Rob. "We've known your mom for thirty five years, I bet. Tell her Rob Wheat and Chick Gandil said hi."

"I will, I will," the officer said. He smiled again awkwardly, and then pulled a paper from his breast pocket. He was clearly uncomfortable with

Chick's social interjections and wanted to get to the business that had brought him there in the first place. Rob looked up at his serious professional expression and they caught each others eyes before the patrolman looked back down at his paper. "Do you know a woman named Irina Kolovitch?"

"Yes, I work with her at the Sea Horse," Rob answered.

"When was the last time you saw her?"

"I don't know…like a week ago. I know she hasn't shown up for work in a while."

"What is your relationship with her?"

"Well, none," Rob said. "I worked with her. I was her housemate for a while."

"You moved out, and then she disappeared at the same time, isn't that right?"

"I moved out. I don't know when she disappeared, or if she disappeared."

"What about Nadia Smolensky?"

Rob looked hard at the patrolman, and then at Chick. Chick stood just beyond the shoulder of the patrolman and leaned against the deck railing. He was smiling, but not convincingly. Rob thought, if this were some kind of serious investigation, why was there not a detective asking him these questions?

"What's this about?" Rob asked quietly. "Why are you here?"

There was an immediate hitch in the officer's stance. He actually took a step back and cleared his throat. Rob bored into the young man's eyes, and Chick picked up on it.

"Yeah, Davy, what's going on here?" Chick asked, coming around to where he could look at him squarely.

The young officer recovered himself quickly. "I was sent by my lieutenant, who had to be in court today. These," he said, holding up the paper in his hand, "are the questions he gave me. I think you better be ready to answer them."

"I did answer them," Rob said. "I don't know what happened to her, or if anything did happen to her."

"But that doesn't change the fact that you were one of the last people to see her before she disappeared. You were seen arguing with her, or at least

22

having a very animated conversation with her, at a party on the night she was last seen."

Rob didn't remember anything of that, not a bit. There was no glimmer of a memory of it. He almost remembered a party. When was that? Was she there? He remembered being drunk, too drunk, typically drunk. He had talked to a lot of people, but he couldn't remember to whom he had been talking, or what the conversations had been about. But he hadn't talked with her, he was sure. He would have remembered her eyes looking into his. He would have remembered her smell. But it was gone.

He shrugged. "I had a buzz."

"So how is your mom?" Chick asked, signaling the conversation was over.

"She's fine. You know, teaching the kids, as she'd say…"

"What ever happened to your dad? I haven't seen or heard about him in fifteen years, I bet."

Officer Davy shuffled, looked from one to the other. "He lives in Florida. He's got a new family and all. He's calmed down a lot. He had a heart attack this spring, not real serious, but he's slowed down."

"Haven't we all? I was just thinking while you were asking Rob questions, remembering you playing baseball when you were a kid. Your dad was the coach, right?"

"Yes. He was big into baseball. I don't know if he still is."

"I heard someone say you were in the Marines. Is that right? And that you went to Iraq?"

"I'm a Marine. I was in Iraq, in '07, in Al Ramadi when it was bad. I mostly stayed behind the wire though…on base."

"You saw some things there though, I bet."

"Yes, I saw some things."

The sun was descending below the tree line, meandering through the clouds there, and the light took a softer glow. The crickets were rosining their bows, and there was a buzz of other insects in the air, along with the evening arguments of the birds. Rob rocked slowly in the chair. He began to realize that Davy was the same age as his daughter, Kelly. Had they gone to school together? They must have, but he couldn't think about that.

Chick turned and called into the dark interior of the house for Tanya to get him another cold beer. "You want one?" he asked Davy.

The young officer shook his head. He folded the paper in his hands and put it in his breast pocket. "Let us know if you hear anything about Irina. We don't want to treat it as a missing persons' case just because then we'd have to bring in their government, but another couple of days and we won't have any choice."

"But you know her," Rob said, again getting the feeling that there was something personal about this visit. "How do you know her?"

"I gave her a courtesy ride one night. The bars had closed and she and her friend, the girl Nadia, were walking home. They were drunk. They gave me their number, I don't know why. But before I could call her, this happened." He went to the stairs. "You all take care. Call us if you hear anything, or remember anything."

He went heavily down the steps and back across the driveway to his cruiser. He opened the door and slid inside where he sat behind the wheel writing something on a pad. Then he backed out and drove slowly down the street.

Rob had not been able to eat his dinner. Tanya worried that it was her cooking, offered to fix him something else, but he calmed her by saying he was just having some gastric distress. After the meal Chick went down to his shop in the garage. Rob stood outside on the deck above, listening to the occasional ringing buzz of the table saw, and the hideous whine when it stopped, watching the yellow square of light from the window become more defined as the outside sky darkened. It was nice to be clean, and to have his clothes clean. He had been able to shave. He looked half-way normal.

He decided to walk down to the beach. It was a larger decision than it used to be. It was a quarter-mile to the highway, which would then have to be crossed against the summer traffic, and then another block, between the highways, it was called, and then across the beach road to the strand itself. Tanya was inside finishing up the dishes. Rob took a step toward the door to tell her where he was going, but then decided against it and went down the deck stairs. It was a quiet beach neighborhood they lived in, with local families that provided the backbone for the tourist and construction economy. It had become quieter in recent years because of the foreclosures. Scattered through the neighborhood were the empty houses of those who had been forced to leave. There were enough of them that Rob wondered where all the people could have gone. Rob shuffled down the street, each step like a sigh. There was no use in hurrying. He would get there when he got there. He had a long wait to cross the highway. He stood there like a statue. When he finally saw a gap in the traffic, he hurried across the still warm pavement.

He went into the convenience store on the corner and bought a six-pack of malt liquor. It was a decision, but he allowed it to make itself. He counted his change. $39. He opened one can and hooked the other five in the claw of his left hand. The first one was gone by the time he walked the block to the beach road. He dropped it by the side of the pavement.

The sea oats waved as he crossed through a gap in the dunes. There was still a thin band of vibrant yellow pressed against the ocean on the eastern horizon and still a bit of pink to the west, but mostly a rich purple was striding from east to west, and more stars were twinkling on by the moment. Tourist families were out strolling after their early dinners, flying kites, tossing Frisbees. Couples stayed closer to the water, holding hands. An anemic shore break lapped against the angle of the beach, running up and then fading back on itself. At one point, as it grew darker, the sand began to glow, yellow and golden, but only momentarily, and then turned gray. The lights of the beach cottages looming over the dunes became more distinct.

It didn't matter which way Rob went. He thought that for a second, but then he knew exactly where he was going. He turned south and began walking. The Avalon Pier walked out on its creosoted pilings in the near distance. Again he realized there was no use in hurrying. In the further distance the adumbrated form of the Nags Head Pier twinkled under points of yellow light. He sidled closer to the water where he hoped the sand would be firmer, but it was loose all the way down.

By the time he got to Avalon Pier fatigue was already upon him. He hadn't planned to stop, but he found himself trudging up the wooden steps to the parking lot. At the south end of the lot, sitting and standing and teetering on the sea wall, was the usual crew, by now wound up and getting rowdy. Most had been there since late morning, drinking beer, smoking joints, doing nothing, looking for more dangerous nothings to do. It was about time for a fight to break out, two drunken middle-aged beach bums with brown torsos and crinkled eyes wrestling and flailing wildly, the other men cheering them on, their skinny meth-addled harridans screeching and whining for adult behavior. Rob didn't need that. He went into the pier house. It cost a buck to walk out over the water, ten if you wanted to bring your gear and fish. He paid his dollar to the grizzled, coughing man behind the counter, who only perfunctorily looked at the cans gripped in his left hand as he passed. Where it was warm and steamy on the beach, a soft cool naked breeze rose from beneath the gaps in the pilings. There were about twenty people on the pier, mostly out toward the end. Some were bottom fishing for spot and flounder. The few at the furthest margin were there for the night looking for shark. An ammoniated whiff of dried bait shrimp rose to his nostrils. It raised a memory of his childhood, of being on a concrete pier in central Florida with his father and brother, the late-morning water pale green and sparkling, the patrons all smiling (at least in the memory) under broad-rimmed straw hats. But somehow the memory had lost its organic element. It was flattened like a pane of glass, without dimension or depth. He could not recall his father's face, and when he plumbed other memories he still could not resurrect it. He immediately thought of Irina and encountered the same dilemma. It brought such a strong anxiousness upon him that he veered to the pier railing for support. He leaned forward, looking down into the dark swirling pool below him. The lights from land on the periphery of his vision alternately faded and stood out brightly.

These bouts of dizziness now sometimes visited him. He practiced the breathing exercises he had learned at the clinic after the stroke and gradually he calmed himself. This was not who he was, not the way he was. This timidity, the hesitation, the fatigue, the confusion... He straightened himself as fully as he could and looked to the south. The lights of the beach town gaily sparkled. He had miles to walk tonight, and that recognition was a start. He did have a plan, or at least the bare bones of one. He finished off the second can of malt liquor and opened a third.

He went back through the pier house, and down the stairs back to the beach with his head down. As he made his way south, he spent half his time looking out to sea and the other half cataloguing the changes that had taken place amid the oceanfront buildings in the dunes. It was hard to recognize and remember now where things had been. There were great swaths of beachfront that in the boom had gone over from the modest family cottages built in the sixties and seventies to the massive oceanfront minihotels with their many bed- and bathrooms, and their overwhelming amenities. A mile south of the Avalon Pier he began to get apprehensive. It came upon him suddenly and without warning that he was approaching the site of the old Croatan Inn, where JP had been killed so many years earlier, a lifetime earlier. He didn't know if he would recognize where it stood, until his eyes were called back from the land to the shore. The telltale marker was just off the beach. If the tide had been higher, he might not have seen it at all. It was the skeleton of an old wooden ship, lying just feet off the beach in the place where it had rested for years, at least thirty because he remembered being on the beach there with Jane and all their friends in the mid-eighties. The wreck was in the shore break even then. Their group would meet on the beach in front of the old Inn every Sunday, soaking up the atmosphere and the sun beneath the cedar shakes and white shutters, playing volleyball, getting cold beers from the cooler at the back screen door, and merely signing for them, trusted to return every few weeks to cover their tabs. He kept his head down and moved on.

A half mile further on he passed the Orville and Wilbur Wright Motel. He remembered the waterspout that came ashore and sliced through the building. That had to have been in the late seventies when he was still a teenager. There was the story of the woman who was driving when she saw it approaching, jumped out of her car, threw herself in the shallow ditch next to the road as she had been taught to do, and then died when a flying refrigerator sucked from one of the motel rooms fell from the sky and landed on her. Another half mile and Rob found himself slowing, pondering the dune line. There were more giant houses, glass-fronted, brightly-lit, with happy, animated figures moving about inside.

Then he remembered…the Merry-Go-Round…a second-hand store that had been there for years. But also on that sprawling lot there had been built, at different times, a six-room motel, a house, and three tiny one-bedroom cottages hunkered down in the dunes. Rob had lived with a friend in one of those un-insulated single-bedroom cottages in the winter of 76-77 when he was eighteen. The friend had the bedroom, and Rob had huddled on the couch in front of the ceramic gas heater, a heater that struggled against that brutal winter. It had been so cold that year that the Sound had frozen, thawed a bit, and then frozen again, pushing up ridges of ice in some places five or six feet high. Rob had worked as a roofer that winter, freezing all day, and then coming home to the cottage where he could only warm himself one side at a time.

Three other friends, acquaintances really, rented the bottom floor of the bigger house on the property. A father and his two teenage daughters rented the apartment upstairs. The friends had bought a cheap wood stove and jerry-rigged it downstairs in their living room, setting it on a bed of loose bricks and jutting the stove pipe out the window through a hole they'd cut in a piece of plywood. Rob and Timmy, his roommate, looked for excuses to visit, bringing gifts of pot or beer to assuage their hosts. One bitter February night they bundled themselves up and crossed the wind-driven lot to the big house. Three hours and a number of beers later they were offered the living room couch and lazy-boy recliner for the night. The stove was stoked to the brim and they all went to sleep.

Later that night, and for no good reason, Rob suddenly awoke. Just inches above his nose there was an undulating gray and orange blanket of smoke. He could feel the heat coming off the stove, which when he looked over was humming, glowing a bright orange, and appeared to be liable to melt on the spot. Rob rolled to the floor, shook Timmy's foot, and then crab-walked back to the bedrooms to wake the others. When he returned to the living room Timmy had opened the front door and the hard icy wind was swirling in and some of the thick gray smoke was swirling out. Rob tried to open a window on the other side of the room, but it was nailed shut and wouldn't budge.

The stove was a violent shimmering red, still vibrating, and was making an eerie hissing sound. If it melted, or fell over, Rob was afraid the house would quickly burn down. He sent Timmy upstairs to wake those occupants, but they were already coming down the outside steps. The smoke had drifted up under the soffit, reformed inside their walls like a ghost, and awakened them. Rob grabbed the tongs, and opened the softening stove door. He pulled it out a burning log and dragged it across the floor and out the door. Sparks hopped onto the carpet and floor, and as Rob came back in, Timmy was stamping around doing an Indian dance to make sure they would not flame up. After pulling out the remaining four logs the glow began to dull and the smoke had risen so a person could almost walk upright in the room.

It was bitterly cold and windy outside. The wind charged down the dunes, and sent sand swirling through the air. The father and daughters from upstairs were dancing on the balls of their feet, the tails of their blankets flapping. The only phone on the property was in the main house where the owners lived, but they were in Florida for a month. There was probably no one else living within a mile of them that winter so there was no where to go to find a phone to call the fire department. Rob sent everyone but Timmy back to their little place, and the two of them made sure the fire was completely out and buried the logs in the side of the dune outside.

As quickly as they could they too returned to their apartment. Everyone was crammed on the couch under smoky blankets, laughing, passing a joint. The father of the teenage girls wore a sheepish smile as he drew a long toke. Timmy grabbed blankets and pillows out of his room and gradually everyone spread out, the two girls and their dad on the couch, and Rob and his three friends trying to get comfortable on the floor. After a while everyone but Rob was asleep. He was still afraid an errant unfound coal might flare up in the house across the way, but it never did.

A half hour later he was approaching the invisible border between Kill Devil Hills and Nags Head. He had finished off his six-pack and was trying not to think of crossing over to the bypass to get another. It was only a little farther. He dragged himself forward, wondering how long his resolve would last. There were fewer people on the beach. The families had returned to their cottages to play backgammon and scrabble, or more likely to grab their mobile devices and ignore each other. A few couples had drifted out, some clambering up onto the lifeguard stands, others crossing in front of him to kick at the shore break, or to toss out shells to awaken the phosphorescent creatures just below the ocean's surface.

Rob kept his head down, moving inexorably south. His plan was to get to the restaurant as it was closing to the public. There would still be another hour or two of clean up for the staff. Staying at Chick's had allowed Rob to make himself presentable enough to be able to sit in the bar as wait people and kitchen staff finished and came out for a beer or a shot, and to plan their evening.

He got to the parking lot, crossed it, and went up the grand stairway to the front door. The clock inside read 9:45…perfect timing for his purposes. The young hostesses were straightening up the entrance area. They stood upright when he came in, but when they realized who he was they ignored him and went on with their chores. The dining room was still a third full. From what Rob could see at the entrance foyer only two or three tables were still eating their entrees, and the rest were in various stages of wrapping their evenings up.

Rob went on towards the bar. A pair of early crew waiters was already perched on stools. They held up their beers to acknowledge him, and then went back to their conversation. Rob went by them and awkwardly lifted himself to a seat at the far end. There was no one behind the bar, the bartender apparently in the kitchen grabbing a late bite or fetching supplies to re-stock the back bar. The lighting was soft and mellow, the music too. There was a votive candle in front of him, the butter-colored flame undulating within a curved wall of colored glass. When the bartender didn't return directly, Rob began to get apprehensive. What had seemed like a good idea, a way to anonymously gather information, now seemed like a long walk that might not turn up anything. But putting things in their proper order, he wanted a drink.

He was glad to see Julie, the lead bartender, coming back from the kitchen, carrying a cup of soup in one hand and bowl of lemons and limes in the other. Beneath her leonine head of hair and hooked blade of a nose, she had the smile of one who knew how to keep your secrets, but might exact a price for it later. She was small, almost petite, but in the last few years she had been given over to a bit of roundness. She was always kind to Rob, although he wasn't sure why. He thought it might have had something to do with Kelly, but he didn't want to think about that.

Julie looked over at him as she set down her things. She was kind to him, but it was her bar and the first thing she wanted was to make sure that he wasn't drunk.

"Hey, Julie," he said, wanting to quickly nip that in the bud.

"Hey, Rob," she said in her throaty bartender's voice. "You didn't work tonight, did you?"

"No, I've been out walking, enjoying the evening." He smiled crookedly, and looked down. God damn it, he thought, relax. He could feel perspiration beading on his forehead, and he wiped it away. He didn't have any reason to be nervous. "How about a beer?"

"Sure," she said. She reached under the bar, pulled a bottle out, snatching off the top in one motion, and slid it to him. "It's on us."

He looked at the bottle, and concentrated on making it last.

The bar wasn't open to the public after dinner service. It was there to handle the overflow of waiting customers during the evening, and then only stayed open afterward to wind down the staff as they came off their shifts. Occasionally a customer would come in off the street. Locals, friends of the restaurant, and young women were usually let in. Everyone else was sent on his way.

Rob worked on putting himself in cipher mode. He didn't want to be seen or noticed. He wanted to listen because he had a strong feeling there were clues to be found among his co-workers. Someone knew something about Irina and her disappearance, whether they knew it or not. Gradually the staff, both from the front of the house and the kitchen, began to drift in. There was a ball game playing out on the TV above the bar. The sound was down, and from where Rob was it looked like small live pieces scurrying across a game board.

The members of the early crew wait staff were the first to come in. They had changed into their street clothes and were carrying their tote bags. They ordered beers or glasses of wine. Depending on the increase of general hilarity and if there was a lack of potential outside distractions, shots might come later. And then, who knew?

Steven Hart walked through the entrance a few minutes later, dressed arch-casually in a pressed pastel shirt and pressed shorts and heavy leather Jesus sandals. He waved to Julie behind the bar and walked past the occupied bar stools toward Rob. There was a serious, etched expression on his face that he was trying to hide behind his forced smile. He came right toward Rob without recognizing him and pulled out the stool one place away. Instead of speaking up and identifying himself, Rob kept his head down and watched him. Steven was a large man whose torso had thickened through the years, though not gone to fat. His hair was thinner than it had been and was going gray at the temples. He was deeply tanned from hours on his boat and on the golf course. Steven looked like what he was, a successful contractor and entrepreneur, one who was comfortable in his clothes, and with his houses and cars and toys.

Staring obliquely at him, Rob saw the tight serious set of his brow, and sensed impatience in his movements.

"Steven," Rob said, turning toward him.

"Rob? God damn. What are you doing these days, man?"

Rob shrugged. "Just this. I heard about Paula," he blurted. "I'm sorry."

Steven shook his head. "We haven't really been close in a while. It's…this has been a long time in coming. Not that it makes it easier on anyone. The kids…her kids, they're taking it hard." He shook his head again. "You know the expression, 'water under the bridge'? After a while, after living as long as we have, it all ends up being water under the bridge, with no chance of stopping it, or even slowing it down. And then something like this happens, and for a moment it does stop…just long enough to let you know your turn is coming, and then the river flows on again." He looked at Rob, the faded blue of his eyes glistening a little in the low light. "Let me buy you a drink. What are you having?"

Rob looked down and saw the beer he had just gotten was already almost finished. "One of these, I guess. Thanks."

"You know what's odd," Steven said, after ordering the beer for Rob and a vodka martini for himself, "Misty, my wife now, she's taking it harder than I am. In the last couple of months she's spent a lot of time over there with Paula. It's changed her. She went from this fun-loving little bundle of cuddles to…I don't know, something more serious. She won't tell me what they talked about. She and the kids, our kids, Paula's and mine, are whispering on the phone all the time. I don't know, man, I'm afraid she may be getting religion." He laughed, quickly and unconvincingly. "Jesus."

"I'm sorry," Rob said again.

Julie brought their drinks, and patted the top of Steven's hand as she deposited them on the bar in front of them. Rob looked over at Steven, held up his glass in thanks.

"How's business?"

"It's coming back. It was great for a while, then nothing. But it's happening again now. That's what I tell myself. Nobody's buying, nobody's building, except the rich. Their money came back…like it always does." He laughed. "A lot of people got over-extended. It was a correction, people will

32

tell you. I know I've been corrected." He sipped his drink, leaning forward and looking sideways at Rob. "How are you? I mean, what happened?"

"I had a stroke last summer," Rob answered. "They don't know what caused it. I'm recovering, but it's a slow road. It's just one side, my left side. My body has to relearn everything. It's a pain in the ass really, because I forget and try to do things, and my body just won't respond. I'm slow and unsteady." He shrugged. "My voice, you can hear it in my voice, the slurring. It's like my tongue is swollen. You were talking about a correction. Well, this has been a correction, or karma."

"Do you feel sorry for yourself?"

"Sometimes," Rob admitted. "I'm not the same person, but it's not like I evolved into this new person. Just one day God came up behind me and hit me with a big stick."

"What a strange day," Stephen said. "Remember the old days?"

Rob remembered. They both sat there quietly then, thinking of Paula and who she had been back then. Both were looking back through their different lenses. There were hard edges to those memories for both of them.

"Let's have another drink," Steven said.

The bar began to fill up with the staff. They were loud. Rob and Steven both watched them, recognizing the unconcern of youth. But then Rob realized Steven was looking for something else.

"Do you know that girl Irina?" Rob asked.

Steven's face turned to stone in an instant. He turned more toward Rob and looked hard at him. "Why are you asking me that?"

"I don't know. She's disappeared. I saw you in here with your family last week. She was waiting on you, and it looked like you knew her." He got the feeling he needed to be more assertive, that there was an advantage to be gained. "I remember her hand on the back of your chair. You did know her."

"Yes, I knew her. She took care of the kids sometimes. Misty knew her, really. I don't know how they connected. They hung out a little, and like I said, went to the beach sometimes, she took care of the kids."

"Well, when was the last time you saw her?" Rob asked, and then quickly added, "I'm only asking because the police came to see me this evening about it."

"About what?"

"About her disappearing. Or at least they think she's disappeared, or nobody has seen her."

"I haven't seen her," Steven said emphatically. "She has boyfriends. The police should talk to some of them, if they can sort them out."

Rob decided he better back off.

"Let's go," Steven said.

"Where?"

"I don't know. Let's just go and see where we end up."

III

Rob awoke on the beach. He was lying on his left side, facing northeast. The clouds he could see were a bruised purple fired with red underneath. The opening of his eyes corresponded with the torch of the sun rising above the horizon. The wind blew in his ears and grains of sand tickled his eyelashes. He found himself in a hollow indention in the sand and he quickly realized he could not get up. He pushed anyway with his left arm and leg. Nothing.

From behind him came the keening, mocking cry of a gull. He didn't know where he was, or how he had gotten there. He remembered leaving the restaurant with Steven, the smell of his new, tricked-out SUV, the slick feel of the leather seats. He remembered the next bar, and the next, and then a party. And then nothing.

Again he realized he couldn't rise. His good right arm was above him, but he couldn't roll himself forward far enough to get it under his torso to lift. Because of the indention, he couldn't push himself backward. In his narrow field of sight he saw no one. Listening carefully, he could hear nothing but the rising and falling of the wind, the droning sound of the shore break slurrying up the sand, and then the repeated cry of the gull. He had to get up… get up, creep away, hide himself and lick his wounds. With that realization came a twinge of desperation, which had been there since the stroke, but which he had mostly been able to keep hidden.

He took his right arm and began to swing it back and forth above him, rocking his body. He lifted his right leg and rocked it too in unison. Gradually his position shifted until after a few strenuous minutes he had rolled himself more completely on his back. But he still couldn't get up. He was a giant turtle turned over on his shell. The sky was a bluing panorama above him, clouds high and fleeing toward the southwest.

Rob was panting hard after his exertion. He could feel his heart pounding in his temples. His brain was like a dry, brittle nut rattling in his skull. A bargain needed to be made. This could not continue. And then there was a face, in shadows because of the brightness beyond it, above him. The face was lumpy, unformed, youthful, but somehow familiar.

"I thought it was you," the boy said

"Help me up, will you?" Rob said, realizing it was Tony, a teenaged busboy from the restaurant.

"I was checking the waves," Tony said. "I saw you down here. Of course, I didn't' know it was you. What happened to you anyway?"

"No, grab the other arm. Sorry, one side just doesn't work."

"You know you're bleeding," Tony said. "Your head is bleeding."

Rob was up, but dizzy and unsteady. He reached up to where Tony was pointing, and traced the length of a three-inch gash, wide enough that he could feel the separation of the skin. His finger came down stained with thick coagulated blood and sand. This was going to be bad. The brightness of the sun was pulsating on him in flashes.

"Help me to the stairs, will you?" he asked. Tony reached out, grabbed him by the elbow, and led him to the stairway that climbed up through the dunes. The tanned sea oats waved in the morning breeze. The east-facing dunes were already reflecting heat back toward the water. "I can't remember. I don't remember."

"What don't you remember?" Tony asked.

"I don't remember what I don't remember," Rob said, shaking his head.

"Have you heard the news though?"

"What news?" Rob asked, feeling a rising impatience as he reached for the stair railing.

"They found Irina," Tony answered, and Rob stopped. "They found a car in the canal off the road between Jamesville and Williamston, and she was in it. Apparently she had been in it for a number of days. That's some weird stuff, isn't it?"

Rob took a step up, raised his trailing leg, and took another step.

"Here, let me help you," Tony said when he saw Rob struggling. He put his Rob's arm over his shoulder and supported him as he rose up the stairway.

Rob couldn't think about Irina, or anything else. All he could do was work to lift his good right foot up and drag the other up behind it. He looked up at the open blue sky at the top of the stairs. That was his only goal.

"Thanks," Rob said when they got to the head of the stairs.

"No problem. You need a ride somewhere?"

36

"If you could… I'd appreciate it. But I don't want to take you out of your way."

"It's no problem, and you really don't look good."

He led Rob to his car, a non-descript fastback with fading paint and rust on the rocker panels. The passenger side floor was covered with fast-food wrappers and drink cups.

"Those are to keep the carpet clean," Tony said laughing, as Rob lowered himself into the seat.

Tony was wearing a bright yellow shirt that glowed in the sunlight. It burned into Rob's skull when he looked in that direction. A hemp and shell necklace dangled from the rearview mirror. It swayed slowly as Tony backed out of the parking space. Luckily he was mostly quiet on the short drive to Chick's house, Rob only speaking to point out the turns. He realized Tony wanted to be rid of him as much as he wanted to be rid of Tony. Both Chick's work truck and Tanya's small car were gone when they got there. Rob thanked Tony and let himself out. He waved as the boy guided his car down the driveway and went slowly up the street.

Alone standing on the concrete Rob again became aware of the throbbing from the gash running along the part of his hair. He heard the hum of the air-conditioning unit behind the house. Down the street he could hear the starting and stopping of a trash truck, its mechanized arm man-handling the big plastic cans that lined the street.

It was dark and cool and quiet in the house, but it smelled of something stale that he couldn't identify. He went down the hall to the room he had been staying in. It was Tanya's sewing room, and she had given it up for him. There was a pull-out couch against one wall. He did not unfold it, just lay on top of the cushions and turned his face to the wall. He was totally fagged out, but he didn't know if he could sleep. He thought of Irina, and then of Kelly, and drifted off to sleep with what felt like a drop of poison on the tip of his tongue.

"Rob…Rob!" He was shaken out of his sleep. "Jesus, Rob!"

He rolled over to find Chick above him, face contorted with anger, fists clenched, his dark form pulsing with menace.

"What?" Rob asked stupidly.

"What happened?" Chick asked. "What happened with you and Steven? Jesus, what happened to your head?"

Rob propped himself up on his elbow. His hand went up to his head and came down sticky with new blood. He was having trouble collecting himself.

"Tanya," Chick called over his shoulder. "Come in here please. Bring the first aid kit." He leaned down and took Rob's arm and got him to a sitting position. Rob saw a dark stain on the fabric where his head had been. He leaned forward and put his elbows on his knees.

Chick turned and paced back and forth in the small room, tossing angry glances at Rob. Tanya came in with the first aid kit. Chick took it from her and fairly pushed her back out the door. "I'll do it," he said, closing the door behind her.

"What time is it?" Rob asked groggily.

"It's five fifteen…in the afternoon."

Chick rummaged through the plastic box, pulling things out and laying them on the floor. Finally he went out to the bathroom across the hall and returned with a wet hand-towel, which he used to daub at the sand and blood-jelled gash on Rob's head. When he had cleaned it, he put some kind of cream on it and then unwound a gauze bandage and wrapped it a few times tightly around Rob's head.

It didn't really hurt, or at least Rob was not connected to the pain if there was any. Chick sat down on the couch next to him. He had calmed himself somewhat, but there was still an undercurrent of anger there, and where there was anger with Chick, there was always the potential for violence.

"So what did you do last night?" he asked. "You left without saying anything to either of us. So give me the rundown."

"I walked on the beach to the restaurant," Rob began carefully. "I had a couple of drinks. I saw Steven there, and we talked. I was trying to get some information about what happened to Irina, find out why she had disappeared. I was going to try to talk to some of the other employees, but I got so involved talking to Steven that I didn't really get to talk to anyone else." Rob looked sideways at Chick. He was straining to remember, but even in his recollections of that early part of the evening there were gaps, and when he skipped forward to what happened later, those gaps became bigger and more jagged.

"So what were you talking about?"

"Life. His life mostly. He talked about his new family. We talked about Paula. He didn't really say it, but I could tell he was down about it. He talked about his money problems." Rob paused. "I wish I had his kind of money problems."

"How long did you stay at the restaurant?"

"I don't know. I got there about nine thirty. The staff was coming into the bar. I talked to Steven, and had a couple of beers. And then Steven said, 'Let's go.' He drove us to Mason's, and then Hattie's, and we ended up at Leaner's. There was a big crowd there for that reggae band. And he kept buying, so I kept drinking. I know we were there late, because the band had stopped playing. And then we were in his car again. I think we went to some party, and it was a long drive to get there, but I can't remember."

"What do you mean, you don't remember?"

"I just don't remember. Something might come to me…"

"You didn't fight with Steven?"

"Who, me? How am I going to fight with anyone? But wait…I remember some kind of problem. It was at a party. It was at a house back on the Sound. One of Steven's friends. I hadn't ever been back there before. There were a lot of people. And there was blow." He looked at Chick and laughed. "It was like the old days."

"But what happened to your head? What happened to Steven?"

"I don't know."

Chick paced in front and above him, and then he stopped and looked down, his face dark and questioning. "They found him, Rob, in the front seat of his car, a bullet hole in his cheek and the back of his head blown off. Someone had tried to make it look like he did it himself, but the police know he didn't."

Rob hung his head. Nothing. He was at that point where he wasn't even going to try to remember. If something were going to come to him, he'd just have to let it come of its own volition. Chick was impatient and getting angrier, clenching and unclenching his fists.

"We've got to get you out of here. You were with him. Everyone saw you with him. It's only going to be a matter of time before they come looking for you."

"They found Irina," Rob said flatly. "The Ukrainian girl. They found her in a canal."

"What does that have to do with this?" Chick asked.

"I don't know. But I think it might have something to do with it. I don't know why I think that, but I do."

Three hours later it was getting dark. Tanya had made Rob something to eat, but he only ate enough to get her to leave him alone. Chick stayed away. He was still angry because he worked so hard to get his life to a place that was simple and safe. There were things that had happened in the past, things he had done, that even after all these years he couldn't afford to come to light. As night approached the throbbing in Rob's head increased, and there were times when he was on his feet that he felt in danger of falling over.

Chick told Rob to get his stuff together. It wasn't much, just a backpack and a smaller gym bag. Chick took them down to the truck. Rob didn't ask him where they were going. Tanya left in her car and after a half hour returned with a few bags of groceries which she transferred to Chick's truck.

It was almost ten when they left. Chick drove south on the bypass to Whalebone Junction, and then west toward Manteo and Wanchese. But he passed both towns and crossed the Virginia Dare Bridge heading west. Mann's Harbor lay nestled against the west side of the Albemarle Sound across the water from the lights of Roanoke Island. Rob suddenly realized where they were going. They passed through the sleeping hamlet and took the road north toward Mashoes. Chick's father had an old house there where he went to get away to fish and drink in the old days. Chick had used it for parties when they were younger. Rob realized he hadn't been there for close to twenty years.

Chick had said almost nothing since they began driving. Rob threw glances at his smoldering profile, but made the decision to keep quiet. In just under an hour they were pulling into the rutted driveway. The dark and the vastness of the sky were a world away from the tourist bustle. The closest neighbor was a hundred and fifty feet further up the road. Rob saw the twinkling of the porch lights in the distance.

"Are the Carvers still in that house?"

"No," Chick answered. "They moved back to Manteo. They're looking to rent it, I think."

Everything had grown wild around the cottage, which hadn't been occupied in a couple of years. Chick would come every few months to check on things, mow the grass, but it was clear he hadn't been there in a while. They made their way to the front porch door, Chick leading, stomping down the higher weeds, Rob following behind. Chick fumbled in the dark for the door key. Outside the crickets trilled incessantly. Chick finally found the key, turned it, and shouldered open the door. He turned on the bare overhead light and the room appeared looking exactly as it had all those years ago. What Rob had forgotten, and what was the most obvious about the main room, were the murals that covered the walls. Chick's dad had painted them on long drunken weekends. They were hunting and fishing scenes, executed bluntly and without talent, painted right on the cinder block walls. On one a rigid hunter aimed what looked like a broomstick at chevron forms meant to represent ducks. On another wall a fisherman with a bending pole leaned back against the pull of an invisible fish. Though they lacked any artistic touch, they were also plainly unapologetic. They were like cave paintings. Chick's father had been a minister in the ghetto in downtown Baltimore. He had taken it for as long as he could, and then he had quit and moved to the Outer Banks. Drinking followed. The murals weren't meant for anyone but himself.

Rob dropped his stuff on the couch. Chick went back outside and returned with grocery bags and put them on the counter in the small connecting kitchen, and then went back outside to get the rest. Rob limped over and began emptying the bags, putting things in the empty refrigerator and in the old dusty cabinet. When Chick came back in Rob stepped aside and leaned back against the old formica counter.

"Chick," he said, "thank you. I know this is a pain in the ass."

"It is what it is."

"I'm trying to put together what happened. I know that sounds weird. It either happened, or it didn't," he said, drifting off.

41

"Now you sound like JP," Chick said. "And you know that's not a compliment."

Nothing was going to help except to be alone with his thoughts. He was only going to remember if he quit trying, and even then things might not come back to him. But he had that guilt, that feeling that he had done something he should at least be ashamed of, and possibly worse. He thought it might have been that night wobbling in the hallway of the employee house, crying about Kelly, speaking gibberish. He remembered Irina's face peering out of her doorway, at first annoyed because it was so late, and then just dumfounded. But that wasn't it. He just needed to get through another couple of hours so he could sleep.

He went into the bathroom and flipped on the light. There was no shower curtain around the old tub. He looked into the cloudy mirror and saw the white swath of bandages around his head. Seeing it reminded him of the pressure beneath his skull, and the throbbing, the pain. He put both hands on the sides of the sink and leaned forward, looking down at the trailing water stain. He turned on the water and splashed some in his face.

When he came back out Chick was standing by the door.

"Lay low," Chick said. "We need to try to figure out what's going on here. I meant to bring you Tanya's phone, although maybe it's a good idea I didn't. I'll get up with you in the next couple of days."

"Thanks, Chick," he said, and then added wistfully, "I wish I didn't need the help."

Then with the clap of the screen door, he was gone. Chick's truck backed out of the driveway, and the beams lit the trees on the highway toward Mann's Harbor. Rob looked around him. It was funny how the memories of a quarter century or more came flooding back, and yet he could not for the life of him remember what had happened twenty-five hours earlier. In the corner was Chick's dad's old stereo. Rob went over and crouched down in front of the line of old LPs. Mostly it was mid-sixties jazz, with a sprinkling of what then would have been called adult easy-listening. Stan Getz next to Ramsey Lewis next to Jobim next to Herb Alpert next to Sinatra. No Beatles, no Mamas and Papas, not even any Simon and Garfunkel. Chick's dad was firmly in the post-World War II crew cut generation. Rob looked at the knobs on the amp. The turntable rested on the shelf above, its opaque plastic cover under a layer of dust. He lifted it and squatted close to the stylus, then with a shrug began sifting through the albums again. Toward the back he found "Time Out" by Dave Brubeck. Here his errant memory kicked back in as he slipped the LP out of the dust cover. Gingerly holding it by the edges with his fingers and spinning it to the horizontal, he placed the hole in the center of the circle. He pressed the power button and a faint buzz of feedback filled the room. He lifted the lever and set the stylus above the outside of the record and then released it. There was a whisper of static and a short intro, and then Paul Desmond's sweet and crystalline saxophone sauntered out of the speakers and swirled around him.

So out in the middle of nowhere, with a broad black sky full of stars swirling above, he listened to jazz music. As he did, he tried to remember. But it was no use. He couldn't get past the horrible apprehension. He was still sandy and ripe, and terribly hung over. There was food in the refrigerator and the cupboards, and he couldn't eat. There was nothing to drink. Although he was too hung over to want anything now, he could anticipate the anxiety he would feel the next day when he had recovered sufficiently to continue on his usual path. He would have moaned then, but there was a germ of strength that wouldn't let him. If I can just put one foot in front of the other, he thought… With a shaking hand, he lifted the needle in the middle of the second song. He couldn't take the frenetic pace of the piano and the rhythm section, especially when balanced by the haunting melodies of the horn. There was a faint fifties sci-fi metal alien insect buzz left hanging in the air. He didn't have the heart to kill it, so he didn't turn the stereo power off. He went into the bathroom, pissed sitting down, rose unsteadily and looked at himself in the mirror again. He went back into the main room, grabbed his bags, took them into one of the small bedrooms, and dropped them on the bed. He went back out and toward the kitchen, panicking now because he knew he had to keep moving or it would catch up to him, and knowing he had nowhere to go. He opened the refrigerator door, looked in as if he expected an oracle's vision in the arrangement of the packages and jars. His vision melted into the interior as the cool air wafted up to his face. He closed the door, realizing that he had almost remembered something.

Then he saw it. On the kitchen counter next to one of the deflated grocery bags was an I-Pod. Where had it come from? The counter was bare when they arrived so Chick must have brought it. He picked it up and looked closely at it. He had never used one before. The small speakers fit snugly in his ears. He looked for the power button, wondered how to use the disc on the instrument's face. And then, without being sure how he had done it, music filled the space between his ears. It was Bryan Ferry and Roxy Music from the late seventies, the lead singer's voice as clear and tremulous has it had been all those years before. Maybe Chick had thought music would relax him.

Without considering what he was doing, Rob headed for the door. Across the road and the sedgy marshland the Sound was a sheet of glass. The light of the filling moon fell on it and lit it white at the edges. He had to walk. He knew that. The song ended. Next was some rap. When had Chick started listening to this? If Rob had known how to change the music, and if he could have seen the mechanism better, he would have looked for something else to listen to. But he was afraid he was going to turn it off. So he let it come as it would.

At the end of the driveway he looked both ways. To the right the road leading back to Mann's Harbor was unlit, empty. To the left he could see the Carvers' house in the near distance, and he knew from experience there were other scattered houses further on. He turned to the left.

He couldn't hear the mosquitos, but he felt their wings tickling his face and neck, and with his right hand he swatted at them where he felt their stings. Once he was walking he felt better. Just put one foot in front of the other, he told himself. Deep inside him was the fear that he could fall over with another stroke, or a heart attack, and that he would lay undiscovered and unmissed, as the life slowly drained out of him. That fear was a palpable taste in his mouth.

He crossed to the far side of the road as he passed the Carver house. There was a low light in the main room behind the curtains, but the occupants, if there were any, must have been asleep. Rob would have had a big dog if he lived so far out of the way, and he took one of the earphones out to listen for one, but all he heard was the symphony of the crickets and the frogs vying with the music in his other ear. He replaced the earphone. As for the music, he didn't recognize much of it. He knew the names of some of the genres; rap, dance (even some old disco), emo, thrash, punk, the oxymoron of some old new wave. He used to know a lot about music.

44

He remembered the lyrics of songs. He remembered the names of members of bands, and if the line-ups had changed over time, and which musicians had played on which albums. Living in Central America had disrupted that, and when he had returned the interest was just gone.

For an hour he walked away from the cottage. He passed more houses, and some of them did have dogs. He wished he had a cane or a stick, for protection first, but also to make him look less a threat. That made him smile, because seeing a picture of himself as if from above, there was no way anyone was going to construe him as a threat. That was the only time he smiled. It was a grim trek, meant only to make the hands of the clock spin. He was tired, sleepy, mosquito-bitten, still stupendously hung over. He was trapped in a place where his memories surrounded him, but they were like the mosquitos, unseen and multitudinous, trying to whisper in his ear.

He walked right out of the hamlet. The narrow two-lane road ran ahead, he knew, for miles until it stopped suddenly when the marshy land simply ended in a thumb surrounded by the Sound. Why anyone had continued building the road out that far, he didn't know. But now it was his alone.

He walked, or limped, as far as he could. He looked up at the stars for a blessing, but they were noncommittal. The music was the perfect, sonic distraction. He was ready to turn, to return, but he kept walking. Who was the writer? Was it Nabokov? He recalled JP telling him the story. It was Vladimir Nabokov, and the story was about how he was afraid to take a walk because when he got to the extremity of it he could not, in his imagination, turn, and have the environment turn mirror-like with him. And because he couldn't turn it in his imagination, he was afraid that it would actually not turn, and he would be a prisoner in whatever dimension he was in when he began to make the turn. Nabokov was afraid there was some kind of crack in the universe, although he didn't know if that fissure was in the whole universe, or only in his small version of it. But not knowing was enough to deter him from taking a chance to find out.

With that, and a propitious change of song that accompanied it, Rob stopped and began to turn. He couldn't rearrange the universe in his imagination either, but it was so dark it didn't matter. Just then the music started, some kind of truncated bass line, chopped and repeated, and then a rap was laid over it.

He turned and all the laws of the universe were obeyed. Everything was where it was supposed to be. If at that moment a star went out in the universe, as one, given their great numbers, probably did, it was a small star, dim and far away. With all those twinkling millions above him, one simply blinked off and did not come back on. He had to figure this all out. First he had to get back. He was already tired, and he pushed himself further. Sleep was essential, and he had been through enough of these episodes that he knew sleep would be long in coming. It would fight him, deny him its benefits for as long as it could.

He felt a tightness in his chest. Fuck it, he thought. If I fall dead on this dark road, so be it. It couldn't be much worse than having to drag himself from place to place, or sweating for hours behind the restaurant's dish machine, or having fallen to a place where he was less than anonymous. Irina was dead. Why? And Steven. Why did it come back to him?

On either side of the low road the marsh grass waved, lit at the tips by the moonlight. Within the margin of the grasses were the silver-tinged ghost trunks of trees, lopped off by the winds of a hurricane that had blown through years earlier. He couldn't see the water of the Sound beyond the carpet of grass, but he knew it was there, shallow, with water the color of weak tea. He had sailed on the Sound, fished for striped bass, shrimped and crabbed. He had plied its margins in canoes and kayaks. He remembered overnight sailing regattas, where in the evenings the boats would raft up, grills would be lit in the sterns, music blaring, margaritas and daiquiris spun in mixers below, joints lit, lines drawn and snorted, general hilarity all around. And sexual tension you could cut with a knife. The proximity kept the actual illicit contact to a quiet minimum, and confined it to whispering couplings between regular partners, but the spillover of affairs in the weeks that followed became legendary.

He finally made it back and opened the door to the old cottage, but he still felt the gnawing tension as he closed it. He went in and filled a glass with water. There was no ice in the freezer so he sipped it at room temperature. He meant to go back to the bedroom, but he ended up first sitting on the couch and then falling over and crashing there, fully-dressed except for his shoes. He tossed and turned, rolled over and back on the narrow area. His head throbbed, and when he reached up, the bandage was damp. He made tentative dives toward sleep, with ersatz dreams preceding

46

the actual fall, jolting him back to consciousness. Perspiring in his clothes, squirming in them, he closed his eyes to keep out any stimuli. He didn't know how long the struggle took, or if he won or lost in the end.

White light, filtering through the pines, splashed on Rob and on the mural on the wall above him. But what woke him were the crows. Their raucous cries and angry conversations finally completely interrupted his escape. He was just suddenly there, on his back, staring. He was famished, which was a good sign. The gauzy curtains waved in the open windows. The breeze coming through was warm, but not oppressive. The crows moved out of the stand of pines in the yard to another further back away from the road. The distance took some of the urgency from their cries.

Rising was less a struggle than he thought it would be. He was on his back, which was never good, and wedged against the back corner, but his good right arm was free and he was able to grab the corner of the armrest and pull himself up. He sat on the edge of the couch, leaning forward looking at the floor, allowing the blood to circulate more evenly through his system before he stood. More birds took up where the crows left off, conversing sweetly in the trees above.

He rose and went into the bathroom to piss and clean up. He felt a bit wobbly standing above the bowl waiting out his bladder. When he was finished he glanced at himself in the mirror, just long enough to know he didn't like what he saw. The blood stain on the bandage had turned brown. He unwound it and dropped it into the small trash can under the sink. He prodded at the swollen wound with his finger. It didn't really hurt. Then he shrugged and turned on the shower. It spat and coughed, spewing tan water on the tub floor, and then cleared itself into a calm throbbing spray. Rob struggled out of his clothes and looked for a safe handhold to steady him as he stepped in. He moved under the stream and let it drum on his head, trying to be careful and not let the water splash onto the floor. He felt the sting of the gash on his part-line. Some of the dried brown blood fell and swirled down the drain. He cleaned the wound gingerly, gently daubing the soft puffy edges on each side of the gash. He took his time, stayed under the spray until the hot water gave out. There was only one threadbare gray towel on the rack. He dried himself the best he could, wrapped it around his waist, and went back to the bedroom.

He rummaged through his bag and put on a t-shirt and a pair of shorts. He went to the kitchen and made coffee and went out on the old sagging porch and sat in one of the two weatherworn rocking chairs. The last time he sat in the chair it had also been 'a morning after.' But it had been twenty years earlier. Chick and Rob had brought girls and drugs out to Mashoes for a hedonistic weekend romp. It was a lifetime ago. Now here he was, rocking gently in the soft morning heat, realizing he was going to have to marshal his strengths and organize a strategy just to be able to rise from his seat. He became aware that he sat with a serene smile on his face, and felt a calm he didn't deserve to feel. He realized it couldn't last. His situation was precarious, not the least because he couldn't bridge the gaps in his memory that now contained two bodies.

The road running in front of the house was quiet. No more than a hundred people lived in Mashoes. It wasn't really even a town. There was no post office, no stores or gas stations, just houses really. Most of the people made their living on the water, crabbing or fishing. There was one small boat-building operation run by a father and son that had been around for many years. They worked slowly, meticulously, turning out a few Sound workboats annually. They were the largest employer. Down the road he heard the gurgle and thrum of a boat going out from one of the canal docks that ran alongside the road. A warm, humid wind rose out of the south.

He gathered himself, rose, and went back into the house. After going through the food in the bags on the counter and seeing what was in the refrigerator, he saw there were four, maybe five days of food. There was no alcohol. Chick's only instruction had been to lay low. This day it would be easy. He would carefully re-introduce himself to food. He had done it before. But there was something different this time. He was optimistic, and that seemed unwarranted. He felt he was within reach of putting everything together, even as he realized at this point he didn't yet have the margins of the puzzle. He found himself thanking an unnamed and hidden deity. He wasn't yet sure entirely what he was grateful for, but he knew it had to do with an infusion of grit.

He ate, just toast and butter. Afterward he went back to the stereo and looked through the albums again. It reminded him of the old days. Then he would have been high already, having grabbed the bong from behind the couch or in the bottom of the closet. He pulled out a double album, and opened it, smiling as he remembered opening albums and having pot seeds dance down the creases and fall to the floor where they would hop and scurry for the corners. He put on a Ramsey Lewis album; clean, concise piano lines over a tripping Latin beat. He bustled around, straightening up. At one point he found himself standing in front of the open bedroom door. He remembered being in that room with a girl many years ago. He couldn't remember her face, although the contours of her body still resonated. It had been a crazy, coke-infused gymnastics contest. He could have sworn they had been swinging from something, although there was only the round globe of the ceiling light above, and they clearly hadn't been swinging from that. A rueful smile crept to his face. When he was younger he had thought of aging, imagined becoming a step slower, visualized the character his face would develop, the gravitas.

But now he was where he was. As he moved forward, it would be by dragging one foot behind the other. One side of his face may have registered serious and mature depth, but the other was a sagging, fleshy mask. Here he was, admitting it baldly, as the Ramsey Lewis Trio happily romped around him. The more serious issue was with his memory. He was worried that there was something organically wrong with his brain. He would acknowledge the effects of the alcohol. It contributed, but there was another disconnect.

He had been on a surf trip to Puerto Rico with Abby. Instead of his usual method of going by himself for three or four months or more, and living off the land, this was a short trip with a chick. He had money from the Rios deal, and he was determined to spend it. They stayed at Dennis' place at Pool's Beach, and he had rented a car so they could get around. The first couple of days it had been flat so they had driven around exploring, swimming in the emerald green sea, bathing in the warm erotic atmosphere, fucking like it was a holy obligation. But then it stayed flat. When he thought clearly back on it, this should have been his first inkling that alcoholism might become a problem. Each day he woke and there were no waves it bothered him more. He began 'Los Rum Drinks,' as they called it with Hemingwayish aplomb, earlier each evening.

Abby was patient for a while. She always had a smile for him, and she was pliant and supple. She was a good conversationalist and she kept him amused with her stories. But finally it got to the point where the thing just broke. They were in one of the bars up on the hill, and she told him this story.

"Memory's a funny thing," she had said. "Did you ever wonder how we store our memories, about where they go and how we retrieve them?"

He had shaken my head. He wasn't listening. She decided to make him listen.

"The brain has billions of nerve cells, but there would never be enough if we tried to store our memories there. After all, every instant, every sight, every sound, smell, taste, emotion… everything holds the potential to become a memory. So if we just think in terms of brain cells, the brain isn't big enough for its memories. If each individual memory were stored in a single cell, then all the cells in the brain and nervous system could only hold a fraction of what we remember, probably no more than a week's worth.

"So where is this storage space? It has to be sub-microscopic. It has to have something to do with the molecules within the nerve cells themselves. One theory is that protein molecules within the cells are involved. They're large enough, and complex enough, and they exist in great enough quantities. There are about thirty thousand billion of them in your brain."

There had been swirls of color around them, glasses clinking, voices talking over each other, music, each a potential memory. Rob began to come around to her, to listen to what she was saying.

"It's known that the shapes of protein molecules can be changed," she continued, "and that they can retain their new shapes. It's also known that electrical impulses, which are what the workings of the brain are all about, can make some of these changes. So as these electrical impulses pass through a cell they might modify the structure of the nerve itself. If you buy into this theory, then memory traces result when protein molecules are altered electrically in certain meaningful ways.

"Now though we come to the apparent paradox," she had said, but then they were interrupted. The lights in the bar had gone down, and a slide show had started on a white screen on the wall, surf shots from the last big swell at Tres Palmas. There had been hooting and whistles, too much noise for her to continue. They had watched with everyone else for a while until the excitement downshifted and only the steepest drops and worst wipeouts got the responses that had greeted all the shots in the beginning.

50

Rob had taken Abby's hand and led her to the back of the bar.

"Continue what you were saying," he had insisted. "How do you know all this stuff anyway?"

"Why shouldn't I know it?"

"I don't know...sorry. Well, go on. You were saying something about proteins carrying memories, and then there was a paradox."

"The paradox is that protein molecules have brief life spans. They only survive a day or two. So if they only last a short time, and they contain our memories, how can we retain those memories for decades?"

"Well?"

"The explanation is that certain giant protein molecules can reproduce themselves. So say your earliest childhood memories once changed protein molecules inside some nerve cells. But those molecules were soon destroyed. The key is that before they passed, they left offspring...and those offspring had the same markings as their parents. What that means is that protein molecules representing a memory from childhood have been reproducing ever since. And under the right conditions they will continue to do so until you're old and feeble.

"And you know something else," she had said, pointing to his drink. "One piece of evidence to support this theory is how the use of alcohol affects the brain. Alcohol can produce radical and permanent changes in protein molecules. The scientific term is called denaturing. This denaturing probably accounts for the hallucinations and loss of memory that occur when people chronically drink too much.

"Also, although protein molecules usually produce exact replicas of themselves, occasionally there may be flaws or differences. If they're serious enough they might account for false memories, recollections of things that never happened, but seem as real as if they had."

"Where did you learn all this?" he had asked again.

She shrugged. "Dad's a doctor. This was part of his 'reasons not to drink' speech he gave when I was fourteen. And it doesn't mean that this is definitely the way it is. All the evidence is circumstantial. But it's intriguing too. And it has some weird connections. The thirty thousand genes that transfer our heredity are also self-duplicating proteins. So are the sub-microscopic viruses that cause infantile paralysis, small pox, even AIDS. So were the first living things on earth. So what if heredity, disease, memory, and the origins of life are all linked? It's strange, almost scary, to think about."

"That's wild," he had said. "What about this? If this is all true, and we know our genes are passed on to our children, how do we know our memories can't be passed in the same way? Think about environments in dreams that are so real and so familiar, but you know you've never seen them. Could these things be locked up in the brain and have come from generations earlier?"

He could still remember his half-drunken wonder. He also remembered Abby in a way he hadn't in a long time. He couldn't help thinking she might have bent him toward something better. She was a remarkable girl and he had let her drift away.

How was this coming to him so easily when he couldn't remember anything of what had happened to him in the last few days? He could recall the smell of her sitting next to him at that bar, the quality of the subdued light, the buzz of both the quiet and exuberant conversations that were going on around him. Honestly, it was so real he could almost touch it. He wondered if the trauma of the stroke had interrupted the connection of synapses, if the stroke had somehow broken the electrical connections. Maybe it was all physical. Maybe it was the organic component of memory that had been affected. He thought of Irina then, and couldn't remember her face.

He spent the day listening to music in the house and sitting on the porch overlooking the road and the marsh beyond. Chick had been right to bring him out here. There were few neighbors, and those who did live in the hamlet minded their own business. Rob was sure Chick had let someone know he would be staying there so they could pass the information on to each other and not worry about the limping stranger in their midst.

By the time evening arrived and softened the light, it had also lightened the stiff south wind that had blown all day. There was a path beaten through the reeds and marsh grasses across the road. Rob crossed the road and followed it to the Sound. A low, weatherworn dock waited at the end with creaking boards and gaps where some of the planks had rotted away. Rob gingerly made his way out to the end and sat, dangling his legs above the water. The Sound spread out before him, turning purple at the edges as the light faded. Far away and to the south he heard the whirr of an outboard motor, but he saw no boats on the expansive vista before him. He could see a few cars crossing the Mann's Harbor bridge. A white heron stood in the shallow water by the grass, walking stiffly, occasionally bending to stab at something below the surface. Dragonflies bobbed and weaved all around him. He stayed until the mosquitos chased him back.

When he came back to the road some movement caught his eye at the Carver's house up the road. There was a woman leaning into her open trunk to pull out grocery bags. She took them into the house and returned for more. Rob didn't know if he should acknowledge her and wave, or pretend he didn't notice her. But she never seemed to see him so he crossed the yard and went back inside. He went to the window facing her house, but by the time he got there her car trunk was closed and she must have gone back into the house.

Rob realized he was alone. Chick had only left him the mysterious I-pod. There was no house telephone, no cell phone, no television or radio. He had no way of getting any outside news, and Chick had not told him when he would be back. He went into the kitchen. At least his appetite was returning.

Four days later Rob was running out of food. He hadn't heard from Chick. He hadn't heard anything. He stuck to the house during the day, avoiding the windows, reading what little was there, plodding through Reverend Gandil's music, napping in the afternoons as if he were on some lazy vacation. His appetite had returned. He wasn't eating a lot, but he was eating regularly. He listened to records and learned how to shuffle the I-pod. The gash on his skull had dried and scabbed over.

He had no doubt that Chick would soon return, but he couldn't help wondering what had happened and was happening in the world across the bridges. He had stopped drilling down into his memory as if he had determined that it was a well that had gone dry. It didn't bother him. In just the few days he was on his way to developing a zen-like serenity. He walked at night, sometimes for miles, wearing himself down until he could sleep. He did not miss alcohol. He could say that, and it was giddily true, although three days were clearly not a full test.

As that fourth day drew on to evening, Rob waited. Every day had been hot, the wet heat pressing down on the roof. Few cars passed on the road in front of the cottage, and none seemed interested, or even noticed, the new occupant. But Rob knew enough to realize that small communities were not long in recognizing changes in their equilibrium. At the Carver house, the only one in view, he had not seen the occupant after the first day. At odd times he would glance over and the car would be gone, and when he looked again it would be back. Now he looked out the window and a woman was walking across the expanse of weeds and random shrubs that separated the houses.

At first Rob felt a stab of panic. He looked around the room, as if he should straighten up, and then smiled at himself. He looked out the window again. The woman could have been anywhere from forty to sixty years old, he thought. She moved at a determined pace, her head down, her long skirt swishing through the brush. She seemed to be talking to herself, perhaps encouraging herself to keep coming.

As she came into the yard and swung around toward the front door, Rob opened it and stepped out on the front porch to greet her.

"Good evening," he said in his most soothing voice.

She stopped abruptly, and a hand came up to her mouth.

"My name is Rob," he said.

"Why are you here?" Rob detected a trace of a Spanish accent.

"I'm friends of the owners," Rob said. "My wife's family owns this house. Do you know Chick Gandil? I know he comes out here sometimes to clean up and mow the grass." He was worried because the woman seemed frightened. She looked at the brown and purple slash in his part of his hair. "Are you alright?" he asked.

"Yes, I'm fine. I just noticed someone was over here. I met Chick…is that his name? I have met him a couple of times."

Rob got the impression she suddenly wished she wasn't there. "Are you related to the Carvers?" he asked, searching for some way to cut through the awkwardness.

"No. I mean yes. I mean, I'm sorry." She could not keep her eyes from his head wound.

"I had an accident. Really, it's not as bad as it looks."

Rob took a step sideways and reached for the deck railing. The woman did look down at his legs then. Her expression changed by the second. There was confusion, but also fear, and lurking underneath was an attempt at a small friendly smile. She seemed frustrated with herself. Her hands danced in small jerks at the ends of her arms.

"Why are you here?" she asked again.

"I'm hiding out," Rob said with a big crooked smile. "No, honestly, I've had a stroke, and I've come here to heal myself. I just felt awkward in front of people. You know how you get an idea of yourself that hangs with you, and you don't think about it until something big happens, and then the idea no longer fits. Well, mine no longer fits."

"I'm sorry," she said.

"I told you my name, but you never told me yours."

"It's Amelia Falcon."

"And why are you here, Amelia?"

"I'm hiding out too," she answered with a small trilling laugh.

Rob could feel her calming down.

"But it's true," she said after a short silence. "My father died. It was some years ago now, but I haven't been able to get over it."

55

"I'm sorry," Rob said.

"Well, we both are apologetic today," Amelia said. "I didn't mean to bother you."

"It's no bother," Rob said.

Just then one of the few cars to be seen in a day drove past, and Rob imagined what they imagined they saw, a middle-aged couple on the front stoop, or country neighbors discussing crabgrass on their lawns, or the dog that was knocking over their trashcans. Rob had hidden out before, been forced to lay low, been wary of whom he saw and who saw him, but here it was different. Even if he were being looked for, no one would think of looking here. They both watched the car as it disappeared around the corner.

Amelia took a few steps back, trying to think of what to say to extricate herself. "If you need a ride or anything..." she began, and Rob saw that she immediately regretted it.

"Thanks. If I do, I'll let you know. It was nice to meet you."

She waved, and then turned and retraced her steps back to her house. Rob knew she felt vulnerable with him watching her back.

He thought about what he had told her of his idea of himself. He had acted as if he had accepted the change, and that was not at all true. He could not admit to himself that he would not ever again be who he was. In his dreams he was the old Rob, solid, strong, whole. But here on this front step in the hinterland, he knew he was vulnerable. He didn't know who might be searching for him, or why. He didn't know if it was because they thought he knew something. He didn't even know if he did know something, and just couldn't remember it.

Nothing to drink. He didn't think about it except when he thought about it. He knew that if there had been alcohol there he would have drunk it. The drying out with Chick and Tanya had only lasted a few days, and then there was the binge with Steven. Once again he silently and sheepishly thanked the unnamed God that was helping him, and then, before he thought too much about it, he went back into the cottage.

He cooked up some rice and sautéed the rest of the vegetables, which were starting to look soft and suspect, and ate as the sky darkened outside. Afterward he sat back on the couch and looked up at the brooding murals on the walls. He thought about putting on some music or looking for something to read, but found he was content just sitting there. The wind picked up after dark and caused the curtains to dance in the window frames. The headlights pulling into the driveway drew him out of his reverie. He felt a sudden dread and apprehension, and then realized it was Chick's work truck.

As he went to the front door, he was surprised when Tanya got out of the cab.

"Come help me with these bags," she said shortly.

Rob shuffled down the steps and went to the passenger door where Tanya stood holding two grocery bags for him. "Where's Chick?" he asked.

"Chick's busy and couldn't come. Apparently my time is more flexible, so I can work all day and then take an hour to shop for you, and then drive it all the way out here."

"Look, I'm sorry, Tanya. I know I've been a pain in the ass."

She shrugged. She reached in to get more bags, and then followed Rob into the cottage.

"I haven't been here in a long time," she said when they got inside, looking askance at the murals and the old-fashioned furniture. "Chick and Jane should sell this place, although I don't know what they could get for it."

"So what's going on in the real world?"

"I brought you a Coastland Times so you can read it for yourself. Obviously with Steven, there has been a lot of talk. Chick did work for Steven, and they know you were staying with us."

Rob put the groceries away. He didn't want to admit it, but he was looking for alcohol. There wasn't any. He felt a strong momentary anxiety, but it dissipated quickly. Tanya went into the bathroom and closed the door. He heard her moving around, tending to her business, and Rob was embarrassed because of the closeness in the cottage. He made a racket of closing cabinets and folding up the paper bags. He heard the toilet flush and water running and then she came out.

"Is that woman still staying at the Carvers'?"

Rob nodded. "I met her today."

"Did she tell you anything about herself?"

"Not really," he said, thinking back to their conversation.

"She has an interesting story. She's from New York, you know? She's a painter. Her father died in the World Trade Center, on 9/11."

"She didn't say anything about that. We didn't talk for long. I think she was just wondering who the hell I was."

Tanya shook her head. She did look tired. "Chick and I went to Paula's funeral one day, and then Steven's the next. It was surreal, that's the only word for it. Paula and Steven's kids, and then Steven's new family…everybody crying and talking a mile a minute, sorry, but wondering what had really happened, and it was clear no one knows anything concrete."

"Did Chick say anything about how long I need to stay out here?" Rob asked. "I mean, if the police aren't looking for me, then why do I have to be out here?"

"They are looking for you. Chick told them he thought you went back to Florida." She looked down. "I think he wishes you would go back to Florida."

"Well, I would, but I can't," Rob said quietly. It was a lie. He wasn't going anywhere. He didn't want to admit it, but this was a chance for him. He needed to know what happened, and why. "Thanks for bringing this stuff."

She shrugged. "I know you two go way back. But he's different now, you know."

Rob nodded, but he knew Chick wasn't that different. He was always looking for an angle. Even now Rob wondered what shims Chick had wedged in to square things for himself. He didn't want to think about it with Tanya standing right there because he didn't know if he could hide the questions he had, even with half an empty expression.

"I'll be back in a couple of days," Tanya said. "Or Chick will."

"Can you get me a cell phone?"

"I don't know. I'll ask Chick. Who would you call?"

Rob laughed. "No one, probably. It's a connection thing. I may not have anyone to call, but I still want to be able to call them."

"I'll ask Chick," she repeated.

Rob stood there, trying to think of something to say to keep Tanya there for a while longer. He noticed she seemed nervous about being alone with him. She scanned the room for her things and then headed for the door. Rob limped after her. "Has anybody figured out what happened to Irina?" he asked.

"No. I don't think so. Why would you ask me that?"

"Because I've been sitting out here by myself with nothing to do but think about it, and I started to think that she's the key. Whatever happened to her, and whoever was responsible for it, is connected with Steven."

Tanya shrugged. "Why? She went off the road and into the canal, and a week later they found her." She shrugged. "But I still don't know why everybody is so worried about that Russian whore."

Rob was surprised at the venom in her voice. There was something pointed and personal in it. He hadn't thought that Tanya knew anything more about Irina than her name, if she even knew that. He followed her out on to the porch, and then down the steps. She moved with hard, sturdy steps. She turned when she got to the truck door. "Chick says he will be coming in a few days. He says stay quiet and keep your head down. That boy cop, the big one, who came to the house, he's been looking for you. He's been over to the house a few times."

"I just don't know what's going on," Rob said. "I keep thinking I'm going to remember something important. I know I have the key to it, I know it."

"Well, then you better get about remembering it," Tanya said. "You know Chick. You can see how he changed, can't you? Once he got into his trim work he seemed to have found this quiet niche, something he was really good at, but it was safe. No more trawl boats, no more long-lining, no more danger. Now this happens, and you put him right back in the middle of it. And the bad thing for me is that he loves it. I just want it to be over."

She got into the truck, waved weakly to Rob, and backed out of the driveway. Rob went back in. He picked the newspaper up from the counter and took it over to the couch. It was a small local rag, two sections, twelve pages each. It was all local news. On the front page were the beginnings of a couple of in-depth stories to be continued further inside. One concerned problems with the long-term availability of fresh water on the barrier islands. Another dealt with the ongoing fight about whether to build the new bridge to Hatteras Island. There was a photo of a group of boy scouts at a jamboree. Inside there were a couple of wedding announcements, church schedules, advertisements for all kinds of local businesses, photos of long-time county employees receiving service awards, photos of fishermen on docks behind lines of yellowfin tuna and dolphin. In the second section there was a sports page with pictures of golfers at a charity tournament, and stories about the chances of the high school football team in the coming season. There were classified ads, and a simple crossword puzzle.

All in all, it was a typical small hometown newspaper, warm and comfortable, almost apologetically informative. It was able to distract and amuse Rob for a half hour. On the last page, along with the final advertisements, was a photograph of a group of men in Confederate uniforms standing in the doorway of a large old house. They were on the front porch, among the columns, some with hats, some without, a nest of muskets on the lawn in front of them, the shadows of horses at the side of the house. There in the middle of the group, hands on his hips, was Harlan Spencer. He was in an officer's uniform, epaulets on his shoulder, pistol on his belt, large soft-brimmed hat swept forward at a jaunty angle. The story beneath told of the group. They were part of a large affiliated network of re-enactors who traveled to different Civil War festivals and remembrances, partaking in sweeping, loosely-choreographed battles from Fort Sumter to Manassas to Gettysburg. Spencer had started this local group, and was quoted in the piece saying that he did it in honor of his great-great grandfather who served as an officer under General Beauregard. The photo showed them just after the annual re-enactment at Brandy Station outside Culpepper, Virginia the week before at a farmhouse Spencer had rented. They were a grizzled group, cocky in their homespun, clearly too well-fed to have been a part of Lee's cavalry in the summer of 1863. Rob could forgive them for that. He recognized many familiar faces among the pretend soldiers. There was Dustin, the Sea Horse chef, and Bob Stennis, the assistant manager. And in the background, his head rising above those of his comrades, was Davy Todd, the policeman who had come to question Rob at Chick and Tanya's house.

He was about to fold the paper back up when he noticed something. Most of the men were on the porch, but inside the doorway, behind the men, was a form. It was little more than a shadow, but as soon as Rob saw it there was something that immediately drew his eyes and attention to it. It was a young woman's upper torso and head. Though the image was indistinct and out-of-focus, Rob recognized who it was. He couldn't be

60

positive, but he realized almost immediately it was Irina. He looked at the date of the paper and saw it was only a day old. He went back to the story and looked through it again. The dates of the Brandy Station reenactment were May 31st and June 1st. Today was the 9th, he thought. It was now almost ten days since Irina disappeared. Rob looked closely at the photo again. The image seemed to waver inside the doorway, first receding into the inner darkness, then stepping forward toward the light. Was it her? And if it was, why was she with Harlan Spencer?

V

Rob passed an eventful night. After turning in, he staged an all-night wrestling match with his top sheet. A number of times he was startled into wakefulness and lay perspiring in the dark, pulse pounding in his head, short of breath, almost panicked. His dreams were swirling, panoramic affairs. He somehow confused civil war battles with the Franco-Russian conflicts of "War and Peace." He heard thundering horses charging unseen columns beyond rolling hills. He felt the rumble of artillery, the staccato crackle of small arms. But he could never quite see the battle. The closest he came was glimpsing puffs of smoke rising above the treetops. He caught images of red-legged Confederate infantry marching at double-time to join the fray. He thought he saw mounted generals with feathered, cockaded hats on far hilltops, telescopes trained on the melee below them. He was alternately afraid that the battle was going to come to him where he was unarmed and unsure of which side he was on, or that it was going to ebb the other way and he was going to miss it.

There was a dull glow of brown light on the eastern curtains when he woke. He had to take a major leak and he almost jumped up from the couch to head for the bathroom, but he restrained himself. Since his stroke he had to be careful about getting up if he had been horizontal for any length of time. A few times he had forgotten and risen too quickly, with the result that he had fallen over. And the problem was that when that happened he crashed hard, with no mechanism to control or mitigate the fall. The numbness on his left side helped to dull the pain, but it still usually hurt. And then there would be the problem of trying to get back up again.

So he sat up and collected himself, and then stood and went into the bathroom. Because he wasn't drinking alcohol he had been drinking a lot of water, so he stood above the bowl for a long time. He was noticing some subtle changes in his metabolism from drying out. That his bladder seemed not to hold as much was one. And his appetite was coming back. He looked in the mirror. Even after the stroke, he still imagined himself through the prism of whom he had been when he was in full strength as a man. He wouldn't recognize himself otherwise. He couldn't.

Had it been a year? In most ways his life had truly been like a dream since then.

He had gotten up that July morning, nervous because he was not hung over, and he knew he should be. That had been happening more and more, the problem being that he had learned it meant the hangover would catch up with him later, fiercely, unremittingly, and last until well into the evening, or longer. His drinking had been taking on a new cast. He had always drunk for a buzz. For years and years, each night he would drink until he was not drunk, but close, and then stop. But lately it began taking more to get to that buzzed state. And by the time he realized he was there, he was actually well past it.

That morning he had driven down to look at the ocean, hoping some surf would postpone the paying of his debt. The colors of that sunrise were still etched in his memory, maybe at the expense of all those other things he had forgotten. Though the wind was hot and strong from the southwest, and it had been flat the evening before, he came over the dune and was greeted with perfect head-high lines marching in. He thought about going home and getting his short board, but he was too jazzed. He popped three ibuprofen, put on his trunks, and slid his nine-foot Takayama off the roof racks. He felt like a thief... because he was on the beach, in the parking lot by himself, on a morning when no one expected there were waves. He went down to the ocean's edge, knelt in the wet cool sand, rubbed wax on the board's deck in wide swirling circles. Suddenly it felt as if a nail had been driven in between his eyes and had lodged at a center point behind them. He closed them tight, and then half-rose, turned, and vomited in the sand behind him. He opened his eyes, or thought he did, but couldn't see anything. There was a warmth and a tingling in his left side that turned into a fiery electricity. Pulses of vision came and went. He forced himself to rise and struggled to drag himself back to his car, for what he didn't know. It was bad, he knew it was bad, but with each struggling step he hoped it would pass. He only got to the margin of the sand and the blacktop when he lost consciousness and collapsed.

He came back two days later. His first hope was that he was dead and just dreaming. The memory of what had happened was gone. But gone also were the memories of many other things. He realized it when the first nurse came in to see him, and he wanted to ask her where he was and how long he had been there. Not only would his mouth not form the words, but he could not think of some of the words he needed to form the sentences. He ended up being silent, and she moved around his bed as if he weren't there. It was his first experience of being a cipher, but he knew it wouldn't be his last.

What followed was…who cared what followed? It was a battle he alternately fought and ran away from. He was in the hospital for three weeks. He still had not paid the bill. They wanted to send him to a rehabilitation center, but he wouldn't go. He went back to the apartment he rented under a friend's house, and stayed there until his money ran out at the end of winter. He couldn't work, which set him up in a bad pattern. He drank and sank down, stopped periodically and tried to rise up. They put him on a recovery regimen, a combination of physical exercise and speech therapy. He spent what seemed like days filling out paperwork. He went to his sessions for a while, but he didn't think they helped and gradually he dropped out. No one seemed to notice or care. He was on his own, but he always had been. But that was the problem too. He had always been self-sufficient. He never needed anything from anyone. But now there were ordinary things he couldn't do. He hated to have to ask for help. He also hated the sound of his own voice. The lucidity of his thoughts came back fairly quickly, but the ability to put those thoughts into words did not. His speech was slurred, words knotted together as if spoken through cheesecloth. He hated the quizzical or patronizing looks he got when he tried to speak. The result was that he spoke less and less. He was restricted as to what he could do for employment, of course. He had done many things over the years, from carpentry to overall contracting when he was in Central America all those years. He had also fished offshore in a panga boat, chartered inshore to help rich guys angle for rooster fish and snook, bought and sold property in Costa Rica, ran a surf camp and hostel in Nicaragua.

Down there he had often in the evenings hiked to the top of one of the steep hills that rose almost directly from the shoreline, timing it so he would have a few moments to watch the sun sinking into the vast Pacific. He would stand there, arms spread unselfconsciously, at the eastern edge of the Ring of Fire, daring whatever gods had swirled that ring into being, daring them to take him. They hadn't.

His visage, which had dissolved in the mirror, reformed itself. There he was, a lumpy shadow of who he had been. He splashed water in his face and brushed his teeth, dragged a wetted comb through his hair. There was something he needed to accomplish today, some task that would lead him closer to the truth. It wasn't about Irina anymore. Well, it was, but there were now clearly new dimensions to it. If she was dead, which is what he had been thinking, he wanted to know why. But if she wasn't dead, what did that mean? What was the connection with Spencer? What was the connection with Steven, who clearly was dead? He shuffled back into the main room, made himself breakfast, and ate it in the burgeoning sunlight.

After he had eaten and cleaned up he realized it was becoming more of a struggle for him to remain cooped up in the house all day. What had started as an unwarranted, and let's face it, a sexual interest in a young émigré, had taken on a life of its own.

He looked across the lawn and saw his neighbor, Amelia Falcon, coming down her front step and heading for her car. She seemed much less harried than she had when he first met her. Without thinking he went outside and shambled as quickly as he could toward her, trying not to appear in any way threatening. He thought that she would hear him as he approached, but when she showed no reaction, he decided to call her name.

"Amelia, Amelia Falcon," he said, and she did turn around. He had stopped in the general area of the property line, and as she turned he tried to offer a soft smile.

The sun was already fierce, and she put up a hand to her forehead to shield her eyes. "Oh, hello," she said, almost cheerily, which Rob had not expected. They both stopped and looked at each other, smiling. And both, within a few seconds, became embarrassed and looked down at their feet.

Rob was the first to look up. "I saw you come out," he said. "I was going to ask if you could give me a ride?" Actually, he had not thought anything about that.

Amelia did become a bit flustered then. "But you don't know where I'm going," she said simply.

"You're right. I'm sorry."

"I'm going to Manteo, to the grocery store. And then I'm going to the post office."

"Could you give me a ride to the newspaper office?" he asked, and realized why he wanted to go there. He wanted to find out about the photograph of the re-enactment, where it had come from, who had taken it, and how had it gotten into the paper in the first place.

"I guess I could give you a ride. I don't know where the newspaper office is." She looked down again.

Rob again heard the faintest trace of an accent. "It's on Sir Walter Raleigh Street," he said. "Downtown."

He looked closely at her, while trying to pretend not to. She was forty-five or fifty, he guessed on closer inspection. Her body was haphazardly lumpy, bulging at unexpected places, and her legs and arms went from being tapered at the hands and feet to thick where they joined the trunk. Her face though was relatively unlined, the skin translucent and olive, and her eyebrows were carefully plucked. Her hair was swept back, clearly dyed, but with a few gray hairs shining through.

They stood in the sunlight, again both suddenly embarrassed.

"I can wait…if you need to get your things together," she said.

"Yes. It will only take me a few minutes. And thank you again. I've been feeling a bit cooped up."

He turned, heading back to the cottage, consciously trying to minimize his limp. Now he felt her eyes on his back. What was he doing, he suddenly wondered? He should be laying low, as he and Chick had decided he would. But the photo in the newspaper had rattled him. He went inside and grabbed his wallet and the keys to the cottage. He picked up his reading glasses. He stopped at the kitchen counter and took up the paper again. He put the photo close to his face, and then backed it away. It was no mistake. There was a female form in the doorway whose outline was familiar to Rob.

Amelia was a careful, tentative driver. Although there was literally no traffic and the road was straight, she drove slowly and kept her right wheels on the shoulder line. Rob sat back, glad to be moving, glad to be going anywhere. The tall, spindly pines rose on both sides of the road, their needles a faded green in the summer heat. There were no clouds in the sky, but it was also washed to a pale blue.

"It's going to be another hot one," he said.

Amelia nodded, but didn't take her eyes from the road in front of her. Rob got the feeling she was regretting her decision to take him. For some

66

reason it became important to put her at her ease. He wanted to tell her a story, but when he thought about it honestly there weren't many stories of his life that would not shock or frighten her. That thought began to make him uncomfortable, and he worried that she would recognize his discomfort, and that would make the tension worse.

"I told you my father died," Amelia said, seizing control of the situation herself. "He was a great man. He came originally from the Nicoya Peninsula in Costa Rica. It's funny. Did you know men who live there live longer than almost anyone else on earth? They did a study. They said it had to do with the diet and the climate, and partly to do with the fact that men there don't take their relationships with women too seriously, so they don't have the stress that comes from that."

"I used to live there, in Mal Pais," Rob said, surprised and delighted at the coincidence. "In the late eighties and early nineties."

"Really? You should have stayed. My father should have stayed too. But he always wanted to come to America. He always wanted to go to New York. So he left us and went. All he did was work. All he wanted to do was work. He would write us about the buildings, and the crowds. He would write about the Parada de San Patricio, who was his patron saint. He loved it because he would wear green, and that reminded him of his home and the green hills falling down to the sea."

"I remember," Rob said.

"For twenty years he worked, always in restaurants. It took him fifteen years to become a citizen. He washed dishes, bussed tables, prepped food, anything. He was quiet and industrious. Finally in 2000 he got the job he wanted. He became assistant to the sous chef at Windows of the World. He sent us photos of the view. He told us the world was at his feet. The next summer he wrote and invited me to visit him. He had a little apartment in Brooklyn, a walk up. It was neat as a pin because he was never there. He showed me the sights of his city. He showed off his English, which was a source of great pride for him. We had a wonderful time together. When I left we were already planning for me to return. Then the planes came out of nowhere and hit the WTC. He was at work as usual. I don't know what he did when he felt the impact, what he thought, whether he was afraid or not. Nothing of him was ever found."

67

Rob didn't know what to say. He went from a pleasant reminiscence of his time in Costa Rica to an immediate recognition of her stunning loss. Not knowing her did not diminish the empathy he felt. He wanted to touch her hand or pat her on the shoulder, but he knew he couldn't do either. But he had to say something.

"I'm sorry. That was not what I expected. I mean… I know you didn't either. I'm sorry."

"I never tell anyone," she said. "You can imagine. I don't know why I told you." She didn't take her eyes off the road, but Rob noticed her hands seemed to relax their grip on the steering wheel. He was afraid she might begin to cry. "I'm alright, really."

"How did you come back?"

"There was a ceremony. There were lots of ceremonies. I was invited the next year to join the other relatives on the anniversary to line up and climb a podium and recite his name. They paid for me to come. I stood in a long line. We were in alphabetical order. The woman in front of me was named Fain. Her husband had worked for Smith-Barney. She had talked to him on the phone after the plane hit. I can't imagine that, but she seemed happy that she had been able to. Mary was very serene. She asked me where I was staying, and then she insisted that I come to New Jersey afterward and stay with her and her two children. I was in a kind of whirring daze so I went.

"Mary had two children…teenagers. She did not get along with them. The girl was always in black. The boy, he was just mean to her. He spoke back to her, and ignored everything she said. She was not so serene at home. They fought. The girl stayed in her room, the boy stayed away from home. She apologized to me, said they acted that way because of the death of their father. I was not so sure, but she was kind to me, and it was not my business. She helped me. I was trying to get a legal status to stay. She helped me with an immigration lawyer, went with me to the meetings. It was complicated. They were not issuing many work visas, and my tourist visa was running out."

If it blows three days…Rob thought to himself. "What did you do?"

"She got it done. I'll hand her that. She would not take no for an answer. She called her congressmen, wrote letters. I know she spent a lot of money helping me, and I will always be grateful for that."

"But?"

"But what?"

"I sensed there was a hitch or a catch."

She laughed. "Isn't there always a catch?"

They were coming to the old Mann's Harbor Bridge, now the back way into Manteo. There were many boats on the water, ski boats, crabbers, and further to the south, a sailboat becalmed in the light winds. To the south, under the new bridge, the heat caused the horizon to melt into the sky. Amelia had stopped speaking so she could concentrate on her driving across the narrow bridge.

In the silence Rob began to feel the crawling worm of a buried thought. As he always did, he immediately, and a bit frantically, tried to change the subject.

"There was a Ukrainian girl I used to work with," he said. "She disappeared. And then they found her body in one of the canals west of here, sunk in a car. An accident. So that was that. Except that yesterday I saw a photograph of her, or someone who looks very much like her, in the newspaper. And the photo was taken after the car she was in was supposed to have gone into the canal."

"You're not sure though if the photograph is of her?" Amelia asked.

"Not positive, no. But I knew her well enough that I think it is," Rob said, and then realized that he didn't know her, that their relationship was one-sided and weird, prurient. "I don't know how it works any more, with everything being digital, but I was hoping I could see the actual photo. It has to be clearer than the one I saw in the paper."

"What does it mean if it is her?"

"Well, then you have to wonder who was in the car? I remembered reading when it happened, 'She was identified...' Who identified her? I didn't think about it then, but it wasn't a member of her family because they're on the other side of the world."

They came down the gentle slope on the east side of the bridge on Roanoke Island. Rob could actually feel Amelia relax.

"You don't like bridges, do you?"

Rob thought of something else. He remembered Irina's friend, Nadia, the one she would stay up late with talking and smoking. They didn't resemble each other facially, but they had the same color hair and they were generally the same height and build.

He wondered if he had said too much. He wondered if he should have said anything. He was glad he hadn't said anything about Steven, because he realized that would have probably really freaked her out. She dropped him at the head of Sir Walter Street. She asked when he would be finished.

"I'm not sure, but I can find my own way back," he said. "Thank you."

She nodded and drove away. On the sunny corner Rob was suddenly aware of how much in the open he was. Manteo was the town seat, and even though it was a small town, there were sheriff's department and police cars everywhere, it seemed. If they were looking for a stumbling, limping middle-aged man, here he was in the middle of the sidewalk.

As he walked down the street he recognized that he had walked the other way years ago. The old county jail had used to be at the end of it, a block from the Sound. He had spent an Easter weekend in that jail more than twenty-five, no, it was thirty years earlier, in another lifetime it seemed now. They had built a new jail complex now, away from the tidy downtown and the tourists.

The newspaper office was in a nondescript storefront halfway down the first block. There was no one in the front office as he went in. He heard conversation and activity coming from the rear of the building and he hesitated, wondering if he should go back. He looked around for a bell or some other way to announce his presence, but ended up sitting in the slick straight-back chair and waited for them to come to him.

He picked up a copy of the newspaper that lay on the table by the chair. He flipped through it. In the second section, on the last page before the classified ads, were the obituaries. There it was. "Stepven A Banks, III, loving husband of Misty, passed away suddenly on June 5. He is survived by…" and then it went on to list his children from both of his marriages. Nothing was mentioned about the cause of his death. Then right beneath it, "Paula Redmond Banks, died after a long illness on June 4. She is survived by…"

He was musing about Stephen and Paula, and their deaths, and the children they left behind, when a woman came in through the door from the back of the building. She was immediately apologetic to find him sitting there. He introduced himself and gave her some cock and bull story about

70

being a part of the re-enactment and wondering if he could get a copy of the photograph they had run in their recent issue.

She led him back to her cubicle, which was in the back corner just inside the door she had come out of. She sat behind the desk and began punching letters on the keyboard in front of her monitor. "Oh, wait. I can't give you a copy because it wasn't taken by one of our photographers. We don't own the rights."

"Well, I only want it for my personal use. I'm not going to reprint it or anything."

She looked over her glasses at him. He knew better than to try to smile. "I don't know," she said. "You said you were part of the re-enactment?"

"I'm part of the group," he said. "I didn't get to make this trip unfortunately. Maybe next year."

She pressed a few more keys and the printer whirred behind her. It spat out an eight by ten photograph that she handed to him. "How much do I owe you?"

She smiled and waved a hand.

He took out his glasses and looked at the photo. It was clearer than it had looked in the newspaper, but the hazy form in the doorway was still elusive. It could be her, he really thought it was, but he couldn't be sure. He looked up and found the woman looking intently at him.

"Thank you," he said, rising and limping gingerly toward the door. "You've been a great help."

"Wait," she said. "Let me get something to protect that." She reached behind her and retrieved a tan folder and handed it over the counter to Rob. He nodded his thanks and left.

He looked at the photo again when he got out into the bright sunlight, hoping Irina would come into view. But she didn't. He put it back in the manila folder. The summer light was broad across everything. He walked back to the highway, and then on the shoulder with the traffic in the sandy groove made by earlier pedestrians. There were houses off the road behind drooping trees, and neighborhoods behind them.

He stumbled along, not in any hurry because it was useless to be in any. He kept his head down, consciously tried not to limp, and tried to bridge the gaps of what he knew and didn't know. Two people, not that he was close to them, but he had shared some proximity, had died, one and perhaps both of them violently. And he kept getting the aching feeling that what he didn't know, especially about Steven, had a lot to do with what he couldn't remember.

Traffic was steady both ways, though it lessened as he increased his distance from the downtown area. He realized he couldn't walk all the way back, but he wasn't ready to stick his thumb out yet. He hoped vaguely that Amelia Falcon would come by and solve his problem. But then suddenly he saw the flash of a vehicle swerve by and come to a stop in front of him. It was Chick's truck. Chick didn't get out of the cab, but waited for Rob to come up to the passenger side, and then moved some papers from the seat so he could get in. When Rob was settled he pulled back out on to the highway.

"What are you doing?" he asked. "What are you doing out here?" He shook his head.

Rob didn't say anything. At first he was going to tell him about Irina and the photo, but something stopped him. "I just had to get out," he finally said. "I needed to do something besides sitting around."

"I told you to stay put," Chick said levelly, but the muscles were standing out in his forearms where he clutched the steering wheel.

Rob didn't say anything. Chick drove north on Roanoke Island, back toward the old bridge. He passed the Gardens and the outdoor theater. Tall pines stood back off the road, their needles pale and blue in the heat. Closer to the pavement, highway crews had planted rows of cherry trees whose deep pink blossoms waved languidly in the breeze.

"I haven't been completely straight with you," Chick said as they climbed the embankment to the foot of the old bridge.

"About Steven?"

"Yes, about Steven. There's more to it, more that you don't know. Steven was sick. He didn't want anyone to know. Other than the doctors, they knew. Things had happened, with his business, his money matters, and then this cancer came up. He told me he knew something wasn't right, but with his new family he avoided finding out until when he did, there was nothing to be done about it."

"He didn't look sick."

"Well, he was. When things started going south with his business, he tried everything. He had the three houses, but none of them would sell.

Nothing was selling. You could give things away, that's all. This was before he knew he was sick. He had no new contracts. He owed money on equipment, to the banks, to sub-contractors. He'd bought toys, and cars, the best of everything. He couldn't bring himself to tell his new wife that they had to change their lifestyle. His whole persona with her was based on him being this high-flying, successful entrepreneur. And he had another family besides. He started liquidating what he could, but it wasn't helping. I know he was desperate for a plan. He began mining his real estate contacts, and his lawyers, anyone…me even. He realized his oceanfront rental house was the key. People were still coming on vacation, and the people with money were beginning to recognize that they were in better shape. More to the point, he realized he wasn't one of them. Those four or five years when he was making a quarter or a half million or more were like a mirage. He realized that those times when things were going so well, when he felt he had things under control… that whole time, he was being used. Someone further up the line had set things up, and he had fallen for the scam just like everyone else."

Rob thought that Chick might be talking about himself.

"So like I said he had his big oceanfront house with the ten bedrooms and bathrooms, and two of every appliance in the kitchen, the one he used to take his little Slavic girls to in the off-season and chase them around the rooms. It was the jewel in his empire, but there was a balloon payment coming, and after that it would all be over. Someone told him about a scam that if he stopped making payments in the spring, and then collected all his weekly summer rentals in cash or checks to a dummy corporation, that the bank probably wouldn't catch up to him with the foreclosure paperwork until after the season was over. With the combination of not making payments, plus the $5000 a week, he was looking at pocketing about $100,000 in hopefully untraceable cash."

"Well, how was that going to really make a difference?"

"It wouldn't really. That was just going to be for ready money, and to stave off what creditors he could." Chick's face was stony, his hands still tightly gripped the steering wheel and he stared straight ahead. "But he was also looking at his insurance policies. His whole thing at the end was about taking care of his wife and his kids. By the time they found the cancer, it was stage four. He knew he was done for, and he wasn't going to put himself through chemo or anything else when he knew in his heart there wasn't any chance. He was keeping it from his family. His wife didn't know anything. It must have been weird for him with Paula sinking so fast. I still wonder if he told her anything."

Rob saw Paula's face, her twenty-year old face, with the mischievous, beckoning smile, her love of the secret thing between them. Now she was gone, totally gone, and he was dragging himself along still, his dead leg trailing behind.

"He told me. When he did, and the way he did, I knew it was going to cost me something. He told Ed Thomas at the bank. He told his lawyer, Sam Scarborough, and he told Spencer. All these old-school guys. He was looking into all these ways to hide and shield his money from the government and lenders. His feeling was that he had worked hard all his life, and the government just wanted to take his money and give it to people who weren't willing to work as hard as he had. He didn't explain his reasons for dumping on the people who had lent him money, and rightfully expected to get it back."

What about Irina, Rob wondered? He looked at the folder in his lap. There were all these gaps in what he was hearing and trying to put together. Steven loved his family, yes, but there were other things involved, other pulls on his emotions and energies. Was Chick trying to say Steven arranged his own death?

Rob felt Chick was struggling with something beyond the story he was telling, that Chick was involved in something further. It made him wonder if Chick was being truthful about this story of Steven's health. Every time he learned anything, it didn't serve to tighten the story, but to expand it.

"Chick, why am I still hiding? Why can't I contact the law, or turn myself in, and just see what happens?"

Chick slammed the heel of his right hand on the dashboard. "Because you don't know how to answer them. Do you think they're going to stand for, 'I don't know,' or 'I can't remember'? They'll try to make you remember."

"Remember what? I want to remember, they want me to remember, but you don't. Why?"

"It's just better that you don't." He looked sideways at Rob with a withering, condescending, dismissive expression.

74

"Fuck you, Chick." Rob immediately felt lightheaded as he sometimes did since his stroke when he became overly emotional. The left side of his body began to tingle, almost hum. He leaned back against the headrest, trying to calm himself.

He would remember. It would all come back. He would retrieve it somehow. He and Chick didn't have anything to say to each other the rest of the way back to Mashoes. When they got there Chick went to the back of the truck and collected the grocery bags that he brought in and set on the counter.

"It won't be much longer, Rob," he said. "Just let me figure it out."

After he drove away, Rob emptied the groceries. In the bottom of one of the bags was a half-gallon of dark rum. Rob looked at the bottle for a long time.

VI

The bottle stayed on the kitchen counter for an hour. Rob sat on the dust-exhaling couch in the other room and ignored it. He listened to music, Herb Alpert, Chet Baker, acoustic Herbie Hancock. He even found a Sun Ra album tucked in the back, which greatly increased his respect for Chick's father. He put it on. He was agitated less by his desire for the alcohol than by his anger and confusion at Chick. The music rose and fell in the heat of the dark room. The coy, stumbling humor of the Arkestra, the crazy, antic chases the instruments would launch into, driven by Sun Ra's plunking piano notes, reminded Rob of a rainy, umbrella-swirling funeral parade... on roller skates. The ceiling fan rattled and sliced overhead, keeping time, prodding the faded curtains into a languid, opiated dance.

The tan folder lay on the table. He slid it over in front of him and opened it. Pulling his reading glasses out of his pocket and slipping them on, he squinted at the photograph. There she was. Perhaps not unmistakably her, perhaps not absolutely her, but her enough in his mind that he was sure. But then again the form was out of focus, its outlines so hazy, that the longer he looked at the photo the less sure he became. He stared again at the other forms of the re-enacting soldiers. Above them on the porch, Spencer dominated all. The look on his face was resolute, his stare steely. He had fallen whole-heartedly into his role.

Rob rose and went into the kitchen. Without hesitating, he took the rum bottle, went to the back door, opened it, and dropped the glass vessel on to the concrete pad at the bottom of the steps. It burst as it hit, sending screaming shards of glass scattering across the concrete and into the grass. The smell of deep dark Caribbean cane rose to his nostrils. Memories flooded back of Puerto Rico, Barbados, Nicaragua and Costa Rica. He remembered tropical nights, the buzzing of insects, the disembodied sounds of surf pounding beyond the tree-lined beaches. He saw stars, untold numbers of them, in a great arcing wheel. Memories of torrid embraces replayed themselves. He heard the deep urgent grunts of howler monkeys, and the frantic chatter of a blur of green parrots flying by. His left side tingled. He went back inside.

Lightning flashed on the darkening skies to the southwest. The rain would wash away the rum and he would clean up the glass later. As he watched the sky he saw colors ranging from the still solid blue above, to purple, brooding pink, black and gray, even lines of tan on the horizon. It was still a few hours until sunset. He brooded over what options he had. He had no money, no vehicle. He was wanted by law enforcement, at least as a witness. He was reliant on Chick for shelter, food, outside information. Chick was protecting him…but from what? Rob had been with Steven the night he died, but he didn't remember anything of consequence. But what did Chick think he could remember? Maybe Chick was protecting himself because he was involved. But was he involved in Steven's death, or something more, or something else?

Amelia Falcon's car pulled into her driveway just as the colors of the day were starting to mute and the storm, which had seemed to be holding back, began to rise above the serrated line of the pines behind the properties. Rob watched through the slats in the blinds as she hurriedly transferred her groceries from the trunk to the house. When he saw the dark gray curtain of rain coming across the marshland a mile to the southwest, he went out the front door and hobbled over to her house. As he approached he saw her in the living room watching him come across the lawn.

"I need your help," he said without any preamble when she opened the door. He felt pressure to explain himself quickly, to bring her into his world. "I …I don't know how to put this…"

"Come in," she said, taking small steps back as she opened the door wider.

"I didn't think, or know, if you would talk to me," Rob said. He was breathless, perspiring. "I don't have anything, no money, no car, and there is something I have to get to the bottom of. No, that's not what I mean. I've become a part of something. I don't know how, or I don't remember how…"

He was trying to read her expression as he spoke. She wasn't smiling, but there was the faintest hint of amusement on her face. He tried to explain to her what his predicament was. He didn't spare her the descriptions of his drinking and homelessness, his porous memory. It came down to two characters, Steven and Irina. One was surely dead, the other, he didn't know. But if Irina wasn't, she surely must have answers to what had happened, and why. His plea and explanations dissolved slowly into confused, incomplete mumbles.

"I will try to help you," she said. "I think you are telling me the truth. It seems too convoluted and bizarre that you would make it up just to get attention. Whether or not the girl Irina is alive or dead seems to be the main question to be answered."

They stood there in the small darkening room, two people approaching the back end of middle age, each with the weight of their separate lives, each essentially unknown to the other.

Amelia waved him into the living room, inviting him to sit on the love seat, as she backed toward the worn armchair. As Rob moved to sit down, he saw an easel set up in the corner of the room. Next to it was an end table with tubes of paint and brushes. He tried to organize his thoughts and what he needed to emphasize.

"But before you go on," she said, preempting him, "tell me about your child."

Rob felt as if all the air was gone from his lungs. How did she know about Kelly? He looked at Amelia's strangely unlined face. She sat erectly in the armchair, her legs together, her hands folded on her lap, as if she had asked the most normal question in the world. He collected the thoughts he had thousands of times before, determined this time to deliver them unvarnished.

"She is in prison in Raleigh," he said. "She had too much to drink one afternoon, and ran a red light, and killed three teenagers. It was a horrible accident. She had her own problems with alcohol…I didn't know the extent of them. But because of the law in North Carolina, she was charged with and then convicted of second-degree murder. There was a lot of publicity. It was in the national newspapers, and the trial was shown minute by minute on the Court TV channel. There were all sorts of narratives to make Kelly fit into whatever box the deliverers of these narratives wanted her to fit in. She was the depraved, remorseless killer. She was the sick alcoholic girl. She was the unrepentant goth witch.

"It's been ten years. She was sentenced to twenty years for each of the deaths, to run consecutively, without the possibility of parole. And it's been

78

ten years. She has fifty years left. I can't make sense of that. She's thirty four now."

He shook his head, trying to imagine what Kelly thought and felt about it. Rob knew he could not have taken it.

"I have not known her for a long time, since she was a young girl really. I can't make any excuses. I dropped the ball, and for some reason thought it was better not to pick it back up. I was gone a lot after her mother and I split. I lived out of the country for many years. I tried to see her the times I came back, but I was afraid of her. She changed so much each time, and I didn't have any control. There were things she did as a teenager that I didn't like when I found out about them, but she let me know I had no right to say anything about it. She never got in any serious trouble with the law, but she wasn't on a good path."

It started raining outside, first large scattered drops, then quickly the torrent fell faster and harder, until after a moment they couldn't hear each other speak. Lightning lit up the woods behind the house, the thunder came in long deep complaints in the distance, and sometimes near enough that the boom of it would shake the house. Rob knew because of the intensity it couldn't last long. He leaned forward and looked down at the carpet. Both were quiet as the noise and the violence of the storm washed over them.

Ten minutes later it was darker and the only sounds were the cascading sheets of the accumulated rain running off the roof. Rob looked up and Amelia was looking kindly at him.

"I have tried to see her. I've written her, but she hasn't written back so I don't know if she reads my letters. Since the stroke things have gone downhill for me. What little money I had to begin with went for treatment, and it's been a struggle just to survive since then." He looked at her, shook his head. "This doesn't even sound like my life really. I don't feel sorry for myself. I don't. Say something, please."

"We should find a way for you to see her," Amelia said simply. "Where is her mother?"

"Jane? Jane lives in Asheville on the other side of the state. She married a developer when Kelly was thirteen or fourteen. They lived here on the beach for a while, but she and her husband have been in Asheville for many years now. Jane and Kelly had it rough with each other when Kelly was a teenager, as I guess is usual, but I don't know if they ever mended their fences."

"You should continue writing to your daughter, whether she answers you or not," Amelia said. "Does your wife visit her?"

"She's not my wife, not for a long time, and I don't know if she has visited her." It had quieted as the storm passed, but now the insects and the frogs began to churn up their evening cacophony. Amelia stood and turned on the lamps at either end of the sofa, and then resumed her seat. "You know, Kelly's frozen for me," Rob continued, "frozen as an eleven year old girl. I want to know her, but I don't want to lose that innocent picture, especially when I think of what I might have to trade it for. But how did you know about her?"

"I saw the crosses on the side of the road at that intersection. That was weeks ago. I asked someone about it, and they told me about the accident so I looked it up on the internet. I read different versions of the story. It was all very sad. And I saw the girl's last name was Wheat, which to me was a very odd name. And then you introduced yourself as Rob Wheat, so I just put two and two together. Now tell me more about your other dilemma."

Rob did, or at least told her as much as he could remember, filling in some of the gaps with his own conjectures, and leaving others blank for Amelia to make her own guesses. It centered on two things; who had killed Steven, and why, and what had happened to Irina? Was that her they had found in the sunken car in the canal, or was that her hidden behind the screen door at the civil war battle enactment? And what did Steven and Irina have to do with each other? And what was Rob's own role in all this? Chick led him to believe that he had been a player, but all Rob could remember was partying with Steven that last night, and then waking up the next morning beaten up and dumped on the beach in Nags Head. The police thought he was part of something, which is why Chick had hidden him here, and had gotten so upset when he'd gone to Manteo. But was it the police Chick was hiding him from? Rob tried to explain Chick to Amelia, the strange combination of moral ambivalence, and real brotherly concern. He didn't mention to her the bottle of rum he had left Rob with the latest batch of groceries.

"But even now, as I'm talking to you, I feel I could be on the verge of remembering something. I've had this feeling before, and it's driving me crazy."

"So what is your plan to deal with all of this?"

"My plan? I don't know. When I say I have no money, it's an exaggeration because I do actually have $26. How far would that get me? And I'm apparently unable to move around freely anyway, and not just in the sense of this," he said, tapping his left leg. "Where to begin? I don't know."

"What about the re-enactors?" Amelia said. "There seems to be a key there, one way or another. That is either the girl, Irina, or it isn't. Who is in this group? Why would they know her?"

"Well, it's run by Spencer," Rob said. "It's his group, I think. I recognized some of the others, from his restaurants, and from the old days. He probably knows Irina, of course, because she worked at one of his restaurants. But he has so much else going on, he might not be aware of her at all."

"Is that the only way they would be connected?"

"I don't know. If they have any other kind of relationship, I didn't hear about it. I thought she and Steven had something going, maybe..."

"Well, I guess we could start there. I don't know how much help I can be. I guess the best help is that I am a non-descript middle-aged woman, who won't draw any attention, and I have a car."

"I don't have any money here, not even for gas," he said, looking at her. She waved her hand. "No, I'll figure out a way to pay you back. I still have money in an account at the Banco National in Mal Pais. I did some land deals before I left, and it's there. I left it thinking I'd be going back. This is strange for me. I've spent all my life being a certain way, living my life my way. I was built for it, mentally and physically. And then this happened. I'm not sure who I am now, or how I'm supposed to be. I don't know what my limits are."

"Life is always like that, isn't it? You don't know until your limits until you bump up against them."

Rob was quiet for a moment. "Chick is going to be pissed."

"Where is Chick in all this?" Amelia asked. "He seems to be straddling a number of positions."

"I don't know. Chick has always been a person whose priorities ultimately devolve to taking care of himself. Even when he took me in and set me up here, hid me here, it wasn't just to protect me. I can feel he is also protecting himself from something."

"And what about these Russian girls?'

"That's another funny thing. When I left here in the mid-eighties, this county was probably eighty percent white Anglo-Saxons. There were blacks who lived on Roanoke Island, but the beaches, Wanchese, here, all white. I come back and it's completely different. It's not just Russians...but Ukrainians like Irina, Latvians, Estonians, Maldovans, Belorussians. There are Greeks and Macedonians and Thais. Hundreds rotate through here every summer with this work exchange program. And then there are Hispanics." He nodded at Amelia. "Not many Costa Ricans. But Mexicans, Guatamalans, Hondurans. Talk about diversity."

"But it's good, isn't it?"

"Good, bad...I don't know. It is what it is."

"Tomorrow," Amelia said, and then stopped. She suddenly seemed embarrassed, and afraid of what she was getting into.

"Why don't you sleep on it tonight," Rob said, getting up. He had to reach back down with his right arm to steady himself.

Amelia stood also and walked with Rob to the door. It was fully dark now, the sky magenta above, with a line of faraway white light to the east and the beaches. Stars had begun to twinkle through the growing gaps in the rising clouds. They said goodnight and Rob walked across the soggy expanse between the houses. Before he went around the corner to go in the front door, he looked back toward Amelia's house. What was he doing, he asked himself? What was she doing? That was the more interesting question. Suddenly, standing there on the porch, with insects swirling around the porch light and buzzing around his head, Rob felt exceedingly drained. He dragged himself the last step to the door and went in, turning the outside light off as the screen door clapped shut.

The block walls almost seemed almost to be dripping. He limped into the bathroom, wrestled out of his shirt and took a cloth, wetted it with cold water from the tap, and rubbed it across his face and shoulders. He felt a wave of dizziness and had to clutch the edge of the sink to keep from falling over. Where did that come from, he wondered, after it had passed?

He didn't go into the bedroom, but fell instead on to the couch again and finally went to sleep.

It was a still gray summer dawn the next day. There was no breeze at all. Rob busied himself with breakfast, and tried to straighten the small house. As he was finishing with the dishes, he saw Amelia crossing the field coming toward him. Several pieces of paper fluttered in her left hand. Rob stepped back into the interior shadows and watched her. She looked like what she was, a middle-aged Hispanic woman, going soft and thickening around the middle. She only lacked the black lace dress and tight shoes to be any of the middle-aged women whose type he knew so well from Central America and the Caribbean. But what was different was the Americanization. She had that unmistakable thing that people got in this country, individualism. It might take a while, but in America people eventually became, if not whom they wanted to be, at least who they really were.

"I've been looking things up on the internet," she said when he met her at the front door and let her in. "And I checked out Spencer's Facebook page. So I've got a schedule for re-enactments coming up. Gettysburg is the obvious choice. Lots of re-enactors, lots of spectators. Can you grow a beard?"

"Hold it, hold it. What are you talking about?"

She stopped to look at him. A little color rose to her face as he challenged her. "I'm sorry," she said, more slowly. "I'm getting ahead of myself. Your photo shows the girl, Irina, at the re-enactment, and that's the only place we know she has been, or think she has been, if she is alive. So is she there with Spencer, or is it someone else? He seems like the starting point to me, that's where I was going with this."

"You're right about Spencer. But what does a beard have to do with anything?"

"I researched a lot about re-enactments last night. They're very popular. I couldn't imagine any group that was really serious wouldn't be planning to go to Gettysburg. It is the oldest re-enactment, the biggest battle. They went last year, to the 150th anniversary. I saw photos. Of course, they are going. There is no reason why we can't go too, blend in to the crowd, and be able to observe Spencer's group, and hopefully find some answers. As for the beard… you grow some whiskers, put on a slouchy hat and a baggy uniform, voila, Rob incognito."

"I don't have money to travel. I don't have money for a uniform."

"Mr. Wheat," Amelia said, smiling, "what kind of name is that?"

Rob remembered someone else asking him that. It was Rios, a lifetime ago.

"Can I call you Rob?"

He nodded, frowning. What she suggested was what he wanted. It had been keeping him awake. It had driven him crazy, recognizing there was no way he could accomplish it. And yet here she was, this woman he barely knew, offering to help him. "I've told you, I have no money."

"I do," she said. "I have survivor benefits from the 9/11 Commission. In 2007 I received a check for $1,780,654. It's been sitting in the bank ever since. I have spent virtually none of it. Now, I'm not looking to waste or throw away money. I'm not going to. But you have a problem, and I think I can help. That's what I'm offering."

"But why?"

"Because I've been sitting in that house by myself. I came here to paint, and I'm not painting. This trajectory I'm on is not good for me. I am not living in this world. I am only biding my time. I need to shake things up. Apparently that's where you come in." She laughed.

"I don't know," Rob said.

"Let's just do this. Let's come up with a plan." She gave a Latin shrug. "No harm in that. There is something going on here. I can see that. There is a mystery, a question, and it's tugging at me. But it's burning in you. You don't even have a choice. You have to accept this offer."

She was right. "The police think I'm involved, and I don't even know if I am or not. That's why I'm here."

"I thought as much. But what can you have been involved in? Honestly, what? I look at the scale of this, and to me it seems there are some big players involved. I read what I could find out about it in the papers. This is not just the suspicious death of a local real estate entrepreneur. It's not just the disappearance of a young Slavic restaurant worker. She's Ukrainian. What about everything that's happening in Ukraine? Does that have something to do with it? They had elections at the end of last month. The

Russians are stirring things up there. There is something else going on here."

"Chick," he said, "Chick has more to do with this than he's saying. He was involved with Steven, and he's involved with Spencer. And there's some kind of involvement with Irina. They're all involved, each holding up some part of something, but I don't know what it is. But Chick and Irina…he's said things about her that have made me wonder."

"What you need from me now is mobility," Amelia said. "I'll drive you if you need to go anywhere, or you can use the car yourself if you need to. I'll start researching the trip to Gettysburg."

"I don't think we should let people know we're doing this together," Rob said.

Amelia smiled. "I don't have anyone to tell, honestly. And this is the kind of thing that if I did tell friends about it, I'm sure they'd be cautioning me not to get involved." She laughed, and something in her laugh let Rob see who she had been as a girl. There was a playfulness in it, and also something vaguely sexual. Then she looked seriously at him. "I know what I'm doing. I mean, I have to trust you to be straight with me."

"I'm not harmless, even like this," Rob said, holding up his clawed left hand. "But I'm not a danger to you. Somebody has put me in the middle of this for a reason, and I intend to find out why."

"We also have to get more information about those girls, not just Irina, but the other one too."

"So you're thinking the same thing I am, that the girl in the canal was not Irina. I know her friend's name is Nadia, but I don't know her last name. There must be a clearinghouse. They've both disappeared apparently, so where are their families, or their governments?"

"Maybe I can try to find out something about that, go to the police, claim to be friends with one of them…"

"Let's wait on that, I think. The police are looking for me. Let's not let them become interested in you."

They sat in his front room for a half an hour longer, exploring options, expounding on theories, until she said there were things she needed to take care of if they were going on the road. Their parting was a bit awkward. They hesitated at the doorway, and ended up shaking hands, which brought an amused smile to both their faces.

Rob knew he could collect his things in ten minutes, so he didn't worry about it. He listened to music on the turntable, and from the I-pod. He sat at the low table and wrote everything he could remember about the situation and everyone in it until the sky darkened outside. When he had finished, he stared at the paper for a while, and then finally folded it and put it in his pocket. It was a deeper dark in the house, where he hadn't turned a light on. Insects buzzed all around. The humidity had returned with a vengeance, and he knew it was going to be hot and sticky trying to sleep in the stillness. He took off his shoes and socks and sat on the couch absently rubbing his numb left foot. He thought about Amelia Falcon. Anyone else, and he would have been wondering what her angle was. But she seemed genuine and sincere. He worried that she was going to push him about Kelly though, and on that front he wouldn't be pushed.

Two hours later he was ready for bed. He was about to turn on the bathroom light to brush his teeth when he heard the faint hissing of tires from the direction of Manns Harbor. He looked through the curtains and saw two sets of headlights slowly approaching. In an instant he realized there was a danger to him. He crouched and fairly ran to the back door and hobbled down the outside steps. Luckily, the porch light was not on. At the bottom, he took a step and felt a searing burn on the heel of his left foot. As he limped on, he realized he had stepped on a shard of glass from the broken rum bottle. He looked over his shoulder as he moved away from the house. The cars had come even with the driveway. Their blue lights came on as they turned in.

Rob had first thought of going to Amelia's house, but now he veered away and made his way across the empty soybean field for the line of trees a couple of hundred yards behind the house. He tripped and stumbled as he went, dragging his bad leg and injured foot, slashing his lower legs on brambles and strings of roots and vines. When he saw the beams of flashlights entering the house, and the lights going on, he fell on his stomach short of the trees, not wanting to risk being seen. His chest heaved as he lay there, and he had trouble regaining his breath. When he did he lifted his head and looked back at the house. All the lights were on, and he saw three or four forms moving through the rooms. He thought he recognized the tall form of the young cop who had come to see him at Chick's house, but he couldn't be sure. He tried to think of what they could find that would do them any good. There was no ID in his stuff, no way to positively identify that it was him. They could fingerprint the place, of course, but he wondered if they would go to that much trouble.

As he was observing them, he caught movement out of the corner of his eye and saw Amelia Falcon come out on to her porch, watching the commotion with a phone in her hand. She must know who it was, Rob thought, but she was pretending she didn't. He saw her punch numbers and then hold the phone to her ear. He heard her voice across the field, but he couldn't understand what she was staying. She spoke to someone for a moment, and then dropped the phone again to her side and resumed watching the cottage.

A moment later, a tall man, Rob was almost positive it was the young cop, came out of the back door, aiming with his flashlight in front of him as he came down the steps. He hesitated at the bottom, playing his beam around the ground area, and then aimed the spot of light out across the field. Rob thought the man might be weighing the option of coming out into the field to search, but he saw Amelia standing under the porch light and guided himself with his flashlight toward her.

Rob lay there, feeling the blood oozing from the wound on his heel. He left the leaves and dirt on the surface of the skin, hoping they would combine to clot and stop the flow of blood. It hurt, but he couldn't tell if it was serious or not. He could still make out three people moving around in the cottage. Their partner had arrived at Amelia's house and they had a discussion, with the moths and other bugs swirling in mad orbits around the light above their heads. Rob wondered what the man might be asking, and how Amelia might be responding to him. He suddenly had an ally he thought he could trust, and he felt a gnawing in the pit of his stomach that this episode might soften her resolve, or frighten her off completely.

Their conversation was brief. Their body language told him nothing. The policeman took his leave and returned to his colleagues. He again lingered at the back steps, even squatting down and picking something up at the foot of the steps. He examined it closely and then dropped it and entered the cottage. Ten minutes later they left. Their two cars backed down the long driveway, and then their headlights could be seen in the far trees, their smoldering taillights receded as they returned to their base.

Rob waited in the dirt, mosquitos bouncing furiously against him, until he was sure they were gone. After ten minutes Amelia came back out on her porch and stood silently until the bugs chased her back inside. After ten more minutes Rob rose and drew a wide arc around the back of her property, approaching in the dark behind the house. She must have anticipated him because she opened the door as he neared even though he knew she couldn't have seen him. He came up the steps and stopped outside the door.

"What did he say?" Rob asked.

"Well, they were looking for you. He said they had gotten some kind of tip, and that you were a 'person of interest', although he wouldn't say what about."

"What did you tell him?"

"Just that I hadn't seen you in a couple of days, and I thought you had moved on. He said your stuff was still there. I told him I didn't know you, hadn't talked to you. You were there, and then you were gone." She shrugged as if to demonstrate how she had responded. She stepped back, opening the door wider.

"I've sliced my foot," he said. "I don't know if the bleeding has stopped."

"Wait here," she said, and went back inside. She returned with an old bath towel. "Wrap this around your foot and come in."

Rob hobbled in, leaning over to keep the towel around his wound, and followed her to a chair she had pulled out in the dining room.

"Don't turn on the light yet," Rob said, "until we know for sure they're gone."

They sat quietly in the dark. With each passing moment Rob had a greater feeling that Amelia might be regretting her involvement with him. He thought he could feel her shrinking further into herself. The clock ticked mechanically on the china hutch. The insects droned outside.

"Why don't you have the air-conditioning on?" He had seen the squarish wall units in various windows, and it was certainly hot enough.

"The heat doesn't affect me, I guess."

They were quiet again, though this time there was a more frantic quality to it.

"Let me look at that foot," she finally said, rising abruptly and turning on the overhead light. When the light came on they both looked at each other, and Rob realized she was measuring him as much as he was measuring her.

She knelt down and removed the blood-stained towel from his foot. She dabbed at it with a clean corner.

"I'm going to need some water and a clean cloth," she said. She didn't look up. Rob was above her, looking at the spidery strands of gray hair spreading among the black hair at her part. She kept her face averted as she rose, and went into the kitchen. She returned through the swinging door carrying a bowl of water and a roll of paper towels. Rob let her guide his foot into the warm water, and then she lifted it and dabbed with the towels. "It's not too deep, at least," she said, putting her face closer to it, "but it's going to hurt a bit cleaning it out."

She was efficient and firm as she nursed him, and in a few minutes the bowl was filled with dirt and bits of floating grass and leaves and rose-colored water. She rose again and left the room, returning with a man's t-shirt and scissors. She cut it in strips and wrapped it over the top of his foot and around his ankle. Rob wondered whose shirt it was.

"Do you think they'll come back?" she asked, looking up at him.

"I don't know. When I think it's safe I'll go back and see if they took anything."

"We're going to have to make some kind of move," Amelia said. "If we're doing this, we need to start doing it. They'll at least check back to see if you've returned. This is what we'll do. Stay here on the couch and get some sleep. Sometime before dawn you go back and get just what you have to have. Leave everything else. We're going on a road trip."

89

VII

They had spent two nights in a motel in Williamston, one hundred miles west of the Outer Banks. They had separate rooms. There was nothing uncomfortable about it for Rob. And he didn't think anything about it bothered Amelia.

They left the morning after the police came to Rob's safe house. Amelia convinced him to leave the house just as the police had found it so if they came back they would think it had been deserted earlier, as Amelia had told them. Rob didn't want to leave the few possessions he had, but he also agreed it made sense. He did sneak back and get two things, the folder with Irina's photograph and the attached article from the paper, and the I-pod.

He left that morning with Amelia and just the clothes on his back. His heel was still swabbed in cloth as he hobbled to the car and got in the passengers' seat. He had developed a dark knobby scab on his head, but it was healing. They drove to Raleigh and went to one of the sprawling malls. Their purpose was to buy Rob clothes and incidentals. Rob was uncomfortable about it at first, but Amelia clearly reveled in the process so he let her run the show. She picked things out for him to try on, and then decided yes or no after viewing him in them. She checked for sale prices, but she was more interested in how the clothes looked on him. She tried not to let him see her face when some shirt or sweater hung strangely on his frame. They left the mall with two large stuffed bags. She had also gotten directions to a Salvation Army thrift store, and they bought more used articles there.

After their shopping and a late lunch, they headed east, ending up at the motel in Williamston, a location halfway between the Outer Banks and Raleigh. They shifted back and forth between their adjoining rooms, making plans. Amelia had laid out some of the clothes from the thrift store on the spare bed in her room. She had begun to cut some of the items up. Rob guessed she was working on her idea for their reenactment costumes.

"Do you think you should try to contact Kelly for a visit while we're so close?" she asked as she pulled needle and thread out of a travel case.

Rob found himself agreeing that maybe he should, and offered that he had been thinking about it on the drive toward Raleigh. "I don't know if she'll see me though."

"Maybe she won't. But you'll never know unless you try. My bet is that she probably will. Think about her situation; day after day after day alone with her thoughts."

Rob had been prepared to be defensive, even hostile about the idea, but he wasn't. Amelia was right. She told him she had looked at the prison website and downloaded the visiting schedule and requirements.

"We have the time," she said, handing him the sheet with the rules and procedures for prison visitors.

He had shrugged, but he knew she had him. And when he began to think about it, it was what he wanted and needed to do. When he went back to his room to turn in, he looked at the sheet and thought about what prison was like, and wondered what Kelly was like and how they would respond to each other. He got into bed weighing dread and anticipation in about equal measures.

After their first night in Williamston, Amelia went alone to the county Sheriff's office to get information on the accident that had killed the young woman who had been identified as Irina. She posed as a concerned friend who wanted to erect a small shrine on the side of the road, and she was convincing enough that the woman at the desk not only gave her the location of the accident, but also the names of witnesses who lived nearby. They followed the directions to the spot, which was obvious once they got there because the many tracks from the police vehicles and oversized tow truck were still in the mud next to the road and the canal. The canal itself was about forty feet wide and apparently deep enough that the car had sunk out of sight and was not discovered for seven days. There were two lonely houses on the other side of the road and about a quarter of a mile west of where the accident occurred. After they viewed the crash sight they went to the closest of the houses, and waited by the road until the large and viciously barking dogs brought someone to the front door to see what the racket was about.

"Hello," Amelia said, waving when she saw the form in the doorway, "hello." She crossed the small footbridge over the ditch on that side of the road. Rob waited by the car, leaning against the passenger door. Gone, apparently, was the woman who had stood in front of him that first day trembling and on the verge of tears. He couldn't help but admire Amelia's new-found aggressiveness, and the way she so deftly hid it with her unthreatening demeanor. She was an actress, Rob realized, and an incredibly effective ally for him. He was watching her now accomplishing something he would have had no chance of tackling alone. In a matter of minutes she had relaxed and disarmed the woman in the house, who now came out on the steps to talk to her. They spoke for a few moments, the woman alternately pointing toward the accident site and then gesticulating toward the road heading west. At one point Amelia turned and pointed at Rob. The woman waved, and Rob waved back, not really knowing why Amelia had drawn attention to him. She took a piece of paper from her purse and awkwardly wrote something on it and then handed to the woman. Then she turned and came back toward the car, stopping on the bridge to wave goodbye.

"That was interesting," she said when she returned. "She said the night it happened she was awakened by the noise of engines and squealing tires. She knows she heard two cars, but by the time she got up from bed and looked out the window, she only saw the lights from one vehicle. It was pulled over by the side of the road, and she thought she saw two forms at the edge of the canal. They stood there for a moment, and then got into the car and headed back to the east." They got back into their own car as Amelia was talking. "She called the sheriff's department that night, and when they came out she told her story. At first they didn't do anything about it. She pointed out the area, thinking they would go investigate, but they didn't. They listened to her story, and then got back in their car and left. They made her think she had over-reacted. She went back to bed and forgot it.

"But then, a week later, when she awoke and looked out her kitchen window, there were four police vehicles parked there, including a state crime lab van and a Dare County Sheriffs vehicle, and a tow truck. By early afternoon they were dragging the sunken car out of the canal. She never left her house, but she saw them remove the body and place it in an ambulance that headed back in the directions of Williamston. They lifted the car behind a tow truck, and hauled it, still dripping muck and mud, back the same way. After that, all she learned was what she read in the newspapers."

"I wonder what led them to come back?" Rob asked.

"They must have gotten a tip from somewhere. But they identified her as Irina...how? We're pretty sure it's not her. There wasn't enough time to complete DNA tests, so how?"

"Someone must have identified her."

"Right," Amelia said, "and we have to find out who that was."

Rob watched Amelia from the passenger seat as she drove back toward Williamston. It was obvious that this quest for answers animated her. When she was in her room or at a restaurant she always had her laptop open, scrolling through websites, trying to categorize what they knew and didn't know in a type of spreadsheet she created for herself. She was continually questioning Rob about the roles of different characters. For the most part she was patient with the gaps in his memory. She learned and remembered the things Rob told her, and he realized that her not knowing the people involved enabled her to look at them with an objective scrutiny he didn't have.

"We're going to have to go back tomorrow," she said that evening as they sat at the BarBQ restaurant waiting for their dinners. "I have an appointment with the coordinator who sets up the foreign workers with their employers on the Outer Banks. Did you know there are over three hundred of them in Dare County this year? And that's down from over four hundred two years ago."

"Sounds like a logistical nightmare."

"Yes, and when you consider that they come from ten different countries...from Russia, to Poland to Latvia, and Ukraine, and Thailand, Peru, Indonesia, and Taiwan. They have to be matched to employers, housed, kept track of. And then remember that they're all in their early twenties, so the challenges of controlling their behavior, and making sure they don't go looking for trouble, or trouble doesn't come looking for them...it's daunting."

"Irina is kind of a different case. She's been in the country for four or five years. Illegally, I think, but I'm not sure of her status. After her first summer she went to New York. They all do that, go to New York, or DC, or Las Vegas, at the end of their stay. Their return flights usually leave from Newark or Kennedy. But she disappeared, and when the plane left that September with all her compadres, she wasn't on it. She was back on the Outer Banks the next spring. I know Spencer had something to do with smoothing out her immigration status. I don't know if he sponsored her, or paid whatever penalty she had, and vouched for her, but she's worked for him since. I've heard she still spends some time in New York in the off-season, but I don't know what she does up there."

"I wonder if she goes to Brighton Beach."

"What's that?"

"It's a place in Brooklyn where a lot of Russians settled in the seventies and eighties. I don't know if there are Ukrainians there too. It's become one hub of a crime syndicate that has tentacles all over the world."

Amelia's comment was off-handed, but it immediately started something gnawing in Rob's gut. It had something to do with his last night with Steven. So much of it was blank, maybe forever, but her conversation loosened something like a memory of a voice, a voice with an accent, from the fog of that night. It was a male voice, speaking English, but the accent was thick and Slavic. And that led him to remember a tattoo, a devil with Lenin's face...but where, when?

"So Spencer must have identified her?" Rob said, trying to remember and keep up his end of the conversation at the same time.

"That's what I'm thinking. I don't know, but I doubt she has family in the states. She could have, I guess..." her voice trailed off.

Their food came, and they were quiet as they ate. As they reached the end of their meal, Rob noticed an agitation in Amelia he had noticed before. It increased as the waitress removed their plates and brought coffee, and with it their check.

"What is it?" Rob asked.

"This," she said, reaching across the table for the bill, which the waitress had set in front of Rob. She leaned forward, her head sinking between her shoulders. "This is awkward for me, to be paying for everything."

"But you are paying for everything," Rob said.

"You know what I mean. It's the Latin thing." She was reaching into her purse as she spoke. She pulled out a bank envelope, slid it beneath the restaurant check, and pushed it back to Rob. "Please, you begin paying."

There were only a few other tables occupied in the place so he took the envelope from her and opened it in his lap. There was a tight bundle of bills, many twenties at the top and down further they turned to fifties, and then hundreds. He didn't count it, but he knew there must have been three or four thousand dollars there.

"We need to find better restaurants," he said.

"I told you, I'm not one to waste money," she said. "I'm trusting you."

"Thank you." He realized she had given him enough to show that trust, but not enough that he could get very far if he decided to take the money and run.

"I've been reading about the Civil War," she said, sipping her coffee. "Such amazing, terrible carnage. I had no idea. Thousands and thousands of men facing each other in place after place. It's terrible to think of three thousand boys dying in Iraq over ten years, but there were many battle in the Civil War where three thousand died in an afternoon."

"No smart bombs then, no drones. But it was just at the beginning of when technology started to make a real impact, rifles that could shoot projectiles much farther, artillery that was more accurate and deadly."

"And the leaders then seem so much more...I was going to say tragic, but I mean tragic in a Shakespearean sense. Lincoln on one hand, Lee on the other."

"And Grant as Lincoln's dark, inexorable avenging angel... I know what you mean. You also have the chivalry and quixotic grandeur of the south, and the moral authority and the brute strength of the Northern cause. It makes this re-enactment scene seem kind of silly and immature to me, like boys playing soldiers."

"Maybe," Amelia said, "but I see it a little differently perhaps. It becomes a chance to take the family somewhere so the children can learn the history, and see it almost first-hand. At Gettysburg, for example, they recreate Pickett's charge, and all throughout the weekend they have speakers to explain what different tactics meant to the overall strategy of the battle. After all, it was such a major turning point. Had Lee been able to prevail and win a battle in the North behind Washington, who knows what could have happened? The North may have lost heart, or some European powers might have played a hand."

"You have been reading up on it," Rob laughed.

"We also have to go back to Mashoes tomorrow," Amelia said as they rose. "I have to get my sewing machine...and my painting things, I think."

"Feeling creative?"

"I was thinking it might be a good cover at Gettysburg. And that's also what I need my sewing machine for. I was reading up on these re-enactments, and the care the participants take to make their costumes authentic. Honestly, some of them are really over the top with the lengths they go to, no artificial fibers, no machine stitching on the garments. And it goes further from there as far as where and how they camp, what they'll eat, and how they prepare it."

"No peanut butter and jelly sandwiches?" he asked, holding the door opened for her as they left.

"No, and no cokes or oreos either, at least not out in the open."

They returned to the motel and said goodnight. After Rob closed his door he sat on the end of the bed and took his shoes off. He vacantly rubbed his left foot, hoping to increase the circulation. As usual at the end of a day, it was numb and clublike. He was drifting in his mind when he heard a faint knock on the door, so faint that at first he wondered if he had heard it at all. But then he heard the rapping again, a bit louder, and he got up and went to the peephole in the door. Amelia was outside, arms wrapped around her torso, swaying in the half-light, and preparing to knock again. Rob took the chain from the lock and opened the door.

"I'm sorry," she said, embarrassed that she had disturbed him, and afraid that she would find him in some state of undress preparing for bed.

"Come in," he said, stepping back. If he would have thought about it then, he would have admitted that he enjoyed her discomfort and wanted to heighten it to see what her response would be. She did come in, stepping gingerly over his shoes, and Rob closed the door behind her.

"I'm thinking about tomorrow," she said. "I think I should go alone. If you come with me, we have to worry about someone recognizing you and what that might entail. Also, I started thinking, maybe it was someone from the guest worker clearinghouse who identified Irina, and if not, maybe I could find out if they know who did. And then, I'm going to the bank to withdraw some more cash. I realized I don't want to use my cash card to finance this. Not to be weird, but I don't want our movements to be too easily traceable."

Rob thought about the wad of cash in his pocket. Again he realized that she had given him just enough so that he could leave on his own and get away. Maybe that was what she wanted him to do. Maybe she was thinking to herself that things were getting out of hand. And Rob realized he didn't know her well enough to know.

She stood in his room, playing with her hands, nervous at their proximity, but enjoying it too. She wasn't trying to get rid of him, he suddenly knew.

"It makes sense," Rob said, but then he was suddenly anxious too, as if the discomfort was a ball they were batting back and forth between them. He immediately began to think of drinking, and realized that if she left him alone, and now with money in his pocket, that it was going to be a serious, dangerous challenge.

Amelia looked around his room. She had something else to tell him, Rob realized. They both stood there, and the length of the awkward silence grew.

"Did you hear the one about the priest, the rabbi, and the Wall Street trader?"

"No," she answered with a small smile.

"I was hoping you had. I've heard it's a great joke. So what is the matter?"

"It's just that I'm feeling out of my element. Not all the time…but when the feeling comes, there is a sense of dread attached to it. I realized that this could be dangerous to us both, and when I look at us, I wonder if we're up to it."

"I think that's just why we are up to it. Who is going to suspect us? We'll get one quick look, and that'll be it. I'm known to some of the people involved, but nobody knows you, and no one is going to put the two of us together."

Without thinking, he reached out and clasped her hand. It was small and dark, spidery thin, and she didn't withdraw from his touch. They looked at each other, and both their misapprehensions dissolved.

"I'm sorry," she said, gently withdrawing her hand and lowering her eyes. "I don't want you to think I'm backing out. I'm not. But I'm a woman, and I have to be able to feel my way through things. You are a mystery to me. I look at you and see one thing, but then I realize there is more."

"More or less, I don't know," Rob said, aware of a bit of spittle forming on the left corner of his mouth. He pointed to his face. "I look at this in the mirror, and I don't even recognize it as me. I dream of myself as I was, doing things I could do, thinking as I thought, and then I wake up to this. It's hard. It's karma, but it's hard."

"Well, they say…"

"Don't say all things happen for a reason, because they don't. Some things just happen. If you want, you can put it down to God's sense of humor, or justice, or sadism. So I'm just going to put one foot in front of the other, or rather drag one foot behind the other until I get the answers I'm looking for. Could I do it without you? Probably not. But that doesn't mean I wouldn't still be trying."

"That's what I'm talking about," Amelia said. "That's what I see in you. Even the first time I met you I recognized that hidden little spark. It burns low and slow, but steadily."

Rob smiled his crooked smile. He knew when she left in the morning that small spark was going to have to grow into a wall of fire between him and the bottle or, oppositely, it would be flamed by the alcohol and immolate him. "Thank you for your confidence," he said slowly. "And I also have confidence in you. Now you need to get a good night's sleep."

He followed her to the door, and held it open for her. "Thanks again," he said. She left and he closed the door.

The next morning he was awakened before first light by the sound of Amelia's door closing. He struggled to get his foot in his pants leg so he could go out and say good-bye. She was turning the key in the ignition by they time he got his door opened.

"Be careful," he said, when he approached the driver's side door and she rolled down the window.

"No one's looking for me," she said. "I'm just out for a pleasant summer drive. But I was thinking before I fell asleep that we need to get you a phone so we can stay in communication. I'll try to look into it when I'm down there."

She put her elbow out the window, and Rob patted it before he thought about what he was doing. She blushed and looked down at the steering wheel.

"Well, be careful anyway."

She backed out of the parking space, and he watched as the red taillights receded into the distance. It was night quiet after she was gone, and to the east was just the barest hint of magenta. He went back into his room. He knew he couldn't go back to sleep, and he thought some trepidation would accompany that realization, but it didn't. After making a pot of coffee he turned on the television, but he was unable to concentrate. He went to the desk in the corner. There was a ball-point pen on the desktop and a pad of paper in the drawer. Before he knew what he was doing, he was writing Kelly a letter. It was a hard chore. With the gaps in their relationship, and with the looming bulk of her conviction and incarceration, he didn't know where to begin. And once he had, he didn't know where he was going. But just the act of forming the letters into words seemed to get him from one place to another, although when he was finished he had trouble seeing how far he had actually come. But it was a beginning.

It took most of the morning. One of the things he realized when he finished was that some of his mental acumen was returning. It wasn't all there by any stretch. It was like fog rising in the trees. Things were clearer near the ground, but the upper branches were still hidden in mist.

The rest of the day was a much tougher slog. He never felt the plummeting panic he half-expected, but there was a serious edginess there. He stayed in the room as long as he could, and then he had to walk. The first thing he did was to leave Amelia's wad of money hidden in the room, and when he went out he turned east away from the center of the town. Within minutes he was in the country. Even two hours drive from the ocean it was flat tidal land. He hobbled down the straight four-lane road that bisected the tall pine forest. The cut on his foot was healing, and he padded it with an extra sock, but it was still tender. He was hot in his long pants and shoes. He remembered not many years before when he never wore anything but shorts and slaps, sometimes a t-shirt, when every day he saw and heard and felt the trade winds in the palm and almond trees. Not many years had now become a lifetime ago, someone else's lifetime ago. He had never been able to feel sorry for himself, and he wasn't going to start now. With spittle on his lip, a hand that was hooking more over time, his forearm atrophying, and his left leg not much more than a supporting stump, unseen organs that seemed to be thickening, hardening, conspiring within him, he put one foot in front of the other.

He wondered what was happening with Amelia. He was surprised how much he trusted her to handle her end of it, even if he wasn't sure exactly what her end entailed. He thought he might get directions to the local sheriff's department and go there to see if he could find out who had identified Irina, but he didn't know if he could pull it off. He didn't know if the police from Dare County had communicated with other jurisdictions that they were looking for him. As if on cue, he saw a car approaching from the east. And as it got closer he saw the rack of blue lights on the roof. There was no way to hide so he drew himself up more erectly and looked directly at the form of the driver, waving his hand as the car passed. Then he stared ahead at the broad yellow light that bathed everything. The car did not slow. The crisis passed. But it made him wonder why he was taking chances to begin with, so he turned around and went back to the room.

He had imagined that Amelia would return sometime in the mid-afternoon, and when she didn't, it put him on edge. There was a wicker rocking chair outside the front door of his room and he sat in it, rocking lazily in the shade, waiting for her. Traffic moved in and out of the town, slowing as it came in, and speeding away as it hit the open road going east. The quick-shifting rigs hauling logs chortled and belched smoke as they headed for the mills in Plymouth. Rob's eyelids drooped as he rocked, and periodically he fell asleep, dreaming in snatches until a spasm would bring him back to consciousness.

It was during one of these napping episodes that he awoke to find Amelia's car pulling onto the motel's gravel parking lot. He collected his faculties and rose to greet her. Even behind the reflective light of the windshield he could see some excitement in her eyes. There was a high flush in her face as he opened the driver side door and stepped back for her to get out.

"I have some things to tell you," she said, modestly turning her legs together and holding down the front of her skirt as she got out. "First of all, I did get the sewing machine and some more fabric. But that's not the important part. I hadn't been there ten minutes when a car came up and parked in front of your house. I stayed in my house behind the curtains and watched. It was the big young policeman..."

"Davy Todd."

"Yes. He walked around the outside of the house, and then went in and spent about fifteen minutes inside. He was obviously looking for something, and he wasn't in uniform or driving a police vehicle so I thought he must be off-duty, and that made me wonder. I was trying to think if I could go over and confront him, you know, ask him what he was doing at the house, what business he had there, when I saw another vehicle coming toward the house. It was a truck I'd seen before when you were there, so I figured it must be Chick. The truck slowed as it approached, but then when the driver saw there was another vehicle in the yard, he went past. But then he returned almost immediately.

"The two of them met in the driveway and talked for a while. From what I could see, there didn't seem to be any animosity between them. After ten minutes or so, Chick got back into his truck and drove away. The big guy went back into the house and I couldn't tell what he was doing."

"Did Chick ever go into the house?"

"No. He stayed outside the whole time."

She opened the back door of her car and slid the sewing machine across the bench seat. Rob stepped forward to pick it up for her. His dilemma was that this was the kind of weight he now had the most problem with. The only strength he had was in the right side of his body, and unlike most people who could use their off side as a counterbalance, his left side didn't work that way. Anytime he leaned too far to the right he was in danger of not being able to correct himself. He struggled, but he did get the machine out of the car and limped with it to her room where she had opened the door for him.

"But I'm not finished," she said. "Ten minutes after Chick left, the back door opened and the big guy came down the steps and started to come toward my house. At first, I just panicked. But then I realized he didn't know anything about me, other than from our short conversation the night of the storm, or anything about my relationship with you, and maybe, rather than him getting something out of me, I might be able to get something out of him.

"First of all, he is really a very pleasant young man. He asked some questions. But then I thought I might turn the tables on him. I told him that I had seen a woman visit you there. I told him I didn't recognize or know her, just that she was young and blonde. You should have seen his face. He tried to get me to be more specific, but I said I hadn't really paid close attention. He asked what she was driving, and I told him I didn't remember."

"Why did you tell him that?" Rob asked, perturbed.

"Just to throw him off his guard and see how he would respond. It doesn't matter because I won't be there if he tries to follow up on it."

"Yes, but now he knows what you're driving and maybe he recorded your plate number, and they can trace you to here if they put out some sort of bulletin."

"I thought of that," Amelia said. "But we won't be here. The Gettysburg re-enactment is in three weeks. Tomorrow, if you want, we can go to Raleigh, check into some place there and try to make arrangements for you to visit Kelly. But that's up to you. You think about it and decide. Then I went ahead and made a reservation for a motel in Frederick, Maryland. I thought we could go up and explore other, closer possibilities for places to stay, become more familiar with the lay of the land, and it keeps us away from any prying eyes."

Rob looked at her with a smile of appreciation. But that's not what he was thinking. He didn't mind her taking charge as long as things were moving in the direction he wanted to take. A few days ago he had no choices. He was in the Mashoes house totally reliant on Chick for food and information. He had no way to plan because he had no way to put any plans into effect. Now that was all changed. He had been freed from that. But now he was also tethered to Amelia's accelerating sense of adventure. Rob had allowed it at first, without letting her know or consider the potential for danger. But now she was thinking and planning on her own, and Rob was beginning to feel he was just along for the ride. He knew he had to slow her down and put things more in perspective. He especially had to make her understand that he had to move slowly on the Kelly front. He intrinsically understood that he had only one chance to rekindle that relationship. It was as if he had only one damp match to make a fire to keep himself from freezing to death.

"Sit down," he said, hobbling over to the spare bed and sinking down on it. She followed and sat opposite him. "I need to make sure you understand things. We are both in danger here. If I knew who we were in danger from, then maybe I could make some judgments about them. But I don't. I do know this though. They beat Steven to death. They didn't just shoot him, or stab him. They beat and stomped him, and then they shot him in the face. From what the woman who lives off the highway said, there was another car present when Irina's car went into the canal. So if was Irina, or if it was someone else, it appears to me that they were helped into that canal."

"I understand that."

"I don't know if you do. There are things happening whose roots are too deep and tangled for me to get to the bottom of, and I know some of the people involved. I want the answers, and I know I can't get to them without you. But I have to make sure you know that this isn't a game. That's all I'm saying."

"Maybe I did get a little carried away," Amelia said, looking down at her hands and turning them over in her lap. "But then, I don't think so. All anyone knows of me is that I'm the lonely, nosey neighbor, standing behind my curtains, watching the world go by. And now I'll be gone." She smiled and pushed her hair back from her face. "Stand up," she said, reaching for the tape measure on the bed. "I have to measure you so I can start working on your costume."

He stood with his hands at his side while she measured him, first around his neck, then across his back at the shoulders, down the length of his arm, his waist, writing the results in a small notebook.

"My inseam is thirty two," he said, and chuckled as she grew red.

They talked a little more, and then Rob went back to his room. He could hear the hum and acceleration of the sewing machine as she began work on their outfits. Later she drove them to dinner. They talked about their trip the next day to Raleigh. He didn't say anything to her about his trepidation about seeing Kelly. When the check came, Amelia nodded to Rob, and he paid with the bills he now had in his pocket.

VIII

The prison was on the south side of Raleigh, a few blocks inside the beltway that surrounded the greater metropolitan area. When it was built in the early 1960s there was no beltway, and it was a few miles outside of the city. As the city expanded, the prison became closer to the commercial and residential areas until it was absorbed in an area of strip malls, and commuter neighborhoods, and pockets of small industry. It was still set off by itself, and no one would confuse the complex for anything other than what it was. The four acres that comprised it were surrounded by fifteen-foot stone walls topped with lights and razor wire. Because of the rolling countryside there were places where you could see into the compound. Twenty yards inside the wall was a sturdy tall chain-link fence, again topped with barbed wire, and at certain distances along its length were much taller guard towers that loomed not only above the fence, but also above the walls that surrounded the whole thing.

Inside the fence were dorms and administration and other buildings, and exercise yards with sports equipment... and trees, mostly tall, gaunt pines, growing throughout the outer area. There was not any shrubbery, probably to prevent it being used as a hiding place for contraband or an escapee. The architecture of the buildings resembled a school campus, but again with the barbed wire and the towers and the fortified steel gate off the busy street, there was no denying its true purpose.

As they pulled off the street and moved slowly toward the closed gate, Rob became increasingly nervous. He used the handkerchief in his right hand to dab at the spittle that formed at the left corner of his mouth. As usual, Amelia was driving. She had done all the research, and explained the requirements and restrictions, and arranged for this appointment for Rob to visit his daughter.

When they reached the guardhouse at the gate Amelia handed the armed and uniformed female guard both of their drivers' licenses, as well as the written permission form they had received from the Department of Corrections. Rob was half-worried that his name was going to be in some database, and once the guard fed their information into the computer, the SBI was going to swoop in and take him into custody.

The gate slowly swung open in front of them and the guard pointed at the road and told them to bear right and follow the signs to the visitor-designated parking area, and from there enter the administration building where they would be directed to the visiting area.

On entering the building they went through a metal detector, and Amelia had to empty her purse on a table where the contents were gone through. The block walls inside were painted a cream color in shiny latex. Everything about the process was coldly efficient. The idea seemed to be to keep the emotional heat on a low burner. While trying not to appear sexist, it was clear that the policies had taken in the potential for feminine melodrama and had assiduously worked to keep it tamped down.

Rob moved steadily through the process, or was led through it, and his emotions alternately ran high and then faded into nothingness. Amelia hung back at his elbow. He felt her hesitation as an organic slowing caused by the too-cold air-conditioning. Although only Rob would meet with Kelly, they were both photographed, and their information again fed into the computer. There was a slight hiccup when it was realized that Rob's driver's license had expired, but Amelia jumped in to explain that it couldn't be renewed because of Rob's stroke, and they had not thought to bring any other form of identification.

Rob knew that part of the staffs' hesitation was that he no longer looked anything like the photograph on the license. His drooping left cheek and eyelid, the nascent beard he was growing for the re-enactment, even his hair, now lusterless and visibly thinning, made identification from the photo something of a challenge. But all that was talked through and worked out, and they were asked to wait at one of a group of bare tables and chairs by the windows. There really was a difference in the light and air outside, where the breezes were free to blow where they might and the clouds could wander unmolested. Again Rob's nervousness came in waves. Kelly had agreed to see him, but the whole process had taken place on-line and in writing. There was no organic component to it. He had no idea what her enthusiasm level for the meeting was, or whether she might have agreed to see him out of a sense of duty, or perhaps because she was just bored and looking for anything to disturb her usual routine.

When he was called he followed the matron to the empty cubicle. There was no longer the phone on the hook that had been the prop of so many movies and TV shows, just a straight back chair with a counter in front of it and the open pane of glass so thick that it had a blue tint to it. As he sat down Kelly was led around a corner opposite, shuffling because her hands and feet were shackled. She was brought to the chair in front of him, her head down, her hair no longer black as it had been, but brown and wispy, and Rob couldn't really tell in the light, but there might have been some gray glinting in it. She sat down as if her body was just a loose collection of bones, and looked up at him. What drew his attention and held it was the simple gold crucifix hanging from the chain around her neck.

They planned together, had their meals together, rode in the car together, and almost as a matter of course Rob and Amelia found themselves in Frederick, Maryland. The heat was oppressive, and without bodies of water to mitigate it, the still air pressed down on them when they were outside whether it was day or night. They had two rooms in a sprawling, flat, sixties-style motor inn set in a curving hillside just off the highway. There was thick pastel ceramic tile in the bathroom, and real glass tumblers wrapped in plastic by the sink. Rob's AC unit hummed and vibrated, rattling to keep up.

After the long morning drive from Raleigh, Rob looked forward to a quiet afternoon alone, napping in the cool air, maybe listening to a little music on the I-pod. He didn't unpack because they had discussed it, and they were just using this location as a base to explore the area in the time leading up to the re-enactment in hopes of finding someplace closer to the action.

His mind kept returning to the visit with Kelly. It wasn't so important to try to make sense of the words they had spoken to each other. The undercurrents of what had taken place on either side of that glass wall that divided them, the ebb and flow of emotions, the raising and lowering of eyes, in Kelly's case the dancing flutter of her lips, the shock of orange fabric against her pale skin, all were clues to the reality of their communion with each other. Their conversation had been kept to mundane things, the food, and the visits from her mother, her schedule, and other inmates she had gotten to know. She spoke with humor and fatalistic bravado, often laughing at her own simple jokes. Rob realized she was trying to put him at his ease. He didn't know what to ask her. Was there anything she needed?

For some reason, lying on his back on the bed, trying to forget Kelly, he remembered the trip he had taken to the Indian Ocean over thirty years earlier.

He had gone alone after dropping out of college and saving his money for a year, blissfully unaware of the possible, and then actual, hurdles. He flew to Singapore, and then quickly fled the painful, enforced cleanliness of that city and headed south.

He hired boats in Indonesia using sign language and painfully drawn pictures until he hooked up with two Aussies who had been exploring the archipelago since the early seventies. In one drunken night in Bali they marked out five places in southern Indonesia for him to go, pointing them out on his already tattered map. Then they pointed north to a group of lonely dots in the Bay of Bengal, the Andaman and Nicobar Islands between India and Burma. They told him that was where they were headed next. By then he could barely keep his eyes focused on the map. When he awoke the next day he was going to ask if he could go with them, but they were gone.

He explored some of the Indo spots they recommended, surfing beautiful, lonely reefs with at most only a few other surfers, always Australian. There was a blond, tanned subset of Aussie everywhere he went in the Indian Ocean. They were lean, loud, and aggressive. All they did was travel, surf, drink and fight. But many, most actually, had an innate ability to communicate with the natives. They reminded him of what their forebears in the holds and brigs of the British Navy of the seventeenth and eighteenth century must have been like. He saw them arrive at a beach and within minutes, with a combination of hand signals, English, and whatever Indonesian words they may have picked up, they could negotiate lodging, hire boats, and locate the surf spots they had heard of, or arrange to explore areas they thought might likely be undiscovered breaks.

After a few months Rob began to tire of the perfection of the waves, the loneliness he felt as the only American, and the urge just to move on and see more.

Rob finally heard that if he went to Phuket in Thailand he could arrange passage on a supply ship heading to India that would stop on its way in the Andaman Islands. That was what he did. If he had looked closely at his map (which he actually did all the time), but if he had looked at the distances, and possible routes, and the likely conditions of those routes, he never would have gone. When he made his decision he was in Padang in Sumatra. He first had to cross that island, and then hop on the ferry over to Kuala Lampur, in Malaysia, and then head north up the peninsula. While it was only about four hundred miles from Kuala Lampur to Phuket, and he took a train to the Thai border, it still took six days to make the rest of the trek. Once he was in Thailand he was on buses the rest of the way. It was an excruciating, brilliantly colored and magical trip. Whenever he thought he had never seen a worse road, the bus he was on would round a bend and there would be a new slick orange slash through the jungle. There were actually places so muddy that there were elephants for hire to pull the buses through the mire.

That trip still ranked as among his most startling and etched memories; the blood- and marmalade-colored clay, the brilliant greens of the jungle, the bright blue sky. But what set off the memory, and overcame it every time it returned, were the sounds of the rise and fall of the Thais' dipthong-heavy language. The guttural chatter never ceased. He knew much of it had to do with speculation about his surfboard. Surfers had traveled through Thailand by then, but not many, and still much of the population was unfamiliar with the equipment. The buses stopped running at dusk, no matter where they were on the road. He spent three of the nights in his light sleeping bag, always within sight of the vehicle to make sure he wasn't left on the side of the road the next morning. One night he followed everyone else to an inn, which was really just a large open bamboo hut, partitioned under the thatched roof like a stable. Everyone found a spot and hunkered down. Soon there were small fires and bowls of noodles passed around, and then murmuring of muted conversations, and then everyone slept.

When he got to the bridge to Phuket, which was the end of the line, and he was taking his board down from the roof, the driver spoke to him, pointing and waving him in the direction of the sea. Rob bowed and nodded, took his backpack and board, and walked down the hill.

Phuket then was just at the nascence of developing into the worldwide tourist hub it has now become. But Rob didn't know that. He saw only Oriental faces that first afternoon when he came over the steep hills and saw the ocean beyond. He went down to the beach by the well-worn trail, found a little shop where he got some kind of fish soup with green that might have been seaweed in it. There were boats in the long scalloped bay, and he wondered if he might get passage to the Andamans on one of them. He slept on the beach that night beneath a million pinprick stars the depth of which were wonderful and disorienting.

The next morning one of the first things he saw down the beach was a tall Caucasian man among a group of Thai workers. Under his direction, they were constructing raised huts just off the glistening white sand back among the mangroves. Rob rolled up his bag, collected everything, and went to introduce himself. The man's name was Georg and he was a German ex-pat. He had been in Phuket for a year. He had found his place in the far-flung world, and by the brute force of his will he was going to mold it into his own image. He spoke to the workers in their own language, which to Rob's ear sounded so oddly inflected it almost seemed made up.

Georg had been in Asia for most of the seventies. He had explored much of India on his initial quest for knowledge and spiritual meaning, gradually drifting from Bombay to Hyderabad to Calcutta. He had searched for enlightenment among the monks, and through drugs, and he was able to survive because his parents were wealthy and would wire him money when he needed it. He told Rob this personal history in impeccable English, all the while working and shouting orders and laughing with the grinning Thais in his employ.

He said he came to Thailand and Phuket because he had a dream. "Oh, it's too complicated to explain," he said, but here he was. He put Rob to work, fed him, sheltered him. When Rob told him of his desire to go to the Andaman Islands, Georg looked at him as if he didn't understand why, but said he would help him find a way. Rob asked if his Australian friends had come through, but Georg said if they had, he hadn't met them. He seemed to want Rob to stay around for a while, but he also seemed used to the peripatetic ways of many of the people who found their way to his remote part of the world, and didn't try to hold him.

It turned out that one of the sailboats in the broad tranquil anchorage belonged to a formerly famous child actor from California. Now in his thirties he was sailing around the world with only his exotically beautiful Canadian wife as his crew. They were leaving for Goa in a few days and agreed to take Rob to Port Blair on south Andaman Island, which was where the first leg of their jaunt was to end. Rob said he had no way to pay them, but they said he could pay by winding winches and hauling sail.

He didn't want to say he had preconceptions about what this Hollywood couple might be like, but he found was that they were two of the most loving, devoted people he had ever met. They were clearly meant to be with each other, happy to welcome him on their adventure, and glad of the chance to take him to his destination.

It was an easy, calm passage to the northwest. Port Blair had been in British hands for hundreds of years, and the island of Andaman had long been a penal colony under them. Most of the prisoners in the twentieth century had been Indian nationalists chafing for freedom from the English Crown. The islands had reverted to India upon independence, although there was no apparent plan for them and they were a backwater, a string of thirty or so islands of various sizes populated by fairly hostile aboriginal tribes, a handful of Hindi merchants, and a few of the old guard English that had run the penal colony. Below the Andaman's was what was called the Ten Degree Channel, and below that were the Nicobar Islands, formerly half-heartedly vied for by both the British and the Danes. There were many more islands in the Nicobar chain, but they were smaller, more remote, less populated, and generally less tolerant of strangers. Rob immediately wanted to go there.

He realized he was on some kind of personal quest, but that was as far as the realization went. He wanted to dig down deep within himself, but the challenge at its base it was ego-driven. He surfed a few breaks on the southwest coast of Andaman, around the corner from Fort Blair, only one of which was much of a challenge. It took him a week to locate someone who was heading south to the Nicobars, a fisherman who agreed to take him for a very modest fee.

It was a day-long trip in an open boat. The Hindi owner of the boat drove, and his three-man crew spent the entire day on their haunches, not interested in Rob or their surroundings. The sea was as tranquil as a lake, a

110

stunning languid oily deep blue, and the sky was a lighter, brighter blue with round clouds hanging like balls of cotton. Rob sat in the bow of the boat, rising and falling with the swells, nodding and dreamy. Once the thought came to him that perhaps they were plotting to fall upon him, steal his few possessions, and toss his lifeless body in the vast sea. But when he looked back at them, they smiled openly with betel-stained teeth and he felt relieved.

In the late afternoon the first islands appeared as if by magic, palm tops first, then the slender black trunks amid the green of mangrove, and finally the firma of the islands, stunning white sand, ringed by a surf-fringed reef, only feet above sea level.

The natives on these southern islands were strange. While clearly related ethnically to their northern cousins, they were totally reserved, disinterested, neither friendly nor threatening. At the island where they had chosen to drop Rob, they only seemed a bit miffed that they could not ignore him altogether. The boat captain helped him negotiate the use of an open-walled thatched shack at the back of a broad white beach. He couldn't or wouldn't tell Rob the name of the island he was being left on.

On the trip into the lagoon through the cut in the reef, Rob had seen waves peeling on either side of the opening. With the swell direction from the south-southwest, the right-hand break to the west looked longer and more forgiving. But Rob was a goofy-foot and the left, though shorter, still had a good length wall, and in the middle of it was a stand-up tube section that looked as if it was just possible to make, by sling-shotting through it to the more carveable flatter wall closer to the channel. Either way though, there was a risk surfing alone. Anywhere he had ever surfed he always felt safer if he knew there were at least two more legs dangling in the water than his own. But there was no one else. He knew people had surfed in the general area of these islands, if not on this very atoll, or else no one would have been able to point him in this direction. But he was alone now, and this feeling of raw trepidation, this daring himself, was what the whole trip was about.

He went to bed just after dark, and was up before first light. He had heard the crack and roar and rumble of the swells hitting the reef all night, sometimes seeming close, sometimes far away. In the brightening morning he ate the last of the dried fish he had brought with him from Andaman, and sipped stingily at his canteen. Rob knew he needed to get up and go before he could think about it.

It was about a half mile out to the break over the calm and shallow lagoon. He was waxing his board for the long paddle when he saw two fishermen down the beach preparing to launch their small open dory. He walked down to them, and after some starts and stops, he arranged for them to carry him out and drop him off at the cut in the reef. He helped them roll the boat over a set of round logs down the beach and into the crystalline water. Their boat had an ancient 30 hp Evinrude outboard attached to the rear gunwale. Where or how they had gotten it, Rob had no idea. It was more suited to trolling for bass on a quiet Florida lake than beating its way through long ocean swells. It looked as if it was held together with baling wire and duct tape, but once the fishermen cranked it up, it wheezed and ticked and chortled out to the reef, cleaving the calm water and sending back a foamy green wake.

As they made their way out Rob looked back at the low island at their stern. He knew it was impossibly tiny in this vast ocean. The waving palms stood above the bright white sand beach. As was typical, as they got closer to the breaking waves the surf proved to be much larger than it had looked from the shore. They slowly motored through the channel and Rob checked out the left, it was clearly three to four feet overhead and the tubing section in the middle was exploding over what was a very shallow section of reef, judging by the eddies and boils churning in front of each wave as it rose and threw out, spitting a plume of white vapor as the tube narrowed in on itself at the end of the section.

Rob almost opted for the more manageable right on the other side of the channel. Using his arm pointing to the sun and then moving to the west, he tried to get an idea of when the fishermen would return. After the captain figured out what he meant, he drew his own arm in a big circle and began another, signaling that they would be out overnight and not return to the next afternoon. Before he could think any more about it, Rob slipped off the port side of the boat, waved to the crew, and paddled directly for the left.

The feeling as he left the boat and it chugged away low on the water was almost indescribable. He was totally alone. His heart beat more quickly with a sense of both fear and anticipation. First he tried to gauge the pull of the

112

current in the channel. The water was running into the lagoon at about mid-tide at a very manageable one to two knots. His plan was to surf four hours or so, which would take him past high tide. His main worry was the rate of the outflow once the tide reversed. He had seen channels through reefs turn into rushing rivers heading out to sea, with the water moving so fast that no paddler was strong enough to keep up in the face of it.

The water was so brilliantly clear he could look down and see the sandy bottom at about ten feet and the rising reef wall as he made his way to it. It was less than a hundred feet to the other edge of the opening and he hoped that width would mitigate the current.

The apprehension he felt quickly became a heightened sense of observation as he made the outer edge of the reef and began angling out toward the peak. Fish broke the surface around him and he hoped they were reef jacks or barracuda. By counting the seconds between the breaking waves he could tell it was a long-period swell, something generated from a storm above Antarctica that had long been pulsing north. It was basically a point set up, meaning he could catch waves anywhere along the line as they peeled toward the channel, and as he felt more comfortable he could gradually paddle back out toward the farthest edge of the reef.

The first couple of waves he caught were in the forgiving end section close to the channel. They had big, flat, workable faces, and he made them easily and felt himself getting his legs properly under him. Each time he went back out he went further toward the mawing section, looking deeper and deeper into the shadowy pit, seeing and feeling the waves explode next to him on the reef. He paddled up at the end section of it and looked down at the dark green outlines of the coral heads just beneath the surface.

The thing that became apparent was that there was no take-off spot in the tubing section itself. The swells came from deep water and stood up too fast to make the drop. He realized the only way it could be done, if it could be done, was to paddle out beyond that section, choose a takeoff spot further out, and try to see if he could gain the speed and momentum to come in from behind the section and backdoor it, hopefully flying fast enough to duck beneath it and escape through the narrowing trap door at the end. So he paddled out beyond it and tried to study the possibilities.

The first two times he attempted it he chickened out, kicking out just before the section began to heave over. He wasn't upset with himself because he still didn't know if it could be done, and he told himself he wasn't going to try it unless the odds were at least even that he could make it out the other side. Finally, on his third try he saw what he thought was his best chance. He paddled into a deep peak, took the long drop and looked up and out at the long feathering section that was the set-up to gain the speed he needed. After a chattering bottom turn, he came up the face, warning himself not to get too high. He came back down to the trough one more time, bent his knees, and threw everything he had into the last critical turn, praying his fin would hold. Rising up and ahead of him was a thick green slab of water. And then it was dark and still (even with his tremendous speed), and so quiet, and he could see the gap of light at the end. But it was just too far, he thought. Then he heard it coming up behind him, a gaining whoosh of air and vapor that caught and enveloped him, and he exploded with it out the end. He barely kept his balance as he flew into the sunlight. He let out a bellow and realized that the moment that had just passed, the one he was already trying desperately to remember with any sense of cohesion or reality, was one point on the long line of his life where everything else either fell before it or after it. But it could never be reclaimed properly, as a memory or anything else.

So what Rob did, of course, was to immediately try to reclaim it. Before his roar of conquest had even dissipated in his ears, he was stroking back out to try again. He still had to make his choices carefully, and he did. He got four or five more tubes, deep, but not as deep, thick, but not as thick, green inside, but not that dark throbbing emerald green. If other surfers had been out, he might have pushed himself harder. But alone as he was, it wasn't about pushing. It was about aligning his mind and body with this pure pulse of nature. There was an intuition in his recognition of the points of energy on a wave. Each movement he made was innately designed to get him from one of those points to the next.

He stayed out for three or four hours, long enough that he could feel it in his arms and shoulders. The tide had crested an hour or so earlier, and as it receded the tubing section got sketchy and too shallow very quickly. He was about to give up on it, maybe try to get through the current in the channel and try a few rights when he saw a large set darkening the horizon. He paddled over the first five waves heading out, and then he really had to scratch harder because there were more waves coming and they were

114

walling up outside. He was angling back toward the channel when he saw the last, largest wave of the set, and it appeared to be setting up much the same way as the first tube he had ridden. He barely got to the peak and turned and stroked, knowing the drop was going to be steep and late. And then he was standing, weightless, freefalling down the face. Somehow he managed to re-engage his fin at the bottom and made his turn. He instinctively knew he was already behind his mark, but he was flying so fast he conned himself into thinking he could make up the lost time and distance. But then he came into the launching section lower and slower than he needed to be, and there was nothing he could do about it. He flew under the curtain, looked up at the green coming over him, and then, when he realized all was lost, he crouched into a full-on Mickey Munoz Quasimodo stance. In the next second, the wave exploded on him. He relaxed as he fell. He didn't want to ball up because he was afraid to sink and hit the reef, but he wanted to abbreviate himself a bit because he didn't want to get hit by his board. He was rag-dolled in the pit, and pushed deep enough that he grazed the coral with his shoulder. At first he thought he was deep enough to be safe, but then the elevator of water drew him up, with him feeling like he was bound in a cocoon of silence, and tossed him over the falls. He again hit the reef, a bit harder, with the point of his hip. The wave still rolled him and he felt pressure building up in his ears and in his lungs because he had been under water for a while, but he still couldn't tell which way was up. He willed himself to relax for a moment longer, and then the swirling and pulsing passed him by. He opened his eyes, gauged where the light was coming from, and swam toward it.

By the time he broke the surface, balls of exploding colored light disrupted his vision. He had thought he had caught the last, largest wave of the set, but he turned now and a wall of rolling whitewater was almost on him. Taking as deep a breath as he could, he dove. Underneath all was quiet and murky white. But when he finally rose into the air again, he was again struck by the impossibly bright colors of everything.

He alternately swam and was buffeted into shallower water. But this presented him with new problems. Out where the waves first broke, they broke over dead submerged coral heads. Further inside where the movement was less violent, and the rolling waves were more an aeration factor in the shallow water, the new reef was alive and growing. He soon

115

found himself flattened out above a bed of impossibly sharp living fire coral. He floated above it, trying to use his fingertips and toes to guide himself toward the channel. He still had not located his board, and he was afraid it would drift to the channel, be caught in the current, and float out to sea.

Finally he saw his board hung up on an island of exposed coral inside of him. He braced himself as another small wave of whitewater washed over him. After it passed, the same wave washed his board over the top of the coral and it was floating again, drifting closer to the channel. Luckily, he made it to the channel the same time his board did, because there was even more current than he expected. Though he was close to being spent, he had enough energy to swim into the outflow to retrieve it. Still he couldn't relax because now both he and the board were in the rip and heading out to sea. Paddling diagonally, he made it to the edge of the reef where the current eddied back to the island, and it was only then that he could finally relax.

Then he saw it. At first it was just a massive dark shadow moving parallel to him in the depths of the channel. Everywhere but in that channel the water was as clear as virgin light. But because of the movement of the fine sand and current drawing the cloudy biological matter from the lagoon, the channel water was murky and clouded. With Rob watching warily, it rose and surfaced fifteen feet away. It was an eight or nine foot tiger shark, and it swam lazily with him as he veered away hugging the edge of the reef, ready to make a mad scramble on to it, fire coral or not, if the thing came too close. But it never came closer. It seemed only vaguely interested. A few times its nearer eye rose above the surface and it stared at him coldly, but then it gradually circled away and headed back to the open ocean.

Rob kept looking over his shoulder and down into the water behind him as he made his way to the inside edge of the reef. Then he halted. It was still a two hundred yard paddle across the lagoon to the beach, and the water was four or five feet deep, and there was no protection from any kind of danger for the whole distance. He waited and thought about it. There wasn't much chance of a boat returning, and there wasn't any other way to go.

Finally, he just began to paddle in, stroking steadily as he normally would, and willed himself not to think. And he didn't, until he saw a broad dark shadow underneath and to the right of him. He inhaled and his whole body lurched inward. Even in the warm water and the warmer air he was chilled until he realized he was above a gliding giant ray. It flew beneath him for a while and then banked away. Twenty minutes later he was walking across the beach to his palapa.

He stayed on the island for three weeks. The Aussies never showed up. He never got close to any of the dark, mysterious natives. They tolerated him, but they watched him sullenly and warily. He lived a life of quiet subsistence, walking to the one store on the island for supplies. Although it was Indian territory, they took his Thai bahts without comment. He smoked the last of his Thai sticks at the end of the first week. He was almost thankful when they were gone because it was such a heavy high, and it could get kind of oppressive, especially in the naked heat of the afternoons.

Rob thought then that his time on the island was a spiritual experience. For a long time, decades, he thought that. He definitely had drilled down deep inside himself. He had been still, and listened, awaited a voice that he never heard. When he slept, he dreamed, and in the long super-heated afternoons, after the winds had picked up and swept through the mangroves and palms, he dreamed with his eyes open. Surfing alone on the reef, at the edge of the great blue depths, he opened his mind. At night, when many more stars than he had ever known existed bumped into each other and crowded themselves across the vault, he lay in his hammock and watched their vaporous explosions beyond the serrated leaves.

What he realized many years later, and it came as a surprise to him, was that he had gained no psychic insights. He left the island the same person he had been when he found it. He still remembered very clearly his time there, and the stark difference between the bright sunlit days, and the depth of the nights' darkness despite the lights of the moon and stars. But the universe shared no secrets, or none that he could decipher anyway.

By the end of the third week he was ready to leave the island. There had been no ocean traffic since he arrived, just the beach-launched boats of the natives. He began to worry that he might be stuck there. He thought about bargaining for passage to one of the gray green islands he saw to the south and west in the clear mornings before the heat and haze rendered them invisible.

Then at the beginning of his fourth week there Rob awoke before dawn to find a gray steel warship, some kind of pocket cruiser, at anchor in the deep water outside the reef. As the sun rose, a launch was lowered. Four sailors clambered into it and it turned in a wide circle before coming through the gap in the reef.

Rob hung back from their landing site as they grounded the craft and hopped smartly on to the beach. Rob guessed they were sailors from the Indian navy because they were quite swarthy in their white uniforms. One, who appeared to be an officer, conversed with a couple of fishermen who had come over to greet them. From their postures and movements he could not detect any problems so he drifted over toward the group. Of course he couldn't understand any of the conversation. He hoped there was some chance of communicating with the newcomers, and he was surprised to be greeted with a flash of teeth in a dark face smiling at him.

"Good morning," the officer said in perfect British English, and with a slight bow. He was somewhat surprised to find Rob there. After getting the particulars about how he had gotten to the island, and how long he had been there, he said, "You know they most assuredly would have killed you, and probably eaten you, only two generations ago. They don't like strangers."

It turned out that it was a routine patrol stop for the cruiser, one made every six months, to keep the islanders who, whether they cared or not, were Indian citizens, apprised of outside happenings. Lt. Ranesh, the CO, passed a mail packet to the headman, along with some boxes of supplies and a few drums of petrol, which had been off-loaded by the launch's crew.

"I've been thinking of moving on," Rob said.

"If you have your passport and your entry permit in order, we can return you to Port Blair," the Lt. said, "but we are on a tight schedule."

Rob scrambled back to his shack, shoveled things into his backpack, took down his hammock, grabbed his board, and headed back to the beach. It felt strange that after three weeks he had no one to say goodbye to. Of the eight or so natives on the beach, none even attempted to meet his eye. Fifteen minutes later he was climbing up the rope ladder onto the hot stippled deck of the sleek gray cruiser.

Late that afternoon he shook hands with Lt. Ranesh and strode down the ramp into Port Blair. As they had entered the small harbor Rob had seen the boat of the sailing couple rolling slowly at anchor. He found them later that evening at sunset on the hill above the Bay of Bengal. They didn't seem as happy as they had been three weeks earlier.

Rob surfed a week on south Andaman, and then sailed with the strangely subdued Hollywood couple to Aragam Bay in Sri Lanka, where he spent the rest of the winter. The waves weren't very good there, but the procession of girls and women from Canada, Sweden, Denmark, the UK, and Germany was, for Rob and the other wandering men who had stopped there, stunning.

The memory of all that femininity brought him back. Amelia Falcon was in the next room. She was the antithesis of them. He stood and hobbled to the mirror. With his hands on the bureau, he leaned forward, tried to get past his face into his own eyes, but he couldn't. What he had been then, those decades ago, was the blank page. He then had the ability to fill the canvas, and he had. But there was no way, these decades later, anyone could look at the painting of his life and see something of beauty. It was not that he hadn't filled the canvas with paint, but the result was more in the style of Pollack or DeKooning, paint flung at the surface, off-handedly, angrily, drunkenly, for whatever reason.

He heard a gentle tapping at his door. Amelia was waiting outside. He grabbed his small backpack, opened the door, and went out into the broad sunlight.

They ended up spending a week in Frederick, going out in the mornings, expanding their explorations, drifting as far south as the Shenandoah Valley, as far west as Harper's Ferry, and north well into Pennsylvania. They visited the battlefield at Antietam.

"I feel like we're in Jeb Stuart's cavalry," Rob said one steamy afternoon. They were travelling on an arcing two-lane road in southern Pennsylvania, west of Gettysburg. Looking at the lay of the land they saw soft hills rising, stands of old-growth trees, wild grass bright green under the fresh summer sun.

Again he was dislodged from the present, and for a few dreamy moments he rode with the Confederate cavalry. He smelled the horses and the wet leather, heard the clank of sabers, the pounding of hooves on the dusty earth.

Any motel room within thirty miles of Gettysburg for the week of the re-enactment had long since been spoken for. It was beginning to look like they might have to use their motel in Frederick as their main base of operation. That meant, they realized, that they were going to spend a lot of time detached from the umbilical cord of their base.

Amelia had been monitoring Spencer's re-enactment website and his Facebook page to keep tabs on their movements. Re-enacting groups were assigned to designated campgrounds in the battle area unless they had made their own arrangements with property owners near the battlefield. Whether assigned or otherwise, most showed up on the main re-enactment website. It turned out that Spencer's group had rented a field west and south of the battlefield. That, at least, would be of some help to Rob and Amelia.

There had been some discussion of buying camping gear, but neither was really interested in pursuing that scenario. Rob was convinced they were stuck with the lodgings they had.

Amelia spent a lot of time on her laptop. She brought it with her at breakfast in the morning, and Rob would see it open on the desk in her room, screen glowing, when he said goodnight to her in the evenings. Rob himself was a Luddite. He had never owned a computer, and his basic knowledge of them was what he had learned sitting in the public library with no real instruction or direction. At the end of their week in Frederick, they sat at a booth in a diner with the remains of their breakfasts congealing on their plates. Amelia's face was just inches from the computer screen.

"What's the plan today?" Rob asked.

Amelia was typing and she held up her hand. Rob got the feeling she didn't want to look up. He sat back and waited. When she finished what she was doing, she closed the laptop and looked at him.

"I don't know how to approach this," she said. "Our motel is good for what we're doing now, getting the lay of the land and exploring, but once the re-enactors start to arrive, it's going to be a burden to us deciding when to leave and when to arrive, and wondering what we're missing when we're not there."

"But I thought all the closer motels were already booked up."

"They are. I have our names on some waiting lists, but..." Her voice trailed off. "This is the thing. I've found a woman who wants to rent a bedroom in her farmhouse. She had never done it before, but she needs the money. Rob, her house is right within the boundaries of the battlefield. Her family has lived there since before the Civil War. It would give us close access to everything. I've been e-mailing her, and we have an appointment to meet her this afternoon."

"So why the hesitation?"

She looked right at him. "Because we have to be married, act married. There is only one room. I've told her we are husband and wife."

"Can't we do that?" Rob asked quietly. "Can't you? I know I can. Look, Amelia, you've been great to me. I'm not quite sure why you're doing all this, what you're getting out of it. I've been afraid to ask too many questions. But I can tell you I won't do anything to make you feel uncomfortable."

"I am uncomfortable already," she said, but with a small smile.

Rob shrugged. "You decide."

After breakfast they went to the Civil War Medical Museum in Frederick. Rob remembered as a teenager he had gotten on a Civil War reading jag. What he remembered about medicine and medical procedures were barns turned into hospitals, surgeries and amputations with screams and without anesthesia, severed limbs in fly-specked piles, slow, lingering recoveries, or creeping inexorable gangrene, or quick deaths from toxic shock.

The truth was apparently somewhat different. Not only a majority, but a vast majority of surgeries were performed with the patient under anesthesia. Many advances in surgical procedures and follow-up treatments were made. It made Rob think about the treatment of injured soldiers from Iraq and Afghanistan, how the numbers of fatalities were so low compared to the number of overall casualties. There were thousands of men, and women, still alive, who in wars as recent as Vietnam would never have survived. But that brought about the larger question of the quality of the life that remained to them. Rob knew how his injuries, received so much later in life, had diminished him mentally and physically. And what of the costs of care of those wounded vets in the long run?

As the time for their afternoon appointment approached Amelia's discomfort showed itself in her silence and the bird-like fluttering of her hands. After lunch they got in the car and drove north toward Gettysburg. Rob didn't want to show Amelia that he was amused at her discomfort, but he was amused.

"What do we tell her about ourselves?" she asked, trying to relax her grip on the steering wheel.

"What do you mean?"

"Well, how long have we been married?"

"How long do you want us to have been married?"

"Be serious, Rob."

"Okay, twenty years," he said.

"Twenty years?"

"Yes, it's my second marriage, your third. Your first husband died under mysterious circumstances. Your second turned out to be gay."

He looked over and she was smiling.

"Alright," she conceded.

"All we have to do is act like we act with each other," Rob said quietly.

"So, twenty years?"

"Twenty years…and you better have a good story about what happened to your first husband."

Half an hour later they were in the country outside Gettysburg. There were fields bordered by split rail fences with horses grazing beyond, deep woods and lonely stands of trees, blue sky, and a white haze on the horizon. As they got closer to the town, they saw evidence of re-enactors beginning to arrive and setting up camps in different fields off the road. With the GPS they easily found the entrance to the property they were looking for. The driveway rose up a hill so the house was not visible from the road. They drove up and at the crest they looked down into a small valley. In the forefront was the house, obviously old-fashioned, but updated. Beyond it were a barn and some other outbuildings, and a field sloping down to woods which ran along the back of the property and spread away in either direction.

As they came down toward the house a woman came out on the porch. She was tall and sturdy, broad in the shoulder and hips. She smiled and waved to them, shielding her eyes with one hand, and then came down the steps to greet them as they got out of the car.

"Hello," she said. "Are you Amelia?"

Amelia nodded and turned to Rob, whose head was coming above the roof of the car. "This is my husband, Rob."

Rob came around the front of the car stiffly, conscious of his limp.

"I'm Kay Yoder," the woman said, holding out her hand. Then she looked back at Amelia with faded blue eyes. "I trust you didn't have much trouble finding the place." When Amelia shook her head, she motioned for them to follow her up the steps.

"Because the house is so old," she said, holding the door open for them, "you might find the rooms small…by modern standards."

It was dark and surprisingly cool inside. The varnish was worn off the ancient wooden floors in high traffic areas and the fringe on Oriental carpet was frayed, but the wallpaper above the chair railing appeared to have been recently hung. There was a dining room to the left as they entered, with a big old table and sturdy chairs. A glass-faced hutch stood against the far wall between two windows, with crystal inside glinting on the shelves. On the back interior wall was a door, presumably leading to the kitchen. To the right was the living room, with opposing love seats separated by a low coffee table. There were moody still-lifes on the walls and chintz curtains trembling in the windows. Straight ahead from the front door was a narrow steep stairway.

"We can sit in here if you'd like," Mrs. Yoder said, extending her arm toward the living room, "and you can tell me about yourselves. Make yourselves comfortable and I'll be right back."

She went into the dining room, and through the swinging door into the kitchen. Rob and Amelia drifted into the living room and took a seat.

"Relax," Rob said when he looked at Amelia's frozen expression. He patted her knee. When she looked at him she had a frantic, frightened glint in her eyes. "Amelia, relax."

Mrs. Yoder came back in with a tray, carrying an old coffee percolator, cups and saucers, cream and sugar, and a plate piled with frosted cakes.

"Your house is like something out of the past," Rob said slowly. "They just don't build things like this any more."

"Thank you," the woman said, pouring coffee in the old-fashioned cups. "The upkeep can be a problem sometimes. For instance, the wiring…the original building is from the 1850s, and the house wasn't wired until the 1920s, and that was ninety years ago. My brother used to help with the electrical and the plumbing, but he's gone to Florida now. You should be glad you're not here in the winter though."

She handed a cup of coffee to Amelia. It tinkled against the saucer as she took it. The smile on her face looked as if it were being forced on her by someone with a gun to her back. Rob worried that she might be having some kind of anxiety attack.

"I guess the re-enactments must disrupt you."

"They do, but it's only for a week or so. I go to the grocery store and stock up, get my medicines, and any other supplies I can think of. Most of the activities are in the daytime, and it's not like it's a Woodstock-like crowd. They generally behave themselves."

"Are there any records about this house from the war or from the battle?" Amelia asked quietly.

"Yes. There wasn't any fighting here. That all took place farther east and north. But apparently the Union army had a supply post here. And there used to be a story about some Confederates who had gotten separated from the comrades and hid in the cellar house, but I think that was just an old story." She looked at Rob. "So what has brought you here?"

"I had to retire because of my stroke," Rob answered. "I guess I got interested because I had time on my hands. And now I've dragged Amelia into it. She paints."

"You're a painter? What kinds of things do you paint?"

"I mostly do landscapes," Amelia answered. Rob could feel her calming herself. "We live near the ocean, so I guess it would be more beach scenes or seascapes really."

"Are you going to paint the battle?"

"I'm going to try, I think. It depends if I can get the right point of view…and not be in the way."

"And what about you, Mr. Wheat?"

"Rob, please. I thought I'd try to join in the re-enactments. I want to try to use it as some kind of therapy…if I can keep up. I'm unaffiliated, but

I've read there is some kind of clearinghouse. Amelia has been working on a Confederate uniform for me, but she hasn't let me see it yet."

They spoke some more about themselves, or the lives they had partially invented for themselves. Mrs. Yoder talked about the area, and how it had been, and how it had changed, and what it was becoming. She spoke about the sprawl, the political arguments about encroaching on the battlefield, the attempts to build a casino near the site, and how it seemed like whomever had the most money usually won the arguments in the end. Amelia calmed and became more herself. After their refreshments, Mrs. Yoder took them upstairs to see the room. Like the other rooms in the house it was small. There was a tall dresser on one wall, and a high, crowned double bed with a beaded cotton bedspread on the opposite wall. The bed was flanked by two high night tables. There was one window on the wall opposite the door, and its white curtains waved in the light breeze. Outside Rob could see the rise and fall of the receding fields and woodlands.

He looked back and Amelia's eyes were transfixed on the bed. A blotchy red had risen unevenly to her cheeks.

"There is only one bathroom up here," Mrs. Yoder said apologetically, "and it's small. We would have to share."

"I don't see that that would be a problem," Rob said. "We should be leaving early and coming back late. I want to immerse myself in this, find out what motivates these people." He felt like he had to keep speaking to keep Mrs. Yoder's attention from Amelia. He took a step forward and pointed out the window. "Is that Big Round Top?"

"Yes," Mrs. Yoder replied, "and to the left beyond it you can see Little Round Top."

"Fantastic!" As soon as the word came out, he smiled, because he didn't think he had ever used it before in that context, and doubted he would ever use it again. "Well, cara mia," he said, and quickly continued in Spanish, "this decision is completely up to you. I wait for you to give this woman your answer."

"I can negotiate a little on the price," Mrs. Yoder said, looking from Rob to Amelia.

"No, I'm sorry, Mrs. Yoder, Rob told me this was going to be my decision. This is perfect for us, and the price is perfectly acceptable. If you'll have us, we'll take it."

Mrs. Yoder was very pleased. She seemed to genuinely like Amelia, and her openness calmed her quickly. The two women went to view the bathroom with Rob trailing behind. The upstairs hallway was dark and narrow. There was an indefinable smell to the place, of dust, and the old stale exhalations of breathing wood.

A half an hour later they were returning to Frederick. Amelia was quiet again on the trip back to Maryland. Rob knew what she was nervous about, and it vaguely worried him too, but he decided to just let it all take care of itself.

"It's perfect," Amelia said, "perfect. I was trying to imagine how I was going to paint...I couldn't make it work in my mind. But with that house as a base, I think I could. As for keeping an eye on Harlan Spencer and his group...perfect."

When they got back to the motel in Frederick, they separated and went to their rooms to pack. It didn't take Rob long. He took his stuff out to the car, and then helped Amelia carry out her things. The last thing he went back for was the sewing machine. In the empty room he could smell what he realized was her peculiar feminine scent. Aside from recognizing it, it had no effect on him.

When they returned in the late afternoon Mrs. Yoder was busy in the kitchen making dinner. She was excited about their presence in her house, and eager to play the good hostess. They gathered in the dining room, with Mrs. Yoder running back and forth through the heavy swinging door to get everything out to the table. When she had gotten everything, she sat with them. At her direction, they bowed their heads and said grace.

Their conversation at dinner flowed easily. Rob and Amelia fell into their roles as husband and wife. Realizing they could get into trouble if they embellished their biographies too much, they directed the conversation to Amelia's childhood in Costa Rica. She spoke dreamily about it, concentrating mainly on its simplicity. She told Mrs. Yoder that one of the hardest things she found when describing it to people was to tell what they had and didn't have. For most of her childhood her family had not had electricity, but then neither did anyone else they knew. No one had cars, but the roads would never have accommodated them anyway. There were animals in their yard, chickens and roosters, and monkeys in the trees, and in those days there were still jaguars in the bush. When she was very young their house had had window frames, but no windows. Sometimes at night bats would fly through the rooms.

"When I think of my life now," she said, "when I'm sitting with my laptop, or listening to the voice of my GPS, it's clear that things have come a long way in my lifetime."

Mrs. Yoder asked Rob about his childhood, and he described it generically, and as he talked he saw that Amelia was also listening, trying to learn more about him, while pretending not to. Mrs. Yoder had made a pineapple upside down cake for dessert, and they ate it with their coffee, Rob realizing that a year ago it was something he would have never thought of eating. When he had first stopped drinking he had worried if his appetite for food would return, but now a few weeks later he realized he might have to begin worrying about how well it had returned, and the small mound of his belly made him think he might need to curb it a bit.

Amelia began fidgeting after the meal as Rob became more and more relaxed. Rob knew why. After dinner they talked more with Mrs. Yoder and moved out to the porch. Then they helped each other get the rest of their things upstairs. Rob went to the bathroom to brush his teeth. When he came back Amelia was wearing a robe and slippers. On Rob's side of the bed was a pair of light blue pajamas.

"I thought you might need those," Amelia said, getting her small toiletry bag and going to take her turn in the bathroom.

Rob quickly changed and got in the bed and under the covers, though he wasn't very sleepy. Amelia came back in and went to the other side of the bed.

"Rob," she said, sitting down, keeping her back to him, "don't try anything funny."

"Amelia, I wouldn't try anything because I'm afraid you would be the only one who would be amused."

IX

When Rob awoke in the morning the sky outside the window was the color of clotted cream. Birds twittered happily against the whitish background. He looked over at Amelia who was still asleep, her mouth partly open, breathing gently through her nose. It was all so strange.

Rob had not slept well, and he knew that Amelia hadn't either. The night had been dark, and all sense impulses came through sound and smell and feel. The sheets had whispered as they rolled and turned, both carefully keeping their positions on their sides of the sloping bed. Rob would awake when Amelia moved and her scent would waft to him, strange and yet familiar. The plastic knob at the end of the curtain cord clicked against the window sash in the breeze.

He had gotten up at one point during the long night to take a leak. He tried to tread lightly, but the floor creaked like a cat being stepped on, and then he ran head on into the edge of the open door. Even in the dark, rays of colored light flashed in front of him and smoldered at the edge of his vision. When he returned he heard Amelia restless under the sheets.

"Are you alright?" she whispered.

"Yes." He could still taste the salt of blood on his lips.

Now he found clothes and went to the corner to change. As he went out into the hallway the floor creaked again, and the stairs groaned under his weight as he went down. He crossed to the front door, undid the locks, and went out to the porch. A blanket of gauzy mist rested on the hillsides. To the east the new day glowed orange behind the hills.

There were now only days until the start of the re-enactments. They had seen people arriving when they themselves got there the day before, and Rob guessed that in the next few days there would be a swelling stream of re-enactors and spectators making their way to this now quiet countryside. He couldn't believe their luck in finding this place.

He went down the steps and around the house to the back. The birds in the heavy green-crowned trees were almost frantic in their singing, chirps and trills and tweets seeming to come from everywhere. The backside of the property sloped down past the looming red barn and outbuildings and, bisected by a pair of fences, ran to the woods that seemed to be running with a stream from southwest to northeast. Rob drifted down, stepping through one fence and opening the gate of the other, until he came to the margin of the trees. He could hear water. Stepping into the cool dark area under the entwining branches he made his way for thirty yards until he came to a brook, shallow and clear, about twenty feet wide, gently chortling over the rocks as it ran south where gravity determined it must. There were some large rocks, boulders almost, at different places along the shore, and beneath the water's surface Rob saw all sizes and shapes of rocks and stones, many of the larger ones flattened on top by the flow. Smaller pebbles ran by, bounced and heckled by the current. Rob followed the stream up its course for a while, negotiating with some difficulty the uneven terrain, though there was an obvious, well-worn path running along the bank.

After a half mile the path suddenly stopped at the base of a twenty-five foot cataract. The water fell gently from above and splashed on the broad flat rocks at the base.

Knowing there must be a way to the top, Rob retraced his steps and found the entrance to a narrow way going up. He went up, moving carefully and gingerly, holding the trunks of trees for support, wedging his feet in among the roots, and with a little difficulty he made his way to the crest of the falls. He went on further for another quarter mile, the path alternately lighter and darker depending on how many trees there were and how thick their foliage was above him.

Rob was panting when he stopped. There had been Rebels in these woods, foraging patrols, or reconnaissance, or deserters. Rob could imagine some poor subsistence farmer from the mountains of North Carolina or Tennessee, his family left at the edge of starvation at home, carried away and finding himself in Pennsylvania fighting for the rights of some rich planters to keep their slave work force. Things were not so different a hundred fifty years later.

The slow trudge back, especially the slippery descent down the trail next to the falls, was much more draining though most of it was downhill. Rob strained as he lowered himself next to the idyllic falls, grasping at saplings with his good right hand. By the time he got back into the sunlight behind Kay Yoder's property he was drenched with perspiration and dizzy from the exertion.

129

He went back to the house in the broadening sunlight. Amelia was up with Mrs. Yoder when Rob got back, in the bright kitchen drinking coffee. They became quiet when he came in, looking at him with veiled looks of feminine conspiracy.

"I was telling Kay," Amelia said, "that we were planning to go to New Jersey today to visit your brother."

Mrs. Yoder had risen when he came in and went to offer him coffee. Rob was jolted by the thought that she could ask him where his brother lived, or what he did for a living, and he and Amelia hadn't worked it out. Hell, Rob didn't even know he was supposed to have a brother.

"No coffee for me, Mrs. Yoder," Rob called after her. "I'm going to go up and shower and get ready, if that's alright?"

"Sure. The hot water should last for the two of you this morning, and I'll take my shower this afternoon."

Rob went upstairs. He knew Amelia wouldn't come up until she was sure he was showered and dressed. He was a bit irked with her fib about him having a brother. They didn't need to make this more difficult for themselves by creating complicated fictions. Their fake marriage was enough to try to keep track of. When he dressed and came out of the bathroom and went back to the room, Amelia was sitting on the bed waiting for him.

"I'm sorry about that," she said. "I had to think of a way for us to leave for a couple of days, and I couldn't wait for you to get back, and then try to get you alone... The thing is, we have to go back to the Outer Banks. Spencer's Facebook page has suddenly gone blank as far as any info about when the group is leaving, or where they'll actually be staying when they get here. I guess I got lazy. Spencer was posting everything...I mean he was very thorough. In his last post two days ago, he said they would have a final list of who was scheduled to come. I realized that with the number of people who are going to descend on this place, if we don't know where their base is going to be, there's a good chance we might not locate them for the whole weekend."

Amelia became more animated as she spoke, and she rose and moved with small, quick steps around the bed.

"I was just taken off-guard," Rob said. "So what's my brother's name?"

"We didn't get that far."

130

"I took a walk in the woods, and while I was there I remembered something. That last night with Steven, we were talking about his wife, Paula, who had just died, and his new wife, I think her name is Mandy or Marnie, something with an M. Misty, that's it. Steven said Irina watched his kids, and that she and his wife were friends. I'd forgotten that."

"Maybe we can figure out a way to talk to her. My main concern is to make contact with Spencer's group so we can find out when they're coming up here and where they are going to stay."

"Maybe I should contact Chick," Rob said. "I feel bad after he and Tanya rescued me, and then I just blew him off."

Amelia didn't say anything, but Rob immediately sensed something in her silence. She was putting some things in a small bag, a few changes of clothes and some toiletries. Rob got his backpack from the closet and began to do the same.

"You don't think I should contact him?"

"I didn't say that."

"No, you didn't say anything."

"Something just seems odd to me. He rescued you, right? But then he hides you. Why? From whom? Why wouldn't he want you to talk to the police?"

"I don't know. I couldn't remember."

"But what does he know? What does Chick think you could remember, and why would he care if you do remember it? You said yourself that he has this quiet life, so friendship of not, why wouldn't he let you deal with the police and wash his hands of it? Doesn't it make you think that he has some kind of involvement?"

All Rob could think of was the bottle of rum, its deep color, the sound of the bottle shattering on the concrete pad, and the aroma of charred cane rising.

And just then, something came to him. It had to do with the memory of the smell of the rum. He began to remember the party he and Steven had gone to. The house was back on the Sound somewhere north in Currituck County. It wasn't a part of any development. There was a paved road heading west off highway 12, and then the paved part ended and there was a gate, and beyond that a sand path into the deeper woods.

Rob could see himself slipping out of the passenger door, sliding off the slick leather seat like it was a carnival ride. He had gingerly gone into the glow of the headlights, giddy in his drunkenness, fumbled with the hook, and pushed open a swinging gate. As he did, he saw the lights of two more cars line up behind Steven. He had trouble climbing back into the SUV. He felt Steven's impatience. The vehicle began moving before he was all the way in and had closed the door. He remembered now that Steven was clearly familiar with the winding trail.

They arrived at the house, which was set back on the waterfront in a large clearing. There were lights strung on poles around the perimeter of the broad manicured lawn. Twenty or twenty-five cars were parked haphazardly in front of the house and across the grass, and behind Steven's car, besides the cars that had been waiting at the gate, two more were now coming out of the darkness of the woods.

The house itself was of a unique design. It rested not on the usual square pilings, but on larger, round piers that not only supported the structure, but rose in haphazard places through the living areas of the house and some through the roof and into the sky like masts. Also, it was a sprawling, single-storey affair. In some places there were split-levels, but nowhere, except for the looming pilings, did it rise more than twenty five feet above the marshy edge of the Sound.

These sudden, clear memories jarred Rob because he didn't know where they came from, and he was desperate to hold and expand on them, but he didn't know if he might somehow do something that would close the gate they were rushing through. He strove to be still and receptive. He felt Amelia looking at him oddly, so he excused himself and went to the bathroom.

Next he remembered climbing the broad front steps with Steven, people milling all around. He was conscious of his limp, and as he moved he tried to hide it. With the urgent dull thud of bass, he felt rather than heard the music pulsing from deep inside the house. Rob didn't recognize anyone among all the faces around him, though many people greeted Steven. Steven himself suddenly seemed less serious and brooding. In fact, by the time they entered the house, he was smiling broadly. Gone was the pensive expression he had worn since Rob first saw him enter the Sea Horse. What replaced it was an expression Rob remembered from Steven's younger days. He openly leered at the young women they saw as they made their way to the back of the house. Rob realized it must be 3 AM, and he wondered what Steven's new wife must think about the empty space next to her in bed.

"Whose house is this?" Rob had asked.

"It's Alexander's," Stephen answered. "Alexander Olsofsky. He's from New York. I built this house for him. Beautiful, isn't it?"

"Where did all these girls come from?" Rob asked.

There were young women everywhere, and not the usual Outer Banks outdoor types. These women were made up, in dresses and heels, placed around the house like pieces of art.

"Alexander flies them down to decorate the place."

"They're doing a good job of it. Who are all these other people? I don't recognize anyone."

"He also flies them down…to populate the place."

Rob's memories were surprisingly lucid considering how drunk he knew he had been. He could clearly remember the high ceiling and the polished wooden beams, a minimalist sculpture in a corner under a beam of strong light. He could remember the rise of the bosom of a beautiful tall woman as she came smiling toward him and then turned sideways as she slipped by. He remembered three or four men wearing black leather jackets, which seemed odd because of the heat. They were stationed at intervals as if keeping an eye on things.

"Alexander is a hedge fund guy from New York," Steven said, with admiration clearly in his voice. "He's originally from Ukraine. When everything on Wall Street went to shit, he stood tall. I don't know if he's here, to tell the truth. He has these parties three or four times a year like this, flies a bunch of people in. It's cool because it's not the people you're used to seeing. And he'll fly them all out tomorrow."

Steven waved at someone across the room, and quickly moved away from Rob. As soon as he was left alone, Rob realized how out of place he was. He didn't recognize anyone. Everyone he saw was wearing designer clothes, and the women wore silk dresses, jewelry, and stiletto heels. Rob was wearing the only decent shirt and pair of trousers he owned, which were decent enough for the Sea Horse, but not for here.

Although he didn't know anyone, many of those who were there seemed to know each other. As new people arrived, they were greeted and welcomed into the group. The tall sliding doors to the Sound side deck opened and closed incessantly as people moved in and out. Rob slid in line behind one group and followed them outside. He guessed correctly that they were looking for drinks, and outside there was a brightly-lit bar on one side of the pool.

As he went behind them, he got the feeling that if his presence were discovered, he would be politely escorted (or maybe they wouldn't be so polite) to the front door and asked to leave. He didn't know where Steven had gone. He tried to listen to the conversations of those around him, but all he could discern was that it was a birthday party, and virtually all the guests had flown in from somewhere else. He found himself behind a woman who was as tall as he was, with her hair up, diamond earrings, a low-cut back, and one of the most beautiful neck-lines he had ever seen. It was long, white, curved like a bow, spreading into soft bare shoulders.

Suddenly as he was remembering this, he also remembered what his girlfriend, Abby, had told him about alcohol and denaturing and false memories. What struck him was that he was sober now, and hadn't had a drink in a couple of weeks. He was drunk in the memory, so he didn't know what the denaturing might have done to the memory at its inception.

When he got to the front of the line, Julie, from the Sea Horse, was tending bar.

"Rob," she said when she looked up, "I wouldn't expect to find you here, of all people."

"I'll let that slide," he said. "Something simple, with rum please. Who are all these people, and whose place is this?"

"Second question first," Julie said, leaning forward, whispering. "This guy named Alexander owns the house. I've done a number of these over the last couple of years. Spencer recommended me. I get a call, they give me a date, and here I am. They start late, so I had time to finish my shift, change, and drive up. These people come from all over. How did you get in anyway?"

"Steven brought me."

"Oh, yeah. He built this house," she said, handing him his drink. "He's got some other kind of business dealings with Alexander. Spencer and

Alexander have some kind of partnership, and Steven has something to do with it."

Rob began to wonder who this Alexander was, and what he looked like. He alternately pictured his as Vladimir Putin fit, or so Bond-villain rotund that he could barely squeeze through his own doorways.

"Be careful, Rob, and try to keep your head down," she said, and then looked past him as a group approached to order drinks.

Tiki torches blazed around the perimeter of the pool, but there was a darkened area in the northwest corner opposite the bar. Rob went there and sat in one of the lounge chairs. From there he could watch the people as they approached the bar, and he could also look through the large glass doors at the crowd milling around in the great room. To his right, under the undulating light, he could see the water of the Sound lying fat and soft and silver under the starlight.

A steady flow drifted in and out from the pool area. Some went to the wooden walkway that led to a gazebo out in the water. By Julie's station, it was like a high-end liquor commercial. The women were truly stunning. And he recognized the predation in those looks. There was some blow around, for sure.

The music that played through the house was an interesting mix, held together by the pulsing beats of the bass lines. A lot of it he didn't recognize, a lot of electronica, and even some of the old music had the bass elevated and had been dubbed into dance mixes.

He sat, with the cool night moisture descending on him, an already-empty drink in his hand, feeling like the interloper he knew he was. A few years ago he could have pulled it off without any worries. No one would have questioned him no matter what he did. Now he had to hide in a dark corner and hope no one looked at him too closely.

He came back to himself in the present with a jarring thump, wondering where these scenes had come from. Again he remembered Abby in Puerto Rico telling him about false memories. But how could these be what she had spoken of when he hadn't had anything to drink? And were these actual true memories, or just tricks of his unconscious?

As soon as he came back, he lost the thread of the memory. It seemed to stop where he had interrupted it, and he could not move it forward. He wondered if he had somehow put himself in a state of hypnosis. That did make sense. His problem now was getting himself back into that receptive state. Amelia was next to him, and had been the whole time. He didn't know what to say to her, or if he should say anything. He was left drained by the whole thing.

He couldn't stop thinking about it on the drive south, but the more he tried to zero in on the memory, the less able he was to move it forward.

He began to realize how much time he and Amelia had spent in the car together, how many miles of blacktop, how much swirling scenery, dry roads, wet roads, head-lighted, following taillights like smoldering devils' eyes. There were interstates and side roads, big green exit signs, lines of rural mailboxes, fast-food signs off interstates on long high poles, and faded signs sagging at two-pump gas stations. Exit ramps and rain ditches filled with weeds and trash and day lilies.

Suddenly he felt a kernel of dread and doubt. What was he doing? How had this accelerated from a curiosity based on an unrequitable sexual attraction into a full-blown investigation of all sorts of people and their possible involvements and motives?

"Put this name down and keep an ear out for…Alexander Olsolfsky."

"Who?"

"Alexander Olsolfsky," he said again, trying to form the name more clearly. "It was his house we went to the night that Steven died. He has a big beautiful house on the Sound in Currituck. It suddenly came to me when I was in the woods. I don't know where it came from."

"That name sounds familiar to me," Amelia said. "I know I've heard it somewhere since this all started."

They both sat back in silence. Rob felt he was on the verge of remembering more, and he hoped that if he remained perfectly still and silent more might come to him. Amelia must have sensed it because though she looked over a few times, and looked as if she might say something, she held her tongue. But the wall remained up in front of him, and he could neither find his way over or around it.

Five hours later they were crossing the bridge from the mainland to the Outer Banks. Amelia had made a hotel reservation in Nags Head, but as they reached the fork that separated the routes to the northern and southern beaches, Rob urged her to take the road north.

"We've got time," he said, "and maybe I'll see something that will help me remember."

They drove through the village of Duck and past Sanderling, around the curve to the road north to the Currituck Outer Banks. The first stretch of land was narrow, only a quarter mile from the Atlantic shore to the marsh of the Currituck Sound. After a few miles it broadened and the land on the Sound side began to show some contours, sandy hillocks with thick bayberry with their dark waxy leaves, low sprawling live oak groves, stunted pines. He began to look for the road. They passed one he knew led to the short narrow landing strip where many of the guests that night had arrived. He didn't remember anything about how long the drive that night had taken. To him it had only been the hiss of tires and tracing antic lights.

"Left here," he said to Amelia, as an unmarked road came up quickly on their left, its new tar dark and steamy under the sunlight. Amelia followed it west under the shadow of the pines. Rob knew it was the right road, though driving it brought no recollection. He knew it for certain when the pavement ended at the gate he had opened that night with Steven. Now the gate was locked, a big chain draped across its face.

"Well?" Amelia asked.

"This is definitely it," Rob said. "At least we know that, and we know where it is. I guess we just put it in the vault with everything else."

"Anything else coming to you?"

"No," he said, perplexed and agitated. "Something somehow opened, and then just as suddenly slammed shut. It's like I can still hear the echo of it in my head."

They sat in the car in front of the locked gate for a few minutes, and then decided to go to the hotel to check in.

He realized as they went that because Amelia always drove, Rob always presented his weak, infirm side to her. His doughy, slack face and shriveling arm were always on her side. Maybe that was good. Maybe it forced her to be more realistic. She had to be able to see that the path they were on, if they followed it to the end, would lead them to the person who had murdered Steven.

"With all of Steven's money problems," Amelia said, as if reading his thoughts, " and if he really was sick, is there a chance he hired someone to take his own life?"

"I've thought of that. I thought maybe there was a suicide clause in his insurance policy, and if he killed himself it wouldn't pay. Maybe he shot himself, and had already arranged for someone to beat him, postmortem. It could have happened that way, I guess, but I don't think it did. That night…I know he was worried about his finances, but he had this optimism too. He would speak about Spencer, and you could just hear the reverence and admiration in his voice. I didn't understand it then, and I don't now, but he thought of Spencer as if he'd found the key to happiness, and the key opened a vault, and in that vault was money…plain and simple."

Amelia had made a reservation at a bed and breakfast hotel in southern Nags Head a half a mile above Whalebone Junction. It was one block back from the beach, between the highways. Rob stayed in the car, slouched down in the passenger seat, while Amelia went to check in. When she returned with the key, they quickly gathered their things and went up the open outside steps to the second floor room.

It wasn't until he was going up the stairs that he recognized it was the Colony Inn, an old hotel built in the '30s. It was one of the first lodging establishments to be built right on the oceanfront. Up until the early eighties it had been located on the beach at Jockey's Ridge. Then, because the owners had been unable to keep up with the taxes, it had been moved to its present location.

Its design hearkened back to the time of its construction, a time before air-conditioning. There had been four connected buildings, broken up by wide breezeways. The rooms had as many windows as were practicable. All had old heavy screen doors, as well as solid wooden ones. Each room had dark pine paneling and pine floors, and ceiling fans that wobbled and whirled as they spun.

Amelia had chosen one room, but unlike the one at Mrs. Yoder's house, this one had two beds. It was a large room on the northeast corner of the north wing with a sprawling view of the ocean. It looked like a spangled cape spread out past the slow moving traffic on the beach road and the massive houses opposite on the strand.

They had gotten to Nags Head and the hotel safely enough, but Rob and Amelia both knew he had to lay low. Just making it from the car up the outside steps to the room had made him feel exposed. Looking out from the cool darkness to the bright, shimmering sunlight, he couldn't get used to the idea that if someone he knew saw him from a distance, provided he wasn't moving, they probably wouldn't recognize him. He looked down at his new clean clothes and shoes, realized his hair was trimmed and combed. His beard was coming in, grayer than he remembered it. Sometimes it made him feel completely detached from himself. He might be nothing more that some invention of Amelia's. The clothes she purchased were on his back, her money in his pocket. And yet she was aiding him in his mission. Every time he got close to really asking why, he stopped himself.

"I called Spencer's office," Amelia said. "He is out of town on business. But the woman on the phone volunteered the information that he is returning tomorrow to prepare for the Gettysburg re-enactment. She said they have a staging area in a warehouse complex he owns on the Currituck mainland. I'm going to drive up there this afternoon just to see what's going on. Maybe I can find out where their Pennsylvania base is going to be.

"Then I'm going to visit Steven's wife, Misty. I called and told her I knew Irina from the restaurant. I feel so badly. Her voice on the phone was so plaintive. She's lost Steven and she's convinced that it was Irina in that car. Just in this short conversation I got the impression that she and Irina were close. If there was anything between Irina and Steven, she didn't know anything about it."

"I guess I have to stay here, out of sight."

An hour later she left. Rob was left alone in the dark room, blind slats slanted, the ceiling fan turning lazily above him. He really wanted to walk on the beach. He fought it. He fought other things. He tried to remember more, but it wasn't happening. Almost before he knew what he was doing he dialed Tanya and Chick's home number. When he heard the clicking interior ring he almost replaced the receiver.

"Hello." It was Tanya. Her voice seemed far away, distracted, brought up from a deep hole somewhere.

"It's Rob," he said.

"God, Rob, where are you? Where have you been? Chicks frantic."

She knew something. When she was at Chick's dad's house, Rob was a pain in the ass to her, plain and simple. Chick told her to bring him groceries, and she did, resentfully. Now Rob realized the resentment was because Chick wasn't letting her in on the why. He had felt the same way.

"I had to get away. Things were closing in on me."

139

"Tell me where you are and I'll have Chick come and get you."

"No. I've been a bother to you, I know, and I'm okay here. Thanks for everything, Tanya, and thank Chick for me too, will you. I'll get in touch with him when I'm settled here."

"But where is 'here', Rob?" she asked curtly.

"I'm thinking it's better you don't know, Tanya." He had to admit he was enjoying this, though he immediately wished he was speaking directly to Chick. "Chick had me tucked away, and now I'm more tucked away, so he should be happy about that."

The silence hung between them then, with Tanya struggling to think of some way to extract his location, and Rob realizing that Chick had had him hidden away, not for Rob's own good, but for someone else's. For whom?

"Can you call back and talk to him, Rob?" she pleaded. "I know he has things to tell you, and, of course, he knows more of what's going on than I do. Take care now. And talk to Chick as soon as you can." The line went quiet. He thought she was going to say goodbye, but instead she said, barely audibly, "We're going to lose the house."

"What?"

"They're foreclosing on the house. I got the letter yesterday. I've owned this house and been living it and paying a mortgage for almost twenty years."

"I'm sorry."

"It's like they suckered us, told us we could lower our interest rate, use our equity. We got a truck for Chick, and tools. He had jobs on the horizon. He had jobs with Steven, and Steven was hooked up with Spencer and Olsofsky. They bought all the land above Swan Beach to the Virginia border."

"But I thought that was federal land?"

"It is, was. They had some kind of deal where they got the land, and donated a small part of it back to the parks service. They also donated some land they had out west, Wyoming or Montana. Spencer had some mineral rights deals out there from way back."

Rob was going to ask how they got the deal, but he could guess how, and it didn't matter anyway. He was also going to ask if Spencer couldn't help them out, but Spencer wouldn't think that was his place, or that it was wise to do something like that. And besides, he was removed by a degree because Chick's deal was with Steven. "I'm sorry, Tanya."

"Yeah, me too. Chick thought he had a big payday coming, but it didn't ever happen like he said it would. The bank has us like indentured servants, or sharecroppers…"

"I've got to go, Tanya."

"Call Chick, Rob."

"I will. I'll call in a couple of days. You take care."

He heard a muffled noise and thought she might have been crying, and he also started thinking she might have been a little drunk, and he quickly hung up before she said anything else.

He sat on the edge of the bed. Once again he'd been given a whole new set of facts to add as another layer to what he already knew. Actually they were less like layers and more like ingredients being folded into a batter.

Amelia returned that evening, tired but full of information. "I went to Spencer's office and applied for a job."

"You applied for a job?"

"Yes, I'm an experienced bookkeeper," she said. "Not really. The receptionist gave me an application and I sat in the outer office and filled it out, trying to figure out what to do next. Considering how busy it was everywhere on the beach, on the roads, in the stores, there was nothing going on in the office. I never saw or heard anyone else, and the phone never rang. The receptionist was on her cell phone, but she was clearly Facebooking or surfing the web. I was beginning to think I wasn't going to get any info when I noticed on one wall there were a number of photographs, showing different arrays of Confederate soldiers in the field. I asked the girl about it, and when I could get her away from her phone, she said it was just the boys playing soldier.

"'That's where Mr. Spencer is now. They're all at the warehouse getting everything packed for the week. They're going to Gettysburg.'"

"Really, where is that?"

"In Pennsylvania, I think," she said.

"No, I mean the warehouse."

"Oh, the warehouse is in Spencer's industrial park in Currituck, just across the bridge."

"She gave me clearer directions and after I handed in my application, I went. It is just on the other side of the bridge, carved out of a pine grove. It's clearly a new complex, six connected warehouses, but only one, the biggest one, had any signage or any activity. And there was a lot of activity…a number of pick-up trucks with trailers, a step van, and a big new vacation travel trailer. Once I turned into the parking lot I was stuck. I couldn't pretend I was interested in renting one of the units, so I just acted like I was lost. There were five or six people moving around outside, and I could hear more in the darkened interior. When I entered the parking lot, their radar definitely went up. As I drove back toward them, three of them immediately approached in a row across, keeping me at a distance from the vehicles and the warehouse. It was a short conversation."

"Did you see Spencer?"

"No, he may have been inside the RV, or he may have been in the warehouse…I don't know. One of the guys who approached me though was definitely in your photograph."

Rob turned and rummaged through his backpack for the folder with the photograph in it.

"Him," she said. She pointed to Stennis, the assistant manager of the Sea Horse. "I just told them I was turning around. After I left I made a list of the vehicles I saw." She handed it to him. "I didn't get any plate numbers."

"No, this is good," he said.

"They're clearly preparing to leave…and soon."

"We're ready if we need to go, right?"

She nodded.

"What is it?" He saw she was thinking of something else.

"I saw Steven's wife, Misty. I told her I worked in the kitchen at the Sea Horse and knew Irina. I was hoping she'd give me some kind of hint that she thought Irina was alive. Misty clearly thinks that it was her in the car in the canal. She wanted someone to talk to. And she talked, and talked. And she's not well…I mean, mentally. She doesn't seem to be grasping things. One minute she seems to understand Steven is gone, and the next she seems to be waiting for him to walk through the door. I don't know if it's medication, or what. And she has some kind of attachment to Spencer. He's apparently taking care of their financial situation, but he's acting as if he's using Steven's money to do it. But Steven doesn't have any money, right?"

"I don't know. I'm confused by that whole thing. Chick said that Steven had some money because he was cheating his creditors by pocketing all the rentals from his oceanfront house and had stopped paying the mortgage on it. But I remember thinking when I heard that, and I still think it, that although that was a lot of money to someone like me, it couldn't have kept his engine running for long."

"Maybe Spencer feels guilty."

"Maybe. I know the plan was for Steven to contract the homes in Spencer's new development. But the thing about Spencer is that he's all business. I don't know."

That evening Amelia went and got takeout that they set up like a buffet on the small desk and ate on their separate beds. They retired early. Rob was awake for a while trying to put things together. Eventually he heard Amelia snoring softly on the other bed.

They were up and packed and on the road before the sun came up. There was not much traffic except for the delivery vans and trucks out early to restock store and restaurant shelves. Fifteen minutes later they were over the bridge and Amelia was slowing as they went past the entrance to Spencer's warehouses. There were lights and obvious activity back at the building Amelia had approached the day before.

They went by and drove to the North Carolina/Virginia border, and pulled into the sprawling border store complex with its souvenirs and cheap cigarettes and Barbeque restaurant and lottery tickets. Both expected that they wouldn't have to wait long, and two hours later Spencer's caravan with its pickup trucks pulling horse trailers and the RV with its Stars and Bars snapping in the wind rushed by. Amelia shifted into gear, and they turned onto the highway to follow them. With Spencer's caravan wrinkling in the heat in front of them, they headed north.

X

"I don't know you," Rob said. He was aware that it was an inappropriate way to begin a conversation. They were again driving through the summer countryside. There were deep green corn fields on the side of the road, and stands of trees, and outbuildings. The ditches were rank with weeds and trash. Billboard signs advertised everything from realtors to personal injury lawyers. It was hot outside the windows and everything was very green.

"Yes, you do," Amelia countered. "You know me. But I've been waiting for you to question it. You're wondering again why I'm doing this, and I've been wondering too. And this is why. My father died quickly, unexpectedly, horribly. Eventually I was given some answers to explain things…but not to the questions I had. When the plane hit the tower, what did my father think, what did he know? How long did he have to think about it? Did he have any idea of what was happening, really? Did he think he would be rescued, or did he know he was doomed from the start? Were there others with him, and did they all die bravely? Did he die bravely?"

There were tears in her eyes, Rob saw, soft tears though, not of frustration, but of nostalgia. They made him almost more nervous.

"But then you showed up next door, mysteriously, after I thought I had found my calm, pat answers. I thought I had everything resolved inside and could go on with my life and painting, but it wasn't happening. And suddenly there you are with questions, and more questions. At first I was afraid, but then I wanted answers. It didn't matter that I didn't know you, or any of these other people. I just knew something was up, and something had been awakened…me."

"So it's not just me."

She shook her head.

"I have another question," Rob said. "How is it that your English is so good? You barely have any accent."

Amelia laughed. "Mrs. Randall. First of all, in the schools in Costa Rica English is a required subject for grades one through eight. In many communities though there is no one to teach it. That was how it was in our school. My father at one point got a job cooking for an American woman, Mrs. Randall, who had built a house and was living in it in Santa Teresa. I didn't understand this then, but she was alone because she had separated from her husband. He was an executive for an American tobacco company. This was in the late seventies. In America it was becoming apparent that tobacco was a health risk, and it also that there were going to be restrictions placed on its sale. The tobacco companies could see that coming. So what they decided to do was go international. They looked at Central and South America and Asia and realized they had millions if not billions of potential customers, and all without the pesky regulations that were popping up in the United States.

"Mrs. Randall came from a wealthy family, as did her husband. They had both gone to Ivy League colleges, and then Mr. Randall had gotten an MBA from Wharton. So their path was set, and the road smooth in front of them.

"Mr. Randall got a job with a tobacco company, and he was transferred first to Panama, and then to Costa Rica. His job was to get the youths of these countries to take up smoking to replace the young smokers the company was losing in the United States. He was a marketing guru and the plan he came up with was genius, and it is one still used by these companies worldwide. First were the billboards and signs on buses and taxis, scenes of young and sexy people being cool and having fun, cigarettes in their slender fingers. That enticed some to smoke. Then there were big promotions held in nightclubs and discos. But then suddenly there was another company marketing their cigarettes in the same way. There was competition. And this competition led to a price war. Cigarettes became so cheap people couldn't afford not to smoke. But what the consumers didn't realize was that both these competing companies were in fact owned by the same larger corporation, the one Mr. Randall worked for. And the sham price war was just their way of setting the hook.

"At this point Mrs. Randall didn't know anything about any of this. Her husband became a vice-president, they had plenty of money, they travelled, they lived the good life, and she had no need to think or wonder where it all came from. But then her father, a life-long smoker, got lung cancer. She flew up to visit him in his last days in the hospital. She told me the condition she found him in changed her forever. He was lying in a hospital bed, shriveled and gray. By this time they had had to remove both of his legs because of circulatory issues, and the surgeons were talking about the possibility of taking one of his arms. He was barely conscious, and so drugged that he didn't know or recognize anyone. But the most shocking thing to her was that in the fingers of his right hand he held a plastic straw the length of a cigarette that they had given him, and every fifteen or twenty seconds he would raise his gray bony fingers to his lips and draw through it.

"Now she realized that her husband's career would culminate in sending millions to the bed her father ended up in. She came back to San Jose and begged him to give up his job, to take his skills and talents to another industry. That was not a path her husband was ready to follow, and consequently their marriage didn't survive long after that. But she loved Costa Rica, and with her settlement she bought some acres in the mountains above the beach in Santa Teresa. She had a big house built and busied herself planting gardens, and made for herself a quiet life.

"So my father began cooking for her. Sometimes he took me. We would have to leave our house in the middle of the night it seemed like, and walk to Cobano where we would wait for the bus, and then take the bus to Santa Teresa where we would be let off to climb the long steep hill to her property. The first time I met her and she spoke to me in Spanish I was in awe. Her pronunciation and grammar, everything was perfect, but also so formal and concise that it was like nothing I had ever heard before. I guess it would be like a rural American hearing a very educated Englishman speak for the first time.

"I was there to work, to help my father in the kitchen and the maid with the housecleaning, but gradually Mrs. Randall took an interest in me. Some arrangement was made with my parents and I became a permanent lodger at her house. I was responsible for some of the cleaning, and for some chores in the garden, but gradually I became more of a companion than anything else. She taught me to speak English the same way she spoke Spanish, pronouncing the words as they were supposed to be, and using them where and when they were supposed to be used.

"I never became close to her, really, but I sensed the opportunity and made the most of it. After four years, by the time I was fourteen, I spoke English as I do now. And then one day, out of the blue, she told me that she would be leaving. And she did. She closed up the house, and a car came and picked up her and her bags, and she never came back."

"What happened to her? Where did she go?"

146

"I don't know. I never heard anything of her or about her again."

Rob looked at her. She stared straight ahead through the windshield, past the road and vehicles in front of her, into the blue distance of the sky.

Amelia followed Spencer's caravan casually and efficiently. Rob kept thinking he would have to tell her to speed up or slow down, but she always maintained a proper distance. It was as if she had done this kind of thing before. Of course, the flagged RV made it easy. The other vehicles sped up and fell behind the RV, like satellites orbiting a sun. It also became apparent as they headed north that there were outriders, a group of half a dozen pickups that joined and left the convoy. They would rev ahead until they were out of sight, and then either slow until they were caught up with, or exit the freeway and wait until they were passed by and come up again from behind.

"In those photos at Spencer's office," Rob said, "how many re-enactors were there in the group?"

"I'm thinking the same thing."

As Amelia drove, Rob began taking a head count of the people in the vehicles that he judged to be part of the caravan. It was impossible to tell how many people were in the RV, and many of the trucks had dark tinted windows. There were also a few vehicles in the ebb and flow of traffic that might or might not have been part of the convoy.

"I've got fifty, mas o menos," he said.

"Maybe there are girlfriends, wives…families."

"I don't see any women, or kids," he replied. "It's all men."

"Maybe Spencer has joined with another group, trying to make a bigger impact."

"That would fit his personality."

Three hours later they approached the sprawl of northern Virginia and DC, and went north into Maryland. Another hour and a half and they were on the Emmitsville Road, and passing the driveway to Kay Yoder's house.

Spencer's group began to slow and turned off to the left into a gated driveway a mile and a half past the Yoder house and on the same side of the road. Rob and Amelia had to wait as the vehicles went into the property and began to park past the split rail fence. Rob sat slouched down with his hat low over his eyes. Amelia pulled off the road to pass the last few vehicles on the right shoulder, and continued toward the town. Rob immediately realized that the stream he had hiked and the woods must be on the back of this property, or bisect it, and that it should enable him to approach Spencer's encampment from the back and still be relatively well-hidden.

Amelia continued for another mile toward Gettysburg before turning to make a circle safely back to Kay Yoder's house. There was much more traffic on the roads. Clearly both re-enactors and spectators were streaming into the area for the big show that was scheduled to begin in two days.

Kay had been so anxious for their return that she was out on her porch waving as they drove up the driveway. She came down the steps and when Amelia stopped the car and got out she and Kay hugged like they were old friends.

Before they had left the beach they had stopped at a seafood market and bought a dozen soft-shelled crabs, along with ears of white corn, and big tomatoes, and zucchini and squash. They had packed the crabs in ice and buried them in the bottom of the cooler. After they had gotten their bags in the house and upstairs, Rob and Amelia went into the kitchen to prepare dinner for Kay. They moved around each other in the small kitchen as if they had cooked together hundreds of times before.

Kay was a bit apprehensive when she saw the crabs, which were still moving lethargically and bubbling around their mouth-parts. Rob gave a look to Amelia who distracted Kay so he could clean the crabs. When everything else was going, Rob dipped them in egg, and dredged them in flour, and then slid them into the heavy frying pan filled with sizzling oil.

Ten minutes later they were sitting in the dining room and Rob was telling Kay, "Yes, you can eat the whole thing...legs and all." They ate crabs, and sautéed squash and zucchini, and tomato slices with salt and pepper and mayonnaise, and ears of the sweet white corn. For Rob, anytime up until a couple of weeks ago there would have also been bottles of wine, or at least coolers filled with cold sweating beer. He tried not to think about it as he drank his iced tea.

Amelia and Kay carried on their easy conversation, flitting from subject to subject. Rob listened absently, thinking about Spencer's group setting up the encampment two rises to the east.

"Who lives three driveways down?" he asked during a lull in their conversation.

"Three? Well, that's nobody. It's just a gate to some pastureland. The Boehnnings own it. They own about the next mile and a half on this side of the road. Why do you ask?"

Rob glanced at Amelia. "We saw a re-enactment group enter through the gate."

"That's a group of real, hard-core re-enactors then, FARBs, the ones who really get into what they're doing. No electricity, only well water. They usually leave their vehicles by the gate, hike back over the rise, and set up camp. They get their firewood from the forest, go back in time. They can ride their horses or march on the back trails to the battlefield. Some of them take this all very seriously."

Just after the solstice, the time from the broad heat and light of afternoon until full darkness was long, as if the sun purposely delayed its departure. And it was only just after five when they finished their dinners and sat back. Kay got up and went into the kitchen to make coffee.

Rob rose from his seat, somewhat too quickly, because he was immediately dizzy and lurched against the edge of the table to keep from falling over. Their glasses shook and the cutlery rattled.

"Sorry."

"Are you alright?" Amelia asked, rising to help him.

"Yes…just dizzy. I got up too fast." He held the table, his head unweighted and floating, shots of light at the corners of his vision. Gradually he settled back into himself. "I'm going to go into the woods back there and follow them to behind Spencer's encampment."

"I'll come with you."

"No, it would be better if just one of us goes. And we don't want to get Kay suspicious about anything." He didn't want to also say that he thought there might be some danger. He saw the tell he now recognized when Amelia was about to argue with him about something. It was a small intake of air and a scrunching of her shoulders, as if her argument was gathering itself to spring from her. "You're not coming, and that's it. Just trust me on this, will you?"

She smiled then, and knew she was thinking the same thing he was…how in a few short weeks they had built a relationship that from the outside, and even to each of them, appeared smoothed as if by years of age and caring, patient experimentation.

149

"Okay."

Ten minutes later he was crossing the field toward the fences, aiming toward the trees. He automatically began to move with as little extra energy as possible to husband his reserves of strength. He was wondering about Amelia's past love life. He hadn't given it any thought until that moment. The sun was angling to the west, but it was still hot and the rain of a few days before was rising from the earth. He could smell the dirt, and shit, and the mineral scent of the rocks that were baking on the surface and drawing the moisture up from below.

As soon as he entered the trees he raised his concentration level. Everything was mottled in the shadows and gave the impression of movement all around him, which was unsettling until he found the patterns. He could hear the stream water moving, the sound coming from a few different points along the line of its flow. Birds were singing close by, and there was a group really making a racket across the stream and back in the darkness where the trees grew taller and closer together.

He went to the stream and followed along the bank as he had earlier. If he heard anything human, he had thought it would be the sounds of someone chopping wood for a campfire. There had been a couple of other drives leading off the road between Kay Yoder's place and the driveway Spencer's group had taken, but he didn't know if there were any re-enactors camping in those intervening fields, or if there might be houses on those properties with people living there. But he didn't have time to find out because he wanted to get to Spencer's campsite with time to observe before it got dark.

He followed the creek-side trail, moving quickly (for him) and quietly, stopping every few minutes to listen. As he went along he spied in the bushes at his feet a long limb, about the length of his body, and as thick around as his wrist. He picked it up. It was sturdy, hard wood, hickory maybe, smooth-barked and heavy. He carried it with him, and supported his weakened left side with it. As he came to the small cataract, he became more careful because he knew the sounds of the falling water would drown out other sounds, and he didn't want to suddenly come face to face with someone and have to explain himself. He followed the hidden trail up around the side of the falls and emerged from the small camouflaged terminus at the top. He furtively poked his head out before he ventured on to the upper trail. From there he went on, following the stream bank, until he thought he had covered enough ground to be behind Spencer's campsite. Crouching, holding his breath, he carefully made his way to the edge of the woods.

As he got to where the thinning trees allowed the sky to brighten above him, he began to hear sounds of human activity, but the sounds seemed to be coming well away from the border of the trees. As he emerged he saw large rocks, some the size of small cars, strewn along the edge of the trees, apparently dug up from the farmer's fields and pastures when the land had been originally cleared in the early 1800s and rolled or dragged to the forest's edge. He moved forward and from behind one of them Rob was able to look down into the broad swale the group had chosen for their campsite.

The camp was set up as a nineteenth century military bivouac, rectangular white tents already up and aligned carefully to form three quarters of a square. At the end of one line of tents was a meal wagon, a big fire burning in front of it, with steaming pots suspended above. Rob had seen the wagon under a tarp on a trailer behind one of the massive pickup trucks on the highway headed north. Everything looked as if it had come out of another era; from the cook wagon, to the corral with a dozen horses bent at the shoulders munching the yellowing grass, to the two lines of troops in gray and yellow homespun, to the muskets in conical arrangements in front of the tents. There were camp chairs and firepits, a long latrine dug well out behind one line of tents, and two artillery pieces up on the crest of the hill. But then, completely ruining the whole effect, at the end of one row of tents was the shining RV, its striped awning flapping at the edges above the steps and the main door. Then, to further weaken the effect, coming around from the back of the RV, Rob saw a man in Confederate clothing, but slung over his shoulder was clearly a modern and powerful automatic rifle. Rob involuntarily ducked further behind the rock when he saw it. No doubt, it was an automatic weapon, and the man was guarding something, or someone, in the RV.

Perspiring in the slanting sunlight, nervously spying on the activity below him, Rob suddenly knew Irina was in the RV. She was a prisoner, Spencer's prisoner, but why? And if Spencer were holding her, why would he take the chance of travelling all this way with her? Why not keep her at one or another of his properties that were scattered across this country and beyond? It didn't make sense that he could be holding her for some kind of ransom. Knowing Spencer for as long as he had, Rob never doubted that he had stretched the rules, probably broken more than a few on his way up. But would he resort to kidnapping, and if he had, what could have driven him to it? Though maybe the man with the AR-15, or whatever it was, was guarding something else. Maybe, after all, they were guarding Spencer himself. But that brought up the same questions. Why? And from whom?

Looking into the indention, Rob was again struck by the number of people, clearly around fifty, and also that they were all men. From his reading about the re-enacting community and its members, in many ways it was usually a family affair. The men dressed up and staged their battles, but they returned to campsites often run by women, also in period costume. And there were often children, barefoot with straw hats, boys rolling hoops, and girls playing with cloth dolls. As Rob had seen with Amelia, it was often the women who seemed to take the greatest care to see that their costumes were historically accurate. That's where the FARB came in. At first he didn't understand what it meant, until he read that it was something like, 'Far be it for me...' followed by a complaint about the inaccuracy or lack of authenticity in a costume. There were websites devoted to finding materials, threads, even buttons, that were accurate to the age. Besides uniform patterns, they sold dress patterns, and offered advice about hoops and bonnets, dress and sleeve lengths, proper footwear, stockings, even petticoats.

Rob wished he had brought pencil and paper so he could sketch the whole layout. He also wished he had binoculars or a camera with a telephoto lens. Instead he concentrated on committing everything to memory, judging distances and proportions, counting heads. He also realized that when he got back he needed to return to the entrance to count and record the numbers and makes of their vehicles, and try to get plate numbers too if that was possible.

He suddenly recognized that he had stayed in the open, with his scant cover, for too long. He retreated, keeping low, dragging his unresponsive leg, his left arm tucked up as if he were carrying a bundle, until he reached the break in the thicket and went back into the woods. After a moment to adjust to the dimmer light, he was off, crab-walking as quickly as he could, leaning again on his stick, pushing himself until he was winded, and then pushing himself some more. By the time he reached the entrance to the trail down the side of the falls, he was nearly spent. He ruefully thought about what his life and his physical capabilities were now, and tried to lay them flat on top of the memory of what they had been only two years before. He had had his aches and pains then, but he could do what he wanted to do when he wanted to do it. He never minded after a certain age if it hurt to do something. He had always been willing to push his body, and that desire hadn't stopped at middle age. Muscle pain was an elixir. But that life and that thinking were long gone now. He left his walking stick in the brush at the top of the trail and went down.

The sky was orange and yellow, with tinges of red and angry bruised purple at the cloud edges when he emerged from the trees at the back of Kay Yoder's property. Rob was perspiring profusely. Drops formed and fell from the tip of his nose, and his shirt clung to him, pressing against his shoulder and back.

"Did you get lost?" Kay asked when he came around to the front of the house and found Amelia and her rocking on the porch like old childhood friends.

"No, I just wandered a bit further than I had planned, and it took longer to get back than I thought it would."

"Let me get you a cold drink," she said, standing.

"No," Rob replied. "You two sit here and continue your conversation. I can get my own drink, and then I think I'll take a shower."

"He can take care of himself, Kay," Amelia said, looking at Rob's face, searching for any clues as to what he might have found.

"It's a beautiful evening, isn't it?" Kay said. She had a way of smiling that made all her features, especially her eyes, enlarge themselves. On someone else it might have seemed strained, or artificial, but coming from her the way it did, like a blossoming, it just pointed to her natural enthusiasm about things. "It's warm," she continued, "but not too humid. If this weather holds you should have some nice days for your battles."

Rob left them on the porch and went in, passed through the dining room and past the swinging doors into the kitchen. He made ice water and took the glass with him, ice tinkling rhythmically against the sides as he rose to the second storey. He got a new set of clothes from his bag and went into the tight old bathroom to undress. On the inside of the door was a full-length mirror gone dark in some areas where the silver had worn off. After Rob undressed he stood and looked at himself in the glass. Talk about the blues of irretrievability. He looked in outline like one of Picasso's women, nothing quite in place, spindly legs, no ass, and too round torso. His penis and ball sack hung like a useless afterthought. His skin was pale, the hair mostly dark on his chest, but his face was blotchy, mottled, although his jowls were darkening where his beard had come in. In his imagination he only saw himself as he used to be, and this was almost too much to bear. His weakened left side sagged, and his arm, even at rest, bent in at the elbow and again at the wrist, and his left leg would not straighten entirely, so there was something almost simian about the whole effect.

He took a cool shower, trying to rinse off the grime and perspiration and the memory of his reflection in the mirror. He had no urge to be philosophical about it. It was what it was. Or now, he guessed, it is what it is.

After he showered, he dressed and combed his hair, avoiding his reflection while pretending not to. He went into their room and sat on the bed waiting for Amelia to come up. He was anxious to tell her what he had seen and get her reaction to it. He sat there, but she didn't come, and finally he got up and went downstairs. Out to the west he could see a bit of gray light, like spent ash, lying on the horizon. The rocking chairs still creaked on the old painted porch boards. He went out the front door and found the women lazily silent. He thought that they may have been talking about him, and if they were he wondered what Amelia might have told Kay, and whether she had had to invent things to round the picture of him out.

"So how were my woods?" Kay asked.

"Yours?"

"No one's more than mine surely, after all these years."

"Well, they were relaxing...quiet...mysterious."

"We used to live in those woods in the summers when we were children. We'd spend whole days in there, making forts with my brothers, trying to catch the little trout and bream as they flashed through in the stream, damming up schools of tadpoles, tromping though the underbrush, finding wood to make rafts, swimming in the cold water, especially in the pool below the falls. Did you get that far? I had my first kiss under those falls when I was fourteen. Joey Grossenkemper. Sweet boy. At least I

154

thought so until I found out what he told everyone else he had done to me, and worse, what he said I had done to him. I was mortified."

"Aside from that," Rob said, looking down at Kay's full broad bosom, and not only imagining what Joey Grossenkemper might have said happened, but thinking there were probably a lot of boys back then who wanted to get a handful of those, "it must have been a great place to grow up."

"And then there were the stories about the war and the woods," Kay said. "I can remember my grandmother, on this very porch, telling me of the ghosts of rebels that her grandfather had seen in those woods."

"I bet there are a lot of old family stories," Rob said, "and I be a lot of them grew with the legend of the battle."

"Yes. And you know what's strange? As a woman, at least I think that's where it comes from, I can sometimes feel the suffering of those men so long ago as if that suffering has a life of its own. I can sense regret and fear, terror... that feeling that if you take one more step forward you know horrible things could happen to you, and yet you can't turn back. That's a male thing, I think, to step toward your suffering. We women like to wait for our suffering to come to us."

They went on like that for a while, reminiscing about their childhoods, and how things had changed. Amelia told more stories of her childhood in Costa Rica, and that led to a geography lesson because Kay couldn't place it in the abbreviated world map in her head. It also led to a discussion of the migrations, legal and illegal, of Central Americans into the United States. There were Mexicans now living in Gettysburg, Kay said. They had their own stores and restaurants, their kids went to the public schools, the men played soccer on weekends at the parks, and fifteen years ago there hadn't been a single one of them. There seemed to be a few less of them since the economy sank, she thought. What bothered her, and she said she didn't want to seem prejudiced, was that they mostly kept to themselves, and many of the adults didn't seem to want to learn English. She would see them in the grocery store, and their kids would be translating for them.

"But that's probably the way it's always been," Amelia said. "It's so much easier for a child to learn a language. Their minds are so open and ready to be filled. I remember my father when he came to this country, it was a terrible struggle for him to learn English, very frustrating."

Soon the mosquitos began to whisper behind their ears, and they moved inside. It wasn't long after that they began to take turns yawning, and Rob an Amelia said their goodnights and went upstairs. Amelia went into the bathroom, and Rob quickly, and sheepishly, changed into his pajamas. He was smiling when she came back into the room wearing a robe and carrying her clothes because he remembered that he hadn't worn pajamas since he was ten years old. After she put her clothes away she came and sat next to him on his side of the bed.

"Well?"

He told her what he had seen, describing their encampment, the disposition of tents and equipment and people. And then of course he told her of the RV and its guard with his decidedly modern weapon.

"What does it mean," he asked, "when they go to all the trouble to be historically accurate, and yet they have a goddamned Winnebago dropped in the middle of everything? And it's being watched over by a guy in Johnny Reb garb carrying a machine gun?"

"I know what you think it means," Amelia said. "And I'm starting to think you're right. But why? Say Spencer is holding Irina for some reason. Why would he take the chance of bringing her along on this excursion when security has to be so much more difficult to maintain?"

Rob nodded. Amelia was raising all the same questions he had.

"How many of those do you recognize from the photograph in the newspaper?"

"Most of them were there, near as I could tell. There was Stennis and Chef Dustin from the Sea Horse. And then there was that big young cop, Davy Todd. And then there were others I recognized from the beach, but I just know them to see them, no names or anything."

"So how many does that leave that you didn't recognize?"

"About half…twenty, or twenty five. But they're military-looking… in shape, tattoos, crewcuts."

"Maybe Spencer just wants to give himself a promotion in the re-enacting sense of things. Maybe he hired some Marines from Camp Lejeune, some guys the big cop knows, or some sailors from Norfolk."

"It could be," he agreed.

Amelia got up and began to pace, her robe swishing as she walked. Rob was half-seated, leaning against the headboard.

"Tomorrow?" she asked.

"I think early tomorrow morning you need to walk down to the entrance of that property where all their vehicles are parked. Just so we have a record, you should get as much info as you can about the vehicles, makes and models, colors, especially plate numbers if you can get them. I obviously can't do it because I could be recognized. At some point tomorrow I need to go back and do some more reconnaissance, but we have to buy binoculars first so I can get a better look at things. We can tell Kay I'm going out in the woods for some bird-watching. And then we need to go to the re-enacting headquarters and find out how many men are signed up under Spencer and where they're to be staged, and what assaults and skirmishes they're supposed to be part of. And I need to get my assignment too."

Amelia went to her side of the bed. Her face was in shadows because she hadn't turned on her light, and her hair fell across her face.

"You seem different," she said, signaling for him to turn off his light.

When he did she removed her robe and climbed under the covers on her side of the bed, and he did the same.

"I am different. I'm much better at making things happen than I am at waiting for them to happen."

Then he reached over and pulled Amelia to him.

XI

Rob snuck out of bed and dressed and crept downstairs as soon as he saw a faint light in the eastern sky. Amelia's side of the bed was already empty next to him. He slipped out the front door and stood on the porch thinking, what an unqualified disaster. When he had reached for Amelia the night before, it was with the first feelings of natural desire that he had felt in months. Those urges had fallen so far down on his scale of priorities, had been suppressed really because of his fear of an inability to perform, that they had been as dormant as ancient Pre-Columbian jungle ruins covered by vines and centuries of accreted dust. And then this thing last night with Amelia was like a long and arduous archeological dig.

Amelia had been patient and understanding. She viewed his initial lack of tumescence as a temporary and surmountable obstacle. (At least he still had his sense of humor.) But then the problem developed into one of maneuverability. He could really not do much more than lie on his back. He had scooped his right arm under Amelia and drawn her to him, but then his brain sent a message to his left arm that went unanswered. Amelia had responded to his summons demurely, but then she waited. Rob continued broadcasting signals until he felt there could have been visible sparks in the darkened room, but the real result was almost nothing.

"I can't move my fucking arm," he said, choking with frustration and embarrassment, and then in the next instant he was laughing. It began quiet and low, but he knew that if he didn't quell it, it would get away from him and he might wake Kay. "I'm sorry," he choked.

And then she was laughing too into her pillow, and punching him lightly in his useless arm.

"I was afraid," he whispered, "that if I swung it over it might be like hitting you in the side of the head with a twenty pound tuna."

"It is okay," she said.

"No, it's not," he almost hissed. "It just is. Come closer so I can kiss you."

She slid next to him. Their lips found each other and they kissed breathlessly, like teenagers at first, and only gradually settled into it. There was another tongue in his mouth for the first time in actual years, and while his carefully prodded, Amelia's moved and darted like a salamander. Rob's brain continued to send messages to his arm, but still to no avail. He became aware of a subtle and clever tingling at the base of his skull, and gradually, in fits and starts, he got an erection. He at first doubted it was real, until he felt it stretching at the fabric of his pajama pants. He had no idea what he could or should do with it, or what he might ask her to do. And then he realized that even acknowledging it was probably not a good idea.

The whole thing didn't last long, though he held his own as far as that went. There were no gymnastics, no fireworks. Amelia provided most of the animative effort. She centered Rob on the bed while removing her clothes and his. Then she got above him and descended slowly. Her skin where he felt it was cool and powdery, her scent that of dried flowers. He looked up at her, but the darkness consumed everything. He was sure she wanted it that way as protection against disappointing him. Was that how little she understood men? They could be fucking under the full white light of a surgical auditorium with anonymous masked faces staring down all around them. It just didn't matter. This act was less a culmination than a natural point on an ascending line. Her girlish trill at the end finally brought him back to the present.

When they were finished she slid into the crook of his arm and lay straight as a board next to him. He realized she was waiting for him to whisper something, but he was liquid, a spreading puddle. He pressed against her and kissed the top of her head.

"Thank you," he said. "I couldn't have done it without you."

"Not with your left hand anyway."

They both laughed again, hoping Kay hadn't heard anything, and wasn't listening. Rob began to think again about what they needed to do the next day. There were now only two days until the start of the reenactments. He couldn't stop thinking about the RV and wondering if Irina was in it. But then maybe none of this had anything to do with any diabolical plan. Maybe he had misconstrued everything. Perhaps he had deluded himself into all sorts of suppositions that didn't have any basis, twisted and magnified events using his clearly faulty and gap-filled memory to create a conspiracy that involved murder, kidnapping maybe, financial shenanigans. But maybe it didn't exist.

159

"You can't do anything about it now, Rob. Go to sleep."

She was right, of course, and his mind did let him drift in a slow stream prelude to slumber, and then he heard Amelia breathing deeply, already asleep. She was stronger and more discerning than he was, and she believed something was going on. She was his barometer. He trusted her measurements of things much more than he trusted his own. He thought he recognized that she wasn't one who would be easily intrigued, or looking to fill her life with unpredictable and dangerous adventure. Would she?

Amelia was not in the kitchen, though there was coffee made, nor in any of the downstairs rooms, nor on the porch. Her car was still there on the parking apron. She must have left earlier to walk down the road to record the information on Spencer's vehicles. He trusted her to be careful, but even so he worried that she might somehow raise their suspicions and put herself in danger.

The sky outside brightened and the edges and faces of objects began to take on their outlines and shapes. Rob went out on the porch. It was already warm and humid. The flowers planted at the base of the porch were dew-filled and leaned toward the rising sun. Small gray and brown birds hopped aimlessly across the yard. There was a woodpecker at work in the oak tree at the left corner of the porch, but it was invisible among the leaves and branches. Rob sat in one of the rocking chairs nursing his coffee. He could hear sporadic traffic hissing by just past the rise in front of him. To his left in the hazy distance was Big Round Top, and sloping down from its left was the knob of Little Round Top.

What was happening on this day one hundred fifty-one years ago? Lee was moving his army north through Maryland, determined to find a place of his choosing to confront the Union army directly, or draw them into a confrontation. To defeat the Army of the Potomac behind Washington DC would surely throw the north into a panic. His army was strong and disciplined, and more importantly, they knew they could defeat the Yankees. He missed Thomas Jackson. There was no doubt about that. He was irreplaceable to both the army and the cause. But that could not be helped. And General Stuart, his eyes, was off riding, drawing great thunderous circles... who knew where? Lee hadn't heard from him in days, and so didn't know where the northern army was, or whether and where it was moving.

Rob was off in this reverie when he heard Kay coming down the stairs.

"Good morning," she said, poking her head out the screen door.

"And to you."

"Is Amelia in the kitchen?"

"No, I think she went for a walk…probably looking for things to paint."

"Have you got coffee?"

He held up his cup.

"Would you like more?"

"No, I'm good…thanks."

When she retreated into the kitchen, Rob thought about going down the porch steps and over the rise down to the road to wait for Amelia. He wasn't in the mood to talk, and he knew Kay would be.

He was just about to make his move when he saw Amelia's head, and then her shoulders, coming above the rise in front of him. She was laboring, he saw, her camera bouncing along as she moved. When she saw him she began to wave him to her. He went down the steps and they met by the cars.

"We have to go," she said breathlessly. "We have to get moving."

"What?"

"They…a whole group of them is going somewhere. I got down there and made observations from the road, trying to be discreet in case someone was watching the vehicles. I snapped pictures, first of the groups of vehicles as I was going away, and when I came back I used the 200mm to try to get what plate info I could. A lot of the trucks and trailers were facing the road so I couldn't see their plates. I was pretty sure no one was guarding them, and I had almost decided to enter through the gate and sneak around the trucks to snap their plate numbers when I heard voices and men began coming over the hill.

"I continued as if I were just on a pleasant early morning walk. All in all, there were about twenty of them. They all had a very military look to them; young, fit, close-cropped hair. The thing is, they're going somewhere, and we have to follow them. Go. Go! Get the keys…and my laptop!"

161

"What do I tell Kay?"

"Anything…go!"

Rob went into the house quietly and up the stairs. Kay was still in the kitchen. He grabbed the wallet off the bureau, and Amelia's purse from the back of the bathroom door. He looked around the room and saw her laptop on the low table under the window. He closed the screen, unplugged it, and put it under his arm. Kay was coming through the dining room when he came down.

"Where are you in such a rush to?"

"Amelia saw something on her walk that she wants to paint. But now it's an emergency because she wants to get a photo of it while the light is right…whatever that means." He hoped he sounded convincing.

He went out the door. Amelia was already in the driver's seat. Rob remembered that when they arrived the previous day that she had insisted on topping off their gas tank, saying cryptically, "you never know." He hobbled over the lawn to get in the passenger side, handed her the keys, and before he could close the door the car was moving.

Amelia drove the fifty feet up the soft rise until they reached the elevation from which the land dropped off and the driveway ran down to the Emmittsburg Road that crossed it like a T at the bottom. Below them, as if on cue, heading in the direction of the interstate, were five double-cab, four door pickup trucks. Some had dark-tinted windows, but where he could see into the interiors, there appeared to be four men in each truck. In the beds were duffel bags and back packs. The sun was rising in the hills behind them, laying out a broad white light, so it was impossible to recognize any of the individuals.

Amelia waited until they had all passed and then eased down the rest of the driveway. Two random cars passed, going in the same direction as the trucks, but that just gave them a disguising buffer.

"Where are they going?" she asked.

Rob just shrugged. These twenty represented a third of the total heads in the camp, so what were the remainder doing? But then his answer was that they weren't going anywhere. It didn't make any sense to bring this whole entourage up and then have them go in different directions once they were here.

"I'm betting," he said, "that those fellows in front of us are not represented in the number that Spencer has signed up for the re-enactments. They are meant to look as if they are when they are in camp, but they're on some other mission entirely."

"When they came out to the trucks they all had big canvas military-looking bags," Amelia said. "And the bags were clearly heavy."

Another intervening car added to their separation when they stopped at the traffic light before the interstate. One by one the trucks eased on to the entry ramp heading north, and when it was Amelia's turn, she followed them.

The highway was thick with traffic as they edged by Gettysburg, but after they passed the town the number of cars thinned and speeds increased and they drove north through the Pennsylvania Dutch countryside.

"I have no idea where we're going," Rob said, after they had driven north for half an hour. Amelia had been tense, and a dark pink had settled on her upper cheek.

"This all seems so elaborate," she said, and let the thought hang there.

They continued north on Interstate 78. Their speed was steady, but the five trucks ahead of them alternately slowed and sped up, exchanging the lead and randomly their places in line. They passed Harrisonburg and Allentown. Thirty miles north of Allentown they all as a group exited into a rest stop. With frantic misgivings, Amelia followed.

She parked in the shade beneath the immense canopy of a poplar tree and turned off the ignition. The trucks were further ahead, bunched close to the main building. The men didn't acknowledge each other as they got out and went toward the rest room. One person remained at each vehicle, either in the cab, or wandering lazily around its perimeter.

"I have to pee," Amelia said.

"So do I."

"You'll have to wait…but I'll bring you back something to pee in."

"Thoughtful."

She pulled the band out of the back of her hair and shook it forward so it draped her cheeks. Then she smiled at him. As she walked away, he tried to graft the squat woman in front of him with the memory of her naked in the darkness the night before, and it didn't all add up. He worried about

163

them noticing or recognizing her, but he realized that in her posture and bearing she made herself anonymous, as if she had practiced it somehow.

Although he was fifty yards away from the nearest truck, Rob kept low in the passenger seat, his eyes just at the level of the dashboard. The men who remained at the trucks were relieved and allowed to take their turns at the lavatory. Rob watched them as they came and went. They were too far away to distinguish facial features, but close enough that he would have recognized them from their general physical outlines, or their manners of movement. He didn't. He also tried to discern who was in charge of the operation, but no one seemed to be giving orders or taking the lead. They all seemed to understand their tasks and go about them with no prodding.

Amelia returned after five minutes. She didn't raise her head until she was ten feet away. She held up her hand, and in it was a plastic cup and top.

"Very funny," he said, as she slid in behind the driver's wheel.

He got out and opened the back door and got into the back seat. He struggled in the tight confines to get his pants down with one good arm, and grabbed the towel from the floor to put on his lap as there were more cars pulling in and parking around them. He got everything adjusted, and the cup situated, and ...nothing.

"Don't say anything," he said.

She shook her head. The seconds added up. He felt an inner pressure, but no relief. Then, slowly, came an anemic trickle.

"I'm not saying anything," she said, anticipating him.

"You better not." He saw her shoulders shake. "And if you laugh, you'll be wearing this."

And then he was laughing too, which seemed to be an aid to the restricted muscles. His flow quickly gained strength and swirled up and around the sides of the cup.

"Oh, oh," Amelia said suddenly. "They're moving."

She started the car and Rob finished and looked for the lid to put on the cup. He sat back, arching as he struggled again, this time to get his pants back up. When he did, he opened the door to put the cup in the receptacle on the other side of the walk. He was less concerned about being recognized because he hadn't seen anyone he knew or recognized. But when he dropped the cup in, he looked at the lavatory building and he saw the young cop, Davy Todd, heading back toward the trucks. Rob immediately went down on one knee as if he were tying his shoe and watched as the policeman did a mental inventory of trucks and passengers and then climbed into one of the cabs. The other trucks then began to back out of the spaces and head back to the interstate.

"Did you see him?" Rob asked.

"That young, polite policeman, yes, I saw him."

"I have no idea what that means...in the scheme of things."

"I guess we have to follow them to find out."

They had left Gettysburg around seven AM. They headed north and by eleven they were approaching the New York border. Neither Rob nor Amelia had any idea where they were headed. Once they left Pennsylvania they both assumed they were going to New York City, but the caravan stayed west and kept to the beautiful countryside that bordered the Hudson River. Then the trucks ducked off the interstate and they followed, staying single-file on the winding country roads, driving beneath canopies of full-leafed trees, and they rose and fell as the land undulated beneath them.

They spent a lot of time worrying whether they were too close, or had fallen too far back. A few times they thought they had lost the caravan, only to then see the taillights of the rear truck rising over a hillcrest a half-mile ahead of them. Soon they were approaching the prosaic old village of Poughkeepsie. Grand houses stood back on hillsides long distances from the road, with rolling fields sprawled out, and majestic rare thoroughbred horses grazing. Old-growth forest dotted the countryside as if they had all been placed and arranged by eighteenth century English garden architects.

Amelia had Rob open her laptop and explained to him how to get on the internet and go to google earth. She gave him the addresses of a number of the houses they passed, and she told him how to enter the information as she simultaneously tried to follow the caravan of trucks and remain unobserved. Suddenly on screen was an aerial view of the land they were driving through.

"Jesus," Rob muttered. "Look at this."

"You can use the bar at the side to pan in or out," Amelia said. "Oh, oh. Look!"

They came over a rise in time to see the first two trucks, and then the third and fourth, turn on to a dirt and gravel road that ran next to a long white fence and rose up a hillside toward a stand of trees. The fifth truck remained at the entrance, and Rob ducked as Amelia drove steadily by.

"Quick," she said when they were a hundred yards by, "move the image ahead and see where we are and if there is any way we can parallel them from the other side of the hill."

Rob could not move quickly enough for her so she pulled over on to the shoulder and took the laptop. She spun the knobs and panned out, scrutinizing the grid before her. Rob couldn't make out anything on the screen except the gray of the surrounding pasture and the darker gray of the tree-filled wooded areas.

"Here," she said, pointing. "The road curves to the left up ahead, and runs up close to these woods. If we can get there and through the woods, this house, which has to be their objective, is just on the other side."

She slammed the car into gear and tore away from the shoulder. They went over a rise, and as the roadway dipped behind it, it did begin to angle sharply to the left, and ran along next to a shallow, idyllic brook.

"This has to be it," she said, pulling off the road and on to the gravel. To their left, fifty yards past a roadside fence, and up a gradual incline dotted with dozens of sheep, was a border of woods. "The house should be straight through there," she said, pointing to a spot after looking down at the laptop placed on the seat between them.

Rob got out of the car and looked up and down the road. There was no traffic in the mile he could view in either direction. The water in the stream gurgled as it moved downhill. The birds he could hear seemed high and far away. Though it was hot, he reached into the back seat and grabbed the tan windbreaker Amelia had bought him and put it on over his white shirt.

"Can you make it alright?"

"I think so," he answered.

Then he was off. He struggled to climb through the fence, and began to make his way up and across the field. He knew better than to try to run. He just put one foot in front of the other, or rather put his good right foot forward, and followed it as best he could with his dead left foot. Halfway up the rise the sheep took notice of him. They peered at him anxiously at first. The adults walked away slowly in either direction, and the young lambs made wild and inappropriate jumps and gambols.

By the time he made the trees his pulse was quick and pounding in his temples. It was cooler beneath the canopy, but deathly still. Perspiration soaked his clothing and pasted is hair to his forehead. He kept moving steadily, and then froze in a momentary panic when he heard a crashing in the underbrush to his right. But when he looked he saw the rump and raised white tail of a deer as it moved deeper in the woods away from him.

Rob knew from the Google map that it was not a thick stretch of woods that he needed to cross, but he was not making the progress he had in his imagination because of the uneven rise of the terrain, underbrush, fallen timber, the sponginess of the earth beneath his feet, and his own damnable weakness. But then he began to see a gradual thinning of the trees in front of him.

When he got to the border the land opened out into a pasture, bisected by a white fence running its full length. It ran as far as he could see left to right, from the top of one hill and into an indention, and then rose to another eminence to his right. The pasture was close to a half-mile wide, with waving blue-green grass, dotted in spots by wildflowers. Six or seven horses were grazing lazily, heads down, munching at the grass.

Across the field, sprawled along the length of the opposite ridge, was a tremendous mansion of brick and white board, with many dozens of windows, black in the sunlight, and a number of chimneys, like sentries, rising above the roof. To the left, or south side of the house, part of the land had been leveled and there was the fenced-in rectangle of a tennis court. He had no doubt there was also a pool behind. Rob could detect no movement in the house. There were three vehicles, two big SUVs and a long sedan, parked along the circular driveway in front of the house, and there was also a large detached two-storey garage to the south rising above the tennis court. One of the bay doors was opened, and the front grille and hood of a car could be seen inside.

The driveway dropped down to another copse of wood a quarter mile below, and through the trees Rob saw three of the pick-up trucks from Spencer's group, stopped and apparently empty, and unseen from the house above.

Rob wished desperately that he had binoculars. He was basically stuck at his vantage point. There was nothing to be gained by moving left or right along the edge of the woods because it wouldn't improve his view, and if he stepped into the open he knew he could be seen both from the house and from the pick-up trucks. His cell phone was in his pocket, but he was afraid to use it, not knowing if Spencer's group had some way to identify or track its signal.

So Rob stayed and watched. He saw no movement, except the grazing horses in the field. He heard nothing above the singing of birds and the buzzing of insects. Finally after ten minutes he detected movement near the pick-up trucks. He identified at least three forms in the shadows, waiting at the edge of the trees twenty-five feet from the trucks.

As he crouched there waiting for something to happen he began to remember the night before. Parts of it seemed like it had happened to someone else. But then he clearly remembered the powdery dry softness of Amelia's skin, and his own fullness when he had entered her, a feeling he had wondered if he would ever feel again. He recalled the impenetrable shadow of her above him, the tips of her breasts grazing his chest. He suddenly felt furiously adolescent, alone, getting a hard-on in the woods.

Then movement at the top of the woods pricked his dream. He saw four crouching figures emerge from the woods and move, bent low at the waist, across the clearing to the back wall of the garage. There was a delay, and then four more men followed. Once they got to the garage there was no way for Rob to follow their progress because there was an eight foot wrought iron fence, hung with ivy, that ran from the garage to the house. He wondered whose house it was, and who was in it, and he felt a twinge of dread at what might be happening to them.

He didn't know what he expected to happen, and the wait quickly became unbearable. Not many minutes later the front door opened and people began coming out. First came one of Spencer's men armed with an automatic pistol. Behind him came a line of female domestics, in uniform, hooded or blind-folded, hands bound in front of them, and all connected by a single line. After them came two more armed men. The servants, clearly terrified, were led away from the house and across the driveway, and forced to kneel in the grass. Rob's mouth went dry thinking that he might be about to witness the murder of these unfortunate people. Another person, a man, was led out of the garage. He was barefoot and in his underwear, and also bound and hooded. He was led across the gravel to join his workmates. Rob heard a raised voice and the captured group quickly sprawled, face first, on the grass. Rob heard terrified feminine crying, and the women huddled close together.

But there was no shooting. Instead they were threatened again, and then the four men in the assault began to move quickly down the hill, on the driveway this time. They were met by the others at the corner of the garage. As they retreated downhill, Rob heard four concussive pops, the tinkling of broken glass, and then for a moment…nothing. Then he saw smoke, and flames, swirling from an upstairs window. He also saw smoke rising above the roof from the back of the building. They had set the place on fire. By the time Rob realized it, they were gone, swallowed by the woods. More flames could be seen in the main house, and it was clear they had torched the garage too. It began to billow black smoke, and then there was an explosion, as if some accelerant had been ignited.

When he was sure the staff was safe, he turned and headed back through the woods, crashing through the underbrush in his haste. He came out of the trees further down the oblique hill, in front of the car. He raised his arms and Amelia started the engine and came up and met him as he crossed the road.

"We have to be very, very careful," he said. He explained what had happened, and pointed to where the smoke was beginning to rise in a broad charcoal gray above the trees.

"Was anyone left in the house?"

"I don't think so. If they were going to kill someone there, they wouldn't have left witnesses. This was a message. We have to get off the road. We can't afford that they may have noticed us on the way up, and if they were to see us here now, I don't think it would be a good scene for us."

Amelia sped ahead and five miles down the curving road they found a shady park and picnic area that ran next to the brook. Amelia entered and drove over the stone bridge and as far back as the road went, and parked behind a rock outcropping that shielded them from view from the roadway. When they stopped Rob saw that Amelia's hands were trembling, and her expression was one of being both dumbfounded and extremely apprehensive.

"Are you alright?" Rob asked, putting his hand on hers. He put down his window and they heard sirens in the distance. "We're fine here, I'm sure."

Amelia was staring at his hand. The heel of it rested on hers, which was engulfed beneath it.

"We can stop this whole thing, you know?" he said.

She looked right at him. "No, that's not it. I'm just trying to get a grasp of everything. Each new part we find adds another layer, more complexity…more size. Originally, I'm thinking, who killed Steven, and why? Was it a revenge thing? A jealousy thing? But now it looks like an ancillary thing, like a side-show…a subplot. What you're describing at that house is like a military exercise."

"That's what I thought," Rob said. "And the guys at the house just now, I didn't recognize any of them, either as residents of the Outer Banks, or from Spencer's photos. Davy Todd wasn't with them for this part of the program. He must have stayed at the road."

"But whose house was that?"

"Exactly. Because whoever owns it, we're not just talking about someone who is wealthy and has done well for themselves. This isn't the one percent, this is the one tenth of one percent."

Amelia opened her laptop and set it between them. "Let's see what we can find out from this. It's too early for there to be any news reports about the fire, but I want to find the site for the local paper so we can bookmark it and check later.

"Also, I'm worried about this car, and how visible it's become. I don't know if it's been observed or noticed, but if it has, we could be putting ourselves in real danger. I was thinking we could find a rental agency, at an airport maybe, and park this and then rent a car."

"That makes sense," Rob said. He had stopped thinking about how things were to be paid for, or how much they cost.

On her laptop Amelia found the closest airport renting cars was across the border in Connecticut, in Waterbury. It took forty minutes to drive there, both of them scanning the road and looking over their shoulders and in the mirrors as they went. They parked Amelia's car in long-term parking, took everything they needed, and went into the terminal. Less than an hour later they were in a new vehicle, a compact Toyota sedan, heading south into New York, and toward the interstate to take them back to Gettysburg.

Barely four hours later they were pulling into Kay's driveway. It was six o'clock, three full hours of daylight left. Amelia had called Kay from the road, told her they'd taken a spur of the moment excursion, and said they'd had car trouble to explain the change of vehicles. They had driven by the entrance to Spencer's campsite as they came back down Emmittsville Road. The trucks of the men who had fire-bombed the house in Poughkeepsie were not there, causing Rob and Amelia to wonder what further havoc they might be wreaking.

On their way back they stopped at a mall and bought a pair of binoculars. "One more thing," Rob said as they exited the camera store. They went into a bookstore and Rob bought a bird-watching book. "It gives me an excuse to be in the woods with the binoculars."

Kay had dinner waiting for them. Because of the hot weather everything except the corn on the cob was served cold. They were all hungry and garrulous in about equal proportions. Rob smiled and kept up his end, but for some reason he was mistrusting the new accelerated intimacy between himself and Amelia, or rather, he was mistrusting himself. He started seeing the thing as if he were looking at it in the rearview mirror.

"…Rob?" It was Amelia.

"Sorry, I'm drifting."

"More of anything?" Kay asked.

"No, I think I might go in the woods to see if I can find some birds."

"And leave us with the dishes?" Amelia asked, smiling.

"No, I'll help with those first."

"You'll do no such thing," Kay said. "Amelia and I can handle them. But did you know she tells secrets about you whenever you leave?"

"Well, you must be very gullible, or not easily bored."

Five minutes later he came down the stairs, binoculars in one hand, and field manual in the other. Amelia mouthed the word 'careful,' over her shoulder behind Kay who was leaning over the sink.

"Good luck then," she said aloud.

"You two do keep busy," Kay said.

Rob knew they could watch him as he crossed the pasture and went down to the entrance of the woods. He tried to keep his posture more erect and his steps more even, but the attempt only delayed him, so he went back to his one leg dominant shamble and quickly entered the dark confines of the trees.

He didn't look for birds, though he listened for their songs and tried to remember them as he moved along. With concentration he could differentiate a vast array of trills, chirps, peeps, squawks and whistles. It was as if the tops of the trees were in communication announcing his arrival and progress.

The binoculars slung around his neck bounced against his chest as he walked until he finally grasped them in his good right hand. He had some trouble getting up the incline at the falls because recent night rain had made the trail muddy, and he had to switch the field glasses to his left hand so he could grasp at saplings as he went up. He was pleased to find the stout walking stick he had left still hidden in the undergrowth at the top.

As he approached the camp from within the shadows of the trees, he again listened for any signs of human activity under the canopy. He moved more slowly and compactly, freezing at various points to scan the treescape and listen. He overshot the point where he had emerged from the trees on his previous excursion, but there were still outcroppings and brooding boulders to hide behind. Again everything at the camp appeared orderly and neatly arranged. He had arrived at dinnertime. Twenty men were seated at a long wood table by the cook wagon.

The binoculars made an amazing difference in Rob's ability to see and identify faces. There was Stennis, the assistant manager at the Sea Horse, who had been in the photograph Rob had first seen in the newspaper. Other faces he saw were more or less familiar, but he didn't recognize any of those from the raid on the house in New York.

The RV was still there, a looming bulk, dark and quiet except for the guard slowly patrolling around it. The whole mystery now revolved around the plans that were developed behind those darkened windows.

Beside the binoculars and the field book Rob had also brought a pencil and small notebook. He took them out of his breast pocket and began making notes. First came the head count, which ran to twenty-six. Then he made a diagram marking the positioning of the camp; tents, RV, meal wagon, fire pits, latrines, woodpiles, corrals. He recorded the names of those he recognized, and as he did he realized that he had never seen

172

Spencer…not on the trip up, or in the camp, and not on the paramilitary excursion to the north. But he had to think Spencer was there.

He was quickly losing daylight. He re-pocketed his notebook and pencil, slung his field glasses over his shoulder, and made ready to retreat back into the woods. Just before he made his move he detected motion on the hilltop to the east. Within a few seconds ten figures rose over the hillside and began to descend to the camp. Rob was sure it had to be the men they followed north. He wanted to stay to find out what would happen when they entered the group, but to do so risked losing all light and becoming lost in the darkened woods. He momentarily thought that if he waited for dark he could either return along the eastern margin of the woods using the moon and starlight to guide his way, or make a big circle around the field to the north over the next hilltop and head back to the road and return that way. Either option meant traversing uneven, rocky terrain on a poorly lit night, and it was too much of a risk to take. Reluctantly he backed into the trees, hesitated to make sure all was still, and then began to make his return to the house.

He had not gone far beneath the murky canopy when he stepped on a dry branch in the path and it made a report like a rifle shot. Rob looked back and immediately a dark figure popped up a hundred and fifty yards behind him. For an instant they stood staring at each other, but then Rob was off, trying to find a gear that would move him most quickly. He had only one chance; to get to the dark cave of underbrush that was the entrance to the trail down next to the waterfall, and hope whoever was following did not know of its existence. As he ran, limped, hobbled, he tried to do the math in his mind, calculating how far he had to go, how long it would take his pursuer to make up the intervening ground, and what could ultimately happen when he did.

He heard the sounds of his pursuer gaining on him, and his destination suddenly seemed farther than he had remembered. I'm not going to make it, he thought, and considered stopping right there to turn and confront whomever it was behind him. And then he was there. He ducked beneath the bush, grazing his face and cutting his cheek in the process. He clutched the shaft of the walking stick. Rob's best chance was the person chasing him didn't know the trail ended at the top of the falls. If he came by quickly enough, with this little light, and didn't know of it, there was a good chance he would go right over the edge. And then the heavy footfalls came and went right past him. Without thinking Rob followed, the walking stick held out in front of him. He rushed forward. His pursuer had seen the ledge in front of him, but it was too late. Rob came up to the man as he turned, his arms extending, rotating. In his right hand Rob saw the glint and flash of a knife, and when it registered, he thrust the stick squarely in the man's sternum and pushed with all his might. Only then did he look at the face, and he realized that behind the mask of terror, the eyes wide open and frantic, the mouth a perfect silent o, it was Chick.

Then he was gone, and a second later Rob heard a sickening thud. He was stunned. There would have been complete silence in the forest, except for the blood pounding furiously in his temples. He knelt, leaning on the stick, trying to get his breath, and then he half-retched. He tried to be still, to will his breathing to slow, but he quickly realized he couldn't stop moving.

He slid down the side trail, clutching the stick for balance, dreading what he would find. It was worse than he expected. Chick was lying on his back, arms out. His left leg was broken below the knee and bent out at an acute angle. He looked pressed flat against the rock. His eyes were open, searching the magenta sky above him. The blood was spreading, fanning out around his head. Rob didn't even want to think about what the back of his skull looked like. Black blood pooled in the fading light, and Rob realized that for the second time in his life he was examining a Rorschach test pattern of it beneath the body of an old friend.

No time, no time. He listened for any other sounds around him, half-expecting to hear the tromp of many feet closing in on him, but it was deadly silent. He looked for the knife that Chick had held, but he couldn't find it. Maybe it had clattered away into the stream. He quickly went through Chick's pockets, making sure not to step in any of the blood. There were keys in one front pocket, and a wad of cash in the other. There was a hundred on top, and when Rob flushed through the stack he realized they were all hundreds, thousands of dollars worth. So Chick was still being Chick. Here was Tanya getting ready to lose her house, and Chick had enough pocket money to forestall it if he had chosen to. In the pocket with the cash there was also something hard, metallic. He pulled it out. It was a pistol, a .22. He put the money and the gun in his pocket, and turned his head so he wouldn't see Chick's face as he strode away.

XII

"Please, please, don't say anything for a minute. My head is exploding."

It was. The pulse of blood throbbing through his temples felt as if it would cause his veins to burst. The fingers on his right hand were tingling, as were his nose and lips. His left side was peculiarly silent. At one point he thought he might keel over, and he turned his head from Amelia, so as not to alarm her any more than he already had. He sat quickly on the side of the bed, his head in his hands.

When he thought back over the last twenty-four hours it seemed like too much had happened too quickly. It was like being swept off his feet in the strong current of a flood, with rocks and debris beneath the surface, fallen trees above with limbs to trap and hold him down.

He had somehow gotten back to the house, hurrying, worried, incredulous. Amelia and Kay were still on the porch, no lights on, enjoying the deepening gloom. He almost hadn't seen them. He rushed by into the house, unable to answer their cheerful greetings because he was so choked with emotion and exertion, trusting Amelia to come up with excuses for him. Kay's "Is he alright?" trailed him as he went upstairs.

All he could see, all he could think about, was the last look on Chick's face before he went over the edge. Had Chick recognized Rob as he was pursuing him? He had to have. It was shadowy and mottled under the trees, and there was some distance between them at first, but Chick had steadily gained on him, and would surely have overtaken him had not the trail ended so abruptly. Chick knew how Rob moved. At some point it must have clicked whom he was pursuing, and yet Chick hadn't called his name. Rob would never have pushed Chick if he had known it was him…never. He might have beaten the shit out of him with his stick, but he would have left him alive enough to answer questions. Rob had known Chick and Steven were connected, and that Steven and Spencer were linked in their construction ventures, but he had never thought to hook Chick directly to Spencer…although it made sense now. Chick had always tried to work things from as many angles as he could, and he wanted every reward, no matter how small.

So when Chick had secreted Rob to his father's fishing shack that effort must have been to keep him on ice for Spencer. But why? Had Spencer killed Steven, and was he afraid Rob had seen or might remember something? And if that were the case, why not just eliminate him? If Rob, as a semi-homeless dishwasher, were found dead somewhere, or simply disappeared, there would have been few questions asked. Or maybe Chick really was protecting him from Spencer, or from somebody else.

Gradually his grainy, hoarse breathing subsided, though his head still thundered and he began to feel a constriction in his chest that he absolutely refused to acknowledge. He looked around the room. The dark, sturdy furniture further deepened the shadows. His confederate uniform was draped from a hook on the bathroom door, shoes neatly below. The incongruity of the battle re-enactments beginning in just days struck him. Playacting the most important battle in American history seemed like an important and even noble thing, except when he put it in context of the real battle that he was involved in, smaller though it was.

That was when Amelia came in. There were two conflicting expressions on her face. One was of concern for him. Rob knew he must not look well, and the pleading smile he gave her surely didn't help. Just beneath that concern though was giddy, unrestrained excitement. So Rob's plea for quiet temporarily deflated her. There was a moment she almost said something sharp to him, but instead she took her make-up bag and went into the bathroom.

Rob stood and walked jerkily to the foot of the bed and had to sit down quickly again. He really wanted a fucking drink. He imagined himself slinking away while Amelia was in the bathroom. He had already taken the car keys from the dresser. He went down the stairs quickly and surely, no limp, no dragging leg in his imagination, and out the front door without being heard by Kay, who was rattling around in the kitchen. He got in the car, started it, backed up, and screamed away down the driveway. He had Chick's money and pistol in one pocket, and he had the money Amelia had given him in the other. He would drive far enough that they couldn't find him, find one of those small old roadside bars, one with a Ham's light outside, and a big jar of pickled eggs on the bar, and soft pretzels, and soothing near-darkness, a few other patrons who minded their own business, and he would drink until nothing was real. He would hear Bruce

Springsteen and J Geils and Billy Joel on the jukebox, maybe Blondie. Then he would buy a couple of six-packs and hit the road, flip over in a ditch, and be found cold stiff and lifeless the next morning. Amelia could go back to looking for answers to the death of her father, and that would be the end of it.

Each second he hesitated Amelia was closer to returning and ruining his plan. But he didn't move. Gradually his breathing calmed, and he was able to put one thought in front of another instead of having them all in a raging jumble in his head.

When she came back into the room she did so timidly and with her eyes lowered. Obviously Rob's demeanor had frightened her, and she returned not sure what she would find. She looked furtively at him with the idea of sitting next to him on the bed, but when he didn't make any movement or look up, she tiptoed to her side of the bed and they sat with their backs to each other at right angles, staring at the walls.

Rob finally roused himself when he heard Kay come upstairs and go to her room. When he heard her TV come on and the garbled noise like voices riding up and down yoyo strings, he stood and went over to Amelia's side of the bed.

"Chick is dead."

"What do you mean?" she asked. "How do you know?"

"I know because I pushed him over the ledge at the little waterfall in the woods. I didn't know it was him until he was going over...I just knew someone was chasing me. He must not have been familiar with the trail because it comes to this overlook and just stops. The trail down is back a ways into the bushes. Someone had seen me and was after me. I went ahead as fast as I could, but he was gaining. I hid in the entrance to the trail going down, he rushed by. I had a big stick. I came out, he was right at the edge teetering, and when I saw a knife in his hand, which is all I really saw, I pushed him in the chest with the stick, and he went over. Right after I jousted him, I saw his face. Chick. And then he was gone."

Amelia didn't say anything. Her toes squirmed in her lavender slippers. They matched her light robe.

"I had just come back from watching their camp when he saw me. I don't know if he was gathering wood, or was on guard duty, or what. He gave chase, and I ran like...well, you can imagine, I wasn't going to get anywhere fast, and he was gaining on me. It was getting dark, but at some point he had to have realized it was me. If he had called out my name, I would have stopped." It still stabbed at him. "He was with Spencer. This whole time, he was with Spencer."

"Are you sure he's dead?"

"Yes."

She seemed uncomfortable. "Well, I don't know if I should tell you what I've found out or what?"

"No, please, go ahead. It can't get any worse."

"Well, from our trip up north, I saved the Google map of the mansion. I was able to find other maps with the route numbers and road names, and finally one that had address numbers. When I typed in the address for the mansion, the name Alexander Olsofsky came up."

Jesus, Rob thought, that's all we fucking need.

"And then I went to the TV news reports for this evening. They get their news out of Newburg. It was the lead story. 'Financier Alexander Olsofsky's home burns today. No injuries reported. Cause is said to be an electrical malfunction.'"

"That's bunk. The fire was started in four or five different places. Some kinds of charges were set. There were accelerants used. They know that."

"Maybe they're keeping mum while they investigate. Maybe they don't want to frighten the neighbors."

"That seems most likely," Rob said, and felt like he was quickly winding down. "So now we have it figured out. It's some kind of thing between Spencer and Olsofsky. Steven, and Chick, and Irina...or whoever was in that car, are collateral damage. We've figured it out. We're done."

"But that's just it. We're not done. If we knew it was Irina in the car that would be different. We could somehow give the authorities the information we have, and wash our hands of it. But neither of us thinks Irina was in that car. Both of us think she is in that RV at Spencer's camp. And until we know why she's in that RV, and if she needs to be rescued from it, we're not done...even if we want to be."

"But what if she doesn't want to be rescued? Maybe Spencer is protecting her from something. The cost is already high, too high. I've made it higher."

Amelia looked down at her slippers again. "The day after tomorrow the re-enactments begin," she said. "Let's just wait and see what happens with them. Or maybe Spencer's marauding band have another mission. There must be some kind of roster or muster so we can find out which engagements his groups is supposed to participate in."

Rob thought about the Walther plinker and the wad of cash in his pocket. He didn't know where the money came from, or who gave it to Chick, but knowing him as he did, he could understand that. But the pistol...what was that for? What was that description he had read of that kind of gun in a novel? It was Saul Bellow, he thought. And he called it a "toy of swift decisions." You would need a lot of luck to kill a moving man with it. You could surely fuck them up if the first shot was a good one. But if you were close enough to do damage and you missed, you were liable to be facing someone really pissed off and capable of a much bigger reply.

"Should we call the police?" Rob asked. "I feel badly about just leaving him there."

"I don't think we can. If we call, there will be authorities all over the place. It will draw attention to us. You're sure...he was dead?" she asked again.

Rob kept his head down and nodded.

"Then we just keep mum, and let them make their move. Maybe they'll think it was an accident. They will find him, and they won't leave him there. Then they'll be looking around to see what might have happened. We have a new car. They won't recognize it. They can't. You'll have to keep your head down."

"That might be a good idea. But I don't want you sticking your neck out."

"No, I won't. I'll take care of finding out what I can about Spencer's group's deployment for the re-enactments, and see if we can find a way to position you close to them. With thousands of people, and the uniforms and hats, and smoke and noise, and your new beard, you should be able to hover under their radar."

"I've been thinking that maybe we're wasting our time concentrating on the re-enactment aspect. After all, what could happen with all those people around? But after what we saw in New York, I don't know if I'd put anything past either side now."

180

"But what are the sides, Rob?" Amelia asked. "It's not like a case of one side wearing gray, and the other side wearing blue. This is bad though because Spencer is likely to think Olsofsky's responsible for Chick. It's another tit for tat."

He just shook his head.

"Rob, I got you something." Amelia stood and went to the small closet. She reached in and retrieved a long Enfield rifle, which she awkwardly handed to him. "I got it at a shop in Gettysburg yesterday, when you went into the woods. I knew you weren't going to ask, but you had to have something."

"It's beautiful," he said, but without much feeling.

"The man in the shop told me it's the kind most re-enactors use." She seemed to want to say more, but she didn't.

Rob wanted desperately to go to bed and escape into sleep and let his dreams sort it all out, but even thinking it, he knew it wasn't an option. Amelia had more questions and theories and musings, and he listened, offering what he could. But he kept seeing Chick's face, the look in his eyes, as he was going over the precipice. There was that instant of stunned surprise followed by Chick's recognition of him. Chick fell to his death knowing full well who sent him there. But that wasn't right. Rob didn't know it was Chick after him until the last instant, but Chick knew it was Rob he was chasing.

As he was talking to Amelia, and in the gradually expanding moments of silence, he kept picturing Chick as he had been in high school. Then his whole aspect, his whole raison d'etre, was to use his looks and personality to carry him from one scam to another. Whether he was trying to get into some shy sophomore's pants, or to get some petty criminal older brother of a friend to front him a pound of pot, his focus was to come up with whatever argument was needed to cut the deal. But he did it with such youthful, open-faced aplomb that Rob thought he had seen then the germination of an entrepreneurial seed that could have grown into a tree of wealth and success. But it hadn't. It wasn't just the hedonism or the drugs that had side-tracked him. It was also a lack of luck. It was an inability to position himself in the right place at the right time. A lot of success in life had to do with that. After only a few false starts and near misses, Chick had meekly surrendered to his place in the world. Rob went to bed thinking about that, and many other things. When Amelia crawled beneath the covers next to him, she intuitively knew to leave him to himself to sort it all out.

Rob woke the next morning and it was the last day before the re-enactments. It was still dark outside the windows, but Rob knew dawn was close because the birds had begun their tentative songs. Amelia was next to him sleeping on her back, her head propped on the pillow, snoring quietly toward the ceiling. There was no other noise in the house.

Rob lay there, almost paralyzed, unable to rise. Chick was there again, but only for a moment before he sent him back to the silence and the darkness. Rob was already thinking ahead. This morning he and Amelia were going to the staging area to get Rob's assignment, and to try to find information on the disposition of Spencer's group. Rob had more and more been worrying that locking himself into the re-enactments could potentially keep him from more important business. First of all, what if Spencer's marauding group had another assignment planned during the battle? Who would keep tabs on them? And if they all were participating in the battle, was there an opportunity to find out if Irina was in that RV?

He again looked over at Amelia. She shifted in her sleep, turning her back to him and heaving a sigh. Sex didn't have to complicate things, but sometimes it did. In this case, he and Amelia had gotten along well before the sexual component became a part of it. They answered something in each other. Whether sex added to that or not, he didn't know, but now external things were beginning to spin out of control and it was clear they were not going to stop spinning any time soon. They were both involved in this other thing, and neither one of them was backing off on that. But women often had trouble turning off the romantic, sexual part of things. He shook his head. He hadn't even gotten out of bed and his mind was already eddying out in a thousand different directions.

He got up and went downstairs, and an hour later Amelia followed him. By eleven they were mingling with the crowds at the staging area. Rob was nervous about being recognized at first, but he wore a wide, floppy hat that kept his face in shadows. By noon Rob had his unit assignment and Amelia had found the orders for the deployment of Spencer's troops for the first day. They drove as close to that area as they could, and walked the rest of the way after getting directions from a man they found standing in the field, already in Confederate uniform. He pointed them to the railroad cut, which was the part of the battle that Spencer and his men would be participating in on the first day. When she explained to the man that she wanted to set up her painting gear near enough to get the best view without being in the way, he whistled through his corncob pipe and pointed to a small promontory further down from the cut. From there, he said, she could get the best view of the Confederate retreat and the Union pursuit of them. Rob's role in the first day's skirmishes was to be a part of General Archer's unit which had formed the southern, right flank of the Confederate advance on that first morning.

What their positioning meant was that he and Amelia were going to be separated by the rise of a hill between them and a mile of distance. Their only feasible means of communication was with cell phones, which were not supposed to be carried during the re-enactments so as not to ruin the sense of realism. Rob and Amelia decided to carry theirs and keep them hidden, and set on vibrate in case of an emergency.

The population of Gettysburg had swollen greatly in the past days. Roads were clogged with people feeling their ways to their destinations, as well as locals trying to do their last minute provisioning so they could hunker down at home for the long three-day weekend. There were traffic tie-ups and fender benders, crying tires and angry horns.

Most of the visitors felt a patriotic anticipation prior to the re-enactments. Because the dates of the battle fell on the Independence Day holiday weekend, everything was wrapped and festooned with red white and blue bunting. Motels and campgrounds were all filled, and there were already many people in their costumes getting an early start on their nineteenth century alter egos.

They returned to Kay Yoder's house late that afternoon. Both had realized the import of Chick's death as it related to their ability to monitor Spencer's group at its command site. There was no way Rob could go back into the woods because even if Spencer's Confederates had found Chick and thought his death was an accident they would tighten their perimeter.

But the simple domesticity of their evening, with the leisurely meal, and the afternoon slowly melting toward nightfall, helped to calm them both. They didn't know if the re-enactments would pass with the expected tramping of feet, the crackling of small arms fire, and the booming of cannon, or if all hell, real hell, was going to break loose. With the evidence of the raid into New York, Rob now knew that Spencer was capable of almost anything. With his single-mindedness and abundance of resources there was no telling what lengths he might go to. As it was, Rob would bet that law enforcement in Poughkeepsie was baffled by what they had to know was a crime. Whatever had happened between Spencer and Olsofsky had clearly developed into a very vicious and personal feud.

While Rob helped Kay clean up after dinner Amelia went upstairs and laid out the clothes they would be wearing for the next few days. When he came up to fetch her to sit on the porch with Kay the outfits were spread out on the bed. Rob was impressed with what she had accomplished with such limited and ordinary materials.

The uniform she had made for him consisted of a faded gray shirt on which she had sewn wooden buttons, a pair of dingy yellowish pants, and scruffy and scratched leather boots. In the corner was his Enfield musket, the slouch hat to keep his face hidden, and a blanket roll of indeterminate green to be slung across his chest.

On Amelia's side of the bed, her outfit was more voluminous due to its dark gray hooped skirt, and layers of white petticoats and bloomers. Her bodice was a lighter, dove gray with rows of small buttons. The bonnet had a broad brim and was the same color as the skirt. The sashes to be tied under her chin were a contrasting dark blue. Her shoes at the foot of the bed were black with small heels and silver cross buckles.

They sat on the porch that evening. There was no wind and the air was heavy and still. Sounds traveled to them over long distances. There was the hiss of tires on far roadways, the rapid pops of a string of firecrackers, and then also the plaintive notes of someone practicing Taps on a bugle.

"The thing I find so hard to grasp," Amelia said, "are just the sheer number of men in the actual battle...and it happened here."

"I told you about the ghosts," Kay said, not then, but later. "There used to be ghosts in those woods back there."

Rob thought about them, and a newer ghost who was now making their acquaintances.

"The boys who fought here," Rob offered, "on both sides, are the same as the boys we have fighting now in Afghanistan, and were fighting a couple of years ago in Iraq. They're fighting to keep something in place that they don't really have a share in, though they think they've been promised a share, or at least a share has been implied."

More and more stars twinkled on in the sky above, and they watched them and listened to the sounds of their creaking rocking chairs, and the other farther away sounds in the night. They could see the glow of the town of Gettysburg rising to the sky in the northeast distance.

The next morning they were up well before dawn and put on their unfamiliar clothes mostly in the dark. They had loaded the rental car with Amelia's painting equipment and Rob's rucksack and musket. They drove in the dark, following the directions they had been given to the re-enactors' parking area. When they got there and had unloaded everything, Amelia gave Rob a spare key, just in case they were separated and he needed to get somewhere.

For the days of the re-enactment, the battlefield at Gettysburg was like a big fair. There were vendors, horse rides for the kids, historical presentations by actors in costume, food tents, souvenir stands, cannon firing demonstrations, mock cavalry charges, military bands and impromptu hootenannies, tours of the re-enactors' military camps of both sides. The whole battle, of course, could not be portrayed. Each year the historical committee would choose which parts of the engagements they would present, and would write scripts that could be delivered over loudspeakers by announcers ensconced in towers similar to those used in golf tournaments.

For Rob's part he had been assigned to General James J. Archer's Brigade. In the real battle in 1863, their first encounter with Gamble's Union cavalry began the conflict. With neither side knowing the strength of the other on that initial day, the fighting was sporadic, the Confederates pushing ahead, and Gamble retreating for a distance, then dismounting to fight a delaying action, then retreating again. There were two main episodes the re-enactors would portray on this, the first day of the 151th anniversary of the battle. Spencer's group would take part in the struggle to control the railroad cut, at first a victory, and then a defeat for the Confederates. Rob's group would show the skirmishes that led to the death of Union General John Reynolds.

Rob left Amelia by the grandstands as the sun was coming up and went to find his assignment. He found the group of a hundred or so men milling

185

around back at a corralled area off the main parking lot. One man in an incongruous over-large orange t-shirt was working to line up the arriving men in rows, trying to get a head count, and another was passing out a printed sheet outlining their overall role and movements for the day. These gathering men, among whom Rob found himself a part, were newcomers to the role-playing. The veterans of earlier re-enactments did not need to take part in this training. They were back in their camps playing their nineteenth century parts for the roaming families who were beginning to arrive en masse on the scene.

The most obvious thing about the group by the parking lot was that they were middle-aged men mostly, overweight a lot of them, perspiring, out of shape, bearing little resemblance to the lean, battle and campaign-hardened Rebels they were going to portray.

The early morning was warm and steamy. As the sun rose, small and red, pockets of mist could be seen in the low areas and above the streams that meandered through the valley. They marched as a group up a rise and then back down into another small valley. It became lighter and the incongruities of the scene became more apparent. There were men driving around in golf carts, checking on the musters of the different groups, and gauging the progress in their training. There were the metal towers, some with platforms for announcers, some mounted with speakers to keep the crowd apprised of the armies' progress. It began to look like a cross between an outdoor rock show and a meeting of two tipsy middle-aged paramilitary units in a march off.

The drill sergeant assigned to their squad was a veteran of eighteen Gettysburg reenactments who hailed from the mountains of Georgia. He was a big man, 6' 3" or so, 250 lbs., with a substantial belly and a wide grin set in a doughy face. By 7 AM, and even though his men were doing all the marching and turning, his face glistened with perspiration and the collar and underarms of his bright shirt were soaked through. The marchers were serious in their efforts, but often the results were delays in responding to orders, men running up on the heels of those in front of them when a halt was called, heads ducking to avoid rifle barrels swinging around recklessly when a right or a left turn was called.

There was a rising excitement among the men in their small group as the mist lifted and it became apparent that there were troops all over the

186

floor of the valley participating in the same drills they were. Company flags fluttered above some of the groups, and occasionally a bugle call could be heard, or the small distant pops and then rise of a shroud of smoke when re-enactors tested their weapons.

All to the west of the shallow stream that ran through the bottom of the valley the colors of the uniforms were gray with dashes of butternut and yellow. On the eastern side and rising gently to the woods beyond, in front of what Rob realized was the wall of Cemetery Ridge, the uniforms were blue. At the base of the ridge, a half-mile from the stream, cannon were being unlimbered. The hastily assembled cavalries of both sides were also drilling, sinuous single- and double-file lines that meandered on the hillsides, bridles jingling, hooves clomping.

The sergeant of Rob's small squad was frustrated. His face became redder and his voice rose in pitch and became more strident. His charges had more trouble concentrating and comporting themselves as more and more re-enactors took to the field. By eight o'clock Rob reckoned their number to be in the thousands. Rob thought that confusion in the field mirrored the confusion that had occurred on that first morning in July over a century and a half ago. In 1863, neither side, as they began making the first tentative contacts with each other, had any idea of the strength of the other. It was almost as if some weird martial magnetism had drawn the armies together.

Suddenly Chick's face was in front of him again and it brought him back to the serious business he and Amelia were about. He usually didn't try to ascribe motives to people. But when he was still, he wondered about her. He looked down at the dirt in front of him and a drop of perspiration fell off his nose and spun lazily to the ground. Amelia should be setting up her easel three quarters of a mile to the north. He looked in that direction. He began to think of music that reminded him of the Civil War; Neil Young, Uncle Tupolo, Drive-By Truckers, the Band. Gradually now the audience was also arriving, obvious because of the brightness of their vacation clothes. Pillowy cotton clouds dotted the long summer sky. The breeze came gently from the south, brushing over the earth, drawing up heat and moisture. It was warm already, but the promise was for a sauna-like heat to be arriving later in the day.

It turned out that their squad leader, Sgt. Barefoot, was not only the veteran of eighteen Gettysburg re-enactments, but had also participated in reenactments at Antietam, Manassas, and Shiloh, in Tennessee. He was a life-long resident of northern Georgia, and a long-time Civil War history buff.

"For those of you who haven't participated before, you have to realize the kind of fighting we're talking about. These battles were basically lines of men marching toward each other, stopping to fire volleys into the opposite line, reloading as they advanced or retreated, and then stopping and firing again. It was reckoned that a competent veteran could reload and fire three times a minute. Meanwhile the opposing artilleries were trying to find the right positions to best strike and annihilate their enemies.

"These men faced death, possibly hell, maybe heaven, sometimes for days at a time. The Union generals knew they could never beat Lee. Their only chance was to keep throwing fresh men and equipment at him because they knew he would eventually run out of both." He pulled a red kerchief out of his back pocket and mopped his broad brow. His hair was wet and his face was flushed. "We are in Brig. General Archer's brigade, in Major General Henry Heth's 2nd Division. We are soldiers from Alabama and Tennessee, probably farmers, probably poor. We don't own plantations or slaves. We have been expressly told over and over again that this fight is not about slavery, it's about states' rights." He shook his head and smiled at something to himself. "That little stream down there is Willoughby Run. We will encounter Gamble's Union cavalry unit who will harass us while they make a slow retreat in hopes that reinforcements will come up to support them. We will press forward against them, cross the Run...on the other side Gamble will be supported by the arriving troops of Major General John Reynolds, including some Michigan troops, the 24th, the famous Iron Brigade. Even with these reinforcements we will force the Yankees to retreat until General Reynolds rides up to rally them. He will come to the front of their line, raise his sword, and be shot dead out of the saddle. That was one of the climaxes of the first day of battle in 1863, and it will be the high point of our day today."

More tourists were arriving, older couples arm in arm, families with kids in strollers. Magnified voices could be heard rising on the wind coming from one of the towers where an announcer was testing the sound system.

188

Rob looked up and down the line he was in. Of the twenty people, he saw two who might have been around thirty. The rest were mostly forty or so, with a few around fifty, and a couple Rob's age or older. Next to him was a tall thin, decidedly young man with a prominent nose and red hair creeping out from beneath his kepi hat. Like everyone else he was perspiring, little rivulets running down from his sideburns. His Adam apple rode up and down as if he were afraid of something, or maybe he was thinking back to an ancestor or someone known from his home area. His eyes shifted under his bushy strawberry brows, and he would mumble something to himself, the same thing, Rob thought, over and over again.

"Are you alright?" Rob asked.

The man looked at him as if he were speaking another language, and then smiled and shook his head. "I'm sorry," he said, his face transforming itself into a more relaxed neutral expression. "I was just overwhelmed for a moment. Two of my direct relatives, my great-great maternal grandfather and his brother were killed here...one hundred fifty one years ago." He looked around. "Was the sky like this that day? Did the fields look like this? The trees?"

"It's overwhelming," Rob said, moved by the man's obvious emotion. "Talk about hallowed ground."

The man on the other side of Rob was listening, and he leaned forward now, nodding his head. "Them damn Yankees, they must've all become bankers now."

Rob and the red-haired man laughed, and so did a few others in the vicinity. But then they heard an order from the sergeant and they were moving forward. They tried to maintain their line over the uneven ground, and keep up with the other lines of the squads to the left and right of them. When he looked to either side Rob was stirred and impressed by the numbers. There were hundreds of men moving forward, flags undulating and flapping in the breeze, sunlight glinting off the metal from the rifles and belt buckles. Behind some of the lines, officers rode prancing horses, the animals apparently aware of their height, and proud of their roles. Rob's sergeant moved behind their group, speeding stragglers up, and exhorting them on.

Within moments many of the middle-aged men around Rob were struggling to keep up. Rob himself moved doggedly forward. The day had just begun. He would not allow himself to think about discomfort. And this was just practice, military drilling, after all. This was only the rehearsal. The performance was for later in the day, evening almost, when it had cooled a bit. All around him was the small padded thunder of marching feet, although it couldn't be said that they were marching in unison. The dust rose from the ground beneath the marchers as they made their way down the slight incline toward the stream, Willoughby Run, which they would cross and then encounter the Union troops.

"Keep that line straight and moving," chided the sergeant.

Beyond the rise to the north Rob heard the popping of small arms fire and saw smoke drift up above the crest. Amelia came back to his mind again, this time with no doubts. She was there, over the hilltop, standing at her easel. He knew her. She had set it up out of the way of the action, and yet close enough that she could see what she needed to see. Spencer was there, somewhere near her, wearing a new uniform, astride his horse. His uniform had some kind of bright accent calling attention to him, and he was erect in the saddle.

As he moved mechanically forward, sweat dripping into his eyes, Rob felt away from the action, like he was on the outskirts of it. His unit gradually made their way down the mild grade, trying to keep some semblance of the lines together. They would encounter the Union troops after they had forded the shallow run. Rob could see it a hundred yards ahead of them, its banks guarded by the low bushes, nourished with the help of the running, bubbling water. Even moving downhill was a struggle, and not just for him. The ground was uneven, with loose rocks everywhere, abandoned animal holes, and natural rises and indentions. Rob kept thinking they would see the Union forces on the other side of the stream, but he guessed they were either drilling in the shade within the margin of the trees, or perhaps beyond the first cut of them. Again he tried to put himself in the place of the Confederate soldiers in the actual battle. He tried to imagine the hardness of the men, the tenacity, the stoic endurance. As he looked ahead of him, he realized that all the marching, maneuvering and fighting after the Willoughby Run would be done uphill. What was even more daunting was that at first the land rose gently, but after the woods the angle moved more and more away from the horizontal, appearing the get to at least 45 degrees further up the hill. Rob knew that the main problem with the Confederate battle plan was that after the first day they had pursued and chased the Union forces uphill and left off the fighting with the Northerners controlling the high ground.

"Halt!" Sergeant Barefoot bellowed.

The men slid and stuttered to a stop, looking around at each other and back at the Sergeant.

"About face!" the sergeant called, and the men turned around. "Now march."

Fifteen minutes later they were back where they started. Sergeant Barefoot allowed them to sit and drink from their round canteens as he went toward the next group to their right to discuss things with the sergeant from that unit. There were officers on horseback further up the hill, but they did not seem interested in what the ordinary troops were doing. As they squatted in the dust, the red-haired man next to Rob pulled a small bag from his breast pocket and began to roll a smoke. Other men pulled chaws of tobacco out of tins and wedged them in the corners of their mouths.

"We'll do shooting now," one of the men said.

"Shooting what?" Rob asked.

"Not shooting anything, just practicing how to shoot once the reenactment begins. It's kind of funny really. You don't aim at them Yankees, and they don't aim at you. It's a safety thing. We aim like we're all shooting at birds overhead."

"And you can't even pretend you're using your ram rod," the red-haired man said. "They don't want any accidents, or any eyes poked out by flying ram rods."

"We just have to get the timing right," the first man said. "They want two, maybe three volleys a minute."

A few minutes later they heard the sounds of multiple small arms firings from over the hill to their right, and a half-minute later they heard another volley, the shots closer together, and the space between the two was punctuated with cannon fire.

Sergeant Barefoot returned from his meeting and the squad did begin firing practice along with the other squads that made up their part of General Archer's Brigade. The men began to cohere into a unit. They became more prompt at following the sergeant's orders, and crisper in their execution. Gradually they began to understand their parts and what was

191

going to be required of them. A few officers on horseback came by to observe. With hands resting on their saddle pommels, they leaned down to offer advice and exchange views with Sergeant Barefoot.

The last part of these morning exercises was to gather the three hundred or so soldiers of Archer's brigade together and have them move as a unit down the hill toward the stream again, this time firing as they went. The increased numbers made their lines more ragged and their progress a bit more halting, but they were believable as they moved forward, stopping to fire at their invisible enemy, and then going forward again. They went down to the stream, turned and retreated up the hill, and then repeated the whole drill.

"Steady, boys," Sergeant Barefoot yelled in a deep resonant voice. "Keep moving down at them…keep that line together now. Be prepared to load and fire!"

At that moment they heard the chatter of small arms fire over the hill to their left, and then an answering fire from in front of those invisible troops, and then the deeper rumble of what must have been Union artillery. Rob immediately got a prescient feeling about what a rebel foot soldier might have felt at the beginning of those most important days of the war.

"Load!"

All the black powder guns they used were stopped, their barrels sealed. Because the blanks caused an ignition and explosion in the barrel chamber, nothing was allowed to be put in the barrel; no ramrods, no wadding. Rob, as well as most of the other re-enactors knew it had taken 20-30 seconds to reload their '53 Enfield muskets, which was the weapon most of them carried. The most common method of approximating the loading process was to kneel and put in their black powder charge and count off the twenty-five seconds. As Rob did it he thought about the soldiers on both sides who had participated in the real battle. Those twenty-five defenseless seconds must have expanded in their minds and spread out.

And they must have realized after their first few times under fire that there was no use hurrying. It had to be done and done right.

And then they were finished with the rehearsal.

"Lunch time," the red-haired man said, as they stood in line waiting to be dismissed.

"Gentlemen," Sergeant Barefoot yelled down the line. "This concludes our training for this morning. We will muster here, at this spot, at 15:30 hours, 3:30 to you civilians, to find our positions for the battle, which will begin at five. I know I don't have to warn you men not to go back to camp and start drinking beer, nor to engage in any other forms of cutting-up or mischief as would impair your ability to perform this afternoon. Dismissed!"

The men looked up and down the line at each other, and then began to step forward and backward out of formation. Within a minute they were all headed in different directions. Rob looked up to where the sun laid a broad shimmering yellow light over everything. He was perspiring heavily in his clothes and the sweat dripping down to his hands made the heavy weapon difficult to hold. His feet were loose in his boots, except around the ankles where they were rubbing the skin raw on his lower shins. He needed to find another pair of socks or some cloth to help his feet fill the boots properly. He thanked goodness for the wide brim of his hat.

He turned and began to make the shallow rise to the north, over which Amelia was supposed to have set up her easel somewhere near the grandstand. There was still sporadic small-arms fire beyond the crown of the rise, though whether they were still rehearsing, or whether it was some kind of demonstration, Rob couldn't tell. The scattered trees on his uphill climb all had their heavy green summer mantles, and the darkness beneath them looked cool and inviting.

As he reached the crest and looked into the next valley he was struck by the incongruity of the panoramic scene spread before him. There were hundreds, maybe thousands, of men in blue and gray scattered across the bed of the broad indention. To his left, toward the west, was a squad of Union cavalry milling around in a large circle throwing up a low dust cloud as the hooves churned up the drying grass. To the east he saw the muzzle flash of an artillery piece, and a second later felt and heard the dull thump of its report.

Then, also from the north, came a line of three golf carts zipping re-enactment officials from one meeting to another. In front and below him were the grandstands, only partially filled now with brightly dressed observers under hats and parasols watching the activities. There was a trail of them moving over the hill to the south toward the re-enactors' camps and vending and demonstration areas. They mingled with the soldiers, both blue and gray, heading back for lunch, or a lecture, or a shopping trip to the sutlers' shops, and maybe a nap.

Rob scanned the expanse for any sign of Amelia. She had said she was going to set up near the grandstands, and that's where he concentrated his search. But she wasn't at either end. He trudged down the path alone, the others of his unit having taken the fork that led back to the re-enactors' camp. As he sometimes did when he was in a broad open space, he thought of Kelly. He had an immediate urge to shut the thoughts off, shunt them like the cars of a train onto an unused track, but instead he relaxed and surrendered himself to them. When he thought about her life now, the edges of it so narrowly protracted, so rigidly determined, it brought out clutching feelings of terror in him if he imagined them trading places. Of course, anybody could get used to anything, but he could not picture himself living within those constraints. The last time he had talked to her mother, a year or so ago, Jane had told him that Kelly had found religion, and had been baptized, and it had transformed her. Rob didn't believe it. He couldn't imagine it. But he could see it from the standpoint of her trying to find something to affix her consciousness on, something outside herself that would at least seem to mitigate her situation.

But then Amelia had arranged for him to visit her. When Kelly first came into the room where he had been waiting nervously, the most obvious thing, aside from the Bible that she held in two hands in front of her, and the simple gold crucifix around her neck, was the serenity. Her smile was guileless, open, and full of grace and forgiveness. And after their long initial discussion Rob realized that, although he didn't think she believed everything she said she believed, she had found some meaning and had gained an ability to expand her consciousness beyond the walls that held her.

He thought about her punishment. They had made an example of her. Part of the reason was because the victims were young and attractive, and two of them were from the Outer Banks. Their families came after Kelly wanting blood. Could he blame them? They made noise and kept making noise. Their grief became righteous hatred. Kelly had to pay. It was ironic because every other year on the Outer Banks some local drunk hit a guest worker riding their bike on the shoulder of the road. None of them stopped. They drove on and left their victims crumpled and broken on the shoulder of the road to be found like cold origami the next morning. The drivers all dumbly claimed the same thing. They thought they might have hit a deer. And they all got off with nothing more than a slap on the wrist. They got off because their victims' families were not near. Rob was also convinced that whatever the federal authority told those families of their tragic loss they also tried to mitigate the circumstances so as not to make the guest worker program, or Americans in general, look bad.

He approached the grandstands, coming down the hill behind it. By now most of the tourists were gathering their belongings, and trying to corral their kids, to join the trail back.

The broad bowl in front of the stands spread out before him. The large swale itself was mostly empty of trees, only a few copses here and there rising from the long grass that in many areas was waving green, but in some spots was yellowing and turning brown and crisp from the summer heat. Squads of cavalry were still drilling, riding in formation, or making broad thunderous charges, pennants snapping furiously, and the dust and broken chaff rising gray and red behind the horses' hooves. In the foreground a squad of mounted artillerymen raced across the flats and up the far rise, small howitzers and ammunition caissons bouncing behind on their stiff wooden wheels.

It wasn't until Rob came around the edge of the grandstands that he spotted Amelia. She was a hundred yards past, her easel and art kit set up beneath a tree. Around her were Confederate horsemen, three mounted, another pair dismounted, holding the reins of their nodding horses. A tall man stood in front of Amelia, broad feathered hat beneath his arm, bowing slightly as he looked down at her. They were having some kind of serious discussion. At one point the man made a sweeping gesture with his hat, pointing to something across the field. Amelia's eyes followed, and she nodded again in agreement at something that was said. From the distance, Rob could only tell that the man was middle-aged and fit, and that he filled out his mustard-gray uniform. He stepped around and looked at her work on the easel, and again he nodded, more animatedly this time. Then he retreated, retrieved his reins from the man on the horse next to his, put on his hat, and mounted. In unison the horses turned and cantered away.

Rob waited until they were far away across the field before he came out from under the grandstand shadows. There were still people filing away on the trail between Amelia and him so he didn't think she could see him. When he was sure the squad of cavalry was far enough away Rob began to hobble forward toward her. He crossed through the line of spectators and saw Amelia was collecting her things, but looking up in his direction as she did so. As Rob separated from the line and made his way closer, she finally recognized him and quickly stood straight up. He couldn't see the expression on her face, but he suddenly felt relaxed by the simpatico between them. Something almost like tenderness rose up in him.

But then, before he could really recognize or acknowledge the feeling, Amelia took a step forward and put up a hand obviously ordering him to halt. He did. He stood there wavering, trying to understand what she was getting at. She stepped back into the shadows beneath the tree and looked out over the field in the direction the horsemen had retreated. When she looked back at Rob, and he was still standing there, she again stepped forward and held out her hand, this time emphatically signaling for him to go back. He turned and retreated, pulling the brim of his hat down and trying to mitigate his limp as he walked back to the grandstand.

When he was beneath the safety of its shadow again, he looked back. Amelia had finished packing her kit, and now across the field, coming back toward her, was the same group of horsemen. But this time they had with them a small buggy with a black bonnet, bouncing along the uneven ground, pulled by a sturdy quarter horse, a man in a t-shirt with a yellow stripe down the leg of his pants holding the reins. When they got to Amelia the man in the buggy got out, helped her load her things, and then helped her up into the seat. He climbed in next to her and shook the reins. The horses and the buggy all turned as one, although this time they didn't return across the field, but went in the opposite direction away from Rob, rising over the hill and disappearing behind it.

Rob stood under the edge of the grandstand in the shade, musket slung over his shoulder. He unscrewed the cap of his canteen and took a long slug of the warm, metallic-tinged water. For a moment, he was at a loss. He and Amelia had not discussed what to do were they to be separated. He didn't know whom she had driven off the field with, although her keeping him away made Rob think it must have to do with Spencer. What had led her to leave with them was a mystery. She had taken some of her painting supplies and a camera, so perhaps she had been approached to make a portrait of them as a group.

After a few more minutes of speculation, he turned and headed slowly back toward the rental car. When he found the car, he left a folded note clipped under the wipers. "Gone to the re-enactment camp to wait it out until the battle. When you finish what you're doing, find me."

XIII

The re-enactment camp at Gettysburg was an amalgam and a series of contradictions. While many of the re-enactors strove slavishly to bring back the realities of Civil War era life, many of the vendors were there just to make a buck, re-load their trailers and panel trucks, and drive on to the next fair or battle stop. But they were doing their entrepreneurial duty. They were giving the people what they wanted. For every small booth displaying hand-stitched period costumes, there was a thin man with a rumbling cough with three day's growth of beard shoving a paper stick in a whirring metal machine and twirling out pink cotton candy. Rob wandered through the crowd, pulling at his gimpy leg as if it were something following him. He drifted to a food stand, stepping around picnic tables where lunch patrons were pulling French fries from cardboard boats and dipping them in runny lakes of ketchup. At the counter he bought a 12 oz. bottled water for $2.50.

The crowd was thick and plodding. All around him were pink and red faces glistening under ball caps and straw boaters. Kids ran screaming under-foot, ignoring their parents' threats and admonitions. Rob kept walking until he passed the last stand and entered the area where the re-enactors were bivouacked. Most of the camps were small, four or five tents set up behind low rope fences. Some had period wagons and horses out back, dark animals with their heads down nosing hay on the ground. A few of the camps were larger, with long straight rows of white tents with nests of muskets by the front flaps and re-enactors walking to and fro, their blue or gray tunics taken off and shirts sleeves rolled up in the heat.

Rob drifted through, perspiring beneath his clothes, using his kerchief to mop his brow beneath the brim of his hat, his musket becoming heavier with each step. At first he was just looking for some cool shaded place to stop and rest, hopefully a tree with spreading branches and a thick canopy of leaves, with a soft, mossy place beneath where he could lean against the trunk, draw his hat over his eyes and sleep within the brightness. However every shaded place in the loose confines of the camp was already occupied; with cooking and eating areas, or set about with camp-stools and benches. Everyone had the same idea.

He stopped in the middle of the dusty walkway, unsure whether to continue on another third of a mile past the end of the camp where a hill rose and there were shade trees scattered about the crown, or return to the vendors' area and sit in he shadow of one of their great tents.

"North Carolina, hey, North Carolina!" Rob heard a basso voice calling from a group of tents. He turned and saw a man in shirtsleeves with suspenders unslung standing amid a group of seated men who were eating lunch. Rob recognized him from the rehearsal that morning. He waved Rob over, and with nothing even like a decision Rob turned and went in their direction. "North Carolina," the man said again as Rob came near, and the others raised their heads from their mess kits and greeted him.

Their seats were arranged in a circle under the branches of an oak tree. Rob came over, dried acorns crunching and rolling under his feet. The man who called him, one of those mustering with Sgt. Barefoot, whose name Rob remembered was Phelps, had retrieved another camp stool from behind the tree and was beckoning Rob to it.

"Mr. Phelps," Rob said as he arrived in the circle.

"What's your name, North Carolina?" Phelps asked.

"Rob Wheat, from Kill Devil Hills."

"Sounds like a good fighting town," one of the other men said, and the rest laughed.

"Sounds like a made-up town," another said.

"Whereabouts is that?" asked another.

"It's on the Outer Banks…"And when he got no reaction, "on the coast."

"We're the 1st Tennessee Provisional Army, under the command of Major Felix G. Buchanan," Phelps said. "Sit, sit Mr. Wheat. Let us get you a plate."

As Rob sat, Phelps went over to the black metal pot suspended above the fire and ladled Rob a plate of stew. Rob wasn't really hungry, but he ate it to be polite, and because he was anxious for the company, and for the opportunity to blend into the scenery.

"You probably want some water too," another younger man said.

Rob nodded and unslung his rucksack, and swung it around in front of him to retrieve his tin cup. The man took it and went to the largest of the tents that made up their unit. In the shadows of it Rob saw him bend from the waist and fill the cup from a five gallon plastic jug set on a stand with a spigot, like you might see set up in some office.

"We're discussing politics," another man said as Phelps and the young man returned with Rob's food and drink.

"I don't know if I can be of much help there," Rob said.

"Mr. Yount was saying," Phelps began, ignoring Rob's demurral, "that he felt like an indentured servant in the house he supposedly owns and has been living in for almost twenty years. Tracy here then says that it's because we live under and at the behest of a closed oligarchy, even though he knows none of us know what that means."

"What it means," Tracy said, and Rob recognized him as the gangly red-headed man from the muster, " is that we're ruled by a very small group of people who have all the money and control the politics and business. They make the rules, or they pay the politicians to have the rules bent in their direction. Have you ever heard of a lobbyist?"

"They've worked hard for what they have," another man said. He was sitting like a Buddha with his round belly straining at his t-shirt. "You just want to tax them and take their money so you can use it for what you want. We have the highest tax rate in the entire world, from what I hear."

"That's what I call the 'Paris Hilton's Bitch' syndrome," the younger man said. His red hair was draped around a face, framing a riot of freckles and a fine blonde wispy beard.

A number of men slapped their knees and hooted.

"What did you say?" the Buddha asked.

"I called it the 'Paris Hilton's Bitch' syndrome. Look at her. You said, 'They work hard for what they have.' Does she? She's not spending money she made, except the money she got in that porno sucking black dick."

Again there were hoots and catcalls.

"This isn't even money her father made," the flushed red-head continued. "She's living like a queen on money her grandfather made! And she's got you chanting, 'Don't raise taxes on the rich. They're the job creators.' How many jobs has she created? How many porno cameramen, hairdressers, chauffeurs, private chefs, steroided up bodyguards do you think she needs?"

"You've just found one crazy example…"

200

"I'll give you another. Who, as a group, makes more income than any other group in the country? Hedge fund guys. Look at the Forbes 500, and there's probably seventy-five or eighty of them in there. These are guys who can and do make hundreds of millions of dollars a year…each. What's their tax rate? Fifteen percent. Capital gains rate, carried interest rate. The richest mother fuckers in the country and they pay a lower rate than you. How? Because they own the politicians who write the laws. We do have one of the highest tax rates in the industrial world, but none of the rich pay that rate. They've got deductions and exclusions that they've had written into the laws, and accountants and lawyers to show them where to find them. Say you win the lottery tomorrow, a hundred million dollars. Well, the government is going to take 50 million before they even write you the check. But a financier, or a hedge fund guy, or a CEO, or one of those hillbilly Walton's, there's ten or twelve of them on that list…he can make a hundred million, and you can bet he's not even paying close to twenty percent, and he'll be bitching about that."

"You sound like a goddamn communist, Red."

"No, I'm just saying, things have gotten skewed. The whole thing about this country is that they say," he said, an then he looked around the group, his eyes shining and earnest, "you can have the American dream. If you work hard and make the right decisions, you can be one of the elite. You can be upwardly mobile. But more and more, that's not true. You might think that it's because of the recession that middle class wages are flat or falling, but they've been falling for thirty years. Productivity has gone through the roof. Tasks that involved forty people forty years ago now require two. And that's fine. But are the two who are left making any more money? No. The wages for those thirty-eight displaced workers have gone straight to the top, to the CEOs and principle stock holders. But there's still three hundred plus million people in this country, and we've now gotten to a position where 80% of the money is going to the top 2-3 percent. How is that right, or even make sense? In the last thirty years the worth of the bottom eighty percent of the country has dropped by twenty percent, and in that same period the worth of the top five percent has increased a hundred fold. Again, how does that even make sense?"

The other men were looking at the speaker, taking in what he was saying and trying to put their own spins on it. Some clearly agreed with him, and some clearly didn't.

"No matter how you look at it, it's a structural problem. They had a similar dilemma in ancient Rome. They had a large unemployment problem, larger than ours, but we're headed in that direction, and they wisely saw a possible danger in social unrest. So they did two things. They distributed food every week, and they opened the circuses where the populi could watch bloody gladiatorial combats or Christian virgins being torn apart by wild beasts. We do the same things, but it's welfare and the NFL on flat-screen TVs."

"It's the goddamn unions," Troy, a tall lanky man said.

"Whoa, whoa, whoa!" came a chorus of voices.

"Don't be saying that," one of them said. "You're a farmer, Troy, and we all respect that. But my daddy was in the union, and I know for a fact that the unions in this country are what made the middle class. Before unions, the boss said jump, and all the worker could say was, how high?"

"North Carolina," Mr. Phelps cut in, "what do you say about all this?"

"Well, first a point of fact. I think Red here has confused Paris Hilton and Kim Kardashian. Paris provided the template for becoming famous using a porno released without her knowledge...or saying it was released without her knowledge. Kim used Paris' guide, and she was the one sucking black dick. Paris was exclusively polishing white nob."

"Point taken, " the red-headed man conceded amid the snickers.

"As for the rest of this, I say, like everything in this world, it's a matter of balance. It's like me trying to walk. Since my stroke, my right side is my strong side, and it's dragging my left side along. So my right side is like the elites in this society. They have the strength and resources, and they choose the direction. But now they're getting resentful, because they say they have to drag more and more dead weight. But they've created that weight by outsourcing and union-busting and inflating bubbles and stratifying the society. So now they've cleverly made allies of the hard-working yobs who still have jobs and believe in the dream that they can make it too. And yet these workers see a portion of their hard-earned wages going to feed and clothe the shiftless and unworthy, forgetting that some of those shiftless and unworthy were working next to them a few months or a year ago, until

202

they were laid off and their workload was added on to those who stayed. And the elites start the chant for lower taxes, and the hard-working masses join in saying, yes, why should I send my money to Washington where a lot of it is wasted? But the elites want the taxes lowered for themselves, even though they've already purchased from the politicians all the exemptions and deductions and exclusions. They don't want the rabble to know that the top two percent control more of the assets than the bottom fifty percent combined."

"You're sounding like Red now," Buddha said.

"I'm just saying what I think," Rob replied, looking at the man. "They say we're in a slow recovery. So let me ask you, have you recovered anything? Are you back to where you were? Did you know that in this slow recovery, which is actually measured in trillions of dollars, that all of it has gone, not to the top 2%, but to the top one percent? All of it. Now we know not every CEO or magnate is a heartless outsourcer, and not every unemployed person is a leech. But there's no balance. We need the politicians in our country, and the thinkers, too, to get their heads out of their asses and start to come up with some solutions."

A couple of heads in the circle nodded, and more than a few kept their eyes to the ground in clear but obvious disagreement. The conversation continued along its predictable pattern, and Rob withdrew within himself. He wondered again where Amelia was, if she had returned to the car and found his note. Was she now wondering through the concession area looking for him among the tourist families? Had she really gone off with Spencer and his group, and if so, where, and why?

The sky washed pale blue above the spreading branches. What breeze there was drifted like a current from above. There began to be more gaps in what had been a lively conversation, and a few men had already risen, cleaned their mess kits, and ambled back to the tents. Rob guessed they would be laying back on their cots, taking herky-jerky naps in the heat, sweating through their short, color-drenched dreams.

Rob stood. Phelps came over and took his tin plate.

"More water, or anything?" he asked.

"No, I'm going to head back and search out my wife. Thanks for the food. See you boys for the muster this afternoon."

Rob slung his haversack over his shoulders and retrieved his musket. He went back into the sunlight and took the dusty path back through the bivouac area, toward the concessions, heading for the parking lot. Though he felt relatively safe because of all the people, he kept his head down and his eyes open. It was about a mile all told back to the car. Luckily the way was fairly straight and level. There were many other sojourners, going one way or the other, re-enactors in Confederate or Union uniforms in groups or alone, laden, like Rob, with packs and canteens and muskets. There was one group of Union cavalrymen on foot, with jaunty feathered caps and knee-high black boots, leading their horses, which clopped slowly behind them, heads down, flanks glistening. And there were tourist families, large and small, with happy kids running wild, still ignoring their parents' orders and pleas. There were even nuns, a pair of them, in traditional outfits with long black frocks and white wimples, carrying parti-colored umbrellas above their heads to shield them from the sun. They were like every other pair of nuns Rob had ever seen, one tall, the other short, both with glasses, smooth ageless skin and beatific smiles.

The concession area was still crowded with people, and doing a brisk business in iced soft drinks, cotton candy, and popsicles. There were barkers in front of some stands, calling out to passersby. Some worked from meal trucks like you would see at any carnival, vans with sliding windows cut into their sides and brightly colored awnings. But some were modified wood conestoga wagons, with big, spindled wheels and arced canvas covers, with steps up to the opening in the back. Rob stopped at one, and spent another $7 for a liter of water to fill his canteen.

By the time Rob passed all that and crossed the meadow to the parking lot, he was again so soaked through with perspiration that his feet were sloshing in his boots. There were guards in reflective yellow security vests patrolling the parking lot, but they didn't pay any attention to him. He got to Amelia's rental car. His note was still there, undisturbed, unread. It was still two and a half hours until muster.

He was a bit pissed standing amid the long even lines of parked cars, but there wasn't anything to be done about it. He remembered that after the morning rehearsal when he had gone to find Amelia that at the top of the rise there was a sparse line of trees. He thought he could find a place where he could see where his part of the battle was to be staged, but also down the opposite slope past the grandstand to where Amelia had her gear set up.

He trudged up the hill. It was just perceptibly cooler at the crest from a wafting light breeze that didn't penetrate to the valley floor. Finding a spot where the spongy grass grew right up to the root nobs, he situated himself against the trunk of a full-leafed maple and leaned back. He found himself wondering if any soldier a century and a half earlier had been under this same tree and looked out at roughly the same surroundings? Most likely it would have been a staff officer, or an artillery spotter, or someone from the signal corps checking troop positions and movements. Rob waited and listened, wondering if he would feel some pull from the past, but it was just the breeze rustling in the upper branches.

Then he slept, dreaming he had been in this spot many times before, not for the battle itself, but for the re-enactments. He saw himself reeling drunk with other men, all in uniform. It was the whole him, without any impediment, the young him, with the strength he never realized when he had it. The day of this dream battle was windy and dark, like a northeaster day on the Outer Banks. He could even hear the waves crashing on some hidden shore, though there was no water anywhere around. And then the sound of water became the sound of battle, and Rob was looking across another field he remembered from somewhere. He was moving toward it, and behind him he heard rasping breaths and the thud of boots. Before him was cannon fire and plumes of smoke erupting amidst lines of troops advancing toward him. But with all the smoke he couldn't see the colors of their uniforms or determine if they were friend or foe. He still marched toward them, and they toward him, but it suddenly felt very wrong, as if a serious and irreparable mistake had been made. It was not a sham or reenactment, but a real battle, and he was in the middle of it being pulled along as if he were in a strong current, knowing it was a desperate and dangerous place he was headed to. Then he was jolted awake and remembered none of it. The brightness around him throbbed close by and shimmered in the distances.

What he did remember was Kelly. But who was she now? His perception of her remained wrapped in an image of her as a young child. He never took the dark raven hair, the kohl make-up, and the goth clothes she had worn the last time he saw her before the accident as anything more than a late adolescent stage. He knew she did drugs and hung around people who sold them, but what was he going to do or say about that? Rob knew Kelly couldn't talk to her mother or stepfather, but she couldn't talk to him either. Rob had left many years earlier. And Jane and her husband had moved to Asheville. That left Kelly, just emerging into adulthood, living at the beach by herself. They had all turned their backs on each other at the same time, sad as that was to say, and Kelly had aimed herself, or drifted, to that day of the accident.

Her face when she sat with him in that bright visitors area at the prison was one of serene scrubbed beatification. She hadn't prosletyzed, but he knew she would the next time she saw him. Her commitment to her Lord and Savior was genuine. She knew she didn't deserve the peace she felt. With tears in her eyes she told him she studied scripture eight hours a day, and it would get to the point where the words no longer mattered.

"I can feel it jump into me," she had said. "It doesn't flow or drift to me. It's like a quick dramatic possession, a seizure. It's not because I think about it, or have thought about it. It comes to me because He knows I need it, that the only way I could live here, like this, was if I were given some purpose. So the Lord came to me, and drew me up, and showed me the path."

Rob remembered looking at her in prison yellow, her face bright and glistening, her hair pulled back, looking older and younger at the same time. He found himself thinking he was not as glad as he maybe should be about the direction she had found. He was reminded that she had latched on to the music of Trent Reznor and Maynard Keynes in much the same way. But he didn't look at her with anything like doubt or derision. He smiled blithely, told her he was just glad she had let him come.

She had heard about his stroke, probably from her mother, and asked him how he was doing. Did he have a therapy regimen, and was he keeping up with it?

"Yes, I do my exercises," he had lied, "but it's hard because the results are so long in coming, if they come at all. The messages from the brain have to find other pathways. Apparently women can recover more quickly because they can find these alternate pathways more easily."

"No traveling? No surfing?"

"No. No money, not here anyway. I'm working at the Seahorse, cooking," he lied again. "Maybe in another year I'll go back to Costa Rica, live like a patrone, take up golf." He smiled through the glass.

"I always wanted you to take me there," she said, looking at him suddenly with an expression of yearning and sadness. For the first time Rob became aware of the people and the voices around them. He only heard snatches of one half of their conversations, and Kelly heard snatches of the other side. If he were watching a movie of this happening to someone else, there might have been tears in his eyes, and hers. But the father and daughter stared at each other stoically.

"Has your mom been to see you?"

"She has," Kelly had answered, looking down at her hands. "She always wants to bring me things, and she always asks what I need. I tell her, and then the she comes, and brings me something else, either something I don't need, or already have, or couldn't possibly use, or something they won't let me have. But she's sweet, and she wants to be helpful. The fact that she's settled now, and comfortable, I think that makes her feel guilty because we were never close, or even understandable to each other when I was young…as if that, in some way, might have changed things."

Rob looked up.

"Don't even say anything," she said, but not unkindly. "We can all trace our paths to exactly where we are. That's probably the most important thing I've learned, and I'm going with it now."

"Is there anything I can bring you now?" Rob asked, as their time grew short.

"No," she laughed. "Thanks to mom, I have more travel sizes of shampoo and conditioner than I can use in six months. All the girls here come to me. And soap, I have lots of facial soap."

Again, all Rob remembered was the blithe smile, the clear eyes. As he'd left the visiting area, he was stopped by Dr. Kroll, who introduced himself as the staff psychiatrist. They stood by a window, looking up at the high fences topped with loops of razor wire.

"Kelly has undergone a remarkable and thorough transformation," the doctor had said. "As a psychiatrist, I'd say I'm skeptical, at best, about dramatic religious conversions. They often occur in people on a behavioral pendulum. They swing from nihilistic licentiousness to piety, but then with most of them, they tend to swing back again. I don't get that with Kelly, and I've spent many hours prodding her, testing her, looking for chinks in her façade."

"She has forty five more years here," Rob said bitterly. "That might have something to do with it."

"You're right, of course. We can't understand all the mechanisms at work." He looked out and up at the tops of the pine trees beyond the fence. "But you'll have to admit to yourself that there's a sincerity in her words, and her demeanor, that seems sturdy, unshakable. I know Father Trainor has spent a lot of time with her. They pray together, and talk. They've become very close. And she probably didn't say anything about it, but her effect among the women here, and I mean some of the real hardcore ones, has been most profound. What's the expression? 'You don't bullshit a bullshitter.' The woman in here, they would know if she was trying to con them."

Rob had trouble concentrating on the man's words as he spoke. Everything had to do with what he did and didn't know about Kelly and her situation and the conditions of her life inside. Even in the airy, sunlit waiting and greeting area Rob knew a lie was being perpetrated. This room was newly painted and shining with enamel, and the cubicles with the speaker connections were disinfected. The prisoners themselves were clean, their orange jumpers creased, their hair pulled back and clamped. But the whole scene belied a bigger truth. Behind the forbidding steel doors where the prisoners actually lived, that sunlight didn't reach. It was the same cold and darkness as any medieval dungeon. Every time a door clanged shut back there, the soul retreated further inward.

Rob didn't know Kelly. As he had sat on the opposite side of the thick glass he kept expecting that recognition would suddenly arise, as if he were a man with amnesia remembering something after a long time. He had recognized Kelly's eyes. They wore the same yearning expression they had in childhood. So the words she had spoken about God and peace and purpose and understanding…well, they didn't ring hollow, but the words she offered had not been seconded by the sureness and insistence of her gaze.

He didn't know her. She was fully a woman now, and he only saw her as a toddler and grammar school girl. After that their contact had been spotty at best. Those years he had been gone Rob had written her beautiful letters, and never mailed any of them. He knew Kelly and her mom had been hard on each other during Kelly's adolescence. The few times Rob had seen them together then, they reminded him of two cats, close and wary, making long deep guttural growls at each other, both very still in the body, but with invisible tails furiously brushing at the floor behind them.

Now Rob didn't know what his responsibilities or uses to Kelly were. While he was drinking it was easy to avoid thinking about it. And immediately after his stroke his world had become so compressed that there was no room for her, or almost anything else, in it. But those excuses were no more. And it was Amelia who had quietly prodded him. She had lost her father in an instant. Everything they had said to each other had been said, and nothing could ever be added. She had used that to nudge Rob in Kelly's direction. He still had the opportunity, the responsibility, to carry on the conversation with his daughter. Kelly was the responsibility of his blood. But all that was abstract to his normal way of thinking. Guilt and responsibility would never motivate him. But now what Rob needed was to get close to the idea of loving his daughter. She deserved it, and probably needed it more now, even if it was just an approximation, than she ever had before.

Then again he was on a Pennsylvania hillside. Though the spot he had chosen was mossy and soft, there were nobs of roots like knuckles thrust up above the surface that were too numerous to completely avoid. He was squirming again to get himself comfortable when he looked up and saw a lone one-horse wagon approaching from the ridge to the north. The driver held the reins loosely as he dipped down into the bowl of the valley and bounced across the field. Next to him, chatting amiably, was Amelia.

XIV

The sky above was blue going to white toward the western horizon. Rob saw it through a smeared pane of perspiration. He was dead on the field, a casualty in the re-enactment of the first day of the battle of Gettysburg. He saw the legs and boots of the still living men in his unit surging past him, and he felt a strange regret, a longing, to still be with them.

He had wondered how it would work. After the re-enactment of the battle started, how would it be decided who would fall when the armies met? Were they going to draw straws, or numbers from a jar? No, Sergeant Barefoot had told them. There were around two hundred of them representing roughly fifteen hundred troops. That first day their casualties were rather low, only about ten percent. That meant that fifteen to eighteen of them would fall during the mock battle. As for who those would be, he would leave that up to them. When he put it that way, a number of the troops looked up and down the line at each other, still confused about how it would actually work out, each thinking to themselves that it wasn't going to be them and wondering which of the others in line with them it would be.

Rob had other things to think about. He had never gotten a chance to talk to Amelia after she returned from her meeting, but he knew instinctively it was with Spencer. He knew she saw him sitting under the tree above her position, but she didn't acknowledge him, or even look in his direction, even after the buggy that had brought her had been turned around and driven back across the field. Even though there was no overt signal, Rob was conscious enough of the situation that he held his spot. He waited for a half hour above her, hoping for some reprieve, but none ever came, and he eventually had to return to his unit for the final muster before the battle.

There was more excitement among all the men as they returned, shouldered muskets waving in the air above them. Eventually the sergeants among them began blowing whistles and gathering their charges, lining them up and inspecting them, going over the plans again, pointing toward the east where the Yankees could be seen through the trees doing the same thing. The young redheaded Fabian was down the line from Rob, his

Adam's apple bobbing up and down above his collar. Rob saw the other men who had shared their lunch with him, and most of the others who had been at the rehearsal earlier. Once they were in line they all became more serious and listened intently to the Sergeant's instructions.

They were in a kind of natural bowl and an audience began to form on the rim above them. There were no grandstands as there were in the next field over, and Rob had wondered how many people would actually come to view their part of the demonstration. But as five o'clock approached and the battle was ready to begin there were at least a couple of hundred, and more still coming, spreading blankets on the hillside above them. The sun was still burning, and the accumulation of the full day's warmth was on all of them now.

From over the hill they heard the distorted announcements from the PA tower next to the grandstands. The officers on horseback who had been meeting in a knot at the end of the line separated with a clanging of bits and bridles and returned to their sergeants to get the troops ready to move forward.

Rob felt the anticipation of those around him, and he felt it in himself. He was filled with a sense of duty to perform his part in the best, most realistic manner he could. Up and down the line he saw serious faces, intent, glistening with perspiration and purpose. Sergeant Barefoot, whose usual demeanor was measured and plodding, now stood erect and moved up and down the line briskly. His eyes took everything in as he straightened his line and steadied it.

From over the hill they heard a squawking smear of an unintelligible announcement and then a barrage of cannon fire. That was immediately followed by bugle calls from both ends of their line. And then, like some giant machine that had been oiled and primed, they were moving forward. For Rob, and he thought the rest of them, it had none of the same feeling that it had in the morning rehearsal. The ground, which had been so uneven and awkward to walk on then, was now smooth under their feet. Even he, with his jerky plodding marionette limp, moved more easily as they marched down the hill toward the stream. At first the only sounds were the trudging of feet and clopping of horses' hooves, and an occasional harsh scream of a sabre being drawn from a scabbard. But over the hill all hell was breaking loose. Cannons were being fired, bugles blown, and a smattering of applause from the grandstands sounded like birds taking flight.

Rob and his unit moved downhill and over the stream. As their boots churned up the water and mud a fecund scent drifted up to them, scents of both life and death. Water sloshed in their boots as they moved forward on the uphill side.

After they crossed the stream they began to see more blue forms moving among the tree trunks and brush at the floor of the woods across the field from them. There was still no rifle or cannon fire on their side of the ridge, although the pops of small arms fire and the occasional rumble of heavy ordnance continued to be heard over the rise. Some of the spectators on the ridge could be seen moving back and forth, trying to catch the action in both theatres.

When they were eighty yards from the woods their blue-clad enemy, who had been moving around frenetically beneath the trees, suddenly lined up and loosed a volley of rifle fire at them. Actually they saw spots of yellow flame, and then rising white smoke, and then heard the sounds of the muskets, but they knew what it meant and what it was supposed to mean.

"Keep moving forward," Sergeant Barefoot called above the din. Rob saw Rebels on the left flank kneel and fire, the staccato reports rushing across the field toward him, and puffs of white and gray smoke rising above the guns' barrels. Those who fired fell behind as they remained to reload and the line stretched like a rope, the right flank, which included Sgt. Barefoot's men, now thrust into the lead.

"Let 'em hear you now!" he croaked above the din, and a ragged rebel yell went up from the troops as they struggled forward.

Just then Rob saw a Union officer on horseback emerge from the trees ahead. The sun glinted on his drawn sword as he rode across in front of them down the length of the Union line. Even the man's horse seemed to recognize their exalted role. Rob knew the officer was General Reynolds, and his presence was like red meat to the pressing Rebel line.

Their pace increased, and now Rob struggled to keep up. All the men around him were screaming, pressing forward, and waiting, as he was, for the order to kneel and fire. But then, after the General reached the far end of the line, before an order came from Sgt. Barefoot or anyone else, the lower edge of the wood ahead lit up with Halloween orange and yellow flame. The sound didn't come with the flame, but with the rising smoke after. Like thunder, the volley rolled across the field to them. Rob was not alone in his shock at the Yankee fusillade. All around him men flinched, and a few fell to their knees, making their line undulate like a sidewinder snake. Sgt. Barefoot showed an unexpected nimbleness as he rushed behind the line bucking up his charges.

"Forward now!" he roared. "No hesitation. Chase them back."

They moved on relentlessly. The Union general across the field, having reached the edge of his right flank, turned, raising his sword so that it glinted as if it had been lit by the Yankee volley. He urged his horse back across the field in front of his troops, rallying and exhorting them. Rob realized that this was truly the way it had happened. The general was either foolhardy, or else had faith that God above would intervene to protect him.

"Prepare to fire," Sgt. Barefoot called. The front row of the charging Rebels stopped and knelt, shouldering their arms. The row behind, Rob included, stood above and just behind them, sighted their weapons toward the treetops as they were taught, and waited for the orders.

"Fire!"

Flames spat out and an acrid gauzy curtain rose so that at first the trees ahead were blurred. But through it Rob and the others saw the generals' horse rear back and General Reynolds sliding off the animal's broad rump and crumpling to the ground. There was just an instant of silence as they watched the grim ballet of it and then a yell went up from the Rebel side, and a rising sporadic volley lit up from the Yankees in the woods.

The troops on the Rebel side did not need to be urged forward. They flooded up the gentle slope toward the trees, their enthusiasm obvious in their throats and their tromping feet. Even Rob felt himself carried along by the throng, not laboring to keep up as he usually did.

The thing he knew he would always remember were the smells of the battlefield, the green, chlorophyllic scents of trampled grass, the musk of men laboring strenuously to move forward in the summer heat, and the acrid assault of gunpowder in the nostrils.

Just as he was thinking that he felt a jolt and saw a flash of white light, and in an instant he was falling backward, musket clattering to the earth next to him, his wide-brimmed hat flying off. He hit the ground with a thud strong enough to expel the air from his lungs. He couldn't remember closing his eyes, but his vision was interrupted somehow. And when it returned, he saw only blue sky and the dark elongated forms of his compatriots passing over him.

He lay there not knowing what to do. For an instant he worried that he might really have been shot, whether by accident or purposely, and the pain had just not registered. He thought that something physical had actually stopped his forward momentum and thrown him backward. Hadn't it? As the sounds of his own troops moving forward diminished he did an inventory. Everything seemed to be in order and he felt no more pain than he usually did. And though he knew he could move, he could not get his body to develop any electrical sequence from his brain to his nerves to his muscles. The blue sky pulsed with depth and grandeur. He found himself staring further and further into it so that he could almost imagine his sight penetrating the atmosphere and pushing into black space with the light of stars flashing by.

Rob realized he was dead on the field of battle, and he realized that his "death" had come to him much as quickly and unexpectedly as it had in reality come to thousands of soldiers in this battle a century and a half earlier. He had made no decision to fall. It had never even crossed his mind. This was where the paths of reality and re-enactment diverged. What had not accompanied him and his companions as they moved forward was the overwhelming, numbing, clutching fear. In July, 1863, whether acknowledged or not, it was there. It might have been blunted by discipline, or numbed by action, or shared in a sense of inevitability with those around you, but it was still a constant companion whenever the enemy was visually encountered. And thinking back on those days and the potential for horrific, maiming carnage, Rob felt better that he could safely sink within himself.

He didn't move. And then, suddenly it seemed, he couldn't hear anything. When he first fell, he heard the sounds of the troops moving away, and the pops of rifle fire, but that had all drifted into nothingness. He knew he must be breathing, but he was afraid to turn his attention to it.

And then, coming like a frantic crowd trying to escape a disaster and tripping over themselves in the process, were his memories. They weren't cohesive or consecutive. Some lacked contour, but others were as close and imminent as if they were happening in real time. There was his childhood, segmented, confused and confusing. His dead parents and dead brother wandered through as if they were lost. He saw glimpses of childhood friends, through windows, or across streets, and he was unable to get to them and ask, "Remember when..?" And then for some reason, or for no reason, he saw doors. They were shut mostly, and some of them were shut and bolted. He heard sounds of other doors he couldn't see slamming. He saw a screen door with a wooden frame, the spring worn and rusted, partially open and drifting back and forth, creaking in a light breeze.

Then there was a window, and in that window he saw Kelly's face. He was looking into the kohl-dark eyes of her goth phase. And then he turned and it was Irina with her blue eyes and blonde hair floating in the wind. She saw him. For once she was looking right at him, and with an expression of recognition and appreciation. But then she was gone, and so were all the other memories. All that remained was the blue sky above him, looking dangerously as if it might fall in on itself.

Rob had no sense of how long it was until he heard footsteps and voices returning toward him. Then he was looking up at the red sweating face and red hair of his liberal lunch companion. The man didn't say anything, just reached down and helped Rob to his feet. Rob saw then that the boy's face was streaked with soot from the smoke of the gunpowder blanks. He came up shakily and awkwardly because of the dead weight of his left side. As he did he saw the other men of his unit returning toward the creek in no semblance of discipline or good order. They all looked finished, spent, disoriented. Other men who had fallen were being helped up. It looked like the raising of ghosts.

Sgt. Barefoot was at the rear of the group walking along the back line herding the men back to their starting point. He too looked exhausted. Beyond him, through the trees, Rob saw the Yankees retreating up the ridge where, 150 years ago, they had set their defenses, controlling the high ground on that flank, and some said controlling the battle after that.

Up on the prominence where the spectators had accumulated, now there were just small pockets and groups collecting their blankets and belongings for the long walk back to the parking lot.

Rob was utterly drained. He walked next to the thin, red-headed man, struggling to keep up, but feeling a lethargy that required he compel himself to take each next step. Even the curiosity to return and find out what had transpired with Amelia and Spencer's group was blunted by his ennui.

"I was surprised when you fell," his companion said. "You were next to me, and we were moving toward the Yankees, and I could feel everybody getting excited.... And then there were a couple of volleys, and out of the corner of my eye I see you falling backward."

"There was no planning to it," Rob said. "It was a surprise to me too."

"But it was the way you fell. It was as if you were a puppet and someone cut your strings."

"By the time I knew what had happened, it had already happened. I wonder how many men, that day and the next and the next, had the same thing happen to them, had themselves instantly launched into eternity."

"Thousands and thousands," the red-headed man said quietly.

They all returned to the staging area, weary now after their exertions. Again Rob was struck that these were not the lean, hard men who would have been at the original fight. These were middle-aged men who drank too many beers and ate too many snacks while watching TV in their recliners. They listened blankly as a mounted officer thanked them formally, and said he would see them the next day when they would give the Yankees hell. This was his applause line, but it only raised a thin tired murmur from the men.

Sgt. Barefoot was flushed as he thanked them for their efforts. He went over his notes for the next day, telling them they would meet under the green flag that would be planted in the northwest corner of the main battlefield.

"Tomorrow we have the Wheatfield and the Devil's Den, and that's what we will be re-enacting. The whole field will be participating, so we are looking at between eight to ten thousand re-enactors, and three times that many spectators. We will meet at 10AM. Be well-rested because we will be drilling hard, then marching hard and fighting hard." He walked up and down the line. "Dismissed."

The men milled around and then began to break up and go their separate ways. They all appeared to be as enervated as Rob was. He had been surprised at himself at how well he had been able to keep up, although part of him wondered if he had fallen because his subconscious knew he couldn't sustain his efforts.

Again Rob followed the trail up the hillside to the ridge that divided the battle areas. The grandstands were empty as was most of the field. A few four-wheelers scurried across the far hillside, stars-and-bars flags flapping on flexible poles behind them. Under the tree where Amelia had set up there was no remaining evidence of her presence. Rob once again made the trek back to the parking lot. The early evening light was softening, turning a bit yellow and orange on the edges of the horizon, displaying the first hints of an approaching luminism.

The trail going back down the backbone of the ridge to the parking lot was worn down by the footsteps of thousands of re-enactors and spectators so that there were only a few yellow nubs and a fine powdery cellulose dust that rose with each step. Rob was behind the vast bulk of the people, and he slowed further looking down into the natural bowl of the parking lot. They were all there, loading up, getting into their cars and trucks, and joining the snaking lines at either ends of the lot that fed the spectators and non-FARB participants back toward the highway.

As often happened since his stroke, Rob was having trouble coalescing his thoughts and the input of sensations into any kind of cohesive pattern. He had begun to realize what a supreme gift it had been to effortlessly differentiate and filter the barrage of sensory data, stressing some parts, demoting others, and molding them into a recognizable and working shape (to him) that he could use to help catalogue his world.

He found he desperately wanted to see and talk to Amelia. He needed the added depth of her two eyes to unflatten things and give them dimension. What had she learned? Because truthfully, if her contact was with Spencer's group, on whatever level, it gave her potentially much more information than Rob had found out marching and drilling and advancing until he fell lifeless and mock-dead on the ersatz field of battle.

He was behind even the slowest stragglers. He knew he was excruciatingly slow, and yet, in the last few weeks he knew he had shown some slight signs that his body was going around some of the neurological pathways that had been blocked, and finding new ways to connect his thoughts and desires to actions. There was some small hope that maybe he could resume some sense of normalcy. Whatever else this insanity with Amelia was, it was turning into effective therapy.

By the time he got to the floor of the parking lot there were large gaps between the remaining cars so they looked like islands in a vast oceanic archipelago. The volunteers, who had kept the traffic moving and held everyone's tempers at bay, had removed their orange vests and were congregating around two white vans under a clump of trees at the margin of the field. When Rob got his bearings and turned, Amelia was standing next to the rental car, trying not to look excited, but leaning forward, standing in the open door as if it were somehow holding her back. When he got close she came to the back of the car and nonchalantly hugged him. In her eyes were excitement, gratification, and a hint of what looked like mischief.

"I have much to tell you," she said, popping the trunk and helping him load his pack and bedroll, "but how was your battle? I'm sorry...I don't know how to begin...your face is so dirty."

"I am one of the fallen," he said flatly, but with the hint of a smile, or in his case a half-smile, on his face. "The last time I saw you, you were getting into a buggy and riding away across the field as if you were in an outtake from 'Gone with the Wind.'"

"And that's almost what it felt like." She took his Enfield and helped him prop it in the back seat. He removed his slouch hat and wiped the perspiration on his brow with his dirty kerchief. It came away brown and red with dirt. "I saw her...and talked to her."

Rob stopped, with his hand on the edge of the door. "What did she say?"

"Wait...first...let me try to tell you the whole story from the beginning." She scrunched up her face as she tried to concentrate and organize everything. "Well, you saw me at first. I had my paints and easel all set up. But I was just going to sketch at first, take everything in...I wasn't expecting anything to happen. There were thousands of re-enactors, thousands of spectators. I wasn't looking for anyone or anything specific because I had no idea where to look. There were Rebel soldiers all around me, going this way and that, troops, flags, dust, wagons, smoke, noise. It was a lot to take in.

"Suddenly, out of all of this, I saw a man on horseback. He was middle-aged, patrician-looking, and he wore an immaculate uniform with a feathered hat, and a sword jangling at his side as he rode straight toward me with three or four more riders. And it was as if the crowd magically parted. I was a little nervous, but as he got closer I knew it wasn't anyone I recognized. He got off his horse and walked around to look at my work. He told me then he was with Spencer's group. Just that, no further explanation, as if I should know what that meant. He said Spencer was looking for someone to photograph and paint his unit. Now, there was no way, just looking at my rough sketches, that this man could have any idea if I had any talent or not."

That's what Rob was thinking. "So you didn't think his approaching you was a coincidence?"

"No, and I was afraid. Did they know who I was, or that we'd been following them? Did they know I was with you?"

"They had to have…"

"Right, and there was no use denying any of it if they asked. I just hoped they didn't know about us following them to New York."

"So?"

"So it was arranged that a buggy would come for me. They'd provide lunch and I could get started on some preliminary sketches and take some photographs of their group. The buggy did come, and driving it was one of the men from the photos in Spencer's office."

They got in the car and Amelia wound it around to the dirt trail that led back to the highway. Rob was trying to process it all, and also trying not to get too far ahead of himself. Part of it was just innate suspicion. How much did he want to believe that a coincidence was a coincidence, on any level?

"We took a trail back on the other side of the hill behind us, heading…south, or southwest, I guess. We forded one little stream, and went on a small bridge over another, in through some woods and out again, and twenty minutes later we were at Spencer's camp. It was just as you described it, all very military, but not, what do they call it? FARB… especially with the RV right there among the tents and wagons. We drove right up to the front entrance of the RV.

"As we pulled to a stop Spencer came out of the RV, still in full uniform, as opposed to most of the rest of the troops, who had stripped down to their undershirts, or just their suspenders, with no shirts on at all. A lot of testosterone there. Everyone was busy, and even as he was greeting me, he was looking over the activities. He seemed very much in charge.

"So the first thing he did, and actually what I least expected, was invite me into the RV. You've seen it from the outside…brand new, gleaming, same with the inside. It looked like it just came of the lot."

"Were any of the men from New York there?" he asked.

"In the trailer, no, but I recognized some of them when we had ridden up. It was only Spencer and me inside the trailer. Anyway, he offered me a cold drink. As he went to get it, I was still looking around at everything, but I also tried to take in and catalogue as much information as I could. There was a sitting area in roughly the center of the RV, with a low table and chairs arranged around it. There were maps and papers on the table's surface, but just glancing at them I couldn't tell if they dealt with the battle or something else. As Spencer was clinking ice in the glasses and pouring tea, I drifted toward the back, admiring the paintings on the wall as I went. There was a closed door, and I hoped to drift close enough to it to try to hear if there was any sign of life behind it. A phone rang up front and Spencer took the call. I could hear his voice, but couldn't make out what he was talking about. I was hoping he would stay on the phone for a while, but then I could hear him wrapping it up so I moved back toward the center of the RV to meet him.

"He came from the front with two glasses of iced tea, and as he approached there was a sharp rap at the side exterior door. The door opened and there was a man with a clear look of concern on his face. At the same time the door behind me opened, and Irina walked out of the back room. She seemed very cool and unconcerned about the whole situation. She gave me a polite patient smile, as I was somewhat blocking her way to the front of the RV, so I turned and stepped back. But with Spencer coming out of the kitchen, and the other man, who had by now entered and closed the door so as not to let out the cool air, we had all congregated in the center of the trailer, and there was clearly not enough room for all of us.

" 'Ah,' Spencer said, 'the one flaw of this floor plan. I'd send you ladies to await me on the second floor, but alas, there is no second floor.' The man who had come in clearly felt it was important to talk to Spencer immediately. 'Let me step outside and talk to this gentleman, and I'll be back directly.'

"He handed one glass of tea to me, and shrugged and gave Irina the other, and followed the other man outside.

"So suddenly I am left alone with Irina. I didn't know what to say, and I waited for her to say something, but she just smiled, and we stood uncomfortably in the center of the RV. She looked at the glass of tea, and then passed me and went to the kitchen in front. I introduced myself and tried to explain what I was doing there. She seemed totally disinterested in my explanation, but I didn't know if it was because she knew why I was there, or that she just didn't care. She put the glass of tea on the counter, and opened the refrigerator and got a beer, although it was still not even noon yet. You never told me how striking she was," she said, and turned to look at him as if she might have gained a new understanding of where this had all started. "If only God had given me legs like that, and her hair…"

"Alright, you've made your point."

"Anyway, my other point is that she didn't seem restrained or constrained in any way. I got the feeling she could have walked out the door at any moment. But I also got the feeling she was not going anywhere because she was being protected from something else on the outside."

The sky was not darkening yet, but it was beginning to pale above as a prelude. Some of the ground shadows were deepening, and the weight of the afternoon heat had lifted just perceptibly.

"Well, did she say anything?" Rob asked.

"First she asked, 'How do you know Mr. Spencer?' which seemed kind of odd and formal. I told her I didn't know him, that we had only just met, and explained that he wanted me to paint the group. I said I couldn't help but notice her accent, and asked her where she was from. She said, 'Ukraine, but I have been living here for a couple of years.' I was going to ask her about all the political turmoil there, but then I thought better of it and just said, 'oh, an ex-pat like myself,' and told her I was from Costa Rica. 'I was there last winter,' she said, and I asked her where, and she said, 'All over. All we did was drive for three weeks. We went from the northwest, near Nicaragua all the way down to Golfito near Panama. It was a surf trip for the guy I was with so it was mostly just going from beach to beach. But I did get him to take me to Arenal, which was beautiful and cooler, and a nice change. The volcano didn't do anything, but we hiked, and saw animals, and did the zip-line thing through the canopy, which was cool'."

Rob was thinking he had no idea whom she might have gone with. When he came out of his reverie they were at a stop sign, and Amelia was looking at him with a less-than-playful smile on her face.

"Reminiscing about Nicoya?" she asked.

"Yes…and no. I'm just trying to figure out how all this works. So when you were there, there were no signs that they were in lockdown mode? No automatic weapons, no obvious guards, no perimeter set up around the camp?"

"None that I could tell. I suppose they could have had people out of sight, inside the border of the woods, or over the hilltops, or in some of the tents, but I didn't see them."

"And the military types?"

"I saw a few of them, but not all. And the ones I saw seemed to just be integrated into the regular group."

They had moved ahead on the main road. Traffic was heavy, but probably not as bad as it had been an hour ago when everyone was leaving the battle scene.

"So I asked Irina if she was planning to stay in America," Amelia continued. "And this is where she finally began to show some anxiety. Her face darkened and she looked down, and said, 'Yes, at least I want to. There are some problems that Mr. Spencer is helping me work out.'

"'Yes, they have tightened up on immigration,' I said. 'With the threat of terrorism, I've had to deal with that myself. I've gone through some interviews where I'm amazed at the breadth of some of what they know, and then at their total ignorance of other, more important things, especially like where you've been and what you've been doing since you entered the country.'

"When I said that, I found her looking at me very seriously, and I sensed she had something she wanted to tell me, and I tried to be calm and not to appear too interested. I could feel the words coming to her lips…and then the trailer door opened and Spencer came back in. He looked at the beer in her hand. This quiet kind of glaze came over Irina's face, and she sat down on the edge of the couch and waited for Spencer and me to continue our conversation."

Amelia went on to say that Spencer originally wanted to do the preliminary sketches on the battlefield itself…but she convinced him that doing it in camp could be more realistic. She hesitated suggesting that they do the portrait from a photograph, because she thought he might protest at the un-FARB-ness of it, but he readily agreed. They left Irina sitting on the edge of the couch and went out and walked through the camp looking for the best setting. The one they chose was under a large, motherly oak tree. It's branches spread out like an invitation, and behind it were the double lines of white tents for depth and background. Spencer began yelling orders, and within minutes everyone was mustered and in uniform and Spencer set them like chess pieces under the tree. By the time she had her camera ready they were all there posed in front of her. And as with many of the photos Amelia had seen in history books, Spencer and the man who had first approached her, who must have been his adjutant or executive officer, were seated in simple straight-back chairs in the forefront. Spencer sat with his legs crossed, his uniform buttoned to the throat even in the heat, his rakish wide-brimmed hat surmounted with a long black feather. He didn't look into the camera lens, but seemed to be staring afar at some dangerous and higher goal.

Amelia said she had to hand it to the other men. They certainly all looked the part. There were the younger ones with their wispy beards, standing straight and cocksure in their poses. And then as the faces grew older, the men's expressions began to appear more aloof and withdrawn, as if knowing and resigning themselves to their fates, or rather the fates of the men who had preceded them by a hundred and fifty years.

She snapped several shots, sometimes zooming in on various portions of the group in order to get a closer view of individual faces and body types. The men were patient with her requests, but all the while she felt as if there was an anxiety in the group, a restlessness to get on with what needed to be done.

When she was finished and the men had been dismissed, Spencer led her back to the trailer. The man who had been his adjutant came with them. They entered the RV and the three of them sat at the low table. Irina was nowhere to be seen, and the door to the back room was closed.

"The man must have been Spencer's lawyer," Amelia said.

"Describe him."

"Medium-tall, gray at the temples, fit, as if he was a runner…he had one eyebrow that arched, as if he was constantly disbelieving whatever you were saying. That was disconcerting. Do you know him?"

"I'm not sure," Rob said.

Amelia shrugged. "We can look at the photos on my card…and see who else you recognize too. He gave me a simple contract to sign stating that for the final portrait in oil I would be paid $7500, based on the satisfaction of the purchaser, and that Spencer retained rights and control to all prints, memory cards, or other images arising from the procedure. Were I to sign, which I did, I would be paid a $2000 retainer, the balance to be paid on completion.

"At the end he asked me for my address, which threw me, but then I gave him the New Jersey address of the woman I told you about who had helped me with my immigration issues. I gave them my real name, and we stood to shake hands. Spencer immediately got an expression on his face as if he had other things to think about and do. He gathered a few things, including his phone, and without saying goodbye, he left the RV. Oh, and I forgot, the other man gave me his business card so we could stay in touch."

They were stopped at a light and Amelia reached into a side pocket of her camera bag, which was on the seat between them, and handed Rob the card.

"William Babson, Esq.," Rob read, "of Wright and Schuman, with a New York City address. It doesn't mean anything to me."

"When we get back to Kay's we can look at my computer and see what kind of law they practice, and there should be some kind of biography of him."

They were now within a mile of Kay's house. Suddenly Rob was overwhelmed with fatigue. But the breadth of his exertions had shown him that he could overcome his slowness, both mental and physical. He was nowhere near normal, but what he had done today, and the few days previously, he could never have accomplished even a few short weeks ago.

XV

At dawn on July 2, 1863, the second day of the battle, both the Union and Confederate armies were present in the vicinity of Gettysburg. Although there had been fighting the previous day, and both sides had suffered real casualties, neither side had a good idea of the actual number and dispositions of the opposing troops. General George Meade, in charge of the Army of the Potomac for only a few days, didn't realize that his forces actually outnumbered the Confederate army, and he had more troops arriving each hour. General Lee, because of the absence of Jeb Stuart's cavalry that had been riding in a large circumnavigating loop around both armies, felt particularly vulnerable because of the lack of real information on the strength and position of the enemy. Lee met with his corps commanders two hours before the sun came up. His plan was to attack the Yankees in the morning before they had a chance to shore up their fortifications, and hopefully before Meade's full army arrived. General Longstreet, who was his most important commander since the death of General Thomas "Stonewall" Jackson, saw that the Federal army held the better defensive positions on the higher ground. He thought they should try to entice the Union army to attack them. Lee was firm. He wanted to attack the left flank of the Union line with artillery support, his plan being that his seasoned troops would roll up that flank and send the Yankees fleeing to the north and east.

Apparently because Longstreet disagreed with the plan there were delays in the implementation. The attack that was planned to begin at mid-morning did not develop until well into the afternoon, and with a combination of daring, adroit leadership, and just plain naked valor, the Union army was able to repel the Rebel attacks with heavy losses on both sides.

That previous night, which was July 4th, there had been fireworks and celebrations of the nation's 238th birthday. After a dinner of sliced ham, green beans, and, as usual, potato salad, warm and redolent of mustard seed, Kay and Amelia and Rob had sat on the porch and watched the riot of color that lit the night sky, and felt the percussive booms of the charges as the rockets were launched, and heard the faraway voices of the crowd cheering in approval.

Both Rob and Amelia were physically and emotionally drained by the time the last screaming explosion faded into darkness with the appreciative applause of the crowd. Rob was so tired his left hand trembled. As they collected their things from the porch before heading upstairs, amateur rocketeers began setting off their much smaller charges. All over the valley were hisses and pops and sizzling white arches through the darkness, and those lights and explosions lasted until well after midnight.

As Kay and Amelia took things into the kitchen Rob slowly climbed the stairs and went into the room and closed the door. It seemed more like fifteen days than fifteen hours since they had last been there. He wanted only to crawl beneath the cool sheets, close his eyes, and be shielded from all distractions. He had not known such fatigue in a while. Going up the stairs his trailing left side seemed as if it only wished to be left behind. He had to drag it up every step, and when he got to the landing he stopped for a moment to regroup before going on to the bedroom.

When Kay and Amelia came up ten minutes later he had already brushed his teeth and put on his pajamas. For all the draining fatigue, he was still proud of himself. He had managed to keep up with his companions the first day, and if not for his sudden and unexpected demise, he knew he could have continued the charge with them and chased those Yankees up that hill.

After Amelia finished in the bathroom she found Rob lying on top of the light blanket. He was drifting, as if in an undulating current, downstream toward sleep.

"I don't think I can move," he said without opening his eyes.

"I'll help you." She reached out and took his hand, and with his limited aid they managed to get him into a sitting position. "There, collect yourself, and when you feel like you can get up, we'll draw back the sheets and get you under them, and I'll tuck you in."

He smiled at her playfulness and obeyed. After he was situated, she turned out the light and went around to her side of the bed and got in.

"I would give you a kiss goodnight," he said, "but I can't really move from this position."

"I'll save you the trouble."

She leaned over and kissed him on the cheek, brushed him with her lips really, and then settled back. Rob's mind was suddenly travelling at a frantic lurching pace, but then his consciousness sputtered out like a candle and he slept.

He came back to himself in the warm birth of the following dawn. He was nowhere near rested enough. His eyeballs felt scrubbed and bleached. Even before he tested his muscles they were crying out in surrender. But he knew he wouldn't sleep again so he prepared himself to rise. There were still two more days of battles.

The curtains hung limp in the window. Beyond them was just a reverse smudge of light. Rob had somehow kicked his sheet and blanket off during the night so he didn't have to labor to do that. After mentally preparing himself he rose slowly and moved toward the bathroom. Every one of his joints seemed either screwed down tightly or was too loose from overuse. There was a light tremor on his left side, which was an obvious sign to him of extreme and dangerous fatigue. He tried to dismiss it as he stood above the bowl, his piss coming in great spastic spurts.

Amelia stirred languidly as he dressed, and he secretly waited for her to speak to him from one of her dreams. It was dark as he came downstairs, and the only light inside was above the stove, and that only left a horizontal bar across the bottom of the closed door into the dining room. As he got to the front door he discerned a pale pink gauze of light to the east. He went out on the porch and leaned against the railing, looking at the dark rising back of Big Round Top in the gray mist. A bird sang in the distance, and another answered, and soon the song swelled as more joined in.

Rob had an enormous amount to think about now that he added the information that Amelia had given him about yesterday. But he was simply not making any headway. He knew what he had seen when he reconnoitered their camp from the woods; a solid perimeter guarded by paramilitaries with automatic weapons, and a tighter perimeter around the RV, equally well guarded. Yet Amelia said there were no weapons visible when she was there. Did that mean the danger had passed? Or were the armed guards just hidden while she was there? And if Irina wasn't being held against her will, as Amelia seemed to be saying, why was she there? More immediately though, and to Rob what seemed more dangerous, was that if Amelia had given her real name, how long would it take them to identify her and find the holes in the biography she had given them?

Amelia rose and they breakfasted and packed and went to the battleground. They left each other in the parking lot. Amelia was going to her spot on the hillock at the western end of the battlefield. She had her photographs of Spencer and his group, but she also wanted to photograph and sketch the battle that would take place in front of her. From her position she would be able to see the entire panorama, the movements of the armies, the charges, the clashes, the retreats. And while the reenactment would in no way portray the actual battle as far as the placements of the corps and the sizes of the units, or the timing of their assaults and retreats, she still knew that the spirit of the remembrance would be there.

In the larger field with so many more re-enactors and spectators, Rob got more of an idea of the grandeur and scale of the battle. When he looked at the numbers of the re-enactors, and multiplied that by twenty, it gave him more of a grasp of the logistics of moving and positioning those numbers across distances and in unknown terrain. He got the idea that both Lee's and Meade's corps commanders must have had a good amount of autonomy and freedom of movement. They had been given instructions and objectives. But communications once the hostilities actually began would have been limited to rudimentary signals with flags, spotters on the eminences, and couriers on horseback scurrying from place to place bringing instructions and returning to report on progress and casualties.

So on the morning of the actual battle there had been confusion and delays. And so there were on the morning of the reenactment. Many of the younger men had clearly been drinking the night before as they viewed the fireworks celebrating the 4th, and so many of them arrived in a thick-tongued stupor. And many of the middle-aged or older re-enactors, like Rob, were experiencing the twinges and strains and pulls of their recently overused muscles. Rob had had to take three ibuprofen to get himself moving. Everyone was also sunburned, it seemed, although some of that color may also have come from the exertion of getting themselves from the parking lot to the rendezvous point on the battlefield.

Sgt. Barefoot alone seemed to be unaffected by the actions of the previous day. Rob thought that as a veteran of many reenactments he had learned to conserve energy and husband his reserves. He was patient with his mostly raw recruits, and as he lined them up for inspection he didn't bark so much as cajole to get them to their marks.

The second day in 1863 was critical to both sides. Though the Union troops held the better, higher defensive positions, they felt they were fighting on even ground, which probably gave an edge to the campaign-hardened Rebels and their brilliant leader. And again, Gen. George Meade had not even been in command of the Army of the Potomac for a full week.

The troops in Rob's group were supposed to reenact the battle in the Wheatfield. Every year wheat was grown there, not to be harvested in the fall, but to be trampled down by clumsy middle-aged men plodding through it. This part of the battle represented the terrible carnage of the conflict. Over the course of an hour that afternoon in 1863 there were charges and retreats, heroic defenses, great acts of individual and group bravery on both sides. There were tales of so much musket fire that the wheat was blown to dusty chaff in the air.

In the reenactment, this part of the battle was portrayed by one side surging forward, chasing the other back, and then the other side counterattacking, and vice versa, until finally General Crawford's 5th Corps of Pennsylvanians charged down the western edge of Little Round Top and chased the Rebels off the field.

Rob felt safe and anonymous within his group. He kept his eyes out for Spencer and his men, but he instinctually knew he wouldn't see them among the throng, especially because what he could see of cavalry were both sides skirmishing on the far side of the field. So Rob tried to forget about them and concentrate on the movement of the men all around him. Although his own group basically consisted of the scrubs and castoffs, many of the other groups in the larger arena were dressed and polished, drilled smartly, and wore uniforms that were tailored and consistent. Their marches, even on rough ground, were triumphs of precision. Their officers sat in saddles as if they rode horses every day of their lives.

Amelia was in her favored position, but it was more that a half mile away from where Rob and his unaffiliated brethren were drilling. He could only just make her out beneath the spreading branches of the lone tree. But he could see how she might have been spotted by Spencer the day before.

The Wheat Field was one of the few parts of the battle that could be reenacted where it took place. Rose Woods, one of the multitudinous knots of forest, was to the west. Also to the west was Stony Hill, whose name described exactly what it was, a gentle rise topped with sparse wild grass and a riot of loose rocks. Below it spreading out in the cool morning was the Wheat Field itself, a tall grass field really. Still and heavy with dew, it did not look expansive enough that on July 2, 1863 over twenty thousand troops from both sides had occupied it, retreated from it, charged to take it again, and then were again driven from it. All told, on that late afternoon there were numerous attacks over two hours by eleven separate brigades. Of the twenty thousand men engaged, six thousand became casualties.

Because of the carnage the Wheat Field had long been known as a center of roaming specters. Well before the reenactments began in the 1960s locals had been witnesses to strange apparitions and mysterious images gliding over the fields and among the trees. Ghost hunters over the decades traveled there to investigate the reported phenomena. Early in the morning and late in the evening ethereal beings could sometimes be seen, hiding in the borders of the woods, or wisping in and out of the mist. Rob didn't know if he believed in ghosts, but he could sense a heavy blanket of tragedy resting over the whole area, as if these thousands of lives cut so tragically short still left something of themselves to remind and caution those who followed.

In any event, it seemed everyone felt it. There were not the jabs at camaraderie, or the bawdy jokes, or the gruff voices and laughter as there had been when they mustered the morning before.

The day itself was just a long swirling blur. They drilled in the morning, although this time as much larger units, learned their new roles as members of Brigadier General GT Anderson's Brigade of Georgians, serving in the 3rd Division under Major General John B Hood. Being from Georgia himself, Sgt. Barefoot was particularly proud of his assignment, and was determined that the men under him knew and performed their roles to perfection.

There was something awe-inspiring about being in the larger arena with thousands more troops. There were more peculiarities of uniforms, more colors, regimental bands playing, rows upon rows of artillery, wild cavalry charges. There were lines and columns and phalanxes of marching re-enactors, bayonets and rifle barrels glistening in the sunlight, white smoke from the volleys of discharging artillery pieces, constant tattooing drumbeats, men shouting, reins jangling, and horses thundering around the periphery of the arena.

Their part in the drama was straightforward. They would drive toward the enemy, and be driven back, drive forward again, and ultimately end in a stalemate where volley after volley would be exchanged with their Yankee opponents with many men falling on each side.

They drilled through the morning and into the early afternoon. When the smoke cleared and the break was called, Amelia was gone from her spot. On this day Rob had brought a lunch that Kay had packed for him, and instead of traipsing back to the vendors' area he found a shady spot on the border of Rose Woods and ate by himself in the sultry humid breeze.

The feeling had been creeping up on him that it was just too convenient that Spencer had found Amelia among the thousands of participants and spectators. It gnawed at him. Coincidences were things that happened to other people, and you half-wondered if they were telling the truth when they told you about them. But then again he would see Amelia in his mind and the suspicions would melt away.

Rob wandered around the battlefield after he ate, looking at the plaques and monuments, the interactive maps, and again marveled at the sprawling area of the battlefield. He thought about the two commanding generals, one tested and in the moment with his genius, the other just the latest in Lincoln's quest for someone who could fight "that man." Lee was famous for pressing the enemy, and then forcing him to attack the Confederates although they held the better defensive positions. But at Gettysburg it was different. It was Lee who went on the attack (to the consternation of Longstreet) because he wanted to get at the Yankees before all their forces arrived, not realizing that they already had. And the rest is...history.

The afternoon was a blur. As Sgt. Barefoot said, once the battle started it would be a continuing drama of attacking, and then being driven back, a swing around to the left flank with a storm of others and attacking from there...and being driven back. It was not just Rob who had trouble keeping up. All around him were sweating, huffing, stumbling men, their faces streaked with perspiration and powder, their eyes a little wild. In this bigger arena there was a lot more of everything. The big guns boomed, rockets

231

shrieked overhead, a dense smoke from the repeated volleys from both sides rose in all directions. All around, after charges and retreats, fallen men lay on the ground. By the end of the mock battle they were literally strewn across the battlefield.

The first day, with the newness and the excitement of being there, the spectators had not shown as much respect as they did on the second day, in the larger arena, with thousands more participants. The announcements from the towers were still distracting, the presenters sounding like country DJs with their folksy drawls, but even though it was contrived, it was with a striving innocence to get things right.

Throughout the rehearsal, and through the chaos of the actual battle itself, Rob had kept an eye out for Spencer's troop of cavalry. He thought even with the great numbers he would surely spot them at some point, but he never did. He wondered if they, or a part of them, had again slipped away, and were causing havoc somewhere else.

That reminded him of Olsofsky and his burnt house. Rob didn't know if this was a tit for tat thing between Spencer and Olsofsky, or to what lengths either of them might still be willing to go. He got the definite feeling that the dying embers of the mansion in Poughkeepsie were not the last hurrahs for either of them. And now Spencer might think it was Olsofsky who killed Chick, and must be paid back. There was something distinctly nasty and vindictive about this contest, and when you thought about the possible resources they could throw at each other, it appeared that it could go on for some time, or drastically escalate into a final bloody climax.

And then, with the pops of small arms fire growing more sporadic, and the great waves of soldiers ceasing to cross and re-cross the field against each other, it was over. Because it was a calm, almost sultry late afternoon, the pall of smoke hung over everything. The re-enactors on both sides began the organized formal retreats. Quickly the Wheatfield was eerily quiet. The spectators who had been loud and raucous in their cheering on of one side or the other, now quietly collected their things for the long march back to the parking lot.

Rob barely remembered anything of the evening. They ate, but he couldn't have said what, Kay and Amelia sat on the porch and talked, and then somehow he was awakening the next day.

232

And then it was the last day and the climax of the battle. Suddenly it was there, and everything leading to it was a blur. Again all of the re-enactors would be on one field for the dramatic culmination of the conflict, Pickett's Charge. Historically, it was probably the fulcrum of the war, after which the balance of power swung in the direction of the Union forces. There had been reams of descriptions and commentaries written about it, and Rob had read a lot of them over the years. But what he had come to think was that it marked the end of individual chivalric warfare, and the angry horrible birth of the war machine. The idea that so many men could fall so quickly, and at distance, had never been seen before, and especially not at this level of carnage. Sure, there had been the awful hell of Antietam, but in much of that battle it had still been possible to see the facial features, even smell the enemy you were fighting. Pickett's Charge was mostly an unhesitating march of brave men across an empty field to certain doom.

Rob thought again about how he had become one of the fallen two days before. It was still strange to think that he had had absolutely no inkling of an intention to do it. He had not stumbled, and then allowed that stumble to morph into a sudden death throe. He had no done it because of fatigue or discomfort, although at the time he had been experiencing both. He had not "done" anything. His false death had a twinge of divine intention to it, although even as he was considered it, he thought that term was too strong. But what if it had been a warning? What if somehow the fragility of his actual existence was being held up and pointed out to him? It made him think again of Chick's expression, or the expression that had been left on Chick's face, at the base of the falls. He might have thought that expression would have been one of stunned outrage...or questioning surprise. But what it had really looked like was terrible pain followed by immediate release. The nerve synapses had not even completed firing before he was dead.

Amelia and Kay came down the stairs together. The groaning and keening of the steps beneath their feet announced them. Rob had begun to recognize and anticipate the noises each stair made as someone rose or descended, but with that came the realization that they would be leaving the next afternoon, and weren't likely to return. So understanding the language of this particular staircase was like being the last speaker of an obscure Inuit or Maori dialect. With no one to pass it to, it was unlikely to be of use in the future and would soon be forgotten.

What would happen tomorrow? Today he would be in the climax of a mock battle with thousands of participants. Spencer and his men, some of them anyway, would be there, but the chances of gaining any useful information, or even seeing them on the battlefield were still probably negligible. Irina would be in the RV, or would she?

What of Amelia and himself? It came down to the fact that he had nothing to offer her. Surely she would realize that soon, if she hadn't already. Might she not look at today as the culmination of their brief and exiting adventure, and calmly go back to her previous quiet life? He knew he didn't yet trust their abbreviated intimacy, and perhaps she didn't either.

It must have shown on his face because when she came out on the porch, she said, "I know what you're thinking." But then she put her fingers to her lips because Kay was coming out right behind her. Amelia went to the smooth wood rail and looked out across the fields. The trees were dipped in a gray cotton-candy mist. The grass was wet with dew. And as it seemed every morning at Kay's house, the squirrels were scurrying at the tree trunks, and the birds above were trilling in the boughs.

"You'll have some heat to deal with today, my dears," Kay said as she came through the doorway, "or at least quite a bit more humidity than we have had. The FARB boys with their wool undershirts will be earning their keep today."

Amelia came from the edge of the deck and sat in a rocker, holding her mug in two hands in front of her. She looked out across the pleasant landscape, now fully bright in the morning, the horizon already undulating with the heat. "Kay, how many of these re-enactments have you seen?"

"Forty or fifty now, I guess. They really didn't start regularly until the sixties. It used to just mostly be the soldiers. Then you started getting generals portrayed. And you knew it was getting big when Lincolns started parading around the grounds. I've seen Abe Lincolns portrayed as he was supposed to be; tall, gaunt, ugly as sin. And then I've seen others who are short and bald, with only the cut of their beard to give a hint of who they are supposed to be.

234

"I once saw a Robert E. Lee so fat he had to have a stairway to get up on his horse. When I was a kid, sometimes there would be only a few hundred re-enactors and a few thousand spectators. But it's grown and grown. It still has its ups and downs, and it's big business now, especially a big anniversary like we had last year. I sometimes wonder how the ghosts of these boys feel with all the people tramping on the places where they fell." She looked up and neither Rob nor Amelia said anything. "Don't misunderstand me. I think it's a good thing. We remember our past, and we make money. It's the American way."

"It's true," Rob said. "We celebrate the violent individualism and the nobility of the defeat of the Rebel cause… and the anti-slavery morality and overwhelming just power of the Union cause. The horrible carnage is just the dross after it has all been burned away to show the true American spirit."

"That's very poetic," Kay said, looking intently at him with her cornflower eyes.

"He's being sarcastic, I think," Amelia said.

"I don't know that I am," Rob protested. "There is not an American type, or rather there are many, but there is a unique American spirit, although I think we're losing some of the most important elements of it. It's brash, energetic, pioneering, creative, extroverted…and violent. Most important, it's relentless and hard working. The tip of the spear of American creativity is this work ethic. For the first time in human history men have been put in a position where they can create their own nobility. It's 'dog eat dog, and devil take the hindmost,' but that's the way of life in any event. And haven't we found a way, when there was an absolute necessity, to come together and work cohesively toward a common goal?" He looked at them, and then out at the historical panorama in front of him. He was enjoying his bombast. "It turns out the answer is, no…or actually only once, during the Second World War. I'm afraid that may have been the pinnacle of our civilization. The hundred years before that war were spent learning how to concentrate wealth in fewer and fewer hands. And the seventy years after, except for the first ten or so where we begrudgingly rewarded those who had risked and sacrificed so much, has been an exercise in concentrating wealth even more."

235

As the sun became stronger, brighter, so did the colors all around…the blue sky, the green grass, Kay's gardens with the brightly colored flowers above newly turned brown earth. The heat might wash it out later, but for now the world was vividly laid out before them.

"See, during World War II many Americans began to recognize that the collectivism of their efforts was what was winning the war. They looked back to the ten years of the Depression, when everyone had suffered, everyone but the very wealthy who had caused it. Sure, a few of them had lost everything and jumped from buildings to end it all. But like our last dip, most of the rich had lost little compared to the rest of us.

"Anyway, during the fifties, this idea of working together and improving things for everyone led to a general turned Republican president who revamped our infrastructure, improving roads, bridges, dams, the electrical grid. And that was followed by the Great Society of the sixties led by Democrats which added a health care safety net to Social Security, and came up with ways to give more aid to the unfortunates who couldn't, or in some cases wouldn't, rise up.

"I think this is where the moneyed interests realized that they needed to come up with a new model. They had bankrolled this societal safety net by allowing their tax rates to be raised, and in most cases they had done it willingly. There wasn't this Ayn Rand selfishness cloaked as self-actualization drone yet. They had also allowed the unions, because they were so full of returning vets, to become stronger and more vocal. So even though the wealthy were still doing well by anyone's standards, they sensed an erosion of their power and treasure.

"So in response they created Ronald Reagan, or as Gil Scott Heron called him, 'Hollyweird.' Here was a smiling articulate grandfather telling us to pull ourselves up by our bootstraps, whatever they were, because that was the American way. But his agenda was to disrupt the welfare state at all levels, to muzzle and marginalize the labor unions, and to cut taxes for those at the top, and therefore government assistance to those at the bottom. This wasn't the beginning of the idea, but it was the beginning of the implementation of voodoo, or trickle down, economics. You free up the tax money that had been coming from the rich and had been used to maintain the social welfare systems, and you allow them to use that money to invest in new businesses, and therefore new jobs, and then those people on the dole can take care of themselves. But more importantly, from this paternalistic point of view, it will allow this lower form of humanity to feel better about itself.

"But a couple of things happened. First of all, it became cheaper to manufacture goods overseas. You can point to a couple of causes for this. Conservatives will say it's because union demands for wages and benefits drove up costs, and some of that is true. But it was also because factory workers in the U.S. had been led to believe that their work would lead them to a life relatively free from danger and want. The wages they were paid were higher than in the third world countries where workers lived in hovels with dirt floors and no electricity or plumbing, and where the factory owners didn't have to worry about minimum wages, or safety, or anything else. Secondly, the tech boom happened. Suddenly companies could be made, revenues generated, or at least the potential for revenues was seen…and this with almost no employees. The idea became the product, and a few people with big ideas became fantastically wealthy. Nothing wrong with that either. But from the trickle down standpoint, because you don't need factories or a large workforce, it puts a kind of dam to the money actually trickling down.

"Then again, as in the twenties, the stock market became a playground for the wealthy. Did you know that the top 10% of earners own 85% of all stocks, and that percentage is rising, and that the bottom 50% own no stock at all. And now the stock market isn't about building or finding good companies that are growing and hiring more people. It's about logarithms and insider deals and split second computer trading that none of us are a part of. So that 15% of stock owned by the bottom 90% of the people, that's our cushion. Or at least we think it's our cushion. But if the stock market takes a tumble like it did a few years ago, it's already arranged that the losses come from that pile first. And if that part of the pile isn't sufficient, then the wealthy run to the government screaming that if they begin losing any part of their pile, it will threaten the stability of the whole system.

"And the real estate bubble, who created that? Again, the conservative folks will say it was the government's doing, Fannie Mae and Freddie Mac, trying to get people into home ownership who didn't deserve it and couldn't afford it. And sure, in the nineties there was an emphasis by government to get more people into homes. But were these quasi-government entities making and backing all the terrible loans? No...not until the very end anyway."

Kay said, "I sense disgust, but I don't sense any real passion, either for the victims, or against the people who pulled these frauds off."

"Well, I am disgusted that people were able to get away scot free. They say it's difficult to prove the 'intent' to defraud, which to me is all the more reason to go after the people at the top. We should have used the Chinese model. Something like the mortgage meltdown happens in China, they take a couple of CEOs out, line them up against a wall, and shoot them. It's a marvelous deterrent to bad behavior. The leaders of these companies claim they didn't understand these mortgage-bundling instruments, and therefore aren't responsible. Bullshit! Sorry. Basically what I think the bank CEOs did, and many of them are still at the helms of their companies today, is got together and said, 'We're going to play musical chairs. We'll ride this thing as long as we can, and when the music stops, we all dive for the chairs. But in our game we'll be short two chairs. We won't have a chair for the mortgage holders, of course, who will watch their home equity drop overnight to zero or less, or for the teacher's pension fund in Norway, or the police pension fund in Albany, or any of the other schlubs who bought the useless bonds we put together, even though we basically guaranteed they were safe and secure. And then one of us, a bank or maybe two, won't be able to find a seat and will also have to go belly up. It's the price of doing business.

"But the rest of the banks, we will go on even bigger than before. We'll go to the government and say, 'You have to make us whole. You can't afford to let anything happen to us.' And if the government asks, 'What about the poor consumer, the homeowner who borrowed the money because you told him his house was worth it? Don't we have to help him too?' 'No, no, you can't help him because that would create a moral hazard. In spite of the false information we gave him, in spite of the fact that over the course of time more and more of us realized the information was false, he should have known better.' 'Caveat Emptor.' So basically the banks are able to siphon most of the equity out of the country's middle-class homeowners' market. Forget the fact that we've been teaching the middle class for decades that home ownership was the most safe, reliable place to park their assets. The banks get propped up by guarantees and actual cash bailouts and the ability to borrow money from the Federal Reserve at no interest, and then are allowed to go on as if nothing has ever happened. The end."

"Nobody went to jail?" Kay asked.

"Nobody went to jail."

Amelia was looking at Rob with an expression of new-found admiration. "Even if you weren't overly passionate about it, that was very well put together. Where did you come up with all that?"

"I just looked at it as it happened, as it is still happening. Remember how I would lock myself in the den and watch the cable news all night?" It was a gentle reminder that she, as his wife, should know where he had picked up all the information. She caught on immediately.

"I thought you were just watching loops of testosterone cream ads."

"Oh, that hurts," he said, clutching at an invisible wound in his side.

"But at least in this country," Kay said, "if you work hard, and you're smart about it, you can rise up the ladder."

Rob looked at her, wondering if he should say anything else. He could tell her that in terms of societal mobility the United States now ranked 33rd, between Nigeria and the Czech Republic, and that a person born black and poor in the U.S. has almost no chance, none, to rise out of his or her situation. So he just nodded and smiled out at the rolling countryside.

The faint stirrings of a breeze carrying moisture from the Gulf of Mexico shivered at the tops of the trees. Rob longed for the smell of the ocean and sniffed again for the hint of it, but as quickly as he had sensed it, it was gone. There was the realization again that they would be returning to the Outer Banks in only days…wouldn't they? What had they come up here to find, and what had they found…each other? He didn't know. They had found Irina, but were really no closer to knowing her true situation than when they had left. They didn't know who had killed Steven…or why. They didn't know who had killed the girl everyone thought was Irina and dumped her in the canal. Why had Spencer sent a mercenary group to firebomb a financier's house? What was their relationship? And given the financier's Ukrainian roots, how was he related to Irina? Did it have to do with the Ukraine's political situation? Had Spencer recognized Amelia, or did he know who she was to begin with? It couldn't have been purely by chance that he had asked her to come paint their group. Had he already connected her with Rob? Then it rushed at him that maybe Amelia was already connected to Spencer. Maybe she had insinuated herself into his life to watch him for Spencer.

He looked over at her sitting next to Kay, both of them rocking gently in their chairs. She caught his eye and smiled, and all his suspicions immediately seemed baseless.

"We should get ready," he said.

Kay rose. "You need a big breakfast. You both go and get washed up and dressed, and I'll make some eggs and bacon."

Rob turned stiffly from the railing. The exertions of the last two days had settled like dull straining knots in his muscles. Aside from the soreness there was an overwhelming fatigue, as if the elasticity was gone and his tendons and sinews could not revert back to their poised and ready positions. He looked over at Amelia and she held out her hand. He knew his shuffling feet made him look old, but even with the soreness, and in spite of the stiffness, he felt some small strength returning. Not unkindly, he waved her hand away.

They went upstairs and washed up and began to don their costumes. The battle was not scheduled until four PM, but a flurry of other activities was scheduled to precede it. It was the last real chance for the vendors to hawk their souvenir hats and t-shirts. The food purveyors were stocked up, not wanting to run out of anything on this last day. The generals, who would be giving their speeches in breathless overheated tents, were going through their final drafts, adjusting the medals on their uniforms, and snipping at the beards most of them wore only this time of year.

There was a nervousness and anticipation all throughout the environs of Gettysburg. It began to dawn on people that it had been more than a century and a half since the most important battle in US history. Thousands of pages had been written about how the generals had felt, and what they had thought, what they had known or not known, and how their plans had been formulated and executed. Reams had been written about the positions of men, and cannon, and cavalry, where and when they had moved, what they had found, how they had fought, where they had gained ground, or been stopped, or beaten back.

Rob and all the other men of his hackneyed unit were to rendezvous with Sgt. Barefoot at the northwest rim the natural amphitheater of the big valley at 10 AM. It was to be a repeat of the procedures of the previous two days. They would learn their muster area, on this day to be specified by large colored flags, which would be set about the field so the particular units of the armies could gather in their assigned positions. They were then to be told their mission, what units would be to the left and right of them, how quickly and how far they should move forward, how many should fall, and for the Rebel side, when and how quickly they should be driven back.

He and Amelia dressed mostly in silence, taking turns in the bathroom, still shyly turning their heads as the other undressed. He helped Amelia with her many buttons, his fingers fumbling and cramping as he tried to connect the studs with the minute loops.

"You're not worried that they'll see you?" Amelia asked as they were finishing up.

"No. I still think it would be extremely unlikely. And with the flow of the mass of people, they couldn't really do anything if they did spot me. I'm more worried about you."

"Well, you don't have to be," she said, taking his arm and smiling. "This is, after all, what I do. I don't have to pretend to be drawing or painting. I will draw and paint."

"But suppose they know who you are-"

"They don't. It they did, and wanted to do something to me, why wouldn't they have done it two days ago? I left the field in a buggy with someone in uniform. There are thousands of men in uniform. Who was paying attention to me, other than you? If I were to disappear, there's no one here to report me missing but you, and you couldn't report it because we don't know if the police up here are looking for you."

Rob was silent. She was right. But he was still worried that they were missing something, something important.

"They are supposed to pick me up at the same place at noon. I'll go there, take my photographs, do my sketches, and try to get some time alone with Irina. I'm still not sure what to ask her, or if she'll tell me anything. Does she know about the girl in the canal, who everyone thinks, or acts like they think, was her? Does she know Steven is dead, or who killed him, or why? Is she with Spencer, or being held by him?"

241

Rob shrugged. They were all the same old questions. Maybe Irina would open up to Amelia. Maybe not.

They both filled up on breakfast, as Kay had hoped they would. Rob knew that he and Amelia were both at the age where it was important to balance the intake of food with the outflow of energy. And while they were both being active, he still knew he was eating more than he had in a long time. He had especially felt it when cinching his belt this morning and finding that it was only with a deep breath that he was able to find his usual hole, and when he did he could feel his gut swelling over the top band of leather.

At any other time of year the drive from Kay's house to the re-enactors' parking lot would take no more than ten minutes. But they knew traffic would likely be heavy so they left at 8:15. Five minutes after they entered the highway they were in a long line of cars in the right lane crawling toward the battlefield. The heat rose sullenly from the packed moist earth, and with it came impatience from drivers in front of and behind them.

"Obviously if I could move faster, I would," Amelia said, looking into her rearview mirror.

"That never seems to matter to most people. They want to get somewhere with a lot of other people who want to get to the same place too so they can all be together, but they don't want to be together on the way."

"And, of course, this being the climactic day," Amelia said, "I assume there will be even more people than yesterday. And I guess there will be some more Fourth of July celebrations incorporated into the festivities too."

"I think there are more fireworks planned after dark." Rob felt a kernel of anticipation in his belly, but it was curdled with dread. "I think there are fireworks planned for after."

"You just said that."

"Preoccupied, I guess," he said absently. "There are going to be a lot of people."

She looked at him again. He thought back to when he had first really seen her, trudging through the weeds toward Chick's father's house; nervous, kinetic, head down, but moving with purpose. And he remembered her speaking to him the first time, watching her struggle to be composed and assertive. It was no struggle any more. And it made him wonder, was it really such a struggle then? Was she the meek and hesitating person he first met, or was she the person he saw now; tactical, sure of herself, ready for adventure?

Had there been some kind of anima-animus swap? Because now he was the one who hesitated and was unsure of himself. It was true that the blunting of his confidence had begun well before he met her, and could probably be traced directly to his stroke. But he was not sure that his relationship with her had arrested his decline completely, although there was some evidence it had slowed it.

Those were his thoughts as Amelia twisted the steering wheel, working through the rows in the re-enactors' parking area. She obeyed the swinging arms and pointing of the orange-clad volunteers and moved further back among the hundreds of cars. Soldiers, both Union and CSA, were retrieving their gear from their vehicles or were already trudging under the weight of their packs and muskets toward the staging areas. Kids were orbiting around their parked family minivans like antic satellites. Amelia was only taking a sketchpad with charcoal and pencils, and her digital SLR camera and bag. When she was taken back to Spencer's camp for more preliminary work on a portrait she never intended to complete, she knew she could fake it with those items.

After gathering everything they walked together to the border of the parking area. She gave him a look of open and genuine fondness, but she didn't try to embrace him. She waved and then moved to the trail that led up to the saddleback ridge and then on to the natural basin where the battle would be held. Rob took the longer trail that first led south and west and gradually wound more to the northwest where he would begin climbing a gentle rise to the area where the Rebels would collect and muster and be given their instructions for the battle.

He moved to the right edge of the trail and trod on slowly, individuals and groups of gray and mustard-clad re-enactors striding by him. There were cotton white clouds in the sky, but they never seemed to cross in front of the sun, though he could see them moving slowly and majestically in a slow arc from southwest to northeast.

It took him most of a half hour to make it around the half-circular trail and up to the staging plateau at the end of it. When he came over the rise

243

he found thousands of men separating themselves under flags that flapped in the breeze and then meekly fell limp again. To the northeast, across the bowl of the arena, there were still thousands more of Yankee re-enactors doing the same thing.

Rob's squad was to march under the green flag, which he could see on the opposite side of the bowl, and with all the milling Rebel humanity between. There was no trail he could see through them, just a palisade of raised muskets waving like a forest of reeds.

He retraced his steps to go around the far side of the throng, and when he did he looked out at the long rolling landscape to the west. The green and yellow fields undulated as far as the eye could see. And among the fields, mostly in the low areas where streams and brook guzzled and murmured along the depressions, were copses of forest in different lengths and depths. Some were just thin lines of trees, branches entwined above their trunks, reaching for moisture in the brown and red earth. Others were great dense fists of timber, green and white in the sunlight at their mantles, with dark bruised purple and old-blood brown in the shadows beneath.

Rob knew that just to the south and west, at a distance of two miles, lay Spencer's encampment. And in that encampment was Irina, who, if she didn't have all the answers as to what was going on, was still close enough that she had to have some solid guesses.

XVI

Without any more thought, he turned back in the direction he had come. There were a few stragglers coming up the hill behind him, and none of them gave him more than a passing nod. When he got back to where the border of the woods was only a few yards from the trail, he ducked to his right into the trees. He thought about ditching his Enfield and pack, but he didn't. The rifle could at least be used as a walking stick if necessary, and the pack was neither heavy nor too cumbersome. It held only a non-FARB blanket and poncho, and a few snacks.

As soon as he got beneath the trees and began moving away, Rob began to feel like a fugitive and a deserter. As he had perceived himself moving toward Spencer's camp, his imagination had not looked down as a bird might at the actual lay of terrain that he now had to cross. He only knew in which direction the camp lay, and leaning forward he aimed himself toward it. After ten minutes he had crossed the first length of forest and came out into a clearing. The field, although the land was sometimes rutted and the footing uneven, was easier to traverse than the stands of trees with knots of underbrush, low-hanging branches, and knobby roots to avoid. But there was a tradeoff. It was relatively cooler in the shadow of the trees. By the time he passed in and out of groups of them and reached the third or fourth clear area, he had sweat through his shirt and his hair was pasted to his head. A quarter of a mile across that field was another wall of trees. He had no idea how far it stretched or how deep it might be, so he decided to skirt around the north edge of it. This of course left him in the sunlight and humid heat.

He had not expected to see anyone, and he didn't. He saw the roof and upper storey of a house on a hilltop far to the north, and he went into the trees as he passed, though he didn't think they would notice him at that distance. The two and a half miles he had judged to Spencer's camp were as the bird flies, but Rob wasn't a bird, and he wasn't flying. No part of it was easy, and no part quick, so he took his time and plodded on. He did notice that although he tired quickly and movement was a struggle, he was gaining more control. His synapses were rerouting themselves, and with each step he was becoming surer on his feet, a bit more balanced and in the moment with his movements. But he realized the work he was doing to make these small improvements meant much more time and effort were going to be necessary to get him back to any semblance of wholeness.

He kept sensing glimpses of movement out of the corners of his eyes as he marched through the variegated, mottled shadows. He unaccountably looked down at the earth for signs of other footprints, and paused to listen for any sounds. He tried to prevent himself from thinking about what his plan would be when he reached Spencer's camp. And at his slow awkward pace, he had plenty of time not to think about it.

It took him almost an hour and a half to cover the distance. The light and heat from the sun was now broad and oppressive. For the last half hour Rob stuck to the woods because it was too warm for the exertion in the naked sunlight. Each time he went into the trees he lost some of his sense of direction. He never knew how deep or broad a stand of woods might be, and his one fear was that he would be in the trees too long and pass the encampment and not know that he had. He trusted his inner compass though because it had proved itself so many times in the past. And so after his slow laboring struggle he reached the edge of the last bit of forest and saw through the trunks and underbrush the outlines of Spencer's camp. He bent low as he moved forward, leaning heavily on his Enfield for support. The red flag with its crossed field of stars and bars stirred lazily on the pole above the camp.

It appeared to be deserted. He could detect no movement or sign of life anywhere. When his eyes were drawn to some motion it was a waving tent flap, or shirts on a clothesline, or the fringed ends of the canvas canopy over the door of the RV. He slid along the edge of the woods, careful to be quiet now, trying to take in more angles of the campsite. Still he saw no one and heard nothing. He had come without a real plan of what he would do when he got there, and now the quiet of the place made him doubly hesitant. Only days before when he had come from the opposite side of the camp, he had seen armed men with automatic weapons patrolling the perimeter, and more closely guarding the RV. Now there was no one. Still he wondered if it might be some kind of trap. He reached down and felt the outline of the small pistol in his pants pocket.

Rob sat for another ten minutes sifting out his options. His planning had really gone no further than getting to the camp, observing what was going on, and trying to make further sense of it. But now the ghost town facade was calling him to decide on some more aggressive course of action. He began to think they must have moved Irina to some other location. With that thought came a sense of dread that she could be gone and he would never see or hear of her again.

He opened his round canteen and drank. Although he had left it in the refrigerator overnight, and it was somewhat insulated by its canvas cover, the water was still slick and tepid. In the far distance, although it was hard to isolate the exact direction, he heard the popping of small arms fire. The battle rehearsal was beginning. He stowed his canteen and rose, the sun spilling through holes in the canopy above him, adjusted his hat, grabbed his rifle by the barrel, and stepped out into the clearing.

He moved across the intervening field to the encampment. Here the grass had not been beaten down by drilling re-enactors or grazed upon by the horses. It came almost to his knees and he tramped through it as he went forward. Among the browning shoots of grass were wildflowers, bright yellow and pale blue. With each step forward he expected a challenge, but none came. As he got closer he saw smoke curl up from a spent cooking fire until it was taken by the breeze and dispersed. Suddenly to his left he saw a flash of moving color, but it was only laundry on the line rising and falling in the intermittent wind.

Then he was in the camp, walking between the neat rows of tents, approaching the trailer. When he still hadn't been challenged he went right to the entrance to the RV, climbed the two steps using his rifle to steady him, and rapped on the glass on the upper panel.

It was the first overt sound since he had left the woods and it startled him. There was no answer. He knocked again more forcefully, and shook the handle of the door. It was locked. But with that action he did hear a sound of movement from inside. He gingerly stepped down and a few feet back out from under the awning and into the sunlight. "Hello," he hailed at the door. The windows were closed and curtained, and the generator and air-conditioning hummed along steadily, but he knew whomever was inside could hear him. He held out his arms, grasping his rifle by the muzzle to show he meant no harm, but still no one came to the door. He began to think that perhaps he had not heard anything at all.

Rob had decided in any event that he needed to get in the trailer, and he thought he could either break the lock with the butt of his Enfield, or use it to break out a pane of glass and then reach in to unlock the door from the inside. He was just about to come forward when he heard the sound of the door being unlocked, saw the handle turn, and the door swing open wide.

Irina was standing in the doorway above him. She was in shadows, protected by the darkness inside and the awning above her. As almost always happened when he saw her, something clutched at Rob from inside. She was beautiful…but it had less to do with that then it did from something else that came from both inside and outside of him. When he had worked with her, and lived across the hallway from her, it had been there. It didn't matter if she knew it or felt it or not. She wore a short light summer dress, and her feet were bare. She looked down at him, hand outstretched to keep the door open, her blonde hair falling to that side. Her face was in the shadows so he couldn't see her expression. But she was still as he remembered her…and yet utterly different. Gone was the world-weary nonchalance and the sureness. Even without seeing her features he could tell that her self-possession had retreated deep inside. It was as if opening the door was a surrender. And then in the same instant Rob realized she didn't recognize him. His eyes too were in shadow under his flop hat, and the facial hair and the whole incongruity of the uniform further disguised him.

"I thought you were dead," he said before he could stop himself.

"No," she answered, and turned back into the shadows, leaving the door open for him to follow her.

He came forward, leaving the Enfield leaning against the wall and taking off his hat as he went up the steps. It was almost cold inside, and the cool air fell out on him. The curtains were drawn, so it was dark except for a lamp lit above the small dining table by the kitchen. Rob suddenly felt insulated, but also paranoid because he had no way of monitoring what might be happening outside. There were the remains of a meal on a plate on the table's surface. Irina moved there, where she apparently had been sitting, and where there was also a notebook and pen and other papers.

"It's me," he said, Rob, and when she looked confused, he added, "from the Sea Horse."

"I know who you are," she said, with her peculiar sing-song accent. "You are with the woman who paints, the Hispanic woman."

Rob felt a rising wave of panic, but he held it down, hoping it didn't show in his face.

"Oh, they don't know it yet," she said, because she must have caught something in his demeanor that cued her. "Chick told me."

"Who was in the car?"

"That was Nadia," she said very quietly. "You knew Nadia. I remember you used to look at her, look at us."

"But why? Were they trying to get you and just made a mistake?"

"It was no mistake. It was a warning." She put her head down, and for a moment, because of the way her shoulders bunched up, Rob thought she might be crying. But when she looked back up at him, her eyes were dry. "Nadia never knew anything about any of this. She thought she was keeping the secret about Steven and me. That was why she was driving my car, so that Spencer would see it, and think it was me, and not be suspicious."

Rob had no idea where any of this was leading. He had had his suspicions about Steven and Irina, and he remembered the way she had stood above him in the restaurant the last night she had worked there in what now seemed like months ago, but was really only a matter of weeks. "But we know Spencer didn't do anything to Nadia," he finally said.

She looked up quickly and bored her eyes into his. She usually spoke in a high running chortle. Now her voice was low, smoky, indistinct. "You really don't remember, do you? Spencer said you didn't. You were there when they beat him, trying to find out where I was. You had to have been. Why they didn't kill you too I don't know. Perhaps because you are pyanucya, a drunk, and it is bad luck to hurt pyanucya. When Chick heard you showed up the next morning beaten and bruised, they thought maybe the bump on your head had caused you to forget, and that it would all start to come back to you, but it didn't. It was Spencer's idea to hide you, and Chick had the house in swamps to the west, so they decided to take you there, to see if you remembered, and to keep you away from the police." Again Rob experienced a temporary vertigo, his left side tingling and throbbing at the same time. He knew he should reach out for something for support, but he didn't dare. "But you clearly had other ideas, Mr. Wheat, didn't you? What kind of name is that anyway?"

"Why did they need me to remember?" he said steadily. "They knew it was Olsofsky."

"No…they didn't. Why would it be? He and Spencer had too many interconnected things going. They had the oil and gas leases out west. They had the partnership in the development in Swan Beach. They had all the politicians lined up so that when the agriculture bill came up they would insert language to get the environmental restrictions eased, and the bridge to Corolla approved, and no one would be the wiser. By the time the environmentalists caught on they would have their "ecologically safe" development plans drawn up and approved, the septic systems and pilings in the ground, and they could brag that they had traded thousands of acres in New Mexico and Colorado to a national trust for a few dozen acres on the coast of northeast North Carolina, even though that land out west will never be good to anybody for anything, and even the animals, with the exception of a few snakes and lizards, can't live there. Spencer and Alexander make more millions of dollars, and all it costs them is some payments and campaign donations to the politicians."

"But Spencer at least thought Olsofsky was responsible for Steven's death. If he didn't, why did he send people up to firebomb Olsofsky's house?"

"Olsofsky was responsible for Steven's death," she said, looking into his eyes and speaking slowly as if she were speaking to a child. "You see, Steven had been working for Spencer, done all his construction work for years, and he had done quite well. There were ups and downs, of course, but mostly ups, and Steven had gotten rich…nothing to compare with Spencer or Alexander, but most of the rest of us would have been very happy with what he had. He built himself a big house, and built others to rent, and he had big cars and boats and toys. But he had big expenses too. He had to take care of his first wife and their kids together, and he had always been scrupulous about paying taxes, and because he wasn't big enough, like Spencer, to have all those taxes waived and minimized, that was a hefty chunk. What I mean to say was that he had assets, but he was becoming cash poor. And he was living a lifestyle where you can't act like it's any burden to spend at all. There are expensive vacations to be taken, and his older kids with Paula were getting ready to drive so they needed nice new cars, and then there was college for them to think of, and it was important to pick the right schools. This was in 2007. This was five years before I had seen America, much less the Outer Banks. He knew what Spencer was up to in Swan Beach, and he wanted to be in on it. He scraped together as much money as he could, almost three million dollars, and gave it to Spencer to get himself in on what he thought was the ground floor. Spencer gave it to his accounting firm who handled all the money. He probably explained what it was, but in Spencer's world, he got paid the profits first, and any losses came from the pool of smaller investors. So when the crash came, it was Steven's money, and the others who thought they were in on something where they couldn't lose, who were the first to be wiped out.

"So all the smaller investors were wiped out. Spencer took some losses too, but he was in a much better position to handle them, and by the time he totaled what those losses were he was already making money again. And Spencer knew as things started to come back, his losses would be the first to be made up because that's the way the system is set up. After all, he is a job creator, although the most important jobs he creates are in your House of Representatives and Senate."

"So how do we wind up where we are today? After all, that was almost seven years ago."

"Steven spent that whole time juggling. What he owed and what he paid were like balls flying through the air. He believed that Spencer would make it right for him. I don't think he realized to the very end that in Spencer's mind, he just couldn't do that."

Irina looked down at her hands in her lap. Rob sensed that part of her struggle was that she had been caught between Spencer and Steven, and that she also had some more serious connection to Olsofsky.

"I don't know why I'm telling you any of this," she suddenly said, and her distain was immediate and venomous. "What happened to you anyway?"

"I had a stroke-"

"No, before that. You used to be someone different. Both Steven and Spencer used to talk about you. With all they had, they used to speak about you as if they were jealous. And then when I first saw you, at the employee house, I couldn't believe that it was you they had been speaking about."

To this he had no answer. He could only remember what he thought and felt seeing her across the dark hallway, backlit by a shaft of yellow light, her back to him, her short nightgown diaphanous, every inch of her outline, even the sun-bleached hair of her arms, starkly visible. She had vibrated in the light, and in his memory she vibrated still, like a single resonant note from a piano. His arousal was like the immediate explosion of a match flame. But then he was back in the present, and she was sitting before him, and he knew she saw it in his eyes. Even to him there was a stain of prurience to it. He turned and rose slowly, and went to the window, his back to her. His groin throbbed. He could think of nothing but ravishing her, until suddenly he realized who he was, and just like that the fever passed. "Well, this isn't about me anyway—"

"Ah, but it is. Your problem is that you don't know what you can't remember." She looked at him with a caustic smile, and then looked down at her hands. "I'm sorry. I'm playing with you a little, I guess."

"I remember the house in Currituck," Rob said, ineffectually willing the synapses to fire. "It has something to do with that house."

"Yes," Irina answered, and then her expression changed and Rob got the idea that she was suddenly tired of the whole thing. She turned and went forward to the galley.

"Could I have a cold drink?" Rob asked when she got there and then seemingly didn't have any idea what to do with herself.

She turned and looked at him blankly, as if she didn't recognize him, or had no notion why he might be there. It was then that Rob realized she might be under the influence of some soporific. She wasn't drunk...he knew that. But Rob recognized that look on her face, the look of waiting for time to catch up with itself, and being half-confused because it hadn't.

"What are you on?" he asked.

"They gave me something to calm myself, something..."

"Who are they?"

"Spencer...and the doctor."

Maybe they didn't need to have guards, Rob was thinking. She stood in front of the small boxy refrigerator, having clearly forgotten his request for a drink. Rob suddenly realized she was utterly vulnerable. He could do anything he wanted to her. Again he remembered the sweat-drenched fantasies he'd had in the room opposite hers. Here she stood in the shadows, while outside broad sunbeams whose light permeated everything. There was a second he thought he saw in her languid movements an invitation. She looked at him, or at least he thought he saw her looking at him, from under the overhang of her brow. But she sat quickly, and he saw that her thoughts were for no one but herself.

"My family comes from Donets'k, in the east of Ukraine," she said out of nowhere. "Ukraine is two parts, as Putin says. The west is fertile… forests, wheat fields, agriculture. But the east is where the industrial resources are, iron ore, anthracite coal, hydroelectric power, factories. Russia wants these resources, needs them. Putin says he has to protect the ethnic Russians in east Ukraine who are so put upon by fascist mobs. Do you know why there are so many ethnic Russians in eastern Ukraine? Have you ever heard or decossackization?"

Rob did not understand the word and asked her to repeat it. She did with not much better results, and when he shrugged she went on.

"For centuries the Cossacks of Ukraine were the backbone of the Russian tsars' armies. Because they were such good fighters, and proved their loyalty, the tsars gave them a good degree of self-rule. Provided they gave service, they were left in Ukraine to live what was in that part of the world a very democratic lifestyle. But then came the revolution. Stalin, when he took power, could not allow a democracy on his doorstep, especially one that had been loyal to the Romanovs. Also as a Georgian he was jealous, of course, of the natural wealth and beauty of Ukraine.

"So he developed the plan of decossackization. The Reds went in, separated the Cossacks, murdered many of them, a few hundred thousand, and sent the rest east into the steppes of Asia. The Soviets had trials and whole families were given sentences, and when those sentences expired, they were simply renewed.

"Meanwhile ethnic Russians were sent in to repopulate the land. And then in the Great War, when they needed coal and iron for the war effort, more came in. So when Putin says he has to protect the persecuted Russians in eastern Ukraine, he's talking about a group that only emigrated there beginning in the late 1920s, a group that stole the houses and lands and businesses of the Cossacks who had been forcibly removed.

253

"My family, we are ethnic Russians. But I grew up though as a Ukrainian. I was born in the year of Ukrainian independence. My father and mother were proud Ukrainians who looked forward to the work of building a new country. They wanted to have relations with Russia, but as one independent country with another. But Putin, with his crying about the demise of the Soviet Union, does not see it that way. After Yanukovitch was thrown out, he saw his influence waning. He had to have Crimea because that is where Russia's warm water port is. He called for the plebescite to protect the Russians in Crimea because the native Tatars there had suffered the same fate as the Cossacks under Stalin.

"But he also looked at the raw materials in eastern Ukraine as an affront to his prestige and he couldn't take it. What could he do to frighten conservative Ukrainians, especially in the east, and strike at the deepest fears of the West? Accuse the new government that deposed Yanokovitch of being in the hands of the same fascists who had joined the Nazis in the Great War and murdered the Jews, and now are coming for them, and they had better look to Russia for protection.

"This is where my uncle comes in."

"Your uncle?" Rob was confused.

"Yes, my father's brother. You know the term oligarch? That is what he is. He was politically connected during the time of the Soviet Union, and when things became privatized in the 1990s he was able to use his business contacts in Russia and Kiev to build a metal manufacturing conglomerate in the east. Through his political connections he was able to buy land, factories and other businesses at fantastically reduced prices. Ten years after the Soviets left, he and a few others controlled the economics of the Ukrainian state. Because of their wealth, there were real questions about whether their loyalties lay with Ukraine or Russia, or simply with themselves. Members of their group began to dominate politics, and as they did they began to question ties they felt with Russia because they saw that their positions and power bases might be eroded if Russia gained more control. After all, Putin has his own pet oligarchs, and any one of them individually could buy and sell all of Ukraine's oligarchs together.

"Some of the Ukrainian oligarchs, my uncle included, began to embrace Ukrainian nationalism. They held international conferences, they built museums and high-rises in Kiev and Donets'k. They traveled. And as they traveled they saw the economic and personal freedoms of people in the West, and they naturally began to lean in that direction. At the same time, because of the internet and social media, the young people began to lean that way too. It's not that Ukrainians want to be in the West, or even be considered a part of it. But they see their value as being a bridge between Europe and Asia. Putin misread that, I think. He only saw them falling out from under his influence and naturally, for him, thought they had to fall under the influence of the West. Many of the problems that have been created, that he has created, are because of that.

"So the oligarchs, while they were building up the cities and the infrastructure, also began to help repatriate the Tatars of Crimea, who, like many of the Cossacks, had been banned to central Asia during Stalin's years.

"Now Crimea is interesting in all of this. As I said, Russia is determined to keep its warm-water port there. When Yanukovitch was deposed, and most of Ukraine was leaning west, or at least thinking it had the freedom to decide, Moscow started agitating in Crimea. You see, there is a pattern. During Soviet times when one or another ethnic group was banished to the Asian frontier, Moscow always made sure that ethnic Russians filled the void left by the deportations. That also meant ethnic Russians filled the houses and took the lands and businesses of those who had been marched away. So when the Tatars or the Cossacks, what was left of them, were allowed to return after the Soviet collapse, they found Russian families on their properties. That caused smoldering resentments that have been growing for years. When the revolution began Putin used those resentments, and ginned up problems and confrontations, and then said he had to send troops to protect the ethnic Russians who were being put upon by fascist gangs. Next came the plebiscite, and, bang, Crimea is part of Russia."

There were parts of what she was saying that Rob had trouble understanding. First of all, there was her accent. Some words didn't resister as she spoke them, but then he would pick them up as the conversation moved along. But that caused him trouble because he had to bounce back and forth fitting words into their proper places. Also, sometimes she spoke slowly, and at others her mind would run ahead of her words.

"The same thing is to happen in eastern and southern Ukraine, from Donets'k to Odessa to Moldova. That part of the land, which is where my uncle's businesses are, has iron and other minerals and metal ores, hydroelectric power, and also the largest deposits of hard coal in Eastern Europe. The rest of the country has fertile lands to grow wheat and timber. As they say, if you want to grow your people, plant wheat. If you want to grow your army, you mine iron ore and coal, and forge steel."

"So what will your uncle do? He has to pick one side or the other, doesn't he?"

"I don't know. He has more money than he'll ever be able to spend, apartments in London and New York, an islet off Greece. He could leave tomorrow and never have a reason to look back. But he loves freedom. He loves the idea of Ukraine and freedom. It hasn't been good for everyone, but freedom has been good for him. He feels a responsibility to his country. And he hates Putin."

At times she would drift into silence. But then she would collect herself, and make an effort to be ready to continue.

"What about Olsofsky?"

She expelled a quick, bitter mouth fart. "Alexander is a pig. He was in that politically connected group when the Soviet Union first broke up and Ukraine became free. He went out to the front with them. But he couldn't keep up. When they first divided everything, he got a share, but it was not like what the others were able to get, and he did not have the patience or foresight to grow it... He was more into the trappings of wealth than securing or growing it. He made bad decisions. He backed the wrong people. And that was important because this group began to control the state and the politics. From their members were chosen the leaders, or if they weren't members, they were hand-picked by the oligarchs. Alexander began to see his wealth melt like snow. But he was good with computers and he understood software. Instead of developing legitimate businesses he moved into the shadows and in a few years developed one of the largest cyber-theft rings in the world. Men in dark rooms, staring at computer screens, trolling for identities. This was the big, messy, business he excelled in. As it grew he reached out for Russian and Ukrainian emigres in western Europe and the United States to siphon the money out. The guest worker programs for students, the way I first got here, was a tremendous boon to him. Suddenly there were thousands of attractive, employed young people from Eastern Europe all over the first world. They could go to ATM machines with account information that Alexander's hackers had stolen and empty them of money. He had others to launder the money, travel with it taped to themselves to Europe, or down to Mexico, or places he had set up in the Caribbean. It was so easy he kept expecting someone from the US government to show up and demand their cut. Of course, there were big security requirements. Who better to use than the Russian speaking second- or third-generation Ukrainians from the east? And I'm sure that put him on the radar, and perhaps in the hands, of Russian intelligence.

"Olsofsky has warehouses in Donets'k, and Odessa where thirty or forty hackers huddle over computer screens looking for flaws in systems all over the world. He also had other scams…Ukrainian brides for unlucky western men, lotto schemes. He became very wealthy again, wealthy enough, he thought, to become a part of the oligarchy itself. He didn't realize that all these men, who had made their money in the nineties and at least somewhat legitimately, looked upon him, who had only developed most of his treasure in the new century, as an interloper. They did not accept him as he thought they would. He didn't understand that part of the reason, a big part, was that he was a gauche pig. So when he was rebuffed he did what any other disgruntled millionaire does…he came to America.

"You know the expression, 'money talks'? Well, he had the money, and he began talking. Without really understanding what he was doing, he invested in all sorts of things…tech start-ups, IPOs, real estate. To him it was like gambling. He had the funds from his internet frauds coming in, so he felt like he was using house money.

"Somehow he came to the Outer Banks. He contacted me the first summer I came to work, because he knew my father, and my uncle, of course. I met with him out of politeness, and through him I met Spencer. For some reason I could never figure out, the two of them had clicked. Within months they were in these real estate ventures in Nags Head, and Corolla, up to Swan Beach…even out west where Spencer had bought oil leases years before. Through Spencer Alexander had met Steven, because Steven was the builder for Spencer's Outer Banks developments. And for some reason he treated Steven the same way the oligarchs in Ukraine had treated him. He dismissed him, or at best, barely acknowledged him…treated him like a servant…even though he built for Alexander that beautiful house. I think Alexander knew from the beginning that he would try to ruin Steven, just for spite."

"So it was Olsofsky who killed Steven?"

She looked at him as if she had just realized he was there. Rob wanted to hear more, wanted to understand what had gone down, but he knew their time was limited. Spencer's group, perhaps bringing Amelia with them, would return from the morning's staging soon.

"We must leave here," she said. "They will be coming."

"Who, Spencer?"

"No, Alexander's men. They'll find me."

"Because Spencer bombed Alexander's house?"

She looked at him, her eyes in shadows under her straw blond bangs. "Spencer said you knew. I didn't believe him…not that it matters. Alexander has other houses. Something else is spurring Alexander on now. He's afraid of something."

"Won't Spencer and his men be back soon? Shouldn't there be someone here guarding you anyway?"

Fear passed through her like an arrow, the shaft humming through the air and meeting only little resistance in her flesh. "That's what we must prevent. Both sides are well-armed. It would not be good to see them firing real bullets through the countryside."

"Do you have a vehicle?" Rob asked.

"I have the keys to a truck parked by the highway," she said, with a dazed, hunted look, "but I wouldn't dare go in that direction."

From the RV they could really see nothing. Anyone could approach and probably get quite close before they were discovered. The fear was emanating off Irina in waves now. Five minutes ago she had been drugged, calm, and haughty.

"I know a way," Rob said, "through the woods. Get what you need."

She went by him, close in the narrow space, and went to the room in the back of the RV. He heard drawers scrape open and close on metal runners. He went from window to window, peering out, searching for movement. All he saw was an empty yellow terrain. Irina returned after a few minutes, a red and white bag bulging with contents.

"That's too bright," Rob said. "Put your stuff in here." He opened his haversack, removed his poncho and extra shirt and took the stuff she was pulling out of the bag and began cramming it into his. It was mostly lightweight summer clothes, but what also appeared to be a brick-sized jewelry box, a zippered cloth bag obviously filled with sheaves of currency, and a bulging manila envelope, paper ends spilling from the top.

Rob slung the bag over his good shoulder and grabbed his hat. Irina looked around, confused…or hesitant.

"There are guns everywhere in this camp," she said, "but none in here."

"I don't think we need a weapon if we hurry," Rob said. "Once we're in the woods…I don't think they'll be coming from that direction."

But as soon as he said that he wondered why they wouldn't come that way. And if they did their obvious ingress would be through Kay's property, or one of the others between her and Spencer's camp. He shook his head.

XVII

"Ready?"

Irina still wore the light summer dress, and she had put on a pair of cloth running shoes. Also, as she bent over to retie one of the shoes Rob noticed that she had put on a pair of shorts under the dress.

They moved quickly across the clearing to the large jumble of stones that hunkered like mute trolls at the entrance to the trees. For the first time Rob thought of Amelia. If she returned with Spencer's group at lunchtime and they encountered Olsofsky's men she could be caught in the middle of whatever might ensue. But there was no way to warn her.

They wended their way among the boulders and entered the trees, stopping for a moment as their eyes adjusted to the thin light that fell from the treetops like confetti. It seemed as if a green and dappled golden curtain had been drawn around them. There were noises everywhere, the rising breath of wind in the upper boughs, the groan of sturdy branches feeling the movement further down. And birds, some trilling contentedly, sweetly, some repeating and improving long and complicated riffs. There was the beating of wings and the dry rustle as they skittered through the underbrush.

They moved forward. Rob could feel Irina wanted to be close to him for safety, but there was something, pride…or revulsion, that kept her at a distance. For his part, he couldn't help thinking that he was in a game and had captured the flag, or found the prize, although now the answer as to what to do with it or what it all meant eluded him.

Irina followed him without questioning his lead. He took her down the barely discernible trail toward the falls. The creek paralleled them to their right. They couldn't see the water, but they could hear it as it hiccupped and mumbled in its slow descent. It seemed a much shorter distance to the top of the falls than it had when he was being pursued by Chick. He didn't recognize it with the same eyes because they were not now arched with fear nor was his body filled with pumping blood and adrenaline.

Irina was confused when he stopped short, but then he used his musket to lift the underbrush and showed her the dark tangled trail leading to the base of the falls. He let her go first because she was the nimbler of the two, but he whispered a warning to watch her footing. He slid in behind her, looking down at the stunning curve of her spine beneath the dress fabric, watching her thin arm reach out for a branch to steady herself, her bare calves moist from exertion.

Rob's musket got wedged between two stones and as he paused to extract it, Irina moved further down and disappeared as the trail turned back toward the falls. When he reached the bottom and stepped out of the underbrush she was standing pensively at the creek edge looking at the flat slab of dry rock where Chick had met his end.

"This is where they found Chick, I think," she said. "That was when everything broke loose for Spencer. He could deal with Alexander skimming and stashing and mis-entering numbers...he had people to keep an eye for that...but this was where and when he realized how cold-blooded he was."

"Olsofsky didn't kill Chick," Rob said, bending to scrape the mud off his boot with a stick. "I did. I killed Chick."

Irina looked at him. She blinked, and wiped the perspiration away from her face. "I don't understand," she finally said.

Rob recited what had happened, purposely speaking in a slow monotone to disallow any emotions to well up to the surface. When he had explained it to Amelia, whenever he thought about it and dealt with it himself, it always ended with the same tired declaration. "I didn't know it was him following me. How could I? But he...he recognized me. Why didn't he let me know?"

As Rob spoke Irina's face at first projected an obvious incredulity. But then, as he recited the events as he said they happened, and she looked up at the outcropping and then down at the broad flat stone now completely washed clean of blood, she realized he was telling the truth.

"Come on," he said. "This place creeps me out."

He kept moving on the rocks, along the striations where heat and pressure and moisture over millennia had beat and sanded them flat, buried them deep in the soil as if they were dropped from the heavens. The place was still. Not much light penetrated...no breeze...only the water dripping in silver ribbons. Irina moved ahead, and Rob followed.

She went along the trail next to the stream bank. It was obvious, worn soft by the footprints of hikers, birders, lovers, kids. There was faded

261

graffiti on the rocks, bits of paper trash, a bottle being swallowed by the creek-side ooze. Rob watched Irina with all his faculties. The futile ache of it vibrated in his brain and groin. Each fantasy that arose was snuffed out like a candle. Each pulsing urge of blood rose and dissipated. At one point as she lifted a long thin leg over a stone encroaching on the trail he thought of clubbing her, knocking her senseless, just to see if he could actually take what he wanted. It was as fleeting and futile as any of his other desires.

Every few minutes she would pause and look back for confirmation that she was moving in the right direction. Ten minutes from the falls they arrived at the fork in the trail that broke off and led to the back of Kay Yoder's property. When they reached the intersection Rob took the lead.

Then they were approaching the white and yellow splashes of light that marked the forest's border. Rob had calculated that Kay would only see them as they emerged from the trees if she were standing at her bedroom window actively looking out. He judged the odds against that were great. As they moved up the meadow toward the house, they avoided the cart path leading to the gate and instead cut across the field, climbing through the slat fence on the way so they could use the old barn to shield them from observation from the house. When they made it to the structure they moved along the back wall to the only door. It was locked. Rob searched for a key...above the lintel, under the milk can next to the door frame, on the shelf below the milky, cob-webbed window. He found it in less than a minute, dangling from the nub of a rusty nail under the window. He worked it carefully into the dry lock. Slowly the mechanism's memory came back and it stubbornly gave way.

The key turned and the door opened into a gloomy semi-darkness. There was a frantic and unsettling scurrying into the corners and deeper into the creases of darkness. Pigeons stirred and clapped their wings, cooed in the rafters.

Rob left the door open as he went in. He had to find a place where he could leave Irina so he could go to the house and plan his next move. Dust motes floated in the meager shafts of light. The heavy cross-timbers above loomed like nautical structures. Light also came in through the gap above the big swinging doors. Just inside them an automobile hunkered under a tarp. The rest of the vast hollow structure was used for the accumulation of a hundred years of storage. Under other circumstances he would have liked to swing the big doors wide, turn on the dangling frosty overhead bulbs, and explore what had been left in there. He knew there were farming and gardening implements, tools and nails and screws, harnesses, leather straps, flowerpots, bales of wire, old hay he could smell rotting in the loft. He thought about hiding her up there, but he wasn't sure of the sturdiness of the structure.

Finally he went to the old car, lifted the tarp over the driver's side door and pulled it open. It groaned and resisted, remembering only rust and peace. More mustiness assaulted his nostrils. Something acrid, but non-organic, wafted up from the upholstery, but it dissipated quickly. He stuck his head in to make sure there weren't any spiders, and looked over the back seat to make sure there wasn't an opossum or a raccoon, or a family of skunks living there.

Then he went and got Irina, who was crouching just outside the door. She took his hand and ducked into the barn, looking around much as he first did. Rob untied the blanket from his haversack and took it to the car where he laid it across the front seat. She crawled in as he pointed for her to do.

"Stay here for now," he said. "I'll go to the house and see what Kay's doing, make sure she's not suspicious. I don't think she comes out here for anything...I've never seen her...so you can probably move around as long as you don't make any noise."

"What are you going to do then?"

"I don't know. I have to think about it...and talk to Amelia. What will happen if she returns to camp with Spencer and the others and you're not there?"

"He'll wonder if I was forced to leave by someone, or if I just got fed up and left by myself. But immediately he'll think it's Olsofsky. He probably won't let her know anything is going on."

"I have to go back. I missed the muster this morning so I have to figure a way to find out what our program is this afternoon."

"Playing soldier still?" she asked. She looked uncomfortable and drawn in on the bench seat of the old sedan.

He didn't answer. He was thinking that he would go back to the re-enactors' camp and find the Buddha and the red-headed man, make some excuse why he missed muster, get the afternoon schedule, and then get back to Amelia before the battle began at five.

He was already worn from his exertions. He had walked four miles, maybe more, and it was just noontime. From Kay's house it was almost three miles back to the muster area, another half mile to the sutlers' camp. The thought of trudging back was daunting because he was afraid he would use all his energy on the trek and have nothing left for the battle itself. Then he realized he could just go to the end of Kay's driveway and hitchhike back. Surely someone seeing him on the side of the road with his uniform and Enfield would stop and give him a ride…out of patriotism, if nothing else.

First though he had to be seen by Kay at the house. He couldn't afford for her to be suspicious about anything, and especially not if she had seen him loitering around the barn.

Finally he had Irina settled. He gave her a granola bar from his haversack and made her take a long drink from his canteen.

"You'll be safe here," he said, not knowing in any way if that were true or not. "We'll be back before dark, and we'll figure out what to do. Stay here. Stay out of sight."

As he said those words he could hear Chick's voice saying them to him. It unhinged him a little thinking how that had ended, and thinking how much needed to be done, but that he wasn't exactly sure what it was, or how it would be accomplished. He looked intently at Irina, looking for some sign of trust, or simpatico, but he couldn't be sure he saw either. She was here, with him, relying on him for her safety. He wouldn't fail. But even as he was tying things up and preparing to leave her, the expression on her face was one of unconcern, or distracted boredom. Again he wondered what pharmaceuticals she had been dosed with, how long the duration of the effects would be, and what her demeanor would be when those effects wore off. He was thinking this as he said goodbye to Irina, leaving her in the stultifying darkness.

Then he was closing the barn door, replacing the key in its hiding place and moving around the stone foundation to walk toward the house. He looked up at the barn's heavy outline, dark against the blue of the sky, and white where the sun bleached the color from it as it was about to cross the roofline. He had to see Kay in case she had already seen him. What was his reason for being there? It was an awfully long way to come, and he had better have a good reason for returning.

He had his Enfield in his hands. He didn't hesitate any longer. He came around the corner and headed directly for the house. He was perspiring everywhere, and not just from the heat. From his feet, to the backs of his knees, to his humid crotch, to the rivulet that ran between his breasts, to the circumference of his hat band that pasted his hair to his head…everywhere water was being leeched from his body. He crossed the field until he reached the lawn area where the grass was cut short and there were flowers and hedges around the bases of the trees. He swung wide across the yard, not wanting to frighten Kay by having her first see a shadow lurking close beneath a window. His mind was ticking like the tumbrels of a lock as his thoughts veered back and forth in his brain looking for the right excuse to be there.

Then he came around to the front of the house and realized Kay's car was not in its usual parking space. As much as she tried to avoid the crowds and traffic, she must have had to go out for something. To be on the safe side he went up the steps to the porch and knocked on the door and called her name, but all in the house was dark and quiet. Without any hesitation, he retraced his steps and headed back in the direction of the barn. His idea was to get behind it and use it as a buffer between himself and the house as he made for the woods. If on the off-chance she returned and saw him, recognized his limping walk in the distance, he would worry about explaining that later.

XVIII

Rob passed the barn where all was quiet and made his way as the field drifted downhill until he was back in the shelter of the woods. He stopped when he entered the shadows beneath the canopy and looked back up toward Kay's property. There was no movement. He couldn't tell if Kay had returned, but he felt confident, though without any evidence, that he hadn't been seen.

There was no time to stop and ponder his next move. He had to get back to the reenactment. An honest assessment of his energy levels and reserves told him he was running dangerously low. No matter how he calculated distances, it was a long arduous trek back to the battlefield. He thought about following the field to the waterfall and then heading south back to the highway and hitchhiking back. That was probably a mile and a half all told. It would put him in the open and require him to have an explanation if he were asked why he was on private property, but he felt like he could handle that if it came to it.

Then he thought about retracing his steps, going back through the woods all the way to Spencer's camp, and from there across the fields and through the palisades of trees that interrupted them until he came to the back of the fair area where he could search out his companions and find out the plans for the evening battle. His main worry in returning by way of Spencer's camp was that he might encounter them returning at the same time for their mid-day break. But he very much wanted to see what their reaction would be when they realized Irina was gone. And if Amelia was with them, he also wanted to see what her response was, as an individual, and as any way a part of their group. Any way he looked at it, there would be miles to go.

With Irina at the barn he felt like a prospector who had found a great nugget or gem and had hidden it hastily, and then wasn't sure if the hiding place was secure. With each step he took further away from her he worried that he hadn't secreted her away carefully enough, and that she would eventually be found, or else run away by herself.

Once he was in the woods he moved toward Spencer's camp. It was as if something compelled him to go. He kept imagining himself veering off to the right and back toward the highway. But his feet kept to the trail. Now

266

things were moving more quickly. He had rescued Irina from those who might do her harm. He didn't know who they were, and aside from some vague assertions that it had to do with the political situation in Ukraine, he wasn't sure exactly why they wanted her. Apparently it was to put pressure on her uncle, although Rob didn't know if he swallowed that whole story. Rob also didn't know if Spencer was just serving as a rescuer from a sense of chivalry, or, as he thought more likely, because there was a bottom-line calculation going on. That he would go so far as to hire mercenaries and arm them spoke to the idea that he took this all pretty damned seriously.

He thought again that the trail was becoming more and more familiar, as were the landmarks along it. He was beginning to recognize where there might be points of danger along the way where he could possibly be ambushed, and he gave these areas a wide berth as he went on.

After he went up the trail next to the falls he realized that in some way the decisions were being made for him. At the top of the falls he immediately began to bear right into the thicker bush. He reckoned that if Spencer's group returned and found Irina gone some of them might be sent into the woods to fan out and look for her. The cover where Rob now headed was dense enough, he thought, that he might be able to hide in the thick warrens of brush even if they passed close by. It was hard going because he had to duck and crouch and keep his musket pointed forward so he didn't entangle it. The briars scraped at his face and arms and tangled around his ankles as he stumbled in.

Just as he got deep enough to be completely hidden, he did hear voices. He crouched and held his breath, straining to hear if they were approaching or moving in another direction. He was so deep in the brush that at first he couldn't see anything but the twining branches and quavering leaves in front of him. When he first heard the voices he assumed they were Spencer's men. But now as he heard them again, though they were carved and chopped by the forest, he realized that they weren't speaking English. All the phrases were clipped, military-sounding, and though he couldn't understand any of the words, the language was clearly Slavic. Whether it was Russian or Ukrainian, or if there was even a difference, he didn't know. But there were foreign, and he assumed armed men, moving through this southeastern Pennsylvania forest. He crouched, looking for signs of movement through the thousands of infinitesimal green and yellow gaps in front of him.

Then he caught sight of them. From the sounds of their voices, and with the seriousness of their mission, he expected to see an eastern European version of the men Spencer had sent north to Poughkeepsie. But the three men he saw were middle-aged, not in particularly good shape, and two of them had cigarettes dangling from their lips. But what sent a surge of memory through Rob was that the same two who were smoking wore black leather jackets, even in the oppressive summer heat. He didn't recognize or remember any of the individuals before him from their features or their movements, but that uniform, if you could call it that…the jackets, black jeans, heavy black shoes, shot Rob's mind back to the night he and Steven had gone to Olsofsky's house on the Sound in Currituck. He also finally discerned that two of them had pistols in their hands, held loosely and pointing toward the forest floor as they drifted through the trees.

They didn't seem to have a specific route or destination from what Rob saw. They loosely followed the obvious trail, but they didn't seem interested or suspicious that someone might have used it to leave the area previously. Rob concluded that they were most likely patrolling the perimeter, and that meant there were probably more of them in Spencer's camp. When he realized the implications, his calm demeanor began to roil. Spencer's men, very likely with Amelia with them, would be returning to camp for their midday meal, and to rest and prepare for the climactic battle reenactment scheduled for the late afternoon. He was fixed and transfixed. Any movement or noise on his part would bring him to the attention of the patrol beneath the canopy. And as would happen whenever he got himself knotted in a huddling form, his left side began to fall asleep…or not asleep, but it was becoming deadened and unresponsive. He heard the frantic scurrying of some small animal, close but unseen in the brush to his left.

Then Rob heard the unmistakable popping of rapid small-arms fire. The men in the woods with him heard it too. They stood stock-still for a moment, and then began to move, walking rapidly back in the direction from which they had come. Very quickly, within thirty seconds, they were gone from his field of vision. Rob had tried to pinpoint the direction of the gunfire, but the forest seemed to toss the sounds from treetop to treetop above, and by the time they descended to him it was a confused and confusing jumble of misleading vibrations.

He knew it had to come from Spencer's camp though. Again he thought of Amelia, who might be returning to the camp with the group to continue her preliminary sketches and photographic arrangements. It was far too dangerous to follow the men along the obvious trail. The thicket he was in ran on in the direction of the camp, but it was too thick for him to try to claw his way through for that distance.

What he decided to do was to work his way through the thicket to the edge of the woods, and then follow the protection of the boulders along he forest's edge until he reached Spencer's camp. The gunfire, which had built and quickly come to a crescendo, had now stopped. He tried to mine his memory to go back and re-count the number of shots, and while he wasn't positive it seemed like there had been twelve to fifteen in all, and that they had come in three separate concentrated bursts.

Rob turned in the tight stabbing confines, keeping his head down to protect his eyes, and pressed and dragged himself through the warren of low animal trails. Sharp branch tines stabbed at him and grasped his belt and any loose folds of his clothing. He still tried to move quietly. He knew the dense foliage would blunt sound, and he thought the men in the forest had moved away, but if he was heard and his position detected, they could come and find him like a fish trapped in a weir.

By the time he covered the twenty-five yards to what was both the border of the thicket and the edge of the forest, there were no sounds at all coming from the direction of Spencer's camp. He emerged among another group of large granite boulders, looking like cast-off dolmens of some forgotten ancient religion.

He moved forward carefully, halting beneath the rocks to listen for voices in the air and try to feel vibrations of any movement in the earth. He still carried his Enfield rifle with the stopped barrel, as he had since he had gotten out of the car early that morning. He kept thinking he should ditch it. But for some reason he kept it with him, still thinking that at some point it still might come in handy.

The sky above was pulsing again with heat and light. Perspiration took any path it could find to flow downward, collecting finally in his socks and boots. Still he moved forward, afraid to stop for more than a quick listen, worried that if he did he might automatically turn and go in the opposite direction. That urge was strong already. But stronger still was the need to know. Something had happened at Spencer's camp, something serious and with possibly mortal consequences.

By the time he caught sight of the edge of the campsite he still had heard nothing. And he should have. It was past midday. The re-enactors had finished their stagings and rehearsals and should have returned to camp to eat and rest up for the big battle. As more of the camp came into view Rob began to relax a bit because, although there were no signs of life, nothing from his vantage point seemed out of place either. There was no fire or smoke from the cooking area so maybe they had made other arrangements for the midday meal. Perhaps they had gone to the sutlers' area, or maybe Spencer had arranged for a catered lunch, or taken them all to a restaurant in town.

But all that was belied by the fact that Rob had heard gunfire. Although he wasn't positive that all those sounds had come from Spencer's camp, it didn't seem logical that they had come from anywhere else. He now approached the edge of the boulder-strewn barrier at the edge of the woods. He looked across the field to the other stand of trees he had emerged from after making his trek from the battle site earlier that morning.

He waited a few more minutes in the shadows of the last sheltering rocks. He took of his hat and wiped at his forehead with his handkerchief. The sun beat down. His view of the campsite wrinkled and danced, shimmered in the heat waves. Nothing. Then he was standing, moving across the clearing, without making any decision about it. His eyes scanned the camp in front of him and the woods both to his right and left for any sign of movement or color. He switched his rifle to his left hand and reached into his other pocket for the plinker, which he drew and kept low and close to his body. He was completely exposed so there was no point in even attempting any evasion tactics, which he couldn't have pulled off in any event. He just kept moving forward.

He was close to the camp, just entering between a line of tents, and on the verge of thinking that nothing at all had happened, when his attention was drawn by a dancing tent flap, and at the corner where the breeze jerked at the stiff fabric, Rob saw a pair of gray legs prone and disappearing into the interior of the tent. He froze and squatted, leaning on the Enfield, holding his real though admittedly humble weapon by his ear.

Finally he crept across the path to the tent where the body lay. The victim, whom Rob didn't recognize, was on his face in the fine dust. There were two large blood-stained holes in the back of his non-FARB t-shirt. When Rob got closer he saw another hair-clotted wound to the base of his skull. Near his right hand was a pistol in the dirt, but it didn't appear to have been fired.

Suddenly Rob heard a noise coming from the field outside the camp and his insides turned to jelly. He stepped into the tent and crouched behind the thin wall, picking up the 9 millimeter pistol as he stepped over the prostrate man. He heard some indefinable sounds, and then a jangling of metal, and then a nonhuman groaning cry. He finally poked his head out and looked down the open aisle between the rows of tents and saw two saddled horses in the field beyond, their flanks wet and quivering, their reins hanging uselessly down. They appeared to be looking into the camp, trying to judge if it was safe to return to their corral. Then further on in the field he saw it. It was the black buckboard wagon that Amelia had ridden on, still attached to the same horse that had pulled it two days before. But the horse had apparently been frightened so badly that when it fled it had veered off and toppled the wagon, which now lay on its side behind the animal. Every few minutes the horse dragged it a few feet.

Rob came out and moved along the line of tents toward the center of the camp. He found another body crumpled against a cot inside another tent. It was Dustin, the chef and manager of the Sea Horse. His empty body looked useless and disposed of, cast off. For the first time Rob wondered how it was that Dustin had been able to get off from work on Fourth of July weekend, not that it mattered. Never again would he dote on his family in the afternoon and then dog the foreign waitresses and prep girls after the shift. No more screaming at the service staff, no more standing behind the line, sweating above bubbling pans. No more tossing, flipping, feeling for firmness, dousing with wine or cognac. No more burns, or cuts, or slices with incredibly sharp knives. No more anything.

Rob began to get angry. He knew there were reasons for this standoff and these skirmishes, that things had transpired that he didn't fully understand. He knew there were competing motives and desires and

271

excuses, misunderstandings, outright lies, shattered trusts, jealousy maybe, lust, greed, envy...who knew what else? But at some point somebody needed to step back and call for a truce. But even as he was thinking it, he realized it was already too late for talk.

He went forward, the found pistol heavy in his right hand, plinker replaced in his pocket, almost dragging the Enfield now, using the butt of it as a support. He came to the end of the tents and the central clearing in the camp. To his right was the meal wagon. Directly in front of him was the RV, its fringed awning still waving above the steps. Beneath the awning the door was cracked open into the interior darkness. As he moved forward Rob saw two bullet holes in the metal wall next to the door, and when he got close enough he saw that the door itself had been knocked of it upper hinge.

There was no time for hesitation now. Whatever he was doing, he needed to do it and then quickly get away from this place. He went to the steps and rose up them, pistol at the ready. Because of the stark contrast of light outside, he could see very little as he first entered. As his eyes adjusted he saw that the place was ransacked. The acrid smell of spent gunpowder hung heavy in the air. On the floor in the kitchen a man lay on his side, his arm up covering his face, blood fanning out beneath his head. Rob moved his arm to look at his face. There was an ugly hole in his cheek, singed black around the edges, as if the gun's barrel had been pressed against the skin when it was fired. Rob didn't recognize the man. He wasn't one of Spencer's military-looking crew. His hair was longish and wavy, black with flecks of gray throughout, but quite white at the temples. Rob remembered Amelia's description of Spencer's New York lawyer and wondered if it could be him.

Then Rob was drawn to the back of the RV, the sleeping cabin where Irina had gone only an hour earlier to retrieve her bag. He passed through the sitting area to corner where the hallway narrowed. It was dark in the hall, but the door in the back was ajar and light came through the edges. Then he was pushing the door open. There was a skylight in the room that bathed it all in a soft yellow summery glow. There were two bodies, one on either side of the bed. At first Rob thought the form on the right side wedged between the bed and the floor was Spencer. He looked to be the right size, but as he got closer and above him he saw the crew cut and the musculature, and he knew it was one of the commandos from New York.

Rob straightened, aware of the tension and fatigue in his neck and lower back, and went to the other side of the bed. There he found her. Amelia was like a crumpled gray and black flower dropped there on the floor. He couldn't see her face, just the back of her head and her dyed black hair, going white and spindly at the part. He immediately hoped, no needed, that there still be life in her. He put the pistol on the bed, and reached under her limp form with his good arm, realizing as he did that the physics weren't right to be able to lift her from the narrow space to get her on the bed. He was a victim of some shadowy optimism because he still didn't see blood, but as his arm slid beneath her it became slippery with the stuff. Somehow he wrestled her onto the bed, turning her over as he did. Her face was expressionless. Her eyes registered nothing. There were wounds in her upper abdomen, but to the side of her breast so they passed through her from left to right, and had only stained the gray bodice of her dress because of her face-down position.

Rob didn't know what to think or do. He had a long look at her lying there on the bed, being careful as he always was not to muster any feelings, but just let them come as the would. He didn't feel rage or fear. He knew that. Sorrow didn't have a chance yet because of the surprise and the still possible danger. But then that face with nothing on it refused to tell him anything, or let him go. He had always known that he couldn't do this without her, and now he was going to have to.

The bedroom, as well as the rest of the RV, were already torn apart, so there was no point, he thought, searching further. He suddenly felt extremely vulnerable. He had only found five bodies which mean that the rest of Spencer's group couldn't have been there at the time of the attack. He didn't know if they were likely to return, but he knew he had no good explanation if he were found there, no matter who might show up. In his mind he was still trying to compose what had happened from the positions of the bodies, but he suddenly realized that didn't matter as much as getting away did. He would go back to Kay's and get Irina…but then what? He looked down again at Amelia who was no longer able to help him. But the thing he realized, and it chilled him when he did, was that she had trained him for just this moment. When he looked at the trajectory of what he had been when he met her and who he was now he recognized that he owed her a great debt. And so he began to cry. There was regret and longing as he backed out of the room and moved to the front of the trailer. But there was also a blossoming sense of the inevitability of it too. There was no God maybe, but there was a gargantuan impulse of the world to form itself, and you ended up either in or outside of what was created. And while Rob was in it, he was determined to have a hand in the final result.

He limped back to the kitchen at the front of the RV. He took off his gray shirt, sticky with Amelia's blood, and dropped it on the floor. He turned all the gas knobs on the stove full on. Immediate with the low hissing was the smell of propane surging into the room. There was a candle and a book of matches on the table under the window. He took them and set the candle on a low end table near the door and struck a match. He lit the candle, which sputtered a little, and then came to its swimming yellow life. Then he quickly stepped back, pulled the door closed behind him, and set off for the woods, bent over and hurrying like the fugitive he was.

Protected and in his element again, he paused under the umbrella of the trees. The noise of his progress trailed him, loud and urgent to his ears, drowning out the birdcalls and anything else. A few minutes on toward Kay's house he began to anticipate the explosion and destruction of the RV. He thought about Amelia in there, and then he didn't want to think about that anymore. As he went on he tried to reconstruct what he thought had happened.

It seemed to him that they, whoever they were, must have been waiting at the campground. They must have come for Irina, of course they had, and found her gone. The first part of the returning re-enactors from Spencer's group began to arrive. Those others, whomever they were, must have been laying in wait.

He was on the trail almost to the cataract when he heard a hissing and then a high whistle. He stopped and cocked his ear, and looked back in the direction of the camp. What he heard then was not a concussive explosion, but a whooshing thud and the accompanying shrieks of the sheet metal thrown out in all directions. The mass of trees between him and the camp prevented any visual observation. He didn't see fire or smoke. He kept moving, heading back to Kay's.

XIX

So he crouched at the edge of the woods and looked up the gentle incline of Kay Yoder's property. It was still only 2:30 in the afternoon. The day so far had been one hellish trek after another. Rob could not come to grips with his overlapping options. First of all, he could hobble back up to Kay's house and get on her phone, call the police, and anonymously explain or at least describe everything that had happened. Let them sort it out.

Secondly, he could go back to Kay's house, grab the extra car keys and Irina and take off, not worrying about directions or destinations. They could get far away and then work through secondary plans and decisions. It would be like a spontaneous adventure, where distance would lead to peace and forgetfulness. Irina would realize who Rob really was, look past the infirmities. He didn't get far with that scenario. That made him think that he could just leave by himself, go to Alaska, or more likely head for the Mexican border.

Finally, he could go back to the re-enactment, search through the thousands of re-enactors until he found Spencer. He would then pull him from the saddle, throw him down, and demand explanations.

That was what he finally decided to do, or some as yet undetermined iteration of it. Again he felt a tremendous inner pain at the death of Amelia. He felt far more and much more deeply than he had at the death of Chick, even though he had known Chick for so much longer, and had so much of their lives had been entwined together. He still didn't understand much of what his and Amelia's relationship had been, but he recognized how long the odds were of finding someone of the opposite sex at his age that he could relate to or care about, someone who was somehow connected to his new sobriety, and this quixotic quest to figure everything out. Her not being there was like a phantom limb a patient experienced after an amputation. Everything about it was there, except the actual limb itself.

Rob was a bit concerned about the contradictory voices he was hearing in his head. He knew the pressure had been building to an almost unbearable level. He was being pulled forward, and drawn back.

Then he stopped in his tracks under the spreading limbs and branches. He remembered the horse he had seen in the field adjacent to Spencer's camp. It had been standing there, forlorn and confused, pawing at the ground. The light, covered buggy lay twisted and overturned behind it. If it had been a matter of getting on a horse and trying to ride it, he would have known it was out of the question. But if there was a way to secure the reins so the animal couldn't bolt, and then lift the wagon back on its wheels. It couldn't be too heavy. If he could get it upright, and there wasn't any serious damage to the frame or the wheels, and the animal wasn't totally freaked out, why couldn't he get in the wagon and steer it back to the battlefield?

But could he go back in the direction of the camp where he had destroyed the RV? The smoke must be visible by now, and someone had surely sounded an alarm and the fire and rescue services would be coming. But even if they were coming, the gate at the entrance where Spencer's group parked was locked, and that was if they even figured out which field the fire was in. Before he had completely made his decision he turned and was hustling back.

Again he listened as he went, trying to separate the natural forest sounds from anything else that might be lurking within the trees. Some of the birds had now accepted him as another resident of the forest floor, and they no longer ceased singing or flew higher in the canopy at his approach. He realized he was still carrying the 9-milimeter pistol, and he moved to the edge of the stream where he lifted a flat stone and deposited the weapon beneath it. Then he continued on. The closer he got to the edge of the forest, the more his anxiety and second-guessing grew. He didn't hear any sirens, but he didn't know if the forest itself might dampen the sound, or absorb it altogether before it got to him.

When he got to the now familiar brooding stones at the tree line the remnants of Spencer's camp were as quiet as when he left them. A pale wisp of smoke, gray and black, rose from the charred remains of the RV. Part of the aluminum shell had been blown away by the gas explosion, and the parts that hadn't had melted into the floor in misshapen heaps. Rob didn't want to think about what had happened to the bodies inside, and he was desperately afraid that he might smell something that would bring to him full-force what had happened to them. The horse with the overturned buggy was still there on the rise above the camp, frightened further off by the violence of the explosion. But now, either accepting it or forgetting it altogether, its head was forward and down munching at the grass.

Rob crossed the open area and skirted around the southern perimeter of the camp, cagy and aware, and then rose up the hill to a point behind the horse where he thought he could approach it and its disarrayed burden. He didn't think the animal would bolt, didn't think it could, but he didn't want to frighten it. As he got closer and the horse became aware of him, it snickered and sent a muscular shiver through its flanks, but it didn't try to move away. Without having much experience, he didn't know if he should talk to the horse as he approached, whether he should approach slowly or quickly, or if he should try to make himself smaller or larger as he drew near. The horse didn't share his misgivings. It leaned forward and down again, rubbery lips moving, big teeth tearing and grinding the tender green shoots closest to the ground. The rope leads trailed away along the ground on either side. Rob walked up and grabbed the rope, patted the animal's flank, and moved back to the wagon. The horse lifted its head as he went by, watching him under bushy eyebrows. The spindly wheels of the wagon seemed intact, and aside from a layer of dust, the wagon itself seemed in operational shape. Luckily the roof was of a canvas material stretched across an aluminum frame. The frame was buckled in a few places, but had held its shape overall. He could not lift it from that side because he was afraid the frame might break away from the base of the wagon. Still holding the lead he went back to the head of the animal, and around the front of it, dropping the one cord and taking the other up gently as he moved to the other side. The horse nodded its head twice as he went around.

He went around to the underside of the carriage. His task was to pull the upper wheel towards himself and down, stepping back as he did so that it would fall forward into an upright position. Still holding the rein, he got a grip on the wheel with both hands and leaned back and pulled down. The horse took a steadying step, which threw Rob's balance off, toward his weaker left side. But he kept leaning back away from the wheel, his legs spread for balance, and with the help of the forward movement the carriage frame lifted and teetered on its edge. He worried the pressure might bend the axle or buckle the lower wheel, but very quickly the whole thing came up, and he had to hobble back to avoid it landing on his legs. The horse looked around and it took a few nervous steps, but then it reached down and munched at the grass again. Rob took the lead he had and secured it to the metal footboard. Then he again walked in front of the animal, ducking under its neck, and retrieved the other lead. In another few seconds he was picking up his Enfield and stowing it behind the seat. He awkwardly stepped up to the bench. Then Rob made a nickering noise, not knowing if it would have any effect, but the horse seemed as anxious as he was to quit the area. It bowed its head up and down and then pulled the wagon forward.

As soon as they began to move Rob understood how the wagon had fallen over. It lurched from side to side over the grassy, rock-strewn terrain as it rose obliquely up the hill. He was afraid the horse had thoughts of its own about where they were going because it headed uphill to the north, while Rob wanted to turn it back east in the direction of the battle. He kept pulling his right hand lead, and while that did turn the horse's head in the right direction the animal still stubbornly insisted on heading up the hill. Then when they got to the broad summit there were two lines of an old cart path heading east-west. The horse turned the wagon right into the grooves and they stepped smartly toward the theatre of the re-enactment.

He thought again of Amelia. He saw her as he had that morning. He couldn't see her on the floor of the RV, crumpled and turned awkwardly against the wall in her gray and black outfit. He felt a calmness come over him then because he knew he was going to make someone pay for it.

His attention came back to the broad rump of the horse pulling him through the fields. And then he was drawn by the variegated colors, dull in the fields, and then more vivid at the borders of the trees in the near distance. The sky was doing its deep unreal blue throbbing dance.

Rob realized as they went that the trail they were on was on the hillside north of the path he had taken to Spencer's camp in the morning. He could look down in the shallow basin and mark his progress the other way. He got the feeling that someone could have been up along this trail and followed him without him knowing it, as he had made his earlier hike. Looking to where the horse was leading him he saw that it was an old well-used trail that had originally been laid out for wagons such as the one he rode in now, just two worn grooves in the rocky dirt, with a raised tufted mohawk of grass between. Off to either side of the trail was the evidence in

278

new scalloped half-moons dug from the earth that horses and riders had also recently come back and forth along it.

The trip back to the battlefield was quicker than he had anticipated, and it didn't give him time to formulate a full plan of what he was going to do when he got there. They were approaching at the northwest quadrant, above the purveyors' area, and opposite from the approaching roads and parking areas. The horse still moved steadily as if it knew where it was going. Rob did no more than hold the reins loosely in his hands.

Ahead was a line of trees that the trail skirted for a while, and then there was a turn to the right and the trail sliced between the tree trunks, crossed branches making a bright canopy over his head. As he entered the woody area the sounds became more immediate and he knew that he would emerge into the broad open area that was the stage for the re-enactments.

Rob's idea was that he would allow the horse to take him where it would, hopefully to the staging area of Spencer's group. But as he saw the trees begin to thin and the sky to lighten through the leaves, he changed his mind. First of all, he did not want to explain or acknowledge what he had seen at the camp initially, or done afterwards. He had, after all, burned away evidence by causing the gas fire and explosion, although he could blame that on someone else. It would obviously confuse law enforcement when they investigated, but he didn't care about that. For him, what was done was done, and his actions were just to erase any evidence of his presence.

So as the horse drew him and the wagon to the border of the woods, Rob took up the reins and pulled back to stop the animal. It seemed surprised at first and nodded its long head vigorously, but then it acquiesced, taking awkward, stiff steps as Rob climbed down from the seat. Then, as he had seen in cowboy movies, he picked up a stick and struck the horse's rump. The horse started, and nodded its head so that the hair of its mane rose and fell, but it didn't move from the spot. Rob was going to hit it again harder, but instead he shrugged and dropped the stick and went around behind the wagon and into the trees. The horse snorted as he moved away, seeming to call him back, but then it shook out its mane and put its head down looking for something tender to graze on.

He made his way down the remains of a trail that ran southeast through the trees. He knew that another hundred feet to his left was the great grass basin where all the re-enactors were staging themselves for Pickett's Charge.

279

Rob still didn't know what he meant to do. Part of him wanted to return to the battlefield, find his unit, and participate in the great mock battle. He thought the noise and the smoke and the movement and the colors, the blue bowl of the sky above and the reeling earth below would allow him to forget.

It was all a dream. He stopped, looking up at the pale green ceiling of leaves above him, and in the space of a long exhalation his mind reeled in thirteen other directions. Then he was moving again. That was the key, he realized. He had to keep moving. Everything had changed. His whole purpose had been to find Irina and rescue her, and he had done that. Now he must keep her safe and find out who was pursuing her and why. She had given him some clues, but there were still gaps and inconsistencies in her story that he had to get to the bottom of.

He kept to the woods and headed in the direction of the parking lot and Amelia's rental car. He would get the vehicle, go to Kay's and collect Irina, figuring out some story to tell Kay if he needed to, and get Irina away to somewhere safe where she could calmly and clearly explain what and how this had all happened. He knew the decision was the right one as soon as he made it. The idea to participate in the re-enactments had only been made to get close to Spencer and his group to get information about Irina. He had that information. He had her. Let them reverse roles. Let Spencer come after her, he thought with sanguine bravado.

Rob crossed over to the big trail that led from the battlefield to the parking lot and overlooked the field. There were thousands of re-enactors and spectators spread out before him. Again he was taken by the almost toy-like movements of the re-enactors in blue and gray looking like they were set on a large rolling game board.

The spectators were like a large quilt thrown on the hillside, alive with color and movement. The obvious glare of the sun shed light that fell whiter and hotter than it had even an hour before. He kept his head down and moved toward the parking lot.

Then he was in the front seat of the rental car. There was just the faintest floating hint of Amelia's scent, but it was gone as soon as he recognized it. He hadn't driven since before his stroke. As he sat behind the wheel he felt he was unbalanced and falling to his left. Everything seemed awkwardly placed. But he reached beneath the wheel and slipped the key in the ignition and turned on the motor. There were immediate bells and beeps, red lights flashing, but by the time he wrestled into his seatbelt, all was quiet. He exited out of the space and wound through the aisles back to the Emmittsburg Road.

Again there was the problem of Kay. What explanation could he give her for his presence? But he would think of something. He had to escape, and with Irina. That was the only final objective.

As he approached the entrance to Kay's property the anticipation increased exponentially. He pulled into the rutted driveway and then off into the grass next to it past the mailbox just as it began to rise. Unconcerned traffic hummed both ways on the road behind him. He sat behind the wheel perspiring and confused. If he continued up the rise and over the top rim and Kay was home, a whole new batch of possibilities and prevarications would undoubtedly arise. If Kay were at home, she would want to know where Amelia was. If he tried to get everything together from upstairs, she would want an explanation for that. Rob didn't think she would buy that they were leaving and Amelia wasn't there to say goodbye to her. And then she would want to know why Rob wasn't participating in the climax of the re-enactments, which was set to begin in an hour's time. Even if he could seamlessly come up with reasonable answers to those questions, how was he going to retrieve Irina without bringing up many more new and pointed ones?

He thought about what he and Amelia had told Kay about themselves. Although they had invented their marriage and filled it with small instances and stories from their past, they had still been clear and open that they had come from the Outer Banks. With anything close to a coherent description of him, he would easily be identified by any number of people. He could try to explain to her what had really happened, and what was happening…but that would never fly. He found himself not sure if he believed it all himself. He was getting nowhere and time was running out.

Just then he heard an engine start on the plateau above him, and before it even registered, much less before he could consider what to do, a big car came careening over the rise, skidding sideways as it came down the hill, so that it almost sideswiped him at the bottom. Rob ducked as it went by but the occupants must have seen him because he saw them, two middle-aged men with salt and pepper hair, bushy mustaches, and leather jackets. They took out the mailbox behind him, and it spun end over end like a giant's axe until it landed with a dusty thud in the ditch. They scraped to a stop at the roadway waiting for a break in traffic. Rob thought they might reconsider and back up to confront him, but at the first gap in the cars, they spun out and headed in the direction of the interstate on-ramp.

Once again Rob was gob-smacked. They didn't have Irina that he could see, though she might have been in the trunk or thrown on the floor of the back seat. Rob squirmed to get his right hand into his pants pocket, retrieved the .22, which seemed even smaller as he set it on his lap. Then he drove straight up and over the rise of the hill.

The house came into view, and then everything spread out in the sloping field beyond it. Kay's car was set where it usually was when she was home, on the gravel apron to the right. Rob detected no movement in the house or anywhere on the property falling behind it. His first thought was to drive right past the house and take the sloping trail to the barn where he could retrieve Irina and then just drive away. But that wouldn't work. He had to get into the house, give Kay some kind of excuse, and remove as much of the evidence of their presence there as he could.

He was frantically thinking of what excuses he could make as he got out of the car. There was no coherent order to the thoughts rampaging in his head. He put the plinker in his back pocket. Then he found himself praying that Kay was alive and unharmed so that he would have to make excuses to her. He went up the porch steps and through the screen door into the foyer, allowing it to clap shut. Everything was as it should be. He tried to take it all in visually, straining to listen for any sounds from the ground floor or coming from above. All was silent.

"Kay!" His voice reverberated from the ancient boards. Looking at the narrow stairs before him, he thought to rise up them, but he didn't. His mouth was dry. Why won't she answer?

Instead of going up the stairs, Rob went into the kitchen. Again everything seemed in order. He looked through the curtained window back toward the barn. There was no movement in that direction save the rising black bulk of three crows flying close together as they swirled up and around the barn, finally landing side by side on the crown of the roof. He was just about to turn away when he heard something inside the house. It was the faint groan of a heavy slow step of someone at the landing at the top of the staircase. It wasn't Kay, Rob knew. Her signature, even with her size, was lighter and more sure. This person now took another step. He was coming down sideways, Rob could tell, because his feet were too big for the narrow steps.

Only Rob's right arm was useful to him. He instinctively knew that the pistol was not large enough to be trusted to stop whomever was coming down. On the stove was Kay's heavy black cast iron skillet gleaming under its layer of seasoning oil. Rob grabbed the handle of it, felt its heft, and came through the doorway into the dining room. Hugging the wall as he moved, he crept to the corner where the wall ended and it opened into the living room. The base of the stairs was just to his left. He had made his way from the kitchen without making a sound. He heard another soft shallow protest from a groaning board. He thought of the analogy he had made of the language of the staircase. The thought came to him that whomever was speaking it now was clearly not native to it.

He stood at the edge of the wall in the dining room, glistening black pan held behind him. Again came the frantic thought that he should reach for the pistol in his pocket, but there was no time. There was a pause as the intruder listened for signs of life, and then he came down the remaining stairs quickly. Rob did not have to think any more. He raised the pan, balanced it with his left hand, which was good for little else. The first thing he saw was a hand holding a pistol. He thought to strike down on it, but realized if he did, even if he broke the man's hand, he might be in a wrestling match with an opponent who could be much larger than he was.

The last thing he realized before he swung with all his power at the face that followed the emerging pistol was that the hand holding it had a tattoo of Lenin's face on the back of it. There was the potential for memory, and then there was a real memory as he swung, but it disappeared instantly with the sound of breaking facial bones and pulverized flesh. The pistol the man was holding went up in the air, and then clattered harmlessly to the floor. The man slumped back on the stairs and then slid down to the foyer floor. Rob had been prepared to hit him again, and had moved around the wall and drawn his weapon back, but he saw there was no need. He thought he might have killed him, but then he heard a bubbling, gurgling attempt to inhale coming from the man's ruined nose and the hole of his mouth with gaudily red and white broken teeth.

He crouched to pick up the pistol. From the corner of his eye he saw movement outside the screen door and saw Irina running around from the back of the house. He pushed open the door and half-stepped on to the porch where she saw him and immediately stopped. She hesitated, looking at the gun in his hand, and what he knew was the taut expression on his face, and then she came forward again, rising the porch steps and going past him into the interior.

"Do you know him?" Rob asked, realizing had had done much to destroy any chance of recognition.

She shook her head.

"I have to go upstairs," he said. He put the man's pistol in his belt and took the plinker from his pocket and handed it to her. "Watch him. If he moves, which I don't think he will, do what you have to do."

He stepped around the man and moved up the stairs. He didn't worry about being quiet. He knew there was no one upstairs, with the possible exception of Kay, and if she were up there he worried about the condition he would find her in. He reached the landing at the entrance to the hallway. He walked past the first closed door where he and Amelia had lived for three days. He kept moving toward Kay's door at the end of the dark hallway. It was slightly ajar so that two lines of yellow light, one vertical from the floor to the top of the doorway, and one narrowly conical at the top, running wide to narrow, showed his way.

He pushed it open. It was the same MO. Kay was lying on her face between the bed and the wall. Unlike Amelia who must have resisted and was shot standing up, Kay had meekly obeyed their order to lie down and then was shot neatly in the back of the head. After all Rob had seen through the day it almost had no effect on him. He could only muster a short breath of regret that because of him these people had found and done this to her. He looked around the room. The bed was similar to the one she had let to Amelia and him. It had the same crown in the center and sloped toward the edges, and a similar beaded spread with tassels dangling over the wood floor. But Kay's bed had four rising wood posts. The bureau against the other wall was of similar dark wood. On its surface was a faded white lace cover, and on that were powders and sprays and antique perfume atomizers. The scent of her hung in the air, but underlying it was the heavy coppery smell of blood.

He took all of it in quickly. They must not have wanted anything from her because her possessions appeared undisturbed. Rob went through the bathroom door, across the tile, and carefully opened the door into the room he and Amelia had shared. Their room was ransacked. The clothes that they had begun to pack were taken out of the suitcases and strewn about the room. The mattress on bed was akilter where they had lifted it to see if anything was hidden beneath it. Drawers were opened, contents spilled out. Rob didn't know what they were looking for, or if they had found it or not. He could only think that they were looking for some evidence of Irina, and then he remembered that she was downstairs. He had an overwhelming sense of fatigue and disgust. Everything had gotten completely out of hand. What could possibly justify all this carnage? And then he looked out the window and saw the shoulder of Big Round Top. Just beyond it now they were beginning the reenactment of Pickett's famous charge. All those middle-aged men were pretending to kill and be killed by each other.

Rob thought again about Alexander Olsofsky, whom he had never met. This was his doing. He had unleashed all of this because of his feud with Spencer. Whether it was over Irina, or something else, really didn't matter any more. Rob just knew he had to make him pay.

Irina was still downstairs, guarding the man with the Lenin tattoo on the back of his hand. He thought about going down and trying to beat the information out of him, but he knew that would be a useless exercise on a number of levels. First of all, most of the man's teeth were floating free in the jelly of his maw. And his jaw was crushed.

Rob went out of the room he had shared with Amelia without looking back. He remembered Kay and the expressions of appreciation on her face when she would greet them. For the first time he wondered if she might have been lonely. He went down the stairs heavily. Irina was sitting knock-kneed on one of the love seats, looking down at the Russian or Ukrainian, the pistol dangling loosely from her fingertips.

"I know what we must do," she said as the man gurgled a low tortured growl and his left leg began to twitch.

"I'm glad you do," Rob said, suddenly so weak he could feel the blood fleeing from his head and shoulders to his lower extremities. He sat quickly, falling back so his tail bone cracked hard on the third step.

Before it registered to him what he was doing, Irina stood and moved toward the prostrate man. She had taken one of the small pillows from the corner of the love seat. Rob looked at her, dizzily trying to get things back to normal speed and focus his thoughts. Irina leaned over the man and very quickly placed the pistol to the side of his head. With the pillow in her other hand she covered it, put it to the man's ear, and fired. There was a resounding metal crack and both the man's feet came off the floor and then fell again. Within the hollow sound of the reverberation, he heard Irina speak.

"Help me get him into the car. We don't have much time."

XX

Their route of retreat mimicked Robert E. Lee's and the troops of the Army of Northern Virginia as they collected themselves and their wounded and headed south on July 5, of 1863. Rob and Irina went through Frederick, but then unlike Lee they bore to the west and crossed the Potomac into Harpers Ferry at the border of Maryland, Virginia, and West Virginia. They had expected to be pursued, run down, and quickly caught. At least Rob did. But just as the Union army had not followed Lee and destroyed him, no one now seemed to come after Rob and Irina. So where the Shenandoah River joined the Potomac they spent their first night.

Rob's state of mind was one of quiet strangling turmoil. He worked frantically to justify what he had done, to collate what he had participated in, and in some cases just to forget what he had seen. Irina seemed grateful, but there was also something that seemed to suggest that if Rob hadn't come to her aid, someone else surely would have. But when Rob looked at her out of the corner of his eye, and when time and again he realized with shock that she was with him, he also realized that she might not need anybody's help as much as she pretended to.

The hollow metallic click of the bullet swathed in the pillow exiting the chamber and entering the man's brain still stunned him every time he remembered it. How did Irina know that the bullet wouldn't traverse his brain and come out the other side? How did she know that there would be so little blood? How and when had she come up with the idea of putting him in Kay's car at the top of the hill and then waiting for a lull in traffic at the bottom before pushing him over the edge and watching the dead man bobbing like a marionette behind the wheel as Kay's car lurched through the gap and almost went airborne before it smashed into the trees on the other side? And how had she so calmly beforehand ordered Rob to get all his and Amelia's possessions from upstairs, take the rental car and park it in the motel lot a half mile away, all the while still in uniform, and then hike into the hills behind it and return to Kay's to help start her car, remove the rocks from under the tires, and put it in gear?

They began to hear sirens as they made their way south and west behind the ridge back toward the motel and the rental car. Rob felt a short sullen wave of admiration for Irina when he realized that all the man's exterior injuries, even the scant bleeding from his left ear, might well be explained as being sustained by the impact with the trees. Of course they would quickly identify Kay as the owner of the vehicle, and that would lead them to her house where they would find her, but maybe that would all be explained as a burglary or home invasion gone bad. Had Kay told anyone else that Rob and Amelia were her guests? They had used their real names, not realizing where all of this might ultimately lead them. If Kay hadn't let anyone know about her guests, then who would know they had been there among the thousands of visitors? Spencer? Maybe. But even if he did, there was really nothing he was in a position to say about it.

Irina stayed in the car as Rob checked into the Harpers Ferry motel. He knew the clerk could see Irina's dark form in the vehicle, and Rob knew what the clerk thought was the arrangement between them, but that worked well for his purposes. He listed the car as a Nissan, and gave it Virginia plates with made-up numbers, counting on the fact that the clerk wouldn't check or notice, and she didn't.

The room was on the second floor in the back where the building sloped to the river. It was sparse and well-worn, with a small bathroom and two dusty beds. Rob felt sure he and Irina would go their separate ways the following day, and in fact he took the keys to bed with him, hiding them in his pillowcase because he thought there was a chance she might bolt sometime in the middle of the night. For all his previous fantasies about what he would like to do to her, he was so fagged out, so overwhelmed by what had happened, that he lay back on the bed and fell asleep almost immediately.

He heard her moving around the room as a sort of supporting character in his dreams. At one point he opened his eyes and she was standing at the mirror in the bathroom, still clothed, but her dark outline left nothing to the imagination. Later he heard the shower running and tried to rouse himself to be awake when she finished, but it didn't happen.

The first thing to enter his consciousness the next morning was dull, unrelenting pain. His whole body ached. He began to hear voices on the television, and it further roused him. He opened his eyes in the slanting partitioned sunlight and saw Irina sitting cross-legged on the other bed. She had a tray of food in front of her, fruit and juice, coffee, bagels, muffins.

Rob felt pitiable. He wanted to move, but he was afraid he would groan if he did. Irina must have sensed he was awake because she looked over at him and then picked up the remote and increased the volume.

"Did you see this?" she asked, knowing he hadn't.

Rob rolled awkwardly until he could see the screen. Pictured was a shot of the Atlantic basin, and in its southern quadrant, some hundreds of miles east of the Antilles, was a large gray blotch.

"That is now Hurricane Armando," she said, "and some of the models head it in the direction of the Carolina coast."

"I had some friends, years ago," Rob said, "and they had a band they named "The Cone of Probability." It was the perfect name for them. Sometimes their music was perfect, well-formed, every note moving in the right direction, everybody in the same groove, loud and terrible and perfect. And then other times they would all be headed in different directions and whatever they were playing would be blown apart from the inside, or sheared off intentionally by what they called their punk sensibilities. What I mean to say is that they were unpredictable, and so are these storms."

"It's early for one, isn't it…especially to be so big already?"

Rob mustered his strength to sit up. He looked blankly at the screen, slowly concentrating enough to be able to take in its present coordinates, and wind speed, and size. The winds were nearing a hundred miles an hour, but what was ominous was the pressure already dropping to 950 millibars with thousands of miles of warm ocean surface water to feed it. It had an eye already too, not perfect and tight yet, but clearly visible in the satellite photo.

"That is pretty impressive. I'll bet Jim 'the boy who cried wolf' Cantore is already packing his waders and big yellow raincoat."

He winced as he rose to go to the bathroom, and Irina saw it.

"Are you alright?"

"I'll be fine," he responded, but he wasn't exactly sure. He got himself up and stood between the beds. As he began to move toward the bathroom, he did so with small, jerky steps, old person steps. They lengthened and became marginally more fluid as he rounded Irina's bed, but his left leg, which had seemed to be unwinding with his new massive exercise regimen, had reverted to its taut and strangled position. The first thing he did after he closed the bathroom door, before he even pissed, was take a handful of ibuprofen.

By the time he came out his body still wasn't working properly, but his mind was. All around outside was moving water. Harpers Ferry was at the confluence of the Shenandoah and Potomac Rivers, and the water rushed down from the Appalachians, met at this place, and flowed east toward the Chesapeake Bay. To the south of them was the Shenandoah Valley. His first thoughts as they fled Gettysburg had been to break west and head across country. But Amelia had to be answered for. He, or they (because he still didn't know if he should take Irina with him, or if she intended to stay with him) had to stay out of sight until they could figure out how things fell. They couldn't just go back to the Outer Banks and hope people wouldn't see and recognize them. But now the storm, Armando, could be the perfect thing to occupy everyone who might be looking for them.

"Anything on the news about Gettysburg?"

"Yes. The lead story is about the murders and explosion at the camp. The authorities are at a loss for a motive, and if I can read anything into it, I'd say Spencer is not giving up anything."

"What's your relationship with him?" Rob asked, going to the window and throwing open the heavy curtains which chattered as they parted. A warm white light bathed the room.

"He protects me," she answered.

"He protects you," Rob said, "but God help anyone around you. I still don't get it. Alexander killed your friend. Why? And then Alexander killed Steven. Why again?"

When Irina hesitated it gave Rob a sinking feeling that almost made him crumple to his knees. She didn't have a ready, true answer. And that meant that Amelia, and Kay…and the other men at the camp, and Steven, and Chick had all perished as the result of some misdirection on Irina's part.

But then she spoke. "Alexander killed Nadia…had her killed. It was supposed to be a warning. I don't even know if he meant for her to die, but the men he hired, the Russians from New York, the same ones from yesterday…they are not good at restraint or subtlety. Because she had been in my car, the Russians mistook her for me. I told Spencer it was Alexander so he took me with him to the re-enactment at Brandy Station. I know he was trying to communicate with Alexander, to straighten everything out.

And then Steven was killed. It all just snowballed from there. Honestly, if you hadn't gotten in the middle of it, they might have resolved it all between themselves."

The rivers rushed into each other outside the window, careening among the rocks, eddying and boiling, swirling with whitewater and spray.

That afternoon they headed south into the Shenandoah Valley. Before they left, as Irina showered, Rob went to the car and searched through Amelia's possessions. It was a sad business. She had been looking for some kind of adrenaline infusion, and she had found it. It had been like riding on the surface of the rapids from the combining rivers that roared on the other side of the bulk-headed parking lot; giddy drops, swirls, and eddies, places where you were pulled under the cold water and couldn't see anything to get your bearings, and long whooshing chutes, all of it with rocks and boulders both above and below the surface.

Rob carefully searched through her clothing and didn't find anything of interest. He took her make-up bag and laptop back to the room. Inside the make-up bag, in a slit in the lining in one corner, he found an envelope with more currency. He took it out of the envelope and shoved it in his pocket as he heard Irina fumbling with the handle coming out of the bathroom door. He followed her in without saying anything and closed the door. He sat on the toilet seat in the swirling gray mist of steam and counted the money. Amelia had already given him $4000. From Chick's pocket he had taken $6800, and now from the envelope in Amelia's make-up bag he counted $5000 more. Taking out what he had spent that still made a total of $15000, more money than he had seen in one place in a long time. It wouldn't last him long in the overall scheme of things, but it might be enough for the purposes of the plan that had just now burst forth fully-formed in his mind.

When he emerged from the bathroom Irina had already begun the task of trying to unlock Amelia's computer. He let her go about that by herself as he loaded and packed the car. He wasn't quite sure of the timing, but they were going back to the Outer Banks. If it weren't for the possible approach of the tropical system, he would be heading in a different direction, probably west. But the storm might provide him with the cover to move without having to worry about the authorities, who would have other pressing issues on their hands.

First they would take a leisurely drive south through the Shenandoah Valley. Along the way he would randomly dispose of Amelia's things, hopefully putting her in a final proper resting place in his mind.

There were two Shenandoah Valley campaigns during the Civil War. The first was in 1862, and led on the Confederate side by Gen. Thomas "Stonewall" Jackson. In a series of brilliant, unexpected marches he chose his confrontations with the much larger Union forces, surprising them, harrying them, defeating them, and finally forcing them to retreat when it began to look like he might threaten Washington itself. So brilliant was this campaign that it is still studied at West Point and other military academies around the world.

The second Valley campaign was led by Gen. Jubal Early in 1864. By then Ulysses Grant was the overall Union commander and finally Lincoln had a man who recognized that the only answer to the Confederate cause was all-out war. The war would be ended by destroying anything the Confederates could use; crops, factories, timber, railroads. Many of those raw materials were in the Shenandoah Valley. So while Grant confronted Lee, and was determined, and backed by a greater supply of everything, to push him step by step back to Richmond, he sent Gen. Philip Sheridan and his cavalry into the Shenandoah to do the same thing Sherman was doing across a wide swath of Georgia.

"This is it," Irina said.

The TV had been on in the background. Now a bulletin with the network logo flashed on the screen. "Carnage at Gettysburg," was the mastline. "Yesterday," the announcer said, "the 151st re-enactment at Gettysburg was marred by two different violent episodes. Authorities are on the scenes, sifting through the evidence, trying to find clues, and also trying to determine if the two episodes are connected. In the first, at a campsite of a group of re-enactors from North Carolina, five bodies were found, two within the confines of the camp, and three in a large RV, in which there had been a gas leak and explosion. Authorities are mum as to the cause of these deaths, but foul play is suspected."

The news announcer, a man in his late thirties or early forties, with a stony smile and knowing expression on his face, that Rob guessed was supposed to suggest concern, actually seemed to be suppressing a giddy excitement at the scope of the drama. Rob looked closely at his facial features. The man almost didn't look real, but more like a blending of handsome cut-and-paste features that didn't work in total. Irina sat on the other bed, head tilted, and Rob honestly couldn't tell if her expression was one of concerned interest, or boredom.

"At the other scene, we got to our reporter, Kayla Metzenburg."

A young woman, holding a microphone in one hand and brushing at the front of her blouse with the other, suddenly appeared on the screen. "Andrew, I'm at the home of Kay Yoder, a lifelong resident of Gettysburg, who was found deceased from a gunshot wound at her home on the Emmittsburg Road. Related to that, authorities say, is a motor vehicle accident on the Emmittsburg Road in front of the Yoder house. Witnesses reported seeing an auto, Ms. Yoder's vehicle it turned out, coming down the steep hill behind me, from the upper part of the Yoder property, careening wildly across this busy road, where it then crashed into those trees on the other side of the highway. Authorities discovered an as yet unidentified man deceased in the vehicle, apparently as a result of injuries sustained in the crash. At this point it is unknown how his death is related to Ms. Yoder's, or whether these deaths are related to those at the re-enactment camp some two miles away.

"To further add to this mystery, an unidentified couple were reportedly staying with Ms. Yoder at her house. Little is known of them except that they were apparently in Gettysburg for the re-enactment. Now back to you."

The camera held momentarily on the young woman's face. With her free hand she dragged at a wisp of hair that had fluttered to her lips. She let the microphone sag in front of her and looked past the camera for a signal that the scene would cut back to the studio. Irina turned off the TV with the remote before it did.

"We seem to be in the clear," she said.

Rob was thinking about the young reporter's face, wondering about her boyfriend or fiancé or new husband and her life away from the camera. "They might just be acting like they're in the dark," he said, but he didn't believe it. He and Amelia had had no contact with Kay's neighbors, and had not been away from the house with her for anything. No one could identify them as being with her. There were fingerprints, of course, and his were on file. They had given Kay their real names, but whether she had written the names down, or told them to anyone, it seemed like it might be a long circuitous route to get back to him, and he was already planning to be miles and miles, if not countries away, by the time anyone did.

But before he disappeared he was going to take his revenge. He knew that Alexander and Spencer were not through with each other. After what had happened at Gettysburg, Spencer would go home to the Outer Banks, and Rob felt sure that Olsofsky would follow him there. Then they would finally have it out, just the two of them…except that neither of them knew yet, and probably didn't suspect, that Rob was also going to be there, and then both of them would pay.

Rob and Irina rode down through the center of the Shenandoah Valley. It was a broad, scalloped bowl with the Blue Ridge Mountains to the east and the Appalachians of West Virginia rising to the west. All around were rolling hills and tentative ridges and green-blue sub-valleys that sparkled in the sunlight.

Rob had determined that they would move slowly south, up the valley as it was called because the overall elevation rose the further south they went. He was looking to time their return to the Outer Banks with the arrival of the storm, although that storm was still a thousand miles and days away as it meandered across the Atlantic. And there was no guarantee if it would maintain its strength, and with the lack of steering currents no one knew what course it might ultimately take.

They drove south to Luray and went to the caverns. Rob thought it would be good to break the trip up, and also that it would be wise to make themselves part of a crowd wherever possible. But as they were queuing up he realized that he recognized people from the re-enactment. He saw couples and families he had seen at the sutlers' area, and then he realized that it only made sense that Gettysburg had been part of their vacation travel and some of them had continued their tour by heading south.

They descended with the tour into the cool dripping underground. They saw fantastic rock formations, bizarre shapes that heat and pressure and dripping water had formed them into. The lighting reminded him of a carnival funhouse. Rob soon lost track of whether they were moving up or down below the surface and allowed himself to be carried along with the crowd. Irina was at his side. In the dark areas she moved closer to him, brushing against him. He didn't know if she was frightened...or sending signals of trust. He didn't care. He was in a constant state somewhere between arousal and vigilance. Everything stood out in stark relief. Shadows were all fantastic, voices seemed to come from everywhere, footsteps were hollow and resounding. Where in some places the caverns went on, the darkness was of the deep and most enveloping kind. It fell in on itself and it seemed to have a magnetism that wanted to draw Rob into its center. The nervous cries of children finally called him back to himself.

They emerged into the sunlight again and saw the hills around them that crowned those caves. Some of them were bare bald rock with only clinging plants in rain-carved crevasses, others covered with soil and thick with trees that were black and blue and green. The clouds were broad white sailing affairs changing patterns and positions in the sky. Some were tinged with gray on the bottom, and along the far southwestern horizon there were other clouds, brooding and darker, moving toward them.

When they returned to the car Irina wanted to drive.

"Drive us somewhere we can talk," Rob said, and handed her the keys.

She drove as if she were born for it. She slid behind the wheel, tilted the backrest to forty-five degrees and angled smoothly out of the space.

Irina drove east up to the Blue Ridge Parkway, and then headed south. After ten miles of winding rises and descents she found an overlook parking area with the valley spread before them. Rob marveled at how the brown and red of the earth and the green of the grass could create such a palette of varied blues. He wished he could have shared it with Amelia. Thinking that, he turned and looked at Irina, folded so lithely in the drivers seat.

"Tell me about Davy Todd," he said. "You know him."

"He works for Spencer, yes..." and when Rob seemed to want more, she added, "I know him."

"What do you mean, he works for Spencer?"

"Just that. With his military training, and the contacts he has, Spencer uses him for security. And other things. At first, it was just if his family went on vacation, or travelled somewhere, Davy would go along, maybe with one of his ex-Marine buddies, as security. Spencer isn't paranoid, but with everything he has, he has to be aware that there are people who might want to get at some of his stuff. I think after he became partners with Olsofsky, that need became more acute. And then after everything with Nadia, Davy brought in more of his friends from the Marines, men he had seen and done things with in Iraq and Afghanistan, and Spencer began to call Davy his "Director of Special Tasks."

"But I still don't understand why Olsofsky would start all this with Spencer. In America, if you have a business dispute, you hire lawyers and sue each other. I look at the assets I'm assuming both of them have, and whatever their beefs were with each other, neither one of them is going to be ruined."

"They don't have to play by normal people rules. There are two big egos involved, and they feel like they're above it all. They don't have to worry about the consequences. They pay people to do that. Neither one of them planned this, but I think on some level both of them are enjoying it."

"And what about you?"

Irina hesitated, bit her lip. "At first I was just being swept along, and I thought I was being protected by both of them. But now...well, I know Alexander wants me dead. And I guess it's clear that Spencer can't protect me, or I wouldn't be here with you."

She started the car. They sat still next to each other, looking across the ridges and undulations, the striated vista before them.

"I need clothes," she said. "These are all I have. We need to go into a town and buy me clothes."

They were in Roanoke. Things were heating up. Rob had counted on the explosion and fire in the RV to delay the identification of Amelia, and thus not point to any connection between him and her. But now she had been identified. In what had become a national news story with all kinds of conjecture and conspiracy theorizing, a lot of pressure had been put on local law enforcement, as well as the FBI and Homeland Security. Part of the story was that her father had been killed at the World Trade Center. After the bombings in Boston the year before, and with terrorist threats seeming to come at the US from everywhere, politicians and the news media had already begun to use the mysterious episodes at Gettysburg to gin up fears of potential lone wolf terrorists and sleeper cells of jihadis among the population. Rob knew though that there were too many layers, and too many disparate actors, for them to be anything but confused at this point.

Irina was mesmerized by the coverage. She sat cross-legged on the different motel beds, hands moving back and forth on her bare thighs and listened to the wild and unreasoned conjectures, considering them as if she didn't know the true story of what was going on. Rob thought that she was disappointed that she hadn't been identified in the drama. One of the things that added depth to the authorities' confusion was that the same day of the explosion at Spencer's camp, and the discovery of Kay Yoder's body, and also that of the unknown man in her car who seemed to be a viable suspect for all the carnage, another woman was found murdered in the town of Gettysburg itself. While Rob and Irina were quite positive that this killing was unrelated, the authorities were not, and the media were trumpeting that killing along with the others as the work of the forward phalanx of an Armageddon of terrorist mayhem.

Meanwhile Rob and Irina acted as tourists. They visited battlefields and museums. They took casual and not too demanding hikes. They sat at a streetside café and listened to bluegrass music at a festival in Harrisonburg. Rob had to draw the line when Irina wanted to do a tour and tasting at a winery. He wasn't ready for that temptation. They talked. From the first time he had seen her Rob had drawn this picture in his mind of Irina as this fantastic and universal object of desire. And it fit. Every man who saw her had to stop and consider her more closely. She knew it. She accepted it as the normal course of her life, and she was adept at using it to her advantage when she could. But there was more to her. In the afternoons she would make Rob stop, or she would stop if she was at the wheel, and she would buy a bottle of wine. In the evening she would drink the wine slowly, always at first seeming to be critical as to the color and nose and flavors. She would twirl her tumbler or plastic cup, and with a soft gurgle she would aerate the wine, and then comment on its quality. But as the level of the bottle fell, an odd sloppiness would become apparent. Rob thought she must be taking pills. Though he had no idea for what they were originally intended, they seemed to exacerbate her dull and unhinged condition. She would arrive at a state of complete vulnerability where she seemed to have no desire or aim other than to accept whatever might happen to her …and then she would sleep. When he was sure she was out, Rob would pour whatever was left of the wine down the drain, and then rinse out the sink. He wanted to thank someone or something for whatever was giving him the strength not to drink, because he honestly felt high every time he knowingly didn't.

After he had rinsed her cup he would go to the bed and stand over her, stare at her as she lay on the top sheet. Then he would try to summon his desires, and eventually they would come. But they came like limping demons, evil, apologetic. The blood didn't rage through his system. It rose and fell like a giant attenuated heartbeat.

Vying more and more with the violent mysteries at Gettysburg for headlines was the approach of Hurricane Armando. The whole of the east coast was put on alert as the storm made its basically linear approach across the southern Atlantic. What worried serious forecasters most was the realization that as it neared the eastern US, if that was the approach it took, there appeared to be a compete lack of any developing steering currents to push it in one direction or another once it got there. The fear was that it might wobble ashore somewhere and just stop. With its strength and size already, and with the possibility that it would strengthen more as it approached, disaster services up and down the coast began gearing up. Plans were reviewed, and equipment requisitioned and put in place.

The thing Rob counted on was that if the storm did approach he could use it as a shield to get back to the Outer Banks. If it began to look like mandatory evacuations might be ordered, they would need to return before they were put in place. They? He looked at Irina. Every time they separated, he thought she might not come back.

So then they were in Lynchburg. The mysteries of what had happened in Gettysburg still held the national attention. It was now called the Gettysburg Massacre. The internet was rife with rumors. One held that there was a nativist survivalist vigilante re-enactor who had deserted his unit and taken to the woods, and that the killings were some kind of vendetta against the commercial exploitation of the battle.

They had identified Kay, or course, having been found in her own home. On the second day the man who died in the auto accident fleeing her home was identified as Sergi Rodopolov, a Russian national who lived in Brighton Beach, New York. It was hinted at by law enforcement that he had ties to the Russian mob. There was no mention that anything other than the auto accident had caused his death. The theory was that he had murdered Kay during a botched burglary and then panicked, fled in her car, lost control on her angled driveway, crossed four lanes of traffic at the base of it, and then smashed at a high rate of speed into the trees at the other side. They still had not tied him to the campsite murders.

Spencer was interviewed about the carnage that had taken place at his base camp. He appeared shaken and incredulous that his camp had apparently been attacked by a group of well-armed men in broad daylight. No, he did not know of any motive, and as the interview continued, the faces of the five victims were shown on the screen. Chef Dustin and Spencer's lawyer, Babson were on the top row, and in the bottom row were two young Marines from Camp Lejeune in southern North Carolina, heroes from the war in Iraq, Spencer called them, who when they heard of his re-enactment group had contacted him and asked to participate. And then there was a photograph of Amelia. It was an older picture, and in it she smiled carelessly.

XXI

The atmosphere seemed to be holding its breath. The clouds moved perceptibly from southwest to northeast, but with no real sense of conviction. And they were layered, separated by different atmospheric influences and considerations. Some were fat and sunlit white, like sprouting mushrooms. At higher levels they were flatter and hung like dirty laundry heckled by the wind.

The path Armando was taking didn't fit with anything Rob had seen before. It moved to the northwest, then stopped, corkscrewed, moved northwest again, stopped again. Winds were at 110 miles an hour, pressure was holding pretty steady at 920 millibars. On the morning of July 9 it was roughly two hundred miles southeast of Cape Hatteras. It was unfortunate for the Outer Banks that all storms in the Atlantic Ocean were eventually measured by their distance from that strand of land. A hurricane might be five hundred miles from Miami, but because they usually headed in a vaguely northerly direction Cape Hatteras became the chosen point of reference.

It was not a large storm in circumference. It didn't have a broad extended wind field. Hurricane force winds spread about fifty miles from the center, tropical force winds maybe another hundred miles outside of that. But it had had days to generate swell, and the long period pulse expanded outward like ripples from a pebble thrown on the calm surface of a pond.

As with most approaching storms, emergency services kept a close eye on Ocracoke Island, knowing all the tourists there had to be evacuated by ferry, a process that could take two days or more depending on the number of people on the island. So Rob kept an eye out too. When the news came that a mandatory evacuation had been announced for Ocracoke, he made his move. They packed and drove straight across the bottom of Virginia to Tidewater and then turned south and headed for the Wright Memorial Bridge.

He didn't know exactly what he would do. He had no idea whether Olsofsky or Spencer would actually be on the Outer Banks, and no idea what he would do to either of them if he did catch up with them there. His planning didn't go that far.

Irina's demeanor remained closed and enigmatic as they got closer to the bridge. A resignation that she must wait and see what happened seemed to envelop her.

"Anything you need to tell me before we get there?" His tone was vaguely mocking. He knew she had more to do with it all this than he might ever understand. He needled her more. "You don't have to come back if you don't want to."

She took his challenges silently. Looking sideways at her, Rob realized he no longer cared about motives or reasons. The only thing he was sure of was that the clock was ticking down…and when it got to zero…

As they came down Highway 158 through mainland Currituck a steady stream of knotted traffic moved north. The call had been made for Ocracoke, and most visitors on Hatteras Island realized their turn was likely next. Even on the northern Outer Banks, visitors, especially those with families and kids, were nervous, not only about the approaching storm, but also about the tremendous clot of traffic, and were making their decisions to get out.

Rob knew evacuations were a crapshoot. How many times had people been forced to flee, traffic up and down the coast snarled, businesses forced to close down and forego revenue at the height of the season, and then all watch the storm turn and head harmlessly out to sea? Or how many storms had made surgical slices into a point of the coast, and then driven deep inland, chasing the fleeing tourists, dropping deluges of rain, upending trees not used to such violent winds, knocking down power lines, so that vacationers who thought they had been prudent by obeying evacuation orders became marooned in inland motels, their cars under water in flooded parking lots, with no electricity for days afterward?

When Rob had lived on the Outer Banks he had always stayed. Many, maybe a majority of the locals, did. Part of it for Rob had just been the adventure of seeing and feeling the power of a storm as it struck at the heart of the eponymous "Graveyard of the Atlantic." He'd been in houses on pilings rocking back and forth so that water sloshed in the toilets. He'd seen fifty-foot pine trees waving in the wind like blades of grass. He'd seen surf crashing so hard against dunes that it sent walls of water three stories into the air, felt thousands of grains of sand peppering his skin as he leaned at forty-five degrees against a hundred mile an hour wind. The visceral experience was what he had stayed for. Many others stayed to protect their property, or their businesses, or like the folks on Hatteras Island, they stayed because storms were just something you dealt with because you lived where you lived.

Some of the hurricane parties in the old days had been legendary, ten or twelve people in a house with all the booze and drugs they could collectively gather, trying for as long as they could to keep things reasonable, but always eventually succumbing to urges made stark and dreadful by the clamor and relentless barrage of the storm outside. He and Paula had spent a storm together at someone's cottage, but there were big gaps in his memory of it. He didn't recall if Steven was with her, or if Jane had been with him. The only thing he was sure he remembered was Paula taking him by the hand in the darkness and pulling him down the outside steps and out to the street where she knelt in front of him and gave him a frantic blowjob while all around the trees danced like banshees and even in his ecstasy he had been afraid a limb or an entire tree was going to come down and kill them both.

"He will be there, I think," Irina said. Her words felt like the point of a knife and he was back in the moment. "Spencer, I mean. Of all the places he could go, this is where he will go to collect himself. You're the same, right. It's a good place to contemplate your existence."

"I guess." Rob wasn't returning for contemplation. He was returning to reset the balance of things.

Very few cars were heading south as they were. They kept the radio on, listening for an announcement of the mandatory evacuation of the northern Outer Banks, which is what they were racing against. If that happened before they made it to the Currituck Sound it would doom their plans because the highway patrol would be posted at the north end of the bridge to prevent anyone except authorized emergency personnel from crossing, and eventually all lanes would be used to shuttle the traffic north.

Rob wasn't sure where they would go if they got across. Spencer's home was on the Sound in Nags Head, and Olsofsky's on the Sound in Currituck twenty-five miles to the north. There was only one way to drive from one to the other in the best of times, and if the beach were closed the State

Police would be patrolling and setting up checkpoints to prevent people from roaming the deserted roads looking for mischief. Rob held both Olsofsky and Spencer responsible for the violence and carnage, and both must be made to pay. They did make it to the bridge and were allowed to cross unmolested. Instead of going south to Nags Head, Rob took the left and headed north on Highway 12.

Rob and Irina crossed the bridge at noon and the mandatory evacuation was announced at one PM. Although Hurricane Armando was not making any kind of discernible directional headway, it was drifting vaguely north and west. The Cone of Probability was no longer a cone at all. The best the National Hurricane Service could do was to draw an oblong bubble around the storm with the Outer Banks under the western part of the circle.

The storm was so peculiar and potentially dangerous, and coming early and at the very height of the tourist season, that it drove the stories of the killings at Gettysburg off the front pages. Cameras in helicopters showed long lines of sputtering traffic snaking away from the coast. Weather Channel personalities prowled the beaches from Charleston, South Carolina to Ocean City, Maryland. Politicians, wishing to seem concerned and responsible, took to the cameras and microphones wherever they could.

Rob decided to head north towards Olsofsky's property. Theirs was one of the few cars headed in that direction. The traffic was already backed up from the intersection at 158, a mile from the bridge to get off the island, through Southern Shores, through the town of Duck, north to the Sanderling Inn, and into the Currituck Outer Banks. There were police cars with flashing lights in Duck maintaining order and trying to keep the flow moving south. They were still allowing cars to go north without stopping or questioning them. At the Currituck County line however, at the curve just past the Sanderling, there were two police cruisers stopping traffic heading north. Rob had his mind working to come up with an excuse for why they were moving against the flow. He rolled down his window as the officer leaned in.

"We know, officer," he said. "We passed you an hour ago heading south. We were almost to Duck when my daughter said she left her ring, the one her grandmother gave her, on the sink in her bathroom."

Irina held up her hand to show that the imaginary ring was indeed not on her finger.

"We'll only be there long enough to get the ring, and then we'll get back in line, probably two hours further back than we were." He looked at Irina, who put her head down, pantomiming guilt. "How much further is the end of the line now?" Rob asked.

"Another couple of hours, I'm afraid," the officer said. Then he stepped back and motioned them through. "Make it quick."

"That was good," Irina said, as they headed north, glimpsing the stolid and exasperated and resigned faces of the drivers creeping south on the other side of the road.

Rob drove toward Corolla, past the airport, through Pine Island and the driveway to the west that led to Alexander Olsofsky's house. The line ended almost five miles past the checkpoint at the county line. Rob kept going north for another mile, then did a u-turn and came back and queued up at the end of the long line.

"I think I have this figured out," he said as he eased up behind the last car. He shook his head, looking in front of him and realizing that this crawling snake of a line was over twenty miles long before it merged with another line coming from the southern Outer Banks and all the main towns in between, all filled with cars loaded with people and their vacation gear trying to escape the storm.

Irina seemed content to sit back and let Rob decide where they were going. She stared placidly as the scenery drifted past, and eventually she leaned her head against the window and fell asleep. Rob could not stop looking at her tanned legs, all length and curves and angles. He did it purposely to arouse himself, and he was aroused. But he could not keep and hold the excitement. It was like he was pumping up a bicycle tire that had a hole in it. As long as he pumped it remained filled, but as soon as he stopped he could feel the air seeping out. Then he saw on her left leg the blue-black sweep of the end of a tattoo, only an inch of it, before it disappeared beneath the hem of her shorts. He was filled then with the desire to see it all, to trace its outlines, to see how it ran with the curve of her hip. Did it rise still after that? Did it blossom up past the narrowing of her waist? Did it curve around below her belly? All these guesses and imaginings suddenly had him bound taut against the fabric of his pants, and only then did he feel the heat of he sun and the hum of other idling engines, and hear a horn blast further up the line around the curve.

Rob didn't know what he had figured out really. He was back on the Outer Banks, a massive storm approaching, and he was stalking a man who could just as easily be on the other side of the Atlantic as be anywhere near him. But he just had this feeling that here was exactly where Alexander would be. Olsofsky still had unfinished business with Spencer, and they both had property and investments that they needed to look after here…and if they weren't looking after them Rob might just have to burn some of those investments to the ground.

An hour later they were drawing even with the road leading to Alexander's place. Irina had awakened and she watched in silence as they slowly went by. Rob took the next left turn toward the ocean. The street ran for a hundred feet to a feeder road running north-south along the border of the seaside dunes, with beautiful and massive ten and twelve bedroom cottages on both sides. They were hidden from the main road by a high hedge of bayberry, gnarled live oaks and stunted pines.

At the stop sign of the east-west road Rob looked up and down the feeder. To the north, six or seven houses up, there were two SUVs in a driveway being loaded up to evacuate. Rob turned south. The feeder road went south the length of twenty houses on each side and stopped at a bulb of pavement, a cul-de-sac where three houses were in various stages of construction. There were no cars in any of the driveways or work vehicles at the building sites. Rob turned into the driveway of the second to last oceanfront house. The cottage loomed above them as he drove beneath the overhang that led to the two-car garage.

After telling Irina to wait in the car he got out and went to the north side of the house and looked down at the dark manicured space between it and the house next to it. He walked the length of the house to the gate that led into the walled area in back between the house and the ocean where the pool was located. The gate door was unlocked and he slipped into the pool area with its aluminum and Plexiglas furniture, gay umbrellas, and inflatable toys strewn all around the perimeter of the kidney-shaped pool, water pale and glistening. Beyond the pool was a cabana with a bar and grill area, more random chairs and a table out front, everything with the look of being suddenly abandoned. Around the corner from the bar a wooden walkway led to a gazebo planted atop the dune, then to steps down to the beach.

Rob tried the house door from the pool deck, but it was locked. There were outside stairs leading to the decks on the second, third and fourth floors. The sliding doors on the second floor leading to the lower bedrooms, the ones reserved for children and the outer perimeter of invited relatives and the nannies and au pairs, were also locked. He grabbed the railing and hobbled up to the next floor. He was familiar enough with the basic floor plans of these houses to know that on the third level were the master suites, probably three or four of them, ostentatious in every way, with amenity on amenity. On this floor the sliding door to the northeast suite slid silently open at his first touch. He slipped into the cool darkness. The curtains on the window were drawn, as were the heavy ceiling to floor shades on the door he came through. He stopped after he stepped in, pulling the door closed behind him. There was a hollow silence except for the hum of appliances that seemed to come from somewhere in the depths of the house. The faint scent of a woman's perfume still clung in the air in the bedroom as he crossed it and went to the door and into the hallway. He went to the stairway on the west side of the house. The outer wall of the staircase was all of glass, and he looked out and saw the roofs of cars beyond the row of low trees and bushes, and as he looked north and south the line of traffic went as far as the eye could see in either direction.

He climbed to the top floor living area with its massive kitchen and cathedral ceilings and east façade of glass looking out to the broad subtle curve of the ocean on the horizon. When he was satisfied the house was empty he went back down.

He didn't realize until he was descending that he was out of breath and his heart was raging high in his chest. He continued down more slowly to collect himself, holding the railing as he went. On the second floor the stairway ended at the grand entrance and he had to cross to the east side for the stairs leading to the ground floor. As he did he passed the elevator. He came down into the billiard and game room, passed through that into the home theatre and then finally into the garage with doors on either side of the massive staircase. He pressed the button to the door in front of the car and it rolled up. He went out and got into the car with Irina, who showed no reaction, and drove into the garage and got out and closed the door behind them.

They took the elevator back to the top floor, each with a personal bag and some of the groceries they had brought with them, not knowing how long they might be wherever the ended up. He didn't know if either one of them had imagined it would be in such flush surroundings.

Irina didn't even attempt to put any of the groceries away when they reached the top. She just left the bags on the counter and drifted to the ocean side and slid down into the soft folds of one of the couches.

The ocean and skies were blue like Maxfield Parrish was having an argument with himself. Rob could see the beginnings of corduroy lines of swell that were being pushed ahead of the storm. The sky was clear, with just a few high clouds scudding north. When he looked to the south and east though Rob saw a darkness clinging to the horizon threatening to press forward toward them. The beach was empty in both directions, a contradiction in the face of such warm weather and such a bright burning sun.

As it turned out both refrigerators in the kitchen were filled with food. While Irina napped on the couch Rob made scrambled eggs and bacon and when the aroma had awakened her, he brought her a plate and they sat on the separate couches and ate silently, watching the spreading vista unfolding in front of them.

"I could learn to live like this," he said.

When she looked up at him Rob could see that her mind was turning quickly, that the possibilities were becoming too real, even after everything that had already happened. She knew that just beyond the trees on the other side of the road to the west was Olsofsky's house and that Rob had chosen the house they were now in for a reason. She had gone from thinking he was not capable of much of anything to worrying about just how far he might go.

"What are you going to do?" she asked as he took the plates back to the kitchen.

"I don't know. They killed Amelia. I'm going to do something."

Irina sat on the couch and stared out at the expanse of the ocean through the floor-to-ceiling glass. She didn't say anything, she didn't move, except to replenish her drink from the well-stocked bar she found in an alcove on the north wall. Rob carefully reconnoitered the rest of the house from top to bottom, pre-planning escape routes, checking for supplies, filling two bathtubs on the second floor with water, collecting towels, finding a stash of bottled water and sodas in the garage. Then he went out to the pool area and dismantled and stowed all the pool toys and furniture. He did it on the off-chance that the rental companies might send their maintenance crews out (if they were allowed to) to secure the properties.

He took the walkway out to the gazebo and went to the edge of the steps that ran steeply down to the beach. He remembered 4-wheeling on the beach heading to Corolla and further north in the early eighties when there was nothing along this stretch but dunes topped with sea oats and bracken. The beach itself then had been four, maybe five time wider. Now it was narrow and severely angled, and on full moon and equinox tides the water came right up to the base of the dune itself. And with the storm that was possibly coming, he didn't know how much power or how much of an assault it would take to wash the dune away. He looked back at the massive façade of the beach house and suddenly felt vulnerable, as if there could have been others also hidden and waiting for a storm they weren't sure would arrive. There didn't seem to be any birds, as if they were already looking for shelter, but there were dragonflies bobbing and darting among the sea oats and out across the beach.

When he took the elevator back up he found Irina where he had left her, melted into the couch, staring at the ocean. She wore the same glazed frozen expression and the blue of her eyes seemed to fade or deepen as she looked up at the sky or down at the almost violet ocean.

As evening came on the dark smudge on the horizon far to the south seemed to be pressing forward and then receding again. If there hadn't been a warning to look in that direction, Rob didn't know if he would have noticed anything. They watched the hourly updates on the weather channel, and contented themselves with the excruciatingly slow progress of the storm in their general direction. A reporter stationed at Frisco on the south side of Hatteras Island had the camera pan out to the ocean and sky beyond him. It was still sunny where he stood and the inshore waters were a startling brown and green color, and brilliant white where the waves broke, but the black that was pressing on the southern horizon was a sheer standing wall of darkness looking to envelope everything in front of it.

Armando was still two hundred miles south and east of Cape Hatteras, and it was a tight storm wound like a watch spring. It had sped up its forward movement to the north from eight to ten miles an hour so it was predicted the eye would be on or near Diamond Shoals in twenty-four hours. The models for its progress after that were still confused and contradictory. A few of the colored spaghetti lines had it hugging the spine of the Outer Banks and heading vaguely north toward the Chesapeake Bay. Others predicted it would do what many early storms had done, clip the edge of Hatteras Island and then wander harmlessly out to sea. But again the meteorologists didn't have confidence in any of their predictions because there was still nothing else in the environment to steer the storm.

By the time the evening light began to fade, there was virtually no traffic on Highway 12. Between eight o'clock and the time it was completely dark at nine-thirty, Rob had seen only two law enforcement vehicles, one from the sheriff's department and one from the state highway patrol. He had gone through the refrigerators in the late afternoon and found an abundance of opportunities for dinner. There were steaks he would like to have grilled, but he didn't dare light the big brick-faced barbeque on the pool deck. He settled for pan-frying them, and then made an ornate and variegated salad. They ate as the horizon was dimming to mauve. While it was still pale retreating daylight before them, the horizon to the south was already blacker than night, rising like a specter, with faraway licks of lightning as another harbinger to the storm's approach.

They had already agreed to a blackout strategy once the sun went down. After they cleaned up from dinner they each claimed a suite on the third floor, and carefully sealed the curtain edges on the windows and sliding doors and then took sheets and spreads from the beds of the other suites to further prevent any light from escaping their rooms. Rob went back to the upper deck after dark and looked at the lines of massive cottages to the north and south of their position. He knew they were all deserted, and most were completely dark. A few still had porch lights burning, or lights on inside where the evacuating visitors had neglected to turn them off. But overall the only light available was from the stars and the rising almost full moon.

After making sure the house was locked up and secure, Rob settled into his suite. There was one large room with a sofa and TV and sound system, gaming consoles, mini-bar and dorm refrigerator. In the bathroom on the north wall there was a walk-in shower and a Jacuzzi. Across the rough granite tile was a vanity with two sinks and yards of counter space between them. He was too drained to enjoy the opulence. He showered, scrubbing the day's travel away. As he took one of the thick robes from the back of the door, and before he put it on, he looked at himself in the full-length mirror. He saw his own brown eyes and his maize-colored teeth, the wispy blond-gray hair that fell on his forehead. He didn't dare smile.

He had been trying to assimilate and understand what had happened, and he couldn't do it. Amelia was gone before he had even been able to decide if he was going to flee from her first. Her presence in his memory represented a peculiar stasis. They had not been moving toward each other or away. They just were together as if nature had written a law for it.

He came back into the sitting room and sat in front of the blank TV. Eventually he became aware of voices, or maybe just a voice, from Irina's rooms. He listened, at first thinking she had her TV on. But then, though he could not understand the words, he knew it was just her voice. She was on her cell phone again, though he had warned her not to use it, afraid that her position could somehow be traced.

The next morning the sun came up in a sky that was still clear to the east and north except for a dull red, foreboding glow. To the south, it was another story. The sky in that direction looked like the bottom of a black cauldron. The sheer height it had risen to was frightening and appeared to be faux cinematic. It just didn't look real. After checking the road to the west and determining it was empty and deserted, Rob went out and walked to the gazebo. The ocean swell had risen considerably. It was still clean because of the light winds, and Rob watched beautiful, rideable rights grinding across the sand bar in front of him. Far out to the southeastern horizon Rob could see whitecaps where the wind was coming around to the east as the counterclockwise flow pushed north.

The sea oats on the dunes were not concerned. They nodded in the breeze, pale stems waving, green oily heads moving languidly above. Rob saw the dragonflies he had seen the evening before, but this morning there were many more of them, thousands more. They moved above the dunes and beach in the spastic, almost electric flight, changing altitudes frequently, not seeming to have any true direction or flight path. They didn't seem to have any aim in common.

Then from the south, hidden at first by the further darkness, Rob began to see dark speeding forms coming northward in diving, angling, banking paths. He realized they were swallows, or martins probably, thousands of them. They pursued the dragonflies until they caught them on the beach in front of Rob. The small birds scissored through the insects, cutting them in two with their beaks. Rob began to see parts and pieces of severed dragonflies falling from the sky, winged sections almost floating as they fell. So fast and numerous were the martins that it was a chore to sight and follow one of the black-blue wedges through a segment of its flight. Their speed and unerring accuracy made the whole thing look choreographed. Rob followed one through the steep arch of a turn, marveling that the animal could hold together knowing the fragile filigree of its hollow bones.

Rob was neutral in the knowledge that there was a parable of nature playing out in front of him. The martins were the hunters and the dragonflies were the prey. One group must die for the other to live on. But as he continued to watch he realized that that was not exactly what was happening. As the severed corpses began accumulating on the beach, the hunters were not returning to eat them, nor could he see that they were eating parts of the dragonflies as they attacked them. He watched more closely and it was true. This wasn't survival. It was sport. Slowly the living cloud passed him and moved up the beach, thousands of carcasses twitching in the sand on the beach after they had gone.

He went back to the house, locked the door behind him, and rode the elevator to the top floor. Irina was seated at the bar, her long legs stretching to the floor. There was a glass of orange juice and her phone in front of her. She was watching the weather channel on the TV.

"It's reached Cape Hatteras," she said. "Winds are 100-110 miles and hour, and it's moving north at eight miles an hour. They just showed some video. It looks like the north end of Buxton is already underwater."

"I wonder if it will re-open the inlet there again. When I was in high school we used to surf at a break north of Buxton called Ferry Stop, which I never understood because it was just an unremarkable stretch of beach. But then someone explained that during the Ash Wednesday storm in 1963, which wasn't a hurricane, but a northeaster, that it had been so powerful

311

that it cut an inlet through there and for a couple of years they needed a ferry to get from Avon to Buxton."

"Eight or nine miles an hour means twelve hours or so until it's here, right?"

"Yes, if it keeps at that speed," he said. "They tend to speed up as they get further north."

She didn't say anything. She seemed hypnotized by the view outside the wall of glass.

"Is he coming?" he asked, looking at the phone she now held in her hand. He wasn't going to specify between the two.

She nodded. "He's already here. He wants to see us both. I told him we were close, but I didn't say exactly where. We're going to have to be very careful."

XXII

The storm did not speed up. It did not even manage to maintain its same forward speed. Armando stalled again, the eye wobbling roughly over Avon on Hatteras Island. There were dire reports of the damage on the lower end of the island, roofs blown off houses, flooding from the rain, and from the ocean, and from the Sound. There were as yet unsubstantiated reports from Frisco of a line of houses falling into the ocean where the surf had chewed away the protective dunes and swirled under the pilings, softening them until the battering waves caused the top-heavy structures to lurch over and crash on themselves. Roads were flooded and impassable, some with waves breaking on their pavement. Electricity was out. The Weather Channel had field reports regularly until even they determined it was too dangerous for their reporters to be outside and so they retreated to the relative safety of their motel rooms. Then the reports began to come from Nags Head, north of Hatteras Island, and roughly between Rob and Irina and the storm.

The face of the storm from their position changed innumerable times during the day. The sun maintained an almost regular presence until mid-afternoon, but the array and disposition of the clouds around it changed drastically through time. In the morning the bright sun and blue sky and dazzling white of the clouds created a stark contrast with the encroaching black from the south. Then rare rogue clouds would escape from the swirling mass and fly by high above them. Those clouds were weightless white tinged with blue, almost violet on their lower margins. Many were large and bulbous, like sails of a fleet pressing before a storm.

Rob did what he could to prepare to meet Olsofsky. He tried to keep an open mind. Amelia and the other men killed at Spencer's camp were murdered by eastern Europeans. He had seen them in the woods and heard them speak. They must have been connected with Olsofsky. It was true that Olsofsky's house had been burned down so that the attack on Spencer's camp may have been a retaliatory effort. But why the overwhelming increase in violence? The killings at Spencer's camp went way beyond tit for tat, unless there were other depredations by Spencer and his personal Marine guard that Rob didn't know anything about.

Rob knew he was completely out-gunned. He had time to try to come up with a McIver advantage, but basically his only arm was a small-caliber pistol with five bullets in it.

The first squall hit at five o'clock that afternoon. It was a frantic, wind-ripped affair, one dark cloud whose fat warm drops smelled of the tropics. It only lasted fifteen minutes, and the sun came out soon after, spangling everything with glistening crystals of light. The wind began to sweep in from the east in the next hour, at first steady, but then cut through with great gusts that flattened the dune grasses below them, and tore through the trees between them and the road, and came full-brunt against the seaside wall of the house so at the height of the top floor they could feel it swaying. By dark the gusts were probably topping seventy miles an hour. The weather reports were still non-committal about an increase in the storm's forward speed, but they had already added the new wrinkle that two nights hence, Saturday, was the full moon, and with the combination of the storm surge and fuller lunar tides the potential for overwash was increasing dramatically. Rob already realized this wasn't going to be one of those storms where you listened with all your imagination as it battered your place of protection, and after feeling the full thrill and fear of it, you fell asleep and woke up the next morning knowing it had passed.

The eye of the storm had passed over the foot of Hatteras Island with untold destruction to the property in the villages there, and now again it hesitated, placed by the meteorologists five miles west of Avon in the Pamlico Sound. That was another added touch to the nightmare scenario because it meant that all those millions and millions of gallons of shallow Sound water were being pushed into the streams and marshes to the west, and they would be returning full force, rushing east again to flood the back side of the island when the storm passed.

All this destruction was casually meandering toward them and there was no chance now that they would avoid it. No cold front was sweeping through from the northwest to push it out to sea. There were no high altitude winds to shear the tops off the towering thunderheads. The Bermuda High, which was usually a predominant feature of the weather pattern in high summer, had shrunk to a small knot of wind far off the east coast.

As the storm showed signs of ramping up around them and the daylight faded after a brilliant sunset lit by clouds at all levels of the atmosphere, Irina began to show signs of increasing anxiety. Rob thought at first she might have run out of whatever medications she had been taking to keep herself on a steady course. But then he began to realize that she had some kind of phobia about the storm itself. After it grew dark outside and the invisible wind buffeted the cottage from all directions she would turn her head toward each new noise. She sent Rob outside a couple of times to check on things. A rhythmic thumping from the floor below turned out to be the cover of the hot tub on the deck on that level not being securely tied down on one side. A high-pitched whine and ungodly clanging was just the metal clips of the flagpole by the pool being tossed to and fro.

"What am I going to find out when I talk to Olsofsky?" he asked, sitting on the couch across from her, watching as her eyes grew large and frantic with each new noise. Gusts of wind swept in, and fat drops peppered the glass on the ocean side wall. The way she turned to look at him, the suggestiveness she added to her movements, told him she was going to lie.

"He doesn't have anything against you," she said "He knows you were just protecting yourself, protecting me. His fight is with Spencer."

"But why?" Rob asked very deliberately. "You said Olsofsky killed Nadia as a warning to you."

"Yes. He knew I was close to Spencer, and Alexander was afraid I would tell Spencer about his other businesses in Ukraine. Spencer wouldn't want to be involved with someone who might be implicated in international business fraud."

That answer seemed soft. Spencer would have done his homework. There was no way he didn't have a good idea of what Olsofsky's other business entanglements might be. He had lawyers and accounting firms, and in that fraternity of wealth and multi-layered businesses and possessions there were few real secrets. "And Steven?"

"I told Steven I was afraid of Alexander. When Nadia disappeared, Steven was like everyone else in thinking it was me. It was only when he couldn't find Nadia to ask her questions about me...when had she last seen me, did she have any ideas of what had happened...that he began to wonder."

How did she know that? She was tucked away by Spencer in the week that Steven lived after everyone thought she had disappeared. If Steven thought Olsofsky had killed Irina the night he dragged Rob to the party at the Ukrainian's house, and even if he had confronted him about it…but he couldn't because Olsofsky wasn't there that night. Was he?

He leaned over and caught a look in her eye, that while it wasn't frantic, it at least showed fear and a determination to change the subject. Suddenly, and without seeming to move, her whole form and aspect became an invitation. She thrust out her bare leg as if she were absently stretching it. She stroked it from her thigh to her knee as if she were working out a cramp in the large muscle there. Rob saw her eyes beneath the pale wispy curtain of hair. They were dark in the shadows, but keen and predatory.

"I don't know what to do," she said, almost as an aside, but also to lead him away from his fantasies so she could return him to them and broaden them. "Spencer won't want to have anything to do with me after all of this. We could never keep it quiet enough. He would always tell me that he was this far from retirement and ready to take me away with him, and we could travel and be together at last. But he'll never give it up. He can't. He's not interested in making money any more except for the challenge and to keep what he has. He's like a king sitting on his throne in a castle, trying to figure out ways to keep the Huns from penetrating his borders."

Rob couldn't worry about anything she was saying. It was mostly like a long tedious drone in his head. He was completely taken by the leg thrust out on the carpet before him. When he got to her thigh all the electrical signals in his brain began automatically re-routing blood to his groin. The building storm outside seemed little more than a whisper in the background.

Suddenly Irina slid off the couch and turned so she was in a crouch in front of it, her legs tucked beneath her, her head buried beneath her forearms and hands. Her shorts hiked up around her buttocks and her t-shirt lifted so that her midriff was exposed and he could see her diaphragm rising and falling as she breathed. He also saw the curving line of a serpent tattoo that disappeared both up into her flimsy shirt and down beneath the waistband of her shorts. He knew where it emerged on her upper thigh, but he had no idea the course it took between. Her movements were so sudden that it made Rob dizzy and he swayed as he tried to see and mark everything in his memory.

The sounds of the storm came back. Pellets of rain chattered against the outside walls. He felt the assault of the wind on the house, felt its dreamlike swaying. Irina, who had fallen out of focus, came raging back. Her head was down, and her eyes were in shadow, but they were a brilliant gray and black, lit somehow from within.

"I need your help with this," she said.

Then he was moving toward her, and his hand reached for and finally touched the skin on the back of her thigh.

Afterward they slept in each other's arms. The storm rose and fell outside. It was impossible for it not to penetrate their dreams, or periodically chase those dreams away. Irina would move closer when it was at its loudest and curled naturally under his arm. Even in sleep her movements had the natural polish of a practiced concubine. Rob spent much of the night awake, trying to suss out his own motives. He never did find any satisfactory answers.

The transition from night to dawn would have been a subtle one except for the orchestra of percussion that accompanied it. Rob slid out of bed and climbed to the fourth floor. There was just a dull red abbreviation of dawn to the east. Everything else was dark gray and black. Even the whitecaps raging against each other in the jumbling froth on the surface of the sea were the color of rubbed charcoal in the stingy light. The wind raged, almost bowing the windows and sliding doors. Horizontal rain splashed against the glass, carry beads of sand from the beach that tinkled as they struck the surfaces. As the light grew somewhat stronger, Rob could see the tumult of the shore break crashing on the beach and running thickly up into the dunes. Three houses to the north the dune had already been breached and the ocean surged through the fence into the yard and swimming pool and then between the houses on to the road beyond. It was clear that with each new high tide there would be further assaults on those protective walls of sand.

Rob turned on the TV. The satellite signal was unavailable owing to the clouds, or perhaps the dish on the roof had been damaged. There was a radio on the counter in the kitchen, and after he started coffee brewing, he turned it on and tried to find a station in the static. He finally found one, a local country station whose DJs were good ole boys known for their forced offbeat humor and fishing reports. Surprisingly both were there and had been on the air non-stop for almost forty eight hours, trying to keep up with announcements and damage reports and grabbing snatches of sleep on the cots they'd set up in the cramped studio.

There was little jollity or banter. They spoke in tired hoarse anxious voices. The present situation was grim, the outlook grimmer still. The news they had already received and substantiated spoke of devastation, especially south on Hatteras Island and Ocracoke. Even being on the weaker, eastern side of the storm, Ocracoke village was largely destroyed. The idyllic harbor was now filled with drifting swamped boats and the debris from buildings and bulkheads razed on the shoreline all around. The news was brought by Coast Guard helicopters from Morehead City, who got as close as they dared this morning, although the winds in the area were still gusting at hurricane strength.

It was impossible to get to Hatteras Island because the storm was now centered south and west of Oregon Inlet, meaning it had moved a total of twenty miles in the last twenty-four hours. Reports from Hatteras Village, and the DJs stressed that these were not confirmed, claimed that the town was gone, with five or six feet of water still swirling through the streets. And because many of the residents, some of whose families had been there for generations, would never consider evacuating no matter how powerful the storm might be, the potential for large numbers of fatalities was growing with each passing hour.

Irina came up the stairs just as the coffee was ready, wearing only a t-shirt and panties, dragging a blanket on the floor behind her. She glided to one of the stools at the counter and draped herself there as Rob handed her a cup. Then he held up his hand so that they could continue to listen to the reports.

"We have heard, and I stress that this is unverified, that the Bonner Bridge has been breached at the south end, and a large part of the high rise section of it has fallen into the channel. Again this is unconfirmed, and not likely to be until the Armando goes by us. Unfortunately, there is still no sustained forward movement of the storm itself..."

"Let me interrupt Bobby here," the other DJ broke in. "We have a report from Buxton that the village is under three to five feet of water and there are a number of fires burning. Also, and we're hoping this is not true…but Emergency Services set up an evacuation center at the Hatteras School there, and early yesterday afternoon buses were sent to Hatteras Village to transport people to the school. The report we have is that the buses were travelling back between Hatteras Village and Frisco and there was water on the road to begin with, and then waves flooded through the dunes near the pier and two of the buses were carried off the road and into the Sound. Again, we're waiting for confirmation, and praying we don't get it. Back to you, Bobby."

"Thank you, Tim. Let's all pause and say a prayer for those people down there, that the Good Lord is watching over them. Up here on the northern beaches…well, most anyone within the sound of my voice can tell what's happening outside. At this point, even if Armando were to stop blowing in the next ten minutes, we know we have major and substantial damage. Power lines are down, dunes are breached from Corolla to South Nags Head. The Beach Road from Kitty Hawk all the way south is now a four-foot deep stream. In many places the By-pass is under water. There is a twenty-four hour curfew in effect, which means you are not allowed to leave your residence or place of shelter. We hope that most everybody, especially women and children, took the opportunity to evacuate when it was available."

They went on to say that Manteo and Mann's Harbor and Wanchese, as well as a number of communities on the western edge of the Sounds had already experienced serious flooding as steady easterly winds had pushed all the water toward them.

Although the DJs sounded tired out, they tried to maintain a cheerful front. They told gentle, self-deprecating jokes, and they asked for listeners to call in and tell of their experiences, and what they could see, and what they had heard. But very few still had land phone service, it appeared, and cell service was almost non-existent. Most of the calls were from the land-side of Currituck County up close to the Virginia border where the storm was just tentatively reaching. Emergency Services called to give what updates they could on the situation. Movement on any roads in the area was difficult, if not impossible, and even police and fire vehicles were on orders to stand down until the power of the storm lessened. They repeated the same warning they had been giving; no rescues would be attempted in the present situation. Visitors and resident alike had been ordered to leave, and anyone who had ignored those orders had done so at their own peril.

Although the view from the fourth floor windows was virtually unimpeded on all sides, with the rain smearing the windows, beading and dancing on the panes, and the gray squalls fed by roaring gusts of wind blowing through loudly and regularly, it was hard to get a real idea of what the storm was doing any further than the houses on either side of them.

But if Olsofsky was at the Sound house, as Irina said he was, then the storm was perfect for Rob's purposes. By his reckoning it was less than a mile from the massive beachside cottage where they hid across the island to Olsofsky's spread. While any movement outside in the elements would be hazardous, he should be able to make his way unimpeded and unmolested.

Rob still didn't know what he would say or do if he was able to confront Olsofsky. He had imagined all sorts of scenarios where he would present the soliloquy that he planned to unloose on the Ukrainian, but he doubted there would be much time for talk on either side. First of all, he didn't know if Olsofsky would be alone, although he doubted that he would be. That made Rob realize that his small plinker with five bullets might not nearly be enough to subdue any opposition he might find. He realized that he would have to do more to arm himself, and aside from perhaps a carving knife in the kitchen or an ice pick in the bar, he didn't know what other potential weapons might be available.

They still had electricity, which was good, but even as he was realizing it the lights flickered and hesitated, but they came right back on again. Apparently their satellite dish was not damaged because periodically the television would flash from the blue screen to an array of pixilated talking heads that would fade in and out, speaking in some kind of unrecognizable digital language, and then the screen would go blue again.

Irina stayed near him while trying to appear not to. The constant raging of the storm was clearly getting on her nerves.

Rob realized that he needed to do a complete search of the house to see if he could find any other ways to arm himself. Other than in the kitchen he didn't expect to have much luck on the top three floors, and that proved to be the case. He did find a knife with a sturdy seven-inch blade in one of the kitchen drawers, but that was all. Then he remembered that in the garage there was a bench with a wall of tools hooked behind it, as well as a locked door he realized was probably the owner's closet, where the principals could leave personal possessions when renters were in the house.

Irina followed him as he took the stairs down. Though he fought against the idea, he found himself trying to minimize is limp as he descended in front of her. He kept his shoulders aligned as much as possible, but it was a sham march. He could feel the opposing sides of his body moving back toward their post-stroke imbalance.

In the garage he found gardening tools, rakes, shovels, edgers, blowers for the driveway and pool area, some fertilizer and empty flower pots. There were also a few tools hanging on a pegboard behind the table; a hammer, a couple of screwdrivers, pliers, wrenches and a hatchet with a canvas cover for the blade. Below on the floor were a couple of steel toolboxes. Everything was neatly arranged and practically new.

Rob unsheathed the hatchet and went to the closet door. The small room was on the north wall behind the billiard room. With a few strokes the edges of the doorjamb splintered and the door swung open. He found the switch and turned the light on. Inside there were bikes and golf clubs, tennis racquets, surfboards, wetsuits, an elliptical machine, a bench and weights. On the back wall was a large freestanding cupboard with sheets, towels, pillows and blankets. There were shelves of toiletries, shampoo and cream rinse, soap, toothpaste and such, and many rolls of toilet paper. Rob was desperately hoping he might find a firearm, but he had no such luck.

As he was backing out of the room he drew one of the irons out of a golf bag. He took it to the tool area and tightened it in the vise on the side of the table. In one of the tool boxes beneath was a hacksaw and within a few minutes he had cut the head off the shaft to a length of about two and a half feet. He shrugged at Irina as he put it down his pant leg. Then he walked across the garage floor. It altered his limp, but not really in any way someone who didn't know him might recognize.

Above them the house was groaning, shuddering. There were precipitous changes in atmospheric pressure as the wind found chinks in the armor of the house. Outside that wind raged unabated, the surf was a continuous deep rumble, and the ratatat of rain on the glass panes upstairs could be heard even down in the windowless depths of the house. They slogged back up the stairs, afraid to take the elevator back to the top floor.

"He's there?" Rob asked.

She held up her phone. "He texted me that he is. He won't answer any more when I call him. I can't go with you if you go there."

"You don't have to come with me."

"But I don't know if I can stay here by myself."

"We don't have to decide anything right now."

"But when? When are you going?"

"This afternoon sometime. Relax."

Rob felt calm himself, even while they listened to the radio and more tales of catastrophe and destruction. There were reports that houses on the beach in Nags Head, on the strip of beach called "Millionaire's Mile", some of them grand, old-school cottages built in the 1930s, had collapsed and been washed out to sea. Everywhere there were reports of locals who stayed and now were in need of rescue, but there was just no way emergency vehicles could get to them. Still the storm refused to move at more than a snail's pace. Usually when a storm met a land mass that would be the start of it breaking up. It would no longer be able to feed on the ocean's warmth and moisture, and the contours of the land would disrupt the cyclonic action. But the Outer Banks were just too thin a line of land and too low. And while Armando's winds were not as strong as some, it was an incredibly tall storm with its own extra reservoirs of strength.

Rob had begun to get a feeling that all this might spell the end for him. He was moving toward something, or being drawn toward it, and it was becoming less clear if he got there how he was going to pull through to the other side. Both Olsofsky and Spencer must have realized the need to surround themselves with people capable of protecting them. Rob had seen Spencer's Marines, and also the black-clad men who did Olsofsky's bidding. But he had no choice. He had to have some retribution for Amelia's life, and for Kay's too. Even Chick's death was a result of this feud.

His plan was to move late that afternoon. He didn't know what he was going to do when he got to Olsofsky's house. Irina said Olsofsky wanted to meet with him. But what the Ukrainians plans were when they did meet was another question.

He got his small arsenal together. All he had was the Walther, the sharpened golf shaft, the carving knife, and a box cutter. He guessed people had hijacked planes with less.

The house continually shuddered in the wind. Things were coming loose on their house and the houses around them. Pieces of shingles would fly by like spinning ninja weapons. A piece of siding on the next house north came loose and slapped at the wall wildly and incessantly until it finally ripped off. The sound of the surf was mesmerizing. At times it was so startlingly loud that it sounded as if were crashing against the house's foundation. Then it would revert to a whisper beneath the whistling void. And then just as suddenly the crash of the shore break would roar like a cannon shot.

More and more news of damage and flooding came in. It was reported that many towns to the west of the Sounds and along the rivers that emptied into them were being flooded. Little Washington, Bellhaven, Plymouth, Edenton, were all dealing with major flooding. What that also meant, of course, was when the storm passed, if it ever passed, the winds would switch to the west and all the pushed-up water would come racing back to flood the west side of the barrier islands.

Tomorrow was Saturday. Rob couldn't believe it was only a week since everything happened in Gettysburg. Also, to add to the concerns about the storm, Saturday night was the full moon and the increased tides would be added to the swells and the storm surge, and there were many weakened areas up and down the coast where that three feet of higher water pounding the beaches might be just too much to take.

By seven-thirty he was ready. This close to the solstice there were still two hours of ostensible daylight left. Irina was fidgeting, fierce red blotches showing high on her cheeks. He half-expected her not to accompany him.

He remembered their soft collision the night before, not as if it were meaningful, or real even, but just the physical mechanics of it. Where with Amelia there had been some shy hesitation, almost a disavowal of the desire, Irina had no such qualms. Rob's inability to maneuver and his sluggish responses were just minor obstacles. Her desire wasn't so much urgent as not to be denied. In her face was an expression that was other-worldly, and that other world had its own rules of physics and purpose.

All that was a distraction now, and he didn't need any distractions. They had seen only one vehicle on the road, a 4-wheel drive sheriff's department cruiser that had driven carefully north past them in the late morning, negotiating standing water and debris, and then returned an hour later. It must have been making preliminary damage assessments, gauging the flooding, checking for major damage to structures.

Now as Rob looked west from the fourth floor, great sweeping gusts bent low the quivering vegetation, and all was quiet on the roadway as far north and south as he could see. While Rob knew that he could not protect himself and Irina against any kind of sustained assault by more than a couple of people, he was armed. And in his right front pocket he had his wad of cash, money donated by Chick and Amelia, enough so that when this was over he could get far away without leaving much evidence that he had ever been there.

"Are you ready for this?"

Irina shrugged and they went down to the garage. Rob had his plastic mac and he gave Irina one of the large green lawn trash bags, cut at the corners for her arms and with another hole in the bottom for her head, and helped her wriggle into it. When they stepped outside everything was in out-sized motion. The light that filtered through from above was gray and stingy. And the noise. The wind raged, swirling against itself from different directions, whooshing down from the darkness of the clouds above, strafing the sea oats and the sand. The ocean, hidden by the diminished dunes, was in a perpetual rage, shaking the earth as it crashed to shore, relentlessly churning away at the shoreline. The trees to the west that blocked the view of the highway were throttled by angry gusts. The feeder road in front of the house was ankle-deep in water. In it floated scuzzy pods of foam from the dune that had been breached and sent seawater over to mix with the flooding from the rain.

Rob took Irina's hand and they moved down the street. They both had flashlights hanging from their belt loops because they would be returning in the dark. They crossed to the highway and went up the middle of it a quarter of a mile until it met the road that led back to Olsofsky's property. There was not a sign of life anywhere. Once they turned on the road that led back to the Sound, they were quickly absorbed by the pine woods that grew up on both sides. The wind still shook the treetops above them, but it was quieter on the floor of the woods, except for the groans of the straining tree trunks and the occasional crack of a tree branch above them. Everywhere on the road and in the woods were fallen pine boughs and needles, brown and eerie green in the light.

When they got back to the gate to Olsofsky's property they found it unlocked and open, creaking in the wind. As they hesitated they heard a squall crashing through the trees behind them. Within seconds they were engulfed by a solid gray curtain of rain. As it swept through it washed away the view of everything in front of them. They put their heads down and pressed on.

The way narrowed inside the gate. The moving trees enclosed above them and pressed down like some special effect from a movie. Rob had no memory of how far it was from the gate back to the house. He remembered opening the gate, and then he remembered coming out of the trees into the expansive clearing, but nothing in between.

He felt Irina's anxiety level rise with each step. There was something at Olsofsky's house that she absolutely did not want to face. But she was tied to Rob to ride out the storm, so as he went forward she could only follow.

Then as they moved through a meandering curve Rob abruptly stopped. He heard something amid the storm 's clamor that did not belong.

"Quick! This way!" he said, taking her hand and pulling her into the underbrush beneath the thin palings of trees growing up next to the long driveway. They ducked low and he dragged her over the spongy ground until the found a tree trunk solid enough for both to crouch behind. Through the foliage and shimmering rain they saw light, and the light was approaching. Gradually it separated into two beams, and they saw an SUV, white or gray, it was impossible to say which, with one dark figure behind the wheel inside. It came slowly by and then receded into the rain, its red taillights washed to pink, and then disappeared into the trees. Rob wasn't sure, but he thought he had seen letters and a logo on the SUV's door.

"Do you recognize that?"

"No, I could barely see it. Who would be driving now? Where would they be going?"

"I could only see one person, and that just the form of the driver. I just hope it wasn't Alexander."

"You don't have to worry about that. Alexander doesn't drive anywhere. He's afraid to drive."

They waited a few minutes longer to see if any other vehicles would follow the first one, and then went back to the road and soldiered on. Now though they kept closer to the edge of the trees. The rain now was just a fine mist, tasting of the ocean's saltiness, drifting and swirling through the air. The clearing was only a hundred yards past where they had seen the mysterious vehicle leaving. There were two SUVs, tricked-out Escalades it looked like, parked up close to the house. The strings of light hung between poles in the yard danced and jerked in the gusts, animating the shadows all around, but after a minute searching every corner of the yard, Rob was convinced there was no one outside.

They moved inside the protection of the trees and made their way to the south end of the sprawling house. Rob watched for signs of movement in the house itself, but even as the angle of their approach changed, the interior light seemed only to shine on inanimate objects. But the lights that were on didn't seem to be those that would be left on in an unoccupied house. Irina followed close behind him. The pine trees and oaks back here grew in sand, ancient eroded dunes, and the drainage was good, but with so much rain it was reaching capacity. In the shallow swales of Olsofsky's lawn great puddles and ponds spread out and glistened on the surface.

Rob gently pulled Irina's hand as they moved around to the back of the house. There were lights on around the raised pool deck, and Rob saw the line of lights above the dock thrust out into the Sound. What was different now was that because of the strength and duration of the strong easterly winds all the water was blown away from the shore. The pier went out a hundred feet into mud, and the mud continued for another two hundred yards past that. Olsofsky's big boat, three quarters of the way out on the dock, secure in its cradle, was fifteen feet above nothing.

They slowly climbed the side stairs to the pool deck, Irina staunchly resisting each step. Rob finally let go of her hand halfway up, put a finger to his lips, and then continued on. On the deck at the level of the pool surface, more light spread out from inside the house. Rob scanned every corner of the deck, but there was no one keeping watch outside.

Then he saw them, two human forms floating face down in the pool, eddying with the wind that dappled to water's surface, gently bobbing, arms outstretched, legs slightly parted, among the stray leaves and branches that had blown there. Rob put his hand on the grip of the pistol in his pocket and moved closer. They were middle-aged men, judging from the gray in their hair, dressed in black and gray. Either could have been among the men Rob saw in the woods by Spencer's camp a week earlier. There was an aura of pink in the water around each body that looked garish as the light shone from beneath.

Rob backed away across the deck until he was against the wall of the house. He pulled the gun out of his pocket and edged along the wall toward one of the glass doors. As he got closer to the first one, he saw it was slightly ajar, and he could hear the high strains of violin music coming from the interior of the house. He crouched next to the opening and listened. He heard the music, eerie and distorted, but nothing else. Before he knew what he was doing Rob slid the door open wider. He stood to his full height and stepped in, disappearing from Irina's sight. Memories of the house came back as he moved further into it. He remembered rooms filled with beautiful people, statuesque women, laughing men. He remembered seeing Steven…it was the last time he remembered seeing Steven…standing across the room, drink in hand, smile of unconcern on his face. He remembered pulsing, throbbing music, so different from the strings that wafted through these rooms now.

The first room he entered was a library. There were bookcases on the walls, and thick vellum spines of sets of books, and two heavy leather chairs, each with a reading lamp. There were portraits on one wall, from the 19th century it looked like, and French landscapes on another. In one corner was a table with bottles of port and brandy and cognac, with the proper glasses and snifters on a rack above. In the center wall was a fireplace, the bricks rising and spreading out across the whole wall. Rob edged through the door at the end of that wall, and looked out into the great room of the house with its distinct levels and juxtaposition of steps, shiny wooden floors, scattered Oriental rugs, sparse furniture, and the random pilings rising through the floors, supporting staircases and ceilings, some rising to the roof line, and some right through into the sky. The pilings were all of different diameters, some infused with the sick green color of salt treatment, some painted in a thick shiny tar meant to look like creosote, but without the acrid, burnt smell. From everywhere came the beautiful scraping of a rosined bow against the violin strings, just that one lonely instrument playing a lonely song. Again he thought what he thought the first time he had seen the room, that it looked like an architectural museum piece. The vertical shadows the pilings threw on the wall were in some cases stark and finely drawn outlines, but in others gave a softer impression.

Rob took two more steps into the room before he saw him. In the center of the great room, on the lowest level, there was a man sitting with his back to Rob in a straight-back chair. At first because of the small size Rob thought it might be a boy, but he could see light shining off his bald head, and a ring of gray hair around his temples. The man's head was down, his chin resting on his chest in what looked like a pose of exhausted resignation. Rob could not stop himself from moving closer, all the while swiveling his head trying to take in any signs of movement or danger around him. He was ten feet away from the man, who he assumed must be Olsofsky, though the figure ruined any imagining he had had of him, when he realized that he was probably dead. He was intricately tied to the chair, and there was a gag, although it appeared he had almost succeeded in removing it. Rob saw that his hands had been horribly and irreparably burned, and when he came around to where he could see his face, it was clear he had been badly beaten. There were pools of blood beneath the chair, as well as spattered blood, dark flung droplets on the floor all around. He had clearly been tortured, though for what information or whether they had gotten it, he didn't know.

Rob had wanted revenge on Olsofsky. He had dreamed and breathed it. But if this was Alexander, it was not the Alexander his imagination had drawn for him. And that made him wonder if perhaps he had made Olsofsky into a form the real man didn't fit. Maybe he was completely wrong about the whole thing. He kept thinking about it as he searched the rest of the house. He got the feeling as he went from room to room that the artwork on the walls and the statuary in alcoves and sudden recesses was expensive and aesthetically valuable. He realized they must represent the taste of the person trussed up in the chair on the lower level.

He came back to himself when he heard a great whoosh of wind and then a loud tearing crack, and then the whole house shuddered. Something very heavy, probably a traverse limb of one of the pine trees above, crashed down on the roof right above him. He hurried back downstairs. There was no longer anything he could do except collect Irina and go back to the beach house. Now Rob knew they must find Spencer because only he could have the final answers to bring this all to a resolution. Rob probably could have guessed that all along.

XXIII

Rob hurried to the back, avoided looking at the corpse in repose on the chair, and went out the same door he had come in. The sky all around was darkening to a bruised violet and purple and he realized they didn't have much time to get back before they would have to use their flashlights, which was something he didn't want to do.

Irina wasn't on the steps where he had left her. He didn't see her in the shadows of the trees by the south side of the house, or anywhere on the expanse of the puddle-strewn lawn in front. She had bolted. There was only one place she could have gone, and that was back to the Oceanside cottage. He automatically began moving in that direction, trudging through the spongy undergrowth, stumbling over sappy pine-scented branches knocked loose by the storm and strewn across the path. With the great noise and clamor, he worried a tree or a branch might fall on him before he could hear it. Some of the branches already on the ground were big enough to easily kill a man if he was in the wrong position beneath one. As Rob got closer to the main road he remembered the truck they had seen leaving the area as they were entering. Rob now immediately thought of Davy Todd and how Irina had said he was an agent of Spencer. Who better to have on your side during a crisis and state of emergency that a sheriff's department official who was able to be out on the roads at any time day or night? Was it Davy Todd in that truck, and had he killed the two men in the pool? Had those two men tortured Olsofsky, and if so, why? Was it to avenge their fellow killed in Gettysburg, or had Olsofsky welched on payments to them? He didn't know.

Rob got back to the road without a tree branch or anything else falling on him. Highway 12 was still deserted, and many of the parts he could see were under standing water, green leaves and pine straw strewn everywhere on the combed and wind-stippled surfaces. When he got back to the feeder road and looked down the street to the cottage he knew he was in trouble. The garage door was open and yellow light spilled out onto the glistening driveway. When he came even with the driveway and looked into the garage, he saw the car was gone. He stood in the bathing light, salt-tinged raindrops falling in an angry flurry, wind still whistling, droning, roaring so he almost didn't hear it any more.

She won't get far, he thought. There must be roadblocks, patrols. The road was probably impassable in many places. He was sure she would have a good story to tell, perhaps that he had kidnapped and held her. She could explain the rental car that way. But they wouldn't come for him during the storm, would they? He doubted they had the extra manpower. But they would be planning to find him after.

It was just another knot in the line of things. He went in, closed the garage door, and dripped on the concrete floor for a while. He took off the raincoat, hung it on one of the tool hooks, and went wearily upstairs. He forgot about the elevator until he was on the second floor landing. As soon as he got to the fourth floor he had to fight the urge to pour himself a drink. The television in the great room was still on, the screen blue and silent.

He turned on the radio and it was the same voices. One of the DJs was giving a new and extensive litany of damage reports; overwash, flooding, trees down, houses blown off their foundations, roads underwater, roads undermined, and still the storm was raging from Cape Hatteras to the Virginia line. The next day, Saturday, was the full moon, which was raising more tidal concerns, and the progress of the storm, as viewed from its center, was still at a snail's pace. The center was still in the shallow water of the northern Pamlico Sound, just a few miles above Oregon Inlet. There were rumors that the bridge at the inlet, which was already something of a sad joke, had been undermined on the south end, and some of the pilings were dangling freely in the current and not connected to the base in any way. That was an old rumor really. There were other reports of its collapse.

The only bright spot in anything the voices were saying was that finally a cold front had worked its way across central Canada and was forecast to dip down into the northeast US, which caused the models to suggest that it could push Armando out to sea where it could drift harmlessly away into the north Atlantic. That scenario, if it played out, would not be until Sunday though. Rob would have to figure something out by then, and now he was just drained and lay back on the deep couch, and slept. The wind whistled and whined, the house quivered, he heard bangs and crashes and thuds, as if the house were a ship powering through heavy seas.

When he woke up in the gray and faded pink that stood for dawn, the TV screen was still blue, and no voices came forth. Through the milky glaze

331

of the glass to the east he saw the ocean still tossed in a raging jumble. More of the dunes in front of the line of houses had been chewed away, and there were some breaches where the waves had crashed through and the foamy whitewater spread as it flowed toward the street. The houses along the line had all taken a beating, screens and shutters torn away, siding split at the nails, everything not tied down scattered up and down the streets.

Rob wanted to believe the light was a bit stronger this day. He had to make himself believe the storm was moving, that while it might be unrelenting and powerful for a while yet, it would pass.

He had awakened thinking the same thing he had been thinking when he drifted off to sleep, marveling at the fact that Alexander Olsofsky was not fat. Olsofsky had been the villain and the bugaboo. Everything had led Rob to believe that Olsofsky was the prime moving force. He had killed Nadia (or had her killed) as a warning to Irina. He had then killed Steven when he got too close. That killing was also a warning to Spencer, whom Olsofsky knew by then to be hiding and protecting Irina.

Rob knew he had to go. He didn't think law enforcement would move against him now, even if Irina had given him up, and even if she had manufactured a list of crimes against him. They would have too many other critical priorities while the storm raged. But they would probably put plans in place to apprehend him after the weather cleared and before they opened the beach back up to residents of visitors.

His battery was running down. He had steadily been on the move since he and Amelia left Mashoes. As he gathered his things together he again realized he was no closer to answers than when he started. There was only one person left to talk to, Spencer.

The rental car was gone. He was going to have to find a vehicle. He would figure out the logistics of making an escape later. He dragged his meager possessions down the feeder road to a house at the north end of the cul de sac. He broke in and went upstairs, made himself a nest by the picture window on the third floor at the west end of the house. That position gave him an unobstructed view looking north and south. The new house he found himself in was the same, but completely different. The floor plans varied with regards to minor things. In this house on the east end was a widow's watch rising on the southeast corner. The appliances in the kitchen were arranged differently. The bar was on the south side instead of the north. The pool outside was an oval instead of kidney-shaped, and the pool house stood at a different angle from it. The only thing the furnishings had in common was that they were of the same high quality and utilitarian style.

Sitting in his perch as the day dragged by, he came up with a plan, or the bare bones of one. He would sneak back to Olsofsky's place in the evening. There were the two Escalades on the lawn. He could take one of them. Or there was a raised two-car garage set back on the north end of the property. Rob felt sure there were probably a couple of nice vehicles in there. He would take one, go back to his new base, and hide it in the garage. After the all clear he would drive north to the village of Corolla, move it from house to house, from store parking lot to shopping center lot until the area filled back enough so that he could make a break for it. He had made no firmer decision about it except that he would head somewhere out west.

All this was based on the belief that the storm would eventually pass. For more than two days it had blown and swirled and roared, and it still showed no signs of abating. The wind was still from the east, which meant the center was still south of him. The dunes up in front of him were sturdier and higher than they were in many places to the south. He thought of Kitty Hawk where there was virtually no natural dune any more even at the best of times, or over the Bonner Bridge on Pea Island where what was left of those bald dunes were washed over and the road flooded during normal northeasters.

Rob saw no traffic. He watched the trees and bushes beneath him rock and buck under the lash of the powerful capricious gusts. He saw squalls veil the land as they moved across the narrow strip. He found an alarm clock radio in one of the bedrooms and fiddled with the tuner for what seemed like hours, but never picked up any stations. He ate food from the refrigerators, just munched on what was available, some fruit, some cold cuts and sliced cheese.

The power went off at 4:15 in the afternoon. Because the sky was an indeterminate gray all day, he only knew it happened because he heard a loud click and suddenly the sounds from inside the house stopped and those outside became even more magnified. He heard the wind whip and

333

flay the exterior of the house. He heard rain tattooing the roof and windows. He decided it was time to go.

With his small bag, and another plastic bag filled with provisions, he put on his slicker and hat, re-checked his sad arsenal, and set off. As soon as he opened the back poolside door and stepped out the wind assaulted him. It pelted him in the face and on the backs of his bare hands. It whipped at the edges of his raincoat and pulled at the underneath of his floppy hat. He stepped around to the north corner and suddenly realized he was in the lee of the wind there. For the previous two days the space between the houses had been like a wind tunnel, adding to the strength of the wind as it swept through the narrow space. Now there were only eddies and whirls of wind, zephyrs that spun through and died. It told Rob that the storm had moved further north. It meant that the eye had to be more west of him.

He went across the highway and into the woods on the other side. The wind still came in great gusts, and Rob began to see more felled trees, as their roots systems and the soil beneath became soaked and soft from the relentless rain so that they could not recover from the continuing gusts. He realized that very few trees were still standing upright. Almost all leaned, mostly to the west.

When he got to the clearing at Olsofsky's house it looked just as it had when he had last left it. He had no doubt that Alexander's corpse was still slouched forward in the chair under the expensive paintings and the gaudy chandelier. This time Rob made his way to the north edge of the woods where standing beneath the drooping boughs was a detached two-car garage built on stilts with a heavy wooden ramp leading up to the great doors. There was a narrow deck that led around to the north side and a door. The door was locked, but Rob was able to open it by slipping the blade of the carving knife between the door-frame and the molding. He then pulled it back and the door popped open. There was no electricity at Olsofsky's place either so he shined his flashlight inside. There were two vehicles. One was the biggest Hummer he had ever seen, and it was painted neon yellow. The other was a limited edition BMW convertible. Neither would serve Rob. The low sports car would never get through the standing water. And the Hummer, while perfect for navigating flooded roads, would be impossible to use as a stealth escape vehicle.

He went out of the garage and closed the door behind him. Neither Escalade by the house had keys in the ignition, and he wasn't going to try to pull the bodies from the pool to see if they might be in their pockets. He didn't know where else he should go to look for a vehicle. There were neighborhoods to the north, but there might also be residents who hadn't evacuated, who might greet a stranger approaching after two days of hurricane weather with a loaded shotgun. It was clear he wasn't going anywhere this night. He would spend the night here and figure out what to do in the morning.

He crossed the spongy lawn to the house in the glowing, almost orange, fading light. The winds still raced in the treetops surrounding the clearing, but it was quieter on the grassy floor. It was amazing what you could get used to. He went around to the back of the house, pointedly refusing to look at the bodies in the pool, and entered through the same door he had the afternoon before. Everything was as he had left it, he was sure, except the music of the single sad violin no longer pierced the air. The first thing he did was go into the great room where the host still sat slumped forward in the straight-backed chair. Rob grabbed the back of the chair by its newelled ends, leaned it back on two legs, and dragged Olsofsky across the wooden floor and into a half bathroom off to the side. He jockeyed him into the confined space, and then stepped gingerly around the body and closed it in the dark.

He used his flashlight to look for food in the refrigerator and went into the library where he sat in one of the deep leather chairs. After he ate he took out the pistol and put it next to him on the chair and looked out at the last strains of evening light. He breathed deeply and sunk back into the leather and waited for sleep to search him out.

He didn't know how much later it was when he awoke. He came to consciousness with a gulping start, and then found he could not fill his lungs with air fast enough. What he saw when he opened his eyes did not make any sense. Before him everything was bathed in a descending broad blue light. From the deck, to the trees, to the dock and gazebo stepping out into the mud of the Sound, everything was meticulously outlined in blue. And it was completely silent. For the first time in days there was no wind, none. Rob clambered out of the chair, with the pistol still in his hand. Then he was smart enough to sit back on the armrest and allow time for the blood to circulate more evenly through his body.

His mind was still not registering what lay before him, but he took short stumbling steps to the sliding door, opened it, and stepped out on the deck. Then he knew. Looking up he saw the great white circle of the full moon spreading its light below. As he came further out on the deck he could see the ragged dark margins where the light shone on the sides of the incredibly high eye wall of the storm. It was such a singular and indescribable sight that he almost forgot everything else. He was stunned at the symmetry of the half-circle of the eye he could see, thrilled at knowing what it held back, but then quickly realizing that it would pass over and the back side of the storm would pound the area from the opposite direction.

Rob immediately felt infinitesimal and alone, not imagining that anyone else could see what he was seeing. Looking up again he even picked out hints of stars in the high haze, and as he looked at the approaching wall of the storm he saw striations and small whorls of wind trying to escape.

Then he knew what he had to do. When the southern eye wall passed, the wind would immediately switch to the west. All the water in the Sounds that for days had been pushed west would flow back, pushed ahead even faster by the reverse winds. The Sound, which was now blue black mud as far as his eyes could see, would return and flood the west side of the Banks as it did. Then the islands, which had been so battered by the ocean, would take another shot from behind, ravaged by a wall of water coming from the swollen streams and marshes to the west.

Rob looked up to see if he could make out any change of position in the moon above the circle of clouds. The storm must be moving north, but its progress was barely discernible. Then he looked out at the pier and halfway along its length he saw the structure of the boat cradle and sling, and moonlight glinting off the polished fiberglass sides of Olsofsky's Sound pleasure boat. If he were able to lower the boat to the surface of the mud, then when the wind switched and the water came back he could crank the engine and make the short two mile dash across the Sound to the land side of Currituck County and try to make his escape from there. He looked back up into the breathless calm and the edges of the storm were undulating as if it were a living, breathing thing. He looked higher and saw the violet portal to the heavens, and thought about those who had tried to enter. In his memory he saw Chick and Amelia, Kay, even Nadia…he had thought they were just gone. He looked at the grandeur and the majesty of the view around and above him. Could it just be an accidental confluence, or was this a moment that was actually meant to speak to him?

The next thing he knew he was on the dock turning the manual crank and slowly lowering the powerboat. It was a Buddy Davis center console with twin three hundred horsepower Yamaha motors, twenty six or twenty eight feet, a beautiful craft that probably ran to $200-300,000. Without electricity cranking it down was a painfully slow process. He knew the back end of the storm was coming when the light shifted more to the north and he began to hear faint whistles and whines coming across the muddy flats. And then he saw the shadow of the towering eye wall approaching, swallowing everything in its path. The light of the moon became gradually fainter, and then it was snuffed out altogether.

The wind as it returned on the backside of the storm was a blasting screaming banshee. It crossed the bare Sound with nothing to temper or mitigate it and within moments the gusts were again in the hundred mile an hour range and Rob had difficulty holding his position on the dock. The heavy boat swung wildly in the sling, banging the wooden frame and threatening to crush his fingers between the gunwales and the wood structure. He finally got the boat down to the mud just as stinging darts of rain began to fly from the low clouds. He climbed down to the boat's deck and crouched behind the transom as he waited for the water to return.

It didn't take long. There was still faint moonlight to the north and he saw it reflect off the water as it crept back. Within ten minutes wavelets were lapping at the bow of the boat, and a few minutes after that the craft was afloat. He turned the key and the motors chortled to life. He used the gaff to push himself away from the dock where he lowered the propellers and dropped the transmission into gear and the boat leapt forward into the oncoming swells.

Rob could barely see anything as he steered straight west across the Sound. Even in calm and ideal times the Sound was notoriously fickle for its shallows and shifting shoals, and Rob knew there was a chance he could run aground and be stuck, or hit something hidden underwater and damage his props beyond his ability to repair them. The rain was driven at him in almost horizontal sheets, and it was so dark he felt in danger of losing all sense of direction. But he still had his instincts. As he bounced and jostled his way through the swells, he mentally gauged where he guessed the north-south channel would be, and as he realized he was approaching it, he suddenly knew he wasn't just going to cross the Sound and flee. Twenty five miles to the south was Spencer's property on the south side of Colington Island. He would go there.

In between and ten miles to the south was the Wright Memorial Bridge that spanned the Sound between the Currituck mainland and bedroom community of Southern Shores. Rob prayed that it was lighted because he dreaded the idea of trying to navigate the pilings in this enveloping darkness. Once he turned south he could see no light anywhere. The boat was mercilessly pummeled and buffeted by cross swells coming across his beam. The twin motors struggled as they churned through the water, with the boat occasionally yawing so heavily that one or the other of the props came completely out of the water with an accompanying high-pitched scream. It was only one of the many noises, made louder by the fact that he could see nothing. Who knew what had dislodged from the western shore and was now floating in the current? He hunkered down behind the plexiglas windscreen and squinted in the black. Now that there was no chance of turning back, he second-guessed himself, and wondered if he should have waited for morning.

His wariness became greater when he knew he must be approaching the bridge. Again, he didn't know if there might be lights on the bridge itself, but he prayed there might be at either or both ends of the span. The problem was that even if there were lights there, visibility was so bad that he didn't know whether he would be able to see them from the central channel. He also kept his eyes peeled for channel markers, but it was still the same dilemma. Then suddenly, looming out of the darkness above him he did see a pattern of lights dotting the sky. He slowed and saw the outline of the bridge's roadbed, but he could still see nothing of the pilings beneath. And then one was there, just to port, too close he thought, but he made it by and through the opening without even seeing the pilon on the other side.

After he passed the bridge, the wind became even stronger. He was entering a wider part of the Sound, with more fetch, and more opportunity to store water at its western edges. The swells became stronger, larger, and more unpredictable. As he would descend into a trough, with the motors whining and gurgling in protest, Rob could feel the swells loom up next to him, and he became deathly afraid that one would break over the side of the boat and swamp him out there, two miles from either shore. He took to turning to starboard to climb the swells, and then as he reached their crest he would swing to port and back into the trough. The action threw him from side to side in the boat and wished he had put on a life vest.

After the bridge he knew he had to navigate more to the west because eventually he had to get by the tip of Colington Island and then find the narrow channel to the south of it that led east to Spencer's property.

Spencer had found the land in the early eighties, and bought it before he really had the money to. It was four or five acres, and it rose from the road to an area of high dunes, before it fell again abruptly to the Sound on the south shore. Navigating there now under these conditions was highly problematic. Rob remembered times past, sailing in the sunlight in these waters in hesitant winds, when everything was tranquil and the surface sparkled with shards of sunlight, and if anything, they had hoped for more wind to come along and fill their luffing sails. Now he was navigating only from those memories, trying to translate the speed and commotion of this transit with the lazy progress of a light wind sail on a clear fall day. His eyes scoured the invisible horizon, looking for any signs of usable light. His temples throbbed, his back ached from trying to hold himself steady as the boat pounded and lurched south.

Time began to take on a frantic pulsing quality based on the rise and fall of the boat from the crest to the trough of each wave. Forward speed was a chimera, the drift and yaw to the west were like sneaky conduits to another dimension. Though he knew he was making progress to the south, he felt like he was wrapped in a weightless womb and everything was moving but him. Then the skiff would crash down, and his legs would come close to buckling, his spine would be compressed, and he would almost lose his grip on the wheel. He would be there again, drenched, looking, listening, everything in his being wound taut.

Then to the east he thought he saw a faintly perceptible purple glow. He realized it as too early for dawn. He looked again and it was gone, and then it was there again. Wherever it came from he could use it. Because of that anomaly Rob began to make out the dark contours of Colington Island, which he would never have been able to see if not for that deep glow. Somehow he had put himself in the ideal position to skirt the westernmost tip of the island, and he felt confident that he would be able to judge when and where he needed to turn to the east into the channel that led to Spencer's property.

The hint of light bothered him. He wondered if the sun, still well below the eastern horizon, was shining up to the cloud tops of Armando which must rise many miles into the atmosphere so that it was sunrise at the storm's ceiling, and this light on the earth's verge had somehow drifted down and diffused so that when it finally reached the surface all it could muster was the dull violet glow.

Then he was past the headland and turning, and he knew he was in the channel with only another mile to go. The rain, which had been steady and relentless for most of the trip, now began to abate, still angled but not in the ferocious angry torrent that had pounded him until then. Even under his slicker he was soaked through, although there was still such a soft southern warmth in the air that he wasn't chilled or uncomfortable.

As Rob came in below the south end of the island he saw the shadows of it change from the flat recovered marshland of the gated community at the western tip to the rising palisades of the pine forest that stood on the back of a dune or sand bluff that reached to sixty or eighty feet. All this central section of the island was Spencer's, and his home was the only building for a mile in either direction. There was one gated entrance at the main road with a number code for security.

There were lights at the house on the bluff, yellow eyes in the dark night. Spencer would have a generator, of course. Rob eased the throttle as he approached, idling the engine, but still feeling the whistling power of the wind pushing him from behind. The gusts roared across the surface of the water. It whirred and growled and moaned above him. All the noise and the pressure were getting to him. He felt as if his brain were swelling beneath his skull. Now though he was thinking it was going to be a matter of less than a hundred feet before he got the answers he was looking for.

After he found Olsofsky dead, though he had to assume Spencer must have killed the Ukrainian, or at least ordered that he be killed, Rob felt much less fear that his life was in danger. Yet Spencer would know that if Rob showed up, as he was about to, that he came looking for answers.

To his surprise he was able to find an eddy and drifted easily to the dock at the base of the sand hill. He tied off and stepped directly onto the dock's surface. It was pitch dark at the water's edge, but he looked up and saw the lights of Spencer's house looming above him. The wooden stairs leading up to the house were a long tortuous affair with two switchbacks and hundreds of steps. By the time Rob got near the top he was out of breath, and he had to grab the railing to get his bum leg up each new step. Everything was wet, dripping, spongy, slick. Looking west he saw a low luminescence, almost green, beneath the clouds on the surface of the Sound. Rob was just wondering if it was related to the purple he had seen moments before when he heard a noise behind him. He had turned half-way around when he received a blow to the back of his head. He saw all manner of flashing light as he fell.

XXIV

"Rob." He heard his voice being called gently, but it sounded as if were being called through a megaphone of gauze. "Rob." When he tried to register the word, he felt a tremendous pressure and pain at the base of his skull. "Put some ice on his neck, will you." It was not a suggestion.

He finally came back to full consciousness quickly, with no idea how long he might have been out. He was in a room high above the water, looking south and west to the Albemarle Sound, and then further south to the mouth of the Pamlico Sound below it. It was still night, black, enveloping, small and large at the same time.

Rob had been in this room years ago when the house was under construction. Spencer had brought him there to show of his new domain. It was the first time that Rob got the idea of how well Spencer was doing. The drive on the long sandy path was winding and impressive. The house itself, then just a framed skeleton, was a sprawling five thousand square feet, more than Spencer, or anyone else, could want or need. There were a few other people on that informal tour. He couldn't remember who they were. It was so many years ago. He knew they were all high, everyone but Spencer, who already "didn't do that anymore."

Rob realized that now he was slumped back in a deep chair. He found it so enveloping he didn't want to move.

"Rob," he again heard Spencer's voice, and saw two forms, one to each side of him. "This is a hell of a fucking situation, isn't it? The whole of Dare County, and the beach side of Currituck County...well, much of value of both counties eradicated. Roads and highways washed away, no less than five new inlets, I've been told. The Bonner Bridge will have to be condemned. They're saying this makes Sandy look like a summer sun shower. I haven't been able to get down there yet, but they say the Sea Horse is gone, nothing left but the pilings."

Spencer came around and walked toward the glass doors with his back to Rob, scanning the broad gray panorama below him. On the other side Davy Todd sat on the arm of a plush chair that matched the one Rob sat in. He looked from Rob in the chair to Spencer by the door.

"It's a hell of a thing," Spencer repeated, and then stopped. He turned and looked at Rob. His face was haggard, his eyes drawn down at the edges.

"I don't want you to think I'm whining about my losses. Hell, this'll end up being another great opportunity for me. But I think about the people who live here, many of whom will have to leave, never to return, and that's a shame." He shook his head. "Davy here said you were looking to come after me, and I didn't believe him…and now, here you are. But what do you want, Rob? Or more specifically, what do you want from me?"

"I want to know why all this happened, and what your involvement is. People are dead…people close to me…"

"Amelia Falcon."

"And Kay Yoder, and Chick, and Steven, and your lawyer, Babson, and chef, and Nadia. Who am I leaving out?"

"Alexander Olsofsky," Spencer said, and Rob could sense he was sorry about that. "But let's start at the beginning, or what you think is the beginning…Nadia. And before I try to go through this, I'll tell you I only just now got the whole story…or what I think is the whole story." A stunning gust blew through, shaking the southern wall of the house and rattling the window casements. "How much longer do we have to put up with this?"

And then a stronger gust came. Rob could have sworn it moaned "Who?" in a long, drawn-out syllable.

"You thought Irina disappeared. We all did. Nobody knew why, or where she might have gone. I tried to find Nadia because I knew she would know, but she wasn't anywhere either. Two days later Irina showed up here. She was frightened, irrational, frantic. She said Alexander had taken Nadia and her one night after work. She gave me some kind of garbled explanation that it had to do with Alex's criminal activities, and the political situation in Ukraine. Irina told me Olsofsky had killed Nadia in front of her eyes as a warning. She described horrible tortures he had subjected her to. If Irina didn't cooperate with him, although he didn't make it clear what he wanted her to do, she would be next. Then he released her.

"Alexander and I are partners. We have a lot of things going. So the first thing I do is try to get hold of him to get his side of the story. But he's not available. His assistant tells me he's in Ukraine and won't be back for another ten days or two weeks. This is news to me because we have two big meetings, one with the Currituck planning board about the development in Carova, and one in Colorado about a deal we're trying to put together there.

But Irina is frantic. She says it doesn't matter where Alexander is, he will send people after her. So I agree to hide her.

"Unbeknownst to me, Steven is also looking for Irina. Also unbeknownst to me, Irina has been fucking Steven. So the next thing I know Steven is found dead, and the word is that you, Rob, were the last person seen with him and might have something to do with it. But again Irina is in my ear. 'No, it's Alexander. He must have found out about Steven and me, and this is another warning.' Then I get a call from Chick. He says he has you, and that he has a place to hide you to keep you under wraps and away from the cops.

"Also the body has been found. Davy gets involved and arranges for me to come and identify the body because Irina was one of my employees. Of course, it is Nadia, but I identify the body as Irina. I felt bad about that because Nadia was a sweet girl. By the time they found her, well, that environment had done terrible things to her body. I just hoped her soul was in a better, safer place.

"So Chick has you at his dad's old place. At first, I can't figure out why he's trying so hard to protect you. I know how far back you two go, an that he used to be your brother-in-law, and that you'd done some crazy shit in the past...but by all accounts, he'd left all that behind. He and Steven weren't close, I didn't think, but Steven had given him a lot of trim work, and it looked like there was more coming, so if he thought you killed Steven, why would he protect you?

"I myself didn't put much stock in the idea the you had anything to do with anything. The last time I saw you was that night at the restaurant, the night this all started, and you looked bad. You looked like death warmed over."

The lights dimmed momentarily, and then came back brighter than ever.

"You look completely different now, Rob," Spencer continued, "even aside from the beard. You're moving better, there's more flesh on you, more color..."

"I stopped drinking."

Spencer looked at Davy Todd and shrugged, as if that must be the answer. Davy stepped forward and stood above Rob casting a broad shadow over him. "So we thought we had you under wraps," the young cop said, picking up the thread of the conversation. "You had no where to go, and no way to get any where. Chick kept us apprised of what you were saying, but it wasn't making a lot of sense. Everyone in Dare County law enforcement was looking for you. You had lived in the room across from Irina, and you were seen with Steven the night he died. I was doing my best to lead things in other directions. I spread rumors that you were seen in Florida, that you'd gone out west. Then I heard news that the sheriff's department was going to raid Chick's dad's house. I tried to find Chick to warn him, but I couldn't get hold of him, so I volunteered to go along. Luckily, you weren't there. I had the feeling you must be close, but then I saw the woman next door, Amelia, and she told us you've left. I never suspected her of having anything to do with you, but then two days later, you're both gone.

"So now I knew something was seriously amiss. We have Irina's story about Olsofsky, which I thought had some holes in it, and then we have you, with seemingly close involvement with Irina, and Nadia, and Steven, and you're suddenly gone. I went back to Amelia's house actually afraid that I was going to find her dead and buried in the back yard, and you gone with her car."

"But meanwhile," Spencer put in, "Irina is ginning up this Olsofsky thing. We had taken her to the Brandy Station re-enactment, and even there her fear had this frantic edge to it. I should have realized the way she was scrambling that something else was up. But I didn't. Instead I got Davy to collect some of his Lejeune friends who he had served with in Iraq to come and augment our presence at Gettysburg because I was committed to that. And I have to admit I began to accept, and almost relish, my position as Irina's protector. Alexander, who I still hadn't been able to get in contact with, began to seem kind of guilty. Irina was taking the political situation in Ukraine, which was, and still is, confusing and contradictory, and she made Alexander into a Russian-connected criminal kingpin. I didn't see it, didn't get it.

"So Steven is dead, and Nadia is dead, and Irina is pointing at Olsofsky. Chick says he has you under wraps, 'til you're suddenly gone. I'm worried that it means you're dead too, but Chick gives me the feeling that he's more worried that you're still alive.

"We're committed to the Gettysburg re-enactment. It's something I've been doing for years, something I take very seriously because of my heritage. I have no idea that you are following me. At this point we only know that you are gone, and we assume that you've run to avoid answering questions about Steven's death. We all go to Gettysburg. I've got Davy's Marine friends as protection, and I'm thinking I'm going to honor the Gettysburg weekend as I always do, and then resolve the issue with Olsofsky after. I get my lawyer, Bill Babson, to come down from New York, and explain that I want all the information I can get on Olsofsky, not just his business in the states, but what else he's involved in, because Irina is telling me he's into everything from internet marriage scams, to all sorts of other cyber-crimes, to being a sleeper agent for the Russians. Chick comes with us too. He's never been interested in the re-enactments, but this had become an "all hands on deck" situation. I get the RV, even though it ruins our FARB status, but I felt it was important to keep Irina hidden and protected, and she requires some creature comforts.

"So we're in Gettysburg, on edge, not knowing where Alexander is, or if he's plotting against us, or what he wants from Irina, or who is ultimately pulling the strings. Irina tells me some really atrocious thing that Alexander had supposedly done, sick inexcusable things, and for some reason I believe her. But I can't find Alexander, Babson can't find him, so Davy suggests we find a way to get his attention. He had the big house in Poughkeepsie so I send Davy and his boys up there." He paused and turned to look out the window at the low clouds and then wind blowing. Looking at his broad heavy back and his thinning gray hair, Rob suddenly got the feeling that Spencer was almost an old man. "I look back at that decision now and I wonder, what the hell was I thinking? Alexander and I were friends, partners. I didn't know everything about him. I knew the rules were different where he came from, that there were different levers to be pulled, different gears to oil...

"Then, that same evening, Chick went out to collect firewood and didn't come back. We went out, it was already dark, and we found him at the base of the waterfall. At first we thought he might have accidentally fallen, but then Davy noticed his pockets had been turned inside out, and at the top of the falls there was more than one set of shoe prints, and to Davy it looked like there had been some kind of scuffle and someone had sent Chick over the side.

"We carried Chick's body back to the camp, and when Irina found out what happened, she immediately starts screaming that Alexander was responsible, and that he is coming for her."

"I killed Chick," Rob said flatly. "It was an accident."

"We know that now," Spencer said with a bitter edge to his voice. "But we had no way of knowing that then. I was thinking we were in the middle of some kind of international incident. I knew about Irina's uncle, thought I knew about her uncle, and it made me wonder if Alexander was somehow trying to get Irina to hold her as leverage in a power struggle. And he had killed Chick. Honestly, I didn't know what to think.

"To add another layer to all this, he and I were working on this big complicated deal. We were both jockeying to make the most advantageous move for ourselves, and I think now one of the reasons he was avoiding me was that he thought I was trying to take advantage of him. So when we go up and burn his house, he ends up thinking it's some kind of strong-arm business tactic, because he had no idea any of this other stuff is going on...no idea.

"The whole time he's incommunicado, I think he's in Ukraine trying to hold his dealings together there, but he's not. He's in Alaska, salmon fishing. He's under pressure from our deal, and from the chaos in Ukraine, so he just went...turned off his electronics, didn't tell anyone...just went. He gets back to the airport in Seattle, turns on his phone, and all hell breaks loose. He hears messages from his people about his house, and then he hears a messages from me, including the one where I'm yelling, telling him why I burned down his house.

"So now it's his turn for a response. I thought Chick was his response, but it wasn't, as you know. If someone burned down this house, and I found out who it was, I would blot out all evidence of their existence. There would be nowhere they could hide from me. Alexander's response was somewhat more muted, at least it was meant to be. After hearing my messages, he knew where the problem lay. So he went to the city, to Brighton Beach, talked to one of the Russian bosses there.

"What I didn't know was that Irina was also frantically trying to get hold of him. What she was afraid of had already happened, that I was going to talk to Alexander and tell him all the things she had been saying about him. She does get hold of him, and she begs him to rescue her from me!

"This is where Amelia comes in. We had no idea where you were after you disappeared. We assumed you had bolted. We had no idea you had anything to do with Amelia, or that she had anything to do with you. But then Davy spotted her on the way to Poughkeepsie."

"At the rest stop."

"Yes," Davy said. "I saw her going to the bathroom. I didn't pay attention to her, but then I knew her from somewhere. Then it came to me. It was from the night we went to the house in Mashoes. I talked to her on her porch. Now she was at a rest stop in northeastern Pennsylvania. I knew it was more than a coincidence. Like Spencer says though, we didn't connect her to you. But from then on to Poughkeepsie while she was following us, we were keeping an eye on her. When we made the turn to Olsofsky's driveway, we dropped one of our guys just out of sight with field glasses, and when she went by we saw that there was someone else in the car with her. We go the plate number and later I got the Sheriff's Department to run it. It was listed to Amelia Falcon, at an address next to your hiding place, so we had a good idea it was you in the car with her."

"But we were asking why?" Spencer put in. "We knew you had been asking questions about Irina's disappearance, and we knew you were with Steven the night he was killed. What were the two and two to add together to give us the answer as to why you were following us?"

"The photo in the Coastland Times," Rob said, and they both looked at him blankly. "The thing that started all this was that I saw a photo of your group at the Brandy Station re-enactment, a photo of all of you at a house. But behind you on the porch was a screen door, and inside the screen door was a woman's form, and I knew it was Irina, and this was after she was supposedly killed. Amelia didn't know it was Irina, but she believed me. It was her idea that we go to Gettysburg because we thought you must either be hiding her from someone, or hiding her for yourself."

"How did you know where we were?"

"We followed your caravan," Rob answered. "We were staying at a farm house just a couple of miles away. And that was just a lucky coincidence, because it was the only place we could find. I was able to go into the woods and spy on your campsite. I never saw Irina, but I saw your guards with automatic weapons. We knew something was happening, but we didn't know what. It had to have something to do with the body in the canal, and then Steven's death. After you went to New York," he said, nodding to Davy, "we thought you must be having some kind of feud with Olsofsky, but we didn't know what it was about."

"But when you were in the woods, you killed Chick?"

"Yes, but it was an accident. I didn't know it was him, but I guess that got the ball rolling. But how did you find Amelia at the battlefield?"

"When we got the rundown from the sheriff's department," Davy said, "her occupation was listed as painter. I remembered when I interviewed her on her porch that I had seen canvases leaning against the wall, and I saw an easel and canvas set up inside her window. The day after Poughkeepsie at the battle rehearsal, I looked across the field, and there under a tree was a woman with an easel set up...and I knew it was her. I told Spencer and we decided to ask her to come paint the group. We were playing cat and mouse. I know she knew who I was, so we sent Babson to talk to her, and her curiosity got the better of her, and she had to agree. I have to hand it to her though. She could have been in serious trouble if we were the wrong kind of people, but she brazenly bluffed her way through. Spencer said we should arrange it so she and Irina saw each other so we could see if there was any kind of recognition or connection there, but there was none as far as we could tell. Our plan was to use her to get to you, but when we returned her to the battlefield, with all the crowds we lost her."

"But what happened at the camp the last day?"

Spencer stepped up again. His expression was drawn and fatigued. Rob realized they were all three of them dead tired. "I told you I had been trying to get hold of Alexander. And Irina was trying to contact him too. I don't know what lies or exaggerations she told you about him...that he was the great cyber-criminal, the sex-trafficker, the Ukrainian spy. She had dozens of them. About her too. Did she tell you the one about how she was the tennis prodigy, and her family had sent her to some big tennis school in Florida where, when she was fifteen she had beat Maria Sharapova, right after she had won at Wimbledon? Anyway, Alexander had first hired the Russians from Brighton Beach to rescue her from me. It had to have cost him a great deal up front, and not just in money, and you saw what it cost him in the end. He had sent these Russians to Gettysburg to retrieve Irina at any cost. So the wheels were set in motion when I finally got in touch with him. By the time we finished our conversation it was clear that the things Irina had told us about each other were the cause of everything. He didn't tell me about the Russians coming to get her, but I know he tried to stop them. Unfortunately for all involved, he was unsuccessful. The climax of the battle was that afternoon, and I was able to pay and send Davy's Marine friends back to Camp Lejeune. Alexander was to drive down that evening after the battle. He and I were going to sit down with Irina and figure everything out."

"Which is why she was alone when I found her at your camp that morning?"

"Yes, and she must have known something was happening when no guards were left with her. The sad irony of this part of the story is that Alexander was not able to stop what he had set in motion. The Russians he hired were supposed to take Irina."

"But what happened?" Rob asked, but he knew his taking Irina from the camp had been a fateful decision.

Spencer nodded at Davy, who left the room. Two minutes later he returned, leading a subdued and shuffling Irina by the hand. As she came into the light and lifted her head, Rob saw one of her eyes was blackened and her cheek bruised, and her upper lip was swollen and hanging over her lower lip. There was sheer resignation in her expression.

"We didn't do that," Spencer was quick to point out, "not most of it anyway."

Davy Todd led her over and sat her on the brick apron of the fireplace. Rob could still sense pity and concern in his expression, though he seemed to be trying to hide it. Irina avoided Rob's glance and looked at her hands resting on her knees in front of her.

"I don't know where she thought she was going, or how she thought she was going to get there. After she deserted you and took the car she went south on Highway 12. I don't know how she got through some of the places she drove through. But she made it all the way to the big intersection at Kitty Hawk. Unfortunately for her, that's where the emergency task force roadblock was set up. She tried to run around it and ended up hitting a power pole. When they got to her she was unconscious so they took her to the Kitty Hawk Medical Center right there because there was no way to get her to the hospital. When they ran the plates it came back to a rental car in the name of Amelia Falcon. When Davy heard Amelia's name and the description of the victim he knew it was Irina. He couldn't tell his colleagues though because everyone in law enforcement still thought it was Irina's body they had found in the canal. So Davy went down to the medical center. Her injuries weren't too serious, and she was still groggy from the pain medicine, and there was a skeleton medical crew and he was able to sneak her out. So he collected her and brought her here."

The three men looked at Irina who sat in front of the dark maw of the fireplace, her head down, wringing her hands. She looked up and traced her glance from one to the next to the next.

"What do you want from me?" she asked in a worn-out, hollow voice.

"Rob wants to know what the truth of all of this is," Spencer said. "After all, he has arguably lost the most, and he's the one who has been looking hardest for the answers. He, at least, deserves to know what the real story is."

Irina shrugged and looked from Spencer to Rob. "It was Chick." Rob heard the name and something fit together in his mind, but he wasn't at all sure what it was. "Steven and I were lovers," she said, looking defiantly at Spencer, who showed no reaction whatever. "We had been seeing each other for a year…more. He said he was going to leave his wife, Misty, but I knew he wasn't. But we had to have each other. We would meet at different places, but mostly at his beach house in the off-season. For some reason he told Chick what was going on. Chick got it in his head that I should invite one of my friends for him and we should go to the house and make a party of it. He knew who Nadia was and he began needling Steven to get me to talk her into it. Nadia was up for almost anything, but how old was Chick…fifty-something?" Rob and Spencer looked at each other and without changing expressions they both smiled inwardly. "So when nothing happened, Chick began, not threatening, but hinting that things would be bad for Steven if Misty found out what was going on with him and me. In the end, it wasn't much of a chore to get Nadia to agree. She wanted some cocaine and some Hennessey, which Chick was glad to supply.

"So it was arranged. We met at the house and went upstairs, sat in the living room looking out at the ocean. We drank Champagne, which Steven always had a supply of, and did some lines. Eventually both couples were making out on the couches. I think Chick may have had the idea that it was going to turn into some free-for-all, but Steven put an end to that by taking my hand and leading me back to one of the bedrooms.

"You keep making that face!" she screamed at Spencer, who shrugged and held out his hands, palms up. "I'm young…I deserve to live my life."

She moved to stand up, and Rob saw real pain in her face as she struggled to rise. She teetered for a moment, and then reached back for the mantle to steady herself.

"From the bedroom we heard noises, but nothing so out of the ordinary. When we finished we took a nap, and when we finally came out, it must have been an hour and a half later. The first thing I noticed was that Chick was sitting on one couch and Nadia was lying on the other. As I came closer I was thinking of something clever to say in Russian that the two men wouldn't understand. But when I got near I saw that she was still naked, sprawled half on the couch and half off it and that her hair was in a terrific tangle around her face. 'Bitch!' that's all Chick said. By now Steven came around and went closer, and pushed the hair from her face. 'Chick, what did you do?' he asked. I only remember crying, asking for someone to cover her please. Chick said something, but the only intelligible word was 'Bitch,' again. I knew we were in real trouble, and Steven started freaking out about 'what did you do in my house?' And Nadia's lying there."

Irina broke down into shaking sobs, and the snuffling and heavy abbreviated breaths were the only sounds in the room, although the storm was still creating a din outside. Rob began putting pieces together, as if the solution to the puzzle he had been working on suddenly became clear to him.

"So the three of you took Nadia west and sunk her in the canal?"

Irina nodded, and then took a longer breath to compose herself. "It was Chick's idea. Steven didn't want to do it, but in the end he agreed. We took two cars, Chick driving my car with Nadia in it. I didn't know where we were going. I was afraid they were going to take her into the woods and bury her. But then we came to this place where the canal ran along side the road. Chick said he knew it was deep enough because a nurse had gone off the road there in the eighties and they hadn't found her body for over a year. He put Nadia in the driver's seat and did something to accelerator so that the car leapt forward into the canal. It floated for only a few minutes, and then it sank.

"As we were coming back, Chick kept saying that we had to stand by each other. That was the only way. Steven was real quiet, and I could already feel that Chick was worried about him. There was no way Steven could say anything without ruining his life, but even I didn't trust that he wouldn't. The story I was going to tell was that Nadia borrowed my car, but then she disappeared and I didn't know where she went. Chick thought it was a story everyone would believe, and there would be no evidence to dispute it. After a while everyone would just forget about it, and if they ever did find Nadia's body, hopefully all the evidence would have dissolved away. The problem I had was that Chick was just so calm about it. And while he's telling us we have to hold it together, I could see in his eyes that he really didn't think that at all.

"So after we all separated, the first thing I did was call Spencer. I told him I was in trouble and needed to see him. I was going to tell him the whole story, but I couldn't admit the part about being with Steven, so I found myself making up this story about Alexander and the political situation in Ukraine and how he was threatening me, and I needed to be protected. But as I was making up this story, I found that I liked it better than the truth. I wanted to make it the truth so I added more and more layers, and in doing so I made Alexander look worse and worse.

"I didn't know anything about you," she said, looking at Rob, "about your trying to figure out what happened to me. I knew Chick must be freaking out when he found I was gone, and I knew he didn't trust Steven. So Chick was keeping an eye on Steven, and then you when he found out you were wondering what happened to me."

"And the night I went to the Sea Horse without telling him where I was going," Rob said. "That was it for him."

"He went out to look for you, calling around as he went, and he heard you were at the Sea Horse bar, with Steven, and he thought you somehow connected and were comparing notes. So he went to the Sea Horse, waited for you to leave, resolving that he was going to take care of Steven right there and then. But then the two of you left together, so he followed you from bar to bar, and finally up to Alexander's house. He could go in, after all he had met Alexander before and worked on some of his and Spencer's projects, but he waited outside. Then he heard noises from in the house, and there was some kind of scuffle, and he saw you being escorted out by two of Alexander's big Russian security guys, who took the opportunity to punch you up and then put you in an SUV and drove you off the property. After they returned he drove out and found you in a heap off the side of the road. He went back and parked near Steven's car and waited for him. When Steven came out looking for you, Chick waylaid him and smashed him in the back of the head. Then he put him in his own car, drove him to the entrance gate, pulled over to the side, and shot him in the head.

"He was going to kill you," she said. "At least that's what he told me at Gettysburg. You were unconscious on the ground, and he had made his decision, but then he couldn't do it. He took you back and dumped you on the beach in Nags Head. He still didn't know what to do.

"So that night my car was found with Nadia in it, although everyone thought it was me. And the next morning Steven is found. Chick had tried to make it look like a suicide, but he wasn't at all confident that it would stick. He went to work that day, knowing he had to find and take care of you, not realizing that you'd already been found on the beach and taken back to the house. When he got back that afternoon, you're there, but he couldn't do anything because his girlfriend-"

"Tanya."

"Yes, she was there. So he couldn't do it. And he wasn't afraid that you saw him kill Steven. He knew you didn't. What he was worried about was that Steven might have told you what had happened to Nadia. He didn't think you were playing a double game with him, but he wasn't sure. So he took you to the house in Mashoes, told you the police were after you because of Steven's killing, and he left you there, with no vehicle, no phone, no way to see or talk to anyone."

Rob thought back to the time at the Mashoes house, now with the realization that at any moment, whether it was out of panic, or despair, or measured calculation, Chick could have come back and ended his life. It was the perfect location.

"Then you disappeared. He thought he had you basically imprisoned, and you made a break. He had no idea where to look for you, no idea if Steven had told you anything, no idea if you were running from him, or the police. And because he didn't know about Amelia next door, he didn't know how you left."

"So he called me," Davy said, coming out of the shadows where he had been watching Irina, listening to her story. "After you disappeared, he called me and said he might have some information about your whereabouts, knowing that we were looking for you with questions about Irina/Nadia's death. He didn't know that we'd already been to the Mashoes house and come to the same conclusion he had, that you had somehow run away. I mentioned that we had spoken to Amelia Falcon next door, and that seemed to surprise him, as if he hadn't realized she was living there.

"So Chick was at a dead end," Davy continued. "You're gone. He doesn't know who knows what, or whom they may have told. But he said that for weeks before you had been wanting to visit your daughter Kelly, and you had been trying to work up the courage to do it. Chick, because he was her uncle, and her godfather, had been in communication with her, writing a few letters, and visiting once over the years. So he called Kelly, and she said yes, you had been there, and that a woman had driven you there, though she never saw the woman, and you hadn't said anything about her as to who she was, and how you had connected with her. You hadn't said much else, except that in a week you were going to Gettysburg for the re-enactments. Chick knew that Spencer and his group were going to be in Gettysburg too, so he knew there must be some kind of connection. He tried to call Spencer to see if he could join the group, but because he had never shown any interest, Spencer ignored the message and didn't return the call. When he didn't hear anything back, he went to the beach office where he was told Spencer was unavailable, and then he remembered the Currituck warehouse and went there. At the warehouse he was confronted by my friends from Desert Storm, so he knew something was going on."

"So we come to Gettysburg," Spencer said, taking up the thread of the story. "And the next day Chick shows up. Everyone from the beach knows him, and they're all wondering what's going on with Davy's friends, and with the RV, which is completely out of character for how we run our bivouacs. So I called a meeting with everyone and explained that Irina is in the RV, that she wasn't dead as everyone had thought, and that we are protecting her. I didn't say anything about Olsofsky. I just said we were a part of something bigger, that I couldn't completely explain. While we are there to participate in the re-enactment, we must also be vigilant in protecting our camp. So all these weekend guys, who were in this quasi-military mood to begin with, were suddenly locked and loaded and ready for action."

"And then you found Chick in the woods and Irina told you it was Olsofsky?"

"No," they both said simultaneously.

"We said it was Olsofsky," Davy said, "and she just didn't disagree."

Rob looked at Irina. She was trying to make eye contact with Davy, trying to lure him. But there was a kind of steeliness in her eyes that made Rob realize that everything with her was transactional. And now Rob also noted how she looked at Spencer and him. There was a barely disguised disgust.

"But then," Spencer said, "after Alexander had unleashed this uncontrolled and uncontrollable force, I finally got in contact with him on the last morning of the battle. At first it was a screaming match, but then we gradually began to see what a misunderstanding it was, and we both knew who was at the bottom of it."

"So that's why no one but Irina was there when I showed up that morning?"

"Yes," said Spencer. "I had agreed to leave her there for his Russian friends, and was willing to let him do what he wanted with her. I washed my hands of the whole thing. But when the Russians from Brighton Beach got there, Irina was gone. They were getting paid for retrieving her, so they're pissed. We were all, for the first time, participating in the final battle rehearsal. I sent men back to begin with lunch preparations. My lawyer, Babson, went with them to contact Alexander and make sure the exchange had taken place, and Amelia went, because by now, we're just keeping up appearances. It was a pretext hiring her to paint us, but I decided to take advantage of the pretext and actually get the painting made. I planned to talk to her when I got back to the group to explain what happened. But as you know, it didn't work out that way."

Rob looked out the window where all had been black, and saw what he first thought was a reflection, and then a mirage. Then he realized it was truly there, a barely discernible gray and deep blue smudge beyond the islets along the southern horizon. Spencer and Davy saw him staring and followed his line of sight, and they saw it too.

"Can that be the end?" Spencer asked quietly.

356

Toward the eastern edge of the light band, the purple and blue began to take on a deeper red tinge. It was just enough light that they could begin to see the roiled water of the Sound marching east. The flood was so full the shores of the small islets and sand banks were completely submerged and in places it looked as if the wind-bowed pines were growing out of the Sound itself.

"If it blows three days…" Rob said.

"If it blows three days, it'll blow five days," Spencer continued the old mot.

"And if it blows five days, it'll blow seven."

"Can it really be ending?" Irina asked.

"Not for you, darling," Spencer said quietly.

"Look at you," Irina almost spat. "You old man. You think because you exercise and dye your hair, and take your little blue pill, you won't get old! You are old! You think I was going to stay with you?"

"Steven wasn't much younger than me."

"And how long do you think I was planning to stay with him?" she said, and began crying softly.

They were all staring out the picture window, and it was unmistakably becoming lighter outside. The rain had stopped. The great gray back of the Sound swelled like a breathing animal.

"You know what I'm going to do, Rob?" Spencer said. "Actually, the idea first came to me with Hurricane Isabel in 2003. At some point the economy on Hatteras Island just wouldn't be viable any more. From the reports we've gotten about the destruction from this storm, that time may be now. As hard as I've been trying to get a bridge built up north in Currituck to Corolla, for a couple of years I've been helping to fund the environmental groups, secretly of course, who are trying to prevent the building of a new bridge at Oregon Inlet. They want to turn Pea Island into an off-limits wildlife sanctuary. Some of them support building a long, low bridge from the north end of the inlet into the Sound and then south to Rodanthe. That satisfies most of them. But I'm opposing that too. I've made donations to state and federal politicians to get them to argue that that option is too cost-prohibitive in this fragile economy.

"The reports we've heard from down south are that the destruction of houses and businesses is widespread and catastrophic. I've heard that there

357

are at least three new inlets on the island. And we're pretty sure that the Bonner Bridge has lost its high-rise span. So not only is Hatteras Island cut off from the outside, but it has also been cut into four or five bite-sized pieces.

"Now I don't care how many hundreds of years the Midgetts or the Hoopers or the O'Neils have been living down there. Their grandparents may have been hard, and their parents, and they may have been hard when they were younger, but I'm betting their kids are not so hard at all. I'm betting those kids are as weak as yaupon tea.

"So say after the storm I go down there and offer to buy out everyone, with a little help from the federal government, or course… make them all offers, figure out a way to get them back on their feet on the mainland or up here on the northern Banks. I can go down and clean up all the wreckage, let the land revert back to its original self. And then I'll be a hero. I'll have rescued the poor islanders and preserved the land.

"Then, in about ten years, if I'm still around, and I know Irina here has her doubts, I'll come back with a plan for the state and federal governments to generate fantastic revenue from the area. I'll show them how I can sell this land at exorbitant prices to all my richest friends, and we'll build an enclave down there like Martha's Vineyard or Jeckyl Island, a fabulous gem only accessible by ferry. We'll have a golf course and a marina. We'll be incredibly particular about building standards…

"But that's all in the future," Rob said. "Look at the light."

More of the southern horizon was being bathed in light. There was the flowing spectrum of the sunrise, but then to the west there was a pale eerie glow Rob recognized as the sliding remnants of the full moonlight.

"How dos this all get resolved?" Rob asked after some moments of awed silence.

"I don't have to resolve anything," Spencer said. "As far as anyone knows I don't have anything to do with any of this. If it ever comes up, I'll just point to some Russian-Ukrainian hijinks. When they find out it's Nadia…well, she Ukrainian. And Olsofsky's house burning, we can place clues that it had something to do with the politics. And the carnage at Gettysburg, at our camp, and at your friend's house…where I know they found a dead Russian…it's all going to be traced back to the Ukrainians. I can explain my part away with incredulous disbelief. You, however," he said, looking at Rob, "are not so lucky. I'm assuming your fingerprints will be found at your friend's house in Gettysburg, where she's dead, and at Chick's father's house, and Chick is dead, and at Olsofsky's house in Corolla, so they're going to be looking for answers from you. You won't be able to go anywhere on your passport because you'll be detained as soon as you present it, but I think we can help you."

Rob's mind started turning. If they didn't kill him, and now he didn't think they would, he would go back to Costa Rica. He wouldn't go there directly. He'd probably fly to Managua or San Salvador, and take buses from wherever he landed. He couldn't go to Mal Pais to stay because he'd be recognized there, but north of there between Mal Pais and Nosara was a hundred miles of rugged coast with bad roads and many rivers to ford or cross. There were little villages dotting the coast and up in the hills. A sad old gringo with a limp could find a shack, or build one, in the hills up above one of the beaches. He could look out at the vast curving arc of the Pacific Ocean, with the green, tree-choked hills rising behind him. And think about how life had led him there.

XXV

That was two weeks ago. Rob now sat in a sliding plastic seat at the Ft. Lauderdale Airport. In his hand, he held a passport, a round-trip ticket to Managua, Nicaragua, though he knew he would never use the return ticket.

He had met Davy Todd the night before at the dust and pastel motel he had been staying at for the last week. As they shook hands Davy handed him the passport and a plane ticket.

"I told you he had a heart attack," he said as Rob examined the middle-aged face, Davy's father's face, on the inner sleeve. He had the same mongrel-colored hair, the same hollow-cheeked expression, the same brown eyes. "He won't be needing it for a while, and if he looks and can't find it, he'll just think it's lost."

Rob looked at the biographical information on the opposite page from the photo. Age, height, weight were all right, or close enough. He was glad he'd kept his beard to hide the difference in the shapes of their chins. If he didn't change his expression he should be able to pull it off.

"In a couple of years they'll have facial recognition software at airports so this won't work, but we should be good now."

The continual spate of news about Hurricane Armando was only just calming down. The sustained barrage of the three-day storm had reduced much of the coast from Ocracoke to the Virginia line to rubble. Hundreds of homes were washed away, and thousands of homes and businesses were flooded or wind or surf-damaged. The villages of Hatteras, Frisco, and Avon were completely destroyed. Highway 12 on Hatteras Island had been eaten away in eight places, and there were six new breaches, including a mile-long gap north of the village of Rodanthe. The governor and the president had flown over the area in helicopters, stunned by the scale of destruction. Over one hundred lives were lost, mostly permanent residents of Hatteras Island who had ignored the evacuation orders. Most of them drowned in the flooding.

After the lurid headlines from Gettysburg, it had died down to stale speculation and rumor. Spencer was right. After a flurry of mentions in the beginning of the investigation, his name had dropped from sight and been

forgotten. Conspiracy theorist now held sway when it came to describing
and connecting the crimes, b for all their efforts, the truth seemed to have
found a safe hiding place.
The next day after storm Davy took Irina and Rob in Olsofsky's
boat across the So .o head up the narrows to the lumber town of
Plymouth. It had arranged that one of Davy's Lejeune buddies would
pick them up and drive them to Florida where they would be
responsible .selves.
They ncer's dock early. Above was a clear sky. The wind still
danced een color, and the water was still a dangerous jumble. The
fun arge and confused, coming from multiple directions one on top
s .er, and the boat slammed and skipped and shuddered its way
Everywhere was debris, tree limbs, large and small pieces of wood.
passed part of a roof floating dangerously low in the water, about ten
twenty feet, with shingles still attached. They saw a couple of swamped
boats being dragged by hidden anchors, leaking rainbows of fuel and
stripped of everything that had been in them.

Irina had been crying since they left the dock. Rob was now just numb
to her. He had already decided when they got to Florida, whichever
direction she went in, he was going the other way.

Then as they began to see treetops rising from the west edge of the
Sound, Davy took the motor out of gear and left it in idle. As they drifted
to a wobbling halt he stepped around Rob back to where Irina cowered in
the stern. With one quick motion he picked her up and threw her into the
churning water, then lurched past Rob and slammed the boat in gear and
they tore away.

At first Irina flailed and thrashed, screaming. But quickly she seemed to
surrender. Rob watched as the distance widened. Her bare head came up
with a swell, and then she sank into a trough out of sight. Perhaps she
might find something to hold and cling to. He turned back to the bow to
mark their progress.